ANCESTOR

ANCESTOR

A
NOVEL

SCOTT SIGLER

BROADWAY PAPERBACKS
New York

BROADWAY

Copyright © 2007, 2010 by Scott Sigler

www.scottsigler.com

Published in the United States by Broadway Paperbacks, an imprint of the
Crown Publishing Group, a division of Random House, Inc., New York.
www.crownpublishing.com

Broadway Paperbacks and its logo, a letter B bisected on the diagonal,
are trademarks of Random House, Inc.

Originally published in paperback in different form in Canada by Dragon Moon Press in 2007
and subsequently published in hardcover in the United States by Crown Publishers,
an imprint of the Crown Publishing Group, a division of Random House, Inc., New York, in 2010.

Library of Congress Cataloging-in-Publication Data
Sigler, Scott.
Ancestor / Scott Sigler.—1st ed.
p. cm.
1. Geneticists—Fiction.   2. Transplantation of organs, tissues, etc.—Fiction.
3. Xenografts—Fiction.   4. Transgenic organisms—Fiction.   I. Title.
PS3619.I4725A83 2009
813'.6—dc22   2009038911

ISBN 978-0-307-59101-2
eISBN 978-0-307-58935-4

Printed in the United States of America

Book design by Chris Welch
Cover design by Kyle Kolker
Cover photography © Anatomical Travelogue/Photo Researchers, Inc.

10 9 8 7 6 5 4 3 2 1

First Broadway Paperbacks Edition

For the Junkies — this one is all for you, and all because of you.

"The Valkyrie at my side is shouting and laughing with the pure, hateful, bloodthirsty joy of the slaughter , , , and so am I."

— FRANK MILLER, *Sin City*

BOOK ONE

GREENLAND

NOVEMBER 7: GREENLAND

PAUL FISCHER HAD always pictured the end of the world being a bit more . . . industrial. Loud machines, cars crashing, people screaming, guns a-blazing. Perhaps a world-breaking bomb shattering the earth into bits. But here in Greenland? Nothing but packed snow, endless rocks, and the towering white vistas of glaciers sitting high on the horizon. No cities burning, no abandoned cars, none of that nonsense. Just a tiny virus, and some pigs.

Paul hopped out of the UH-60 Black Hawk helicopter and onto a snow-covered field lit up by the breaking dawn. A woman in an air force jacket waited for him, fur-lined hood tight around her head to ward off the cold and the stinging wind.

She snapped a salute. "Colonel Fischer?"

Paul nodded and casually returned the salute.

"Second Lieutenant Laura Burns, Colonel. General Curry is waiting for you. This way, sir."

She turned and walked toward three white Quonset huts, their curved roofs blending into the landscape. Two tunnels connected the huts, completing the little human hamster town that had gone up less than twenty-four hours earlier. He heard the hum of a diesel generator, saw the curve of two satellite dishes mounted on top of the huts.

Paul followed the girl, their shadows blending together as a long, broken gray shape moving across churned-up white snow. He wanted to get inside, hoped it was heated — these cold temps raised hell with his left knee. Paul absently wondered if the young lieutenant was married, if she was the kind of girl his son would find interesting. He was starting to wonder if the boy would ever settle down and get to the business of making some grandchildren that Paul could spoil rotten.

Overhead, a pair of F-16s shot by, their jet roar echoing off the valley floor. Probably a squadron out of Reykjavík, in to enforce a no-bullshit no-fly zone that had gone up shortly after Novozyme sounded the biohazard alarm.

As he walked, Paul looked out into the shallow valley. Two miles away, he could make out the Novozyme facility: a main building that contained research labs and housing for the staff, a landing strip, light poles, metal guard tower, two small, unblemished sheet-metal barns for the pigs and a head-high electric fence that surrounded the entire compound.

The girl — *Second Lieutenant Burns,* Paul mentally corrected himself — led him to the middle hut. No airlock. There hadn't been time to set up a full temporary biohazard center, so the guys at Thule Air Force Base had shipped out the communications and command part of a portable Harvest Falcon setup. Not that it mattered much. Intel was almost positive that the viruses hadn't escaped the Novozyme facility.

The key word being *almost.*

Paul opened the door and stepped into the heated interior. General Evan Curry looked up, waved Fischer over to the bank of monitors that covered the rear wall. Several American soldiers sat at consoles in the cramped space. A few ranking Danes stood and watched.

Curry had the permanent scowl and gray-peppered buzz cut of the typical Hollywood general, but he strayed from the script with his five-foot-five stature and deep-black skin. The only image that mattered, however, was the shine from his four stars.

"Hello, Paul." Curry extended his hand for a firm shake. "I'd love to say it's good to see you again, but this is just as bad as last time. That was . . . what, three years ago?"

"Three years to the day," Paul said.

"Really? You've got a good memory."

"Kind of a hard thing to forget, sir."

Curry nodded gravely. People had died under his commands as well. He understood.

The general turned to the Danish brass. "Gentlemen, this is Colonel Paul Fischer of the United States Army Medical Research Institute for Infectious Diseases, or USAMRIID." Curry pronounced the acronym *you-sam-rid.* "He's from the *special threats* division, and where we go from here is his decision. Any questions?"

The way Curry said the words *special threats* and *any questions* made it clear he really didn't want to hear any questions at all. The Danes just nodded.

Curry turned back to Paul. "I got a call from Murray Longworth. He said you've got the ball. I'm here to implement your orders, whatever they may be."

"Thank you, General," Paul said, although he wasn't very thankful at all. If someone else could have been trusted to make these choices, he would have gladly passed the buck. "What are we dealing with?"

Curry simply pointed to the Quonset's large main monitor.

Paul had somehow expected the images to be fuzzy. In those apocalypse movies, scenes of carnage came with ample amounts of static, flickering lights and sliding doors that randomly open and shut. For some reason, every doomsday vision seemed to be marked by substandard electrical work.

But this wasn't Hollywood. The lighting was fine, the pictures perfectly clear.

The screen showed the high-angle view from a security camera. A lone man slowly crawled across a laboratory floor. He coughed over and over again, deep and wet, the kind that ties up your diaphragm for far too long, makes you wonder if you might not actually draw in another breath. Each ripping cough kicked out chunks of yellow-pink froth to join the wet bits that coated his chin and stained his white lab coat.

With each crawl, one arm weakly over the next, he let out a little noise, *eeaungh.* The bottom of the screen read DR. PONS MATAL.

"Oh, Pons," Paul said. "Goddamit."

"You knew the guy?"

"A little. I've read his research, was on panels with him at a few virology conferences. We had beers once. Brilliant man."

"He's going out hard," Curry said, his jaw rigid and grinding a little as he watched the man. "What's happening to him?"

Paul knew that answer all too well. He'd seen people die just this way, exactly three years ago. "Doctor Matal's lungs are filling with mucus and pus, making them stiff. It's hard for him to draw air. He's drowning in his own fluids."

"That's how he'll die? *Drowning?*"

"Could be. If the tissue erosion is bad enough, it can cut into the pulmonary artery. He'll bleed out."

"How do we know if that happens?"

"Believe me, you'll know," Paul said. "How many survivors?"

"There are none. Doctor Matal there is the last to go. Twenty-seven other staff members at the Novozyme facility. All bodies accounted for."

Curry nodded to one of the soldiers manning the small consoles. The main monitor stayed on Matal's futile crawl, while smaller screens flashed a series of still images. It took Paul a second to realize the images weren't pictures — they were live video, but no one was moving.

Each image showed a prone body. Some had pinkish-yellow stains on their shirts, just like Matal. Others had blood on their mouths and clothes. A few showed a more apparent cause of death — bullet wounds. Someone, probably Matal, had decided the flu strain was too deadly. That someone had stopped people from leaving the facility whether they showed symptoms or not.

The images made Paul's stomach pinch — especially images of women. Pink froth covering their mouths, dead eyes staring out. They reminded him of the incident three years ago. Like Pons, Paul had been forced to make a call . . . and Clarissa Colding had died.

Paul took a breath and tried to force the thoughts away. He had a job to do. "General, when was the first confirmed infection?"

"Less than thirty-six hours ago," Curry said, then checked his watch. "Based on Matal's notes, he shot seven. Twenty died due to infection. Whatever this bug is, it moves fast."

An understatement. Paul had never seen an infection move that quickly, *kill* that quickly. No one had.

"The facility's contamination control readings are in the green," Curry said. "Only two ways in, negatively pressurized airlocks and both fully functional. Air purification systems online and A-OK."

Paul nodded. Negative pressure was key. If there were any breaks in the facility's walls, doors or windows, fresh air would push *in* as opposed to contaminated air escaping *out*. "And you're sure the entire staff is accounted for?"

Curry nodded. "Novozyme ran a tight ship. The administration helped us locate anyone who wasn't in the building at the time of lockdown. They've all been quarantined, and none show symptoms thus far. It's contained."

On the screen, Matal's crawling slowed. His breaths came more rapidly, each accompanied by the ragged sound of flapping phlegm. Paul swallowed hard. "Did Doctor Matal make any disease-specific notes for us?"

Curry picked up a clipboard and passed it over. "Matal said it was a new Flu-A variant. Something from the pigs. Zeno zoo nose, I think it was."

"Xenozoonosis," Paul said, pronouncing the word slowly as *zee-no-zoo-no-sis.*

"That's it," Curry said. "Matal said it was worse than the Spanish flu of 1918."

Paul quickly flipped through the notes. Matal hadn't had time to properly type the virus, but he'd theorized it was an H5N1 variant or a mutation of H3N1. Paul scanned the lines, dreading what he'd see and wincing when he finally did — Matal's staff had tried oseltamivir and zananivir, the two antivirals known to weaken swine flu. Neither had done a thing.

"I'm not a scientist, Fischer," General Curry said. "But I know enough to realize a virus isn't going to kill *everyone*. I'm surprised a civilian like Matal would shoot his own people."

"He saw how fast it spread, had no way to stop it. Matal decided the death of him and his staff was preferable to the potential death of millions."

"Oh, come on," Curry said. "I'm not about to go licking that pinkish goo off Matal's chin or anything, but how bad can it be?"

"The 1918 epidemic killed fifty million people. World population was just two billion people back then. Now it's almost seven billion. Same kill-rate today, you're looking at *seventy* million dead. No planes back then, General. There weren't even *highways* yet. Now you can fly anywhere in the world in less than a day, and people do, all the time."

"But we just had a swine flu," Curry said. "That H1N1 thing. That killed, what, a few thousand people? Regular old, standard-issue flu kills a quarter million people a year. So pardon my layman's approach, Fischer, but I'm not buying into the H1N1 *pandemic* crap."

Paul nodded. "H1N1 wouldn't have killed *anyone* in the Novozyme facility. They have medical facilities, doctors, antivirals ... they knew what they were doing. This isn't a third-world shit hole, this is a world-class biotech facility. And *pandemic* is just a term to describe infection over a wide area. The first H1N1 case was reported in Mexico. Just six weeks after that report, it was confirmed in twenty-three countries. It was global. Had that been Matal's virus, you'd be looking at a seventy-five percent lethality rate across the whole damn world. You know how many people that would kill?"

"Five billion," Curry said. "Yeah, I can count. Can you believe they actually make you pass math to be a general?"

"Sorry, sir," Paul said.

Curry watched Matal. The general seemed to chew on imaginary gum for a few seconds before he spoke. "Fischer, you paint a fucking scary picture."

"Yes sir. That I do."

Two more chews of imaginary gum, then a pause. "I know what I'd do if I was in your shoes. I'd go all-in. Balls-deep."

"And if I want to go all-in, General," Paul said, opting out of the phrase *balls-deep*. "What are the choices?"

"We've got the full cooperation of the Danish government and Greenland's prime minister. They want this thing wiped out, so they'll back up whatever story we provide. Thule's got a Bone online with eight BLU-96s."

Paul nodded. A *Bone*, meaning a B1 bomber. BLU-96s were twothousand-pound fuel-air explosive bombs. At a predetermined height, the bombs opened and spread atomized fuel that mixed with surrounding air, creating a cloud of highly volatile fuel-air mixture. Once ignited, the temperatures reached around two thousand degrees Fahrenheit, incinerating everything in a one-mile radius — including the viruses and anything they were in, or on.

"General, do we have any other options?"

"Sure," Curry said. "Two more. We can deploy teams in biohazard gear to examine the place, take the risk of some minor, careless act letting the virus get out, or we can cut our losses and go Detroit on it."

Paul looked at the general. "A *nuke*? You've got a nuke?"

"Less than a megaton," Curry said. "But you can kiss everything within a three-mile radius adios. I've got evac choppers standing by. We get our people to a safe distance, leave everything here, then light the Christmas tree."

Curry was serious. A damn *nuke*. Fischer looked at a monitor that displayed a view just outside the Novozyme facility. It showed the pigs mucking about outside one of the barns. Matal and Novozyme had hoped to turn these pigs into a herd of human organ donors. They had been studying *xenotransplantation*, the science of taking parts of one animal and putting them into another. Hundreds of biotech companies were pursuing similar lines of research, and each line carried a remote danger. Remote, but real, as the scene before them so aptly demonstrated.

Ironically, the pigs didn't look sick at all. They looked as happy as pigs can — eating, digging at the half-frozen, muddy ground, sleeping. Paul felt oddly sad that the animals had to die.

"How long for the B1 to drop the fuel bombs?"

"Two minutes from my order," Curry said. "The Bone is on station now."

Paul nodded. "Do it." He hoped the bombs would land soon enough to end Matal's pain before the lungs fully gave out.

Curry picked up a phone and made a simple order: "It's a go."

On the monitor, a new coughing fit clenched Matal's body into a fetal position. He thrashed weakly, then rolled onto his back. His arms reached straight up, his fingers curled like talons. He managed one more ragged breath, then another cough shook his body. Blood shot out of his mouth like a spurt from a fire hose, so powerful it splashed against the fluorescent lights above. His body went limp, wet red still burbling up on his lips and dripping down on him from the ceiling.

"Man," Curry said. "That is truly fucked up."

Paul had seen enough. "I need a secure line out."

Curry pointed to another phone, this one built into the equipment-thick control panel. "That's a straight line to Langley. Longworth is waiting for your call."

Murray Longworth. Assistant director of the CIA and dotted-line boss of Paul's special threats division of USAMRIID. Longworth oversaw an unnamed group combining elements of CIA, FBI, USAMRIID, Homeland and other departments, a force tasked with combating biologically related threats. The legality? Questionable, at best. The secrecy? Absolute. The authority? There was never really any question about that, not when Murray Longworth spoke with the voice of the president himself.

Paul picked up the phone. His boss answered on the first ring.

"This is Longworth. What's your call, Colonel?"

"I've ordered General Curry to use the fuel bombs."

There was a slight pause. "I still can't believe this," Longworth said. "From a goddamn *pig*? How can a pig virus infect people?"

Paul sighed. Longworth ran the show, but he didn't get it. Probably never would. One of the main monitors switched from the steady procession of the dead to a shaking, blurry, bird's-eye view of the Novozyme facility. Bomber-cam.

"The pig genome was modified to include human proteins," Paul said. "That has to happen if you want to make the pig organs transplantable into humans. A new swine flu variant incorporated those proteins and it jumped species."

"Put it in terms that I can understand."

"Fast-moving, airborne, no known treatment, three out of four people die horribly. Goes global within eight weeks. On a scale of one to ten, this is an eight, and my *ten* is the complete extinction of mankind. We need to go scorched Earth here, sir."

Paul heard Longworth's heavy sigh.

"Finish up there as fast as you can, then get your ass back to D.C.," Longworth said. "President Guttierez is calling a black meeting. All the European nations, India, China, everyone capable of this kind of work. We're shutting everyone down until the WHO can put monitors in place. I need you at that meeting."

"I see," Paul said. A *black meeting*. A disaster of biblical proportions was just a broken airlock away, and the world's leaders would meet in secret to discuss the options. No one would ever know.

Not even Matal's family.

On the bomber-cam monitor, Fischer recognized the field he'd just walked through, then the white Quonset-hut hamster town. A fraction of a second later, he heard the roar of the jet's engine. Only seconds now.

"After the D.C. meeting, you go after Genada," Murray said. "We're shutting everyone down, but we get Genada's facility at Baffin Island first."

The monitor switched to a view from a camera that must have been mounted up with the radar dishes on the Quonset's roof. The Novozyme facility was there for a brief second, then a giant orange flash filled the screen. The ground shook. A small mushrooming cloud lifted into the dawn sky.

"Sir," Paul said, "I think I should be on hand for the Monsanto facility in South Africa, or Genzyme's Brazilian installation."

"Genada first," Longworth said. "We already know those fucking Paglione brothers were conducting human experimentation. They're a proven threat. Any progress finding the Russian girl?"

The Russian girl. Galina Poriskova, PhD. She'd threatened to blow the whistle on Genada's human experimentation. She'd contacted Fischer, met with him and claimed to have evidence, but the Pagliones had paid her off before she delivered.

"Just tracking some financials," Paul said. "Investments and the like. NSA is pretty sure she's in Moscow, but we can't get the Russians to cooperate."

"I'm guessing they'll cooperate now," Longworth said. "I'll escalate it to the State Department. P. J. Colding made the human experiments vanish the last time we were chasing Genada. He also took Poriskova right out from under your nose. So we start with Genada before he can do that shit again."

Paul swallowed, closed his eyes. He should have known P. J. Colding's name would come up.

"I understand, sir," Paul said. "But I remind you that I have an asset on the inside at Baffin Island. I can send a message. If anything looks amiss, the asset can cripple transportation, stranding Colding and the entire project."

"Still rubs my ass raw you won't tell me who your asset is."

"Until your people find out how Magnus and Danté Paglione get inside information from the CIA, it's best I'm the only one to know."

"I said it rubs my ass raw, I didn't say it wasn't the right strategy. But, Colonel, can your asset get a message *back* to you?"

Paul ground his teeth. He knew exactly where this was going. "No sir."

"Which means you won't know when the Paglione brothers find out about the bomb you just dropped. They'll figure out what happened, and when they do, Colding will take the Genada project on the run. I'm not about to tell the president that there's a rogue xenotransplantation element unaccounted for, not after what just went down. While you do the D.C. meeting, I'll call up the special threats CBRN platoon. You'll go in with them."

The special threats CBRN team. *Chemical, biological, radiological and nuclear.* Paul didn't know much about those men, he wasn't cleared to know, but they would be much more than just enlisted soldiers in hazmat suits. They'd be special forces. Whip-smart killers.

"I'll have a flight for you out of Thule," Longworth said. "Tell your asset to take out all transportation so Colding and the Genada staff can't get away."

From bad to worse. That action would leave Paul's asset with no support until the CBRN team touched down. Considering the caliber of Genada's security forces, that could be very bad indeed.

"Sir, I suggest we just wait. They've got fifty animals in the facility . . . they can't go far in ten hours."

"Colonel Fischer, we're done here. As soon as I get approval from the Canadians, you order your asset to destroy all transportation, take out any research data and kill the baboons."

"Cows, sir," Paul said. "Monsanto is using baboons. Genada is using cows."

"Then kill all the cows. Stop arguing with me."

Paul rubbed his face in frustration. His ex-wife, Claire, used to tell him that the movement made him look like a little kid who needed a nap. He'd never broken the habit, and now every time he did it he immediately thought of her nagging at him to stop.

"Colonel Fischer," Longworth said. "Will you follow my instructions, or not?"

"Yes sir. I'll send the order as soon as you give the green light."

BOOK TWO

BAFFIN ISLAND

NOVEMBER 7: DREAM A LITTLE
DREAM OF ME

STOP IT, HANDS.

Her fingers brushed long black hair out of her eyes. The hair fell back, slowly, almost floated into place, and she pushed it away again. Her small hands seemed to move of their own accord, grabbing, stitching, sewing.

Stop it, hands, she wanted to say, but she couldn't speak. She could only watch.

It was *wrong*.

It was *dangerous*.

It was what she *deserved*, deserved for being bad. A dulled sense of dread filled her mind, a metallic-gray cloud of doom.

Her hands held a fuzzy, stuffed, black-and-white panda. But her favorite toy wasn't exactly the way she remembered. It was the panda's body, all right, but it had no arms, no legs, and no head.

The possessed hands reached down and came up with the orange-and-black arm of a stuffed tiger, fabric torn where it had once joined at the shoulder, white fluff hanging out in long strands. Liu Jian Dan's hands began sewing. The needle flashed again and again. The tiger arm joined the body.

She felt a pinprick of pain.

Jian looked at the possessed hand. A rivulet of blood trailed down her tiny, chubby finger. The droplet pooled in the joint between her fingers, then fell onto the panda body, staining the fuzzy white fur.

Fear sent a wash of tingles over her skin, like a billion bites from a billion carnivorous bacteria. Her small body shivered.

Her hand reached down again. This time it brought up a long, dangly, gray-and-white leg from a sock monkey.

The needle flashed. More stings. Possessed hands fixed the leg to the panda body, now black and white marked with thin red streaks.

"Shou, ting xia lai," she managed to say finally. *Stop it, hands.* But the hands ignored her.

Why had she spoken Mandarin? She used it so rarely now. But no, that wasn't right, because she was five years old and it was the only language she had ever known.

A lion's tawny leg.

More pain.

More blood.

A pinkish arm from a plastic baby doll.

More pain.

More *blood*.

"Shou, ting xia lai," she said, tears filling her eyes. "Qing ting xia lai."

Stop it, hands. Please, stop it.

The hands ignored her. They reached down again, but this time they didn't find fake fur or plastic. This time they came up with something cold and solid.

A small, severed head. Greasy black fur streaked with wet blood. Wide mouth, dead black eyes. Nothing like this had ever lived, nor would it. Not unless someone created it.

Jian started to sob.

The hands kept sewing.

THE VID-PHONE LET out its unignorable, shrill blare: P. J. Colding jerked awake. He squinted at the glowing red clock set in the vid-phone's base — 6:14 A.M. The time was bad enough, but it also showed the date.

NOVEMBER 7.

Fuck. He had hoped to sleep most of this day away. He slowly reached out and clicked the *connect* button.

Gunther Jones's tired, melancholy face appeared on the flat-panel display. The guy's big lips and sleepy eyes always made him look high.

"She's at it again," Gunther said, his voice sounding only marginally more awake than Colding's. "Fifty-two years old and she has nightmares like a little kid."

"Nothing she can do about it, Gun. Cut the lady some slack. Give me the live feed to her room, maybe it's not that bad this time."

Gunther looked down, hands seeking buttons somewhere offscreen. He usually worked the night-shift watch. Ensconced in the security room, he monitored two dozen cameras that covered the barren area surrounding Genada's Baffin Island facility, the oversized hangar that housed the cows and vehicles, and the main building's hallways and labs. The main building's eight apartments also had cameras, but those were deactivated on Colding's orders. Jian's room was the exception — her cameras were always on. Gunther spent most of his shift writing crazy vampire romance novels, but always kept a close eye on Jian. That was the man's main shift responsibility, really, to make sure Jian didn't try to kill herself.

The vid-phone picture changed from Gunther's face to a high-angle, black-and-white image — an overweight woman tossing and turning on her bed, heavy black hair covering much of her face. Colding could see her lips moving, see her look of fear.

There would be no going back to sleep this time. "Okay, Gun. I'll go take care of her."

He hit the *disconnect* button and the screen went black. Colding slid out of bed, his bare feet hitting the frigid floor. No matter how high they turned up the temperature, the floor remained perpetually ice-cold. He stepped into his ratty flip-flops, pulled on a robe and slid a small earpiece onto his left ear. He tapped the earpiece once, turning it on.

"Gunther, radio check."

"Got you, boss."

"Okay, on my way. Holler if she comes out of it before I get there."

Colding left his Beretta in the nightstand drawer. No need for the gun. He headed for Jian's.

HER BLEEDING FINGERS had turned the panda from black and white to black and red. Panda body, tiger arm, sock monkey leg, lion leg, plastic baby-doll arm and the black head with a mouth full of pointy teeth. Her possessed hands held the strange creation, a misshapen, mismatched Dr. Seuss Frankenstein.

"Not again," Jian's little-girl voice whispered. "Please, not again."

She begged, but like watching a familiar old rerun, she knew what would come next. She started screaming a moment too early, just before the black eyes fluttered open and looked right at her. Primitive, unfeeling, but clearly hungry.

Something shook her, *shook* her. The hodge-podge stuffed animal opened its mouth and seemed to smile. The devil's smile. Mismatched arms — baby-doll plastic pink and tiger-stripe orange and black — reached up and out for her.

Just as the creature opened its mouth to bite, that something shook her even harder.

COLDING GENTLY SHOOK Jian one more time. She blinked awake, the expression of terror still fixed on her confused face. Sweat and tears matted her silky black hair against her skin.

"Jian, it's okay."

He'd watched this woman for two years, tried to help her both because it was his job and because she had become his good friend. For Jian, some days were better than others. The bad days hurt Colding, made him feel incompetent and powerless. He always reminded himself, however, that she was still alive, and that was really something. She'd tried to kill herself twice; he'd personally stopped both attempts.

Jian blinked once more, perhaps trying to see through the hair, then threw her arms around Colding in a crushing hug. He returned the hug, patting her fears away as if she were his daughter and not twenty years his senior.

"I have dream again, Mister Colding."

"It's okay," Colding said. He felt her tears on his neck and shoulder. Jian called every man *mister,* although with her thick accent it always sounded like *mee-sta.* He'd never been able to convince her to call him by his first name.

"It's okay, Jian. Why don't you see if you can get back to sleep?"

She pulled away from him and wiped tears with the back of her hand. "No," she said. "No sleep."

"Jian, come on. Just try. I know you haven't slept more than six hours in the past three days."

"No."

"Can't you at least try?"

"No!" She turned and slid out from under the covers, surprisingly graceful for a woman who carried 250 pounds on a five-foot-six frame. Colding realized too late that she wasn't wearing any pajama bottoms. He turned away, embarrassed, but Jian didn't seem to notice.

"As long as I up, I get some work done," she said. "We have another immune response test this morning."

Colding rubbed his eyes, partially because it kept him from looking like he was trying *not* to look. He stared at the familiar chessboard sitting on her dresser. She'd beat him ninety-seven times in a row, but who was counting?

Her bottle of medication sat next to the chessboard. A clear strip running down the bottle's side let him see how much fluid remained. Across the strip, written in neat black letters, were dates in descending order: Nov. 1 on top, Nov. 30 on the bottom. The fluid leveled out at Nov. 7.

"Yes, I am taking my meds," Jian said. "I may be crazy, but I am not stupid."

But *was* she taking them? Things had been getting worse, her nightmares growing in frequency and intensity. "Don't say that about yourself, Jian. I don't think you're crazy."

"You also do not think you are handsome," Jian said. "This proves your judgment is questionable."

The *zip* of a pants zipper told him it was okay to look her way once again. She was pulling on a Hawaiian shirt — lime-green with yellow azaleas — over her sweat-stained, white T-shirt. Heavy black hair still hung wetly in front of her face, but through that hair he could see the dark rings under her bloodshot, haunted eyes.

She walked to her bizarre computer desk, sat down and switched on the power. Seven flat-panel monitors flared, coating her in a whitish glare. The setup surrounded her in a semicircle of screens. Three down at desk level, the side monitors angled in. Four monitors in the row above that, slanted down and around her so she actually had to turn her head from left to right to see them all.

Colding put the medicine bottle back and walked over to the computer station. All seven screens showed flowing strings of the letters *A*, *G*, *T* and *C*. Sometimes the letters themselves were in different colors, sometimes bright hues lit up long strings, sometimes both. To Colding, it looked like multicolored digital puke.

The immune response was the hurdle that the scientific trinity of Genada's geniuses — Claus Rhumkorrf, Erika Hoel and Jian — simply couldn't surpass. It was the last big theoretical hurdle that stood between Genada and saving hundreds of thousands of lives every year. Now that Jian was awake, she'd prep for the test, or, more likely, prepare for yet another failure and the resultant wrath of Dr. Claus Rhumkorrf.

"You need anything?" Colding asked.

Jian shook her head, her attention already fixed on one of the big monitors. Colding knew from experience that she probably wouldn't register another word he said. Without looking away from the scrolling letters, Jian opened a small dorm-room fridge that sat under her desk and pulled out a bottle of Dr Pepper. Her hand shook a little as she opened it and took a long drink.

"Well, I guess I'm off to bed," Colding said. "Holler if you need anything, okay?"

Jian grunted, but Colding didn't know if it was a reaction to him or to a piece of data.

He'd almost made it out of the room when she stopped him.

"Mister Colding?"

He turned. Jian pointed to one of the computer screens.

"I see the date is November seventh," she said. "I am sorry. I wish I had known her."

Tears welled up instantly. He swallowed against the knot in his throat, clenched his teeth against the pain in his chest.

"Thank you," he said.

Jian nodded, then turned back to her multimonitor array. Colding left before she could see him cry.

Three years to the day since Clarissa had died. Sometimes it seemed like a tick of the clock, like he'd kissed her just yesterday. Other times he had trouble remembering what she looked like, as if he'd never really known her at all. At *all* times, though, every minute of every day, the ache of her absence hung on him like an anchor.

He pretended to cough, giving him an excuse to wipe at his eyes in case Gunther was watching him on the hall cams. Colding walked toward his room. The research facility still reminded him of a school building: cinder-block walls painted a neutral gray, speckled tile floor, fire extinguishers paired with fire axes in each hall. There were even little handles with the words PULL HERE mounted shoulder high, although those weren't for the fire alarm — they would close the airlocks tight in case of any viral contamination.

Colding reached his room and shut himself inside. "All secure, Gun."

"I like the part where she said she's not stupid," Gunther said. "The understatement of the century."

"Tell me about it."

"Get back to bed, boss. I'll keep an eye on her."

Colding nodded even though he was alone in his room. No way he'd get back to sleep. Not today. Besides, Jian's dreams were getting worse. The last two times that had happened, she'd started hallucinating a few weeks later, then finally tried to kill herself. For her most recent attempt, she'd locked herself in a bathroom and filled it with nitrogen gas. Her assistant, Tim Feely, realized what she was doing and called for help. Colding had broken in far ahead of the proverbial "nick of time," but how close she came to success wasn't the point — the pattern was the thing. Nightmares, then hallucinations, then a suicide attempt. Doc Rhumkorrf had already adjusted Jian's meds, but who knew if that would work?

Colding had to report this. Claus Rhumkorrf was brilliant, Erika Hoel was a legend, but without Liu Jian Dan, the project simply ceased to exist.

NOVEMBER 7: EVEN FUCKING COLDER

SHOULDERS SLUMPED, COLDING walked into the secure communications office and sat down at the desk. He'd put on his clothes for the day — jeans and snow pants, snow boots and a big, black down jacket embroidered with the red Genada *G* above the left breast. Wouldn't do to talk to his boss while wearing a bathrobe.

This terminal was the facility's only way to call in or out. It connected to a single location — Genada's headquarters outside of Leaf Rapids, Manitoba. A Genada logo screensaver spun on the monitor. Colding hit the space bar. The computer was designed to do only one thing, so the logo vanished and the connection process began. Right now, Danté's cell phone was ringing a special ring, telling him to get to his own secure terminal.

Colding waited patiently, wondering how to phrase his message. In just over two minutes, Danté's smiling face appeared.

"Good morning, P. J. How's the weather?"

Colding forced a grin at the hackneyed joke. On Baffin Island, latitude sixty-five degrees, there were only two temperatures — *Fucking Cold*, and *Even Fucking Colder.*

"Not that bad, sir. Mind you, I don't go outside much, but at least everything is working great in the facility."

Danté nodded. Colding had learned long ago that his boss always liked to hear something positive, a process Colding referred to as "giving a little sugar." He couldn't blame Danté's need; if Colding had spent nearly half a billion dollars on a project, he'd want to hear some good news as well.

Danté's skin held the rich tan of a man who can afford a private spa even in the deepest, darkest isolation of Manitoba. His thick raven-black hair looked like he'd just stepped out of some Hollywood hairdresser's chair, and his bright-white grin looked like it had put an orthodontist's kids through college. The crazy-big jaw featured prominently in caricatures and political cartoons. This was the face of a billion-dollar biotech company, the face that kept investors pumped up and enthused.

"I was just about to call you," Danté said. "We acquired some additional mammalian genomes. Valentine is flying them out as we speak. He should be landing at your facility in about thirty minutes. Make sure you're ready for him, I need him back right away."

"Consider it done," Colding said.

Danté leaned toward the camera, only slightly, an expectant look on his face. "So since you called me, I'm assuming you have good news about the latest immune response test?"

"They're starting it now," Colding said. "We won't know for a few hours."

"It has to work this time. Has to. If not, I think it's time to bring in more people, top-level people."

Colding shook his head. "I still strongly recommend against that. We're secure right now. You bring in more people, you open the door to a CIA plant."

"But we have background checks—"

"Let it go, Danté," Colding interrupted, not wanting to have this conversation yet again. "You hired me for this reason. We're a lean operation. Four scientists, four security people and that's all we need."

"Clearly that's *not* all we need!" Danté said, his face morphing into a narrow-eyed snarl.

"I know this team. I saved this project once, remember?"

Danté sat back, took in a big breath, then let it out. "Yes, P. J. You did save the project. Fine. So if you're not calling me with good news, you must be calling me with bad."

"It's Jian. She's . . . she's having nightmares again. I wanted to let you know."

"As bad as before?"

Colding shook his head. "No. At least, not yet."

"What's Rhumkorrf say?"

"He's adjusting her meds. Doesn't think it's a major problem, and he's sure we can control it."

Danté nodded, the muscles of his big jaw twitching a little. "That old woman drives me crazy. No wonder the Chinese dished her off like that."

What a prick. *Dished her off?* Danté had all but begged the Chinese for permission to add Jian to the Genada staff. "Come on, Danté, you know we got the better of that deal."

"It's only a *good deal* if she makes it happen and we turn a profit. And if she doesn't, a lot of people are going to die miserable deaths."

"I'm more than familiar with the consequences of failure, Danté."

Danté's scowl softened a little. "Of course, P. J. My apologies. But we can't keep funding this bottomless pit forever. Our investor demands results. Call me if anything else comes up."

"Yes sir," Colding said, then broke the connection. The spinning Genada logo returned. Genada had many investors, but only one that actually worried Danté — the Chinese government. For Danté to snap like that, the Chinese had to be pushing for a return on their significant, if covert, investment.

And that meant time was running out.

NOVEMBER 7: TASMANIAN WOLVES

COLDING WALKED OUT of the main building's airlock and into the morning cold. Even after many months, he couldn't get used to these temperatures. He ran the awkward run of someone trying to stay tucked inside his coat, quickly covering the fifty yards to the hangar.

The hangar looked completely out of place on the snowy, barren landscape. Seven stories high at the peak, 150 yards long, 100 yards wide. Two huge sliding front doors allowed for a plane that would never really come, which was why the hangar doubled as the barn for the cows, and tripled as the garage for the facility's two vehicles. At the base of the left-hand sliding door was a normal, man-sized entrance. Colding waddle-ran to it and slipped inside.

Inside, *heat.* Thank the powers that be. He walked to one of the heaters and pressed the *higher* button again and again, cranking it up to full. He heard natural gas hissing through the PVC pipe as he stripped off his gloves and held his hands in front of the grate. The security-room computer controlled this heater and the fifty or sixty just like it that were spaced along the ground and up on the ceiling, but the temporary override was like heaven.

"Oh, come *on,*" a high-pitched voice called out. "You're turning up the heat? It's frickin' toasty in here."

"That's because you're a mutant from Canada," Colding called over his shoulder. "You were probably born in an igloo." He jerked his hands back as the heat nearly burned him. There, that was better.

Colding put his gloves back on, trapping the heat radiating off his warm skin. He turned, saw the thick-bodied Brady Giovanni start up the diesel engine of the small tanker truck they used to refuel Bobby Valentine's helicopter.

The hangar wasn't exactly *toasty,* as Brady had said, but it was well above freezing. The seventy-thousand-square-foot building held fifty Holstein cows at the far end. They were over sixty yards away, a testament to the building's size. The big black-and-white animals chewed on feed.

Occasionally one of them let out a *moo* that echoed off the hangar's sheet-metal roof some seven stories above.

On this end of the hangar sat the fuel truck and a Humvee. The Hummer saw very little use other than weekly eyeball checks of the off-site data backup, which sat at the end of the facility's one-mile long landing strip, and for taking Erika Hoel to weekly checkups of Baffin Island's two backup herd facilities. Each facility was a miserable thirty miles away — a sixty-mile round-trip with Hoel was about as much fun as a barbed-wire enema.

Brady eased out of the fuel truck, leaving the engine to idle. "All set for Bobby," he said. "I'll start refueling his chopper as soon as he lands."

"It's cold as hell outside this morning," Colding said. "After you open the doors, make sure you adjust the heat so the cows don't get chilled."

"Sure thing. I'll crank the heat for them. You might say it will be a hot time in the old town . . . this *morning*."

Brady laughed at his own joke, as usual, leaving Colding to smile and nod vaguely as he politely tried to grasp the humor. Brady's laugh sounded much like his voice: high-pitched, more at home in the body of a fifteen-year-old girl than a six-foot-four, three-hundred-pound man. As a security guard, Brady cut an imposing figure. No one understood his jokes, not even Gunther or Andy Crosthwaite, who had both served with the man in the Canadian Special Forces.

Speaking of Andy . . . Colding checked his watch. A little past 10:30 A.M. Imagine that, Andy "The Asshole" Crosthwaite was late.

"Brady, you heard from Andy?"

Brady shook his head.

"Shit. Well, he'll be out here soon to help you with the refueling. I'm gonna step outside for a second. Hold down the fort."

Brady laughed his high-pitched laugh. "Hold down the *fort*. That's good!"

Colding smiled, nodded. Hard enough not getting Brady's jokes — now he apparently didn't get his own.

He walked out of the hangar's small personnel door and back into the subzero morning's blazing white. His feet scrunched the facility's packed snow as he walked away from the hangar, until they sank calf-deep into undisturbed drifts. He stood alone, staring out at the white expanse of Baffin Island. With his back to the lab, there wasn't a building in sight.

Three years. Fuck sleeping, he should be *drunk*. Maybe he'd hang with

Tim Feely after the morning's experiment. Tim was always down for a drink and always seemed to have a bottle close at hand.

Three years.

"I just wish I had you back," Colding muttered. But Clarissa couldn't come back, no matter how bad he wished for it. He couldn't blunt the pain permanently lodged in his chest. What he *could* do, though, was make this goddamn project work . . . and by doing so, spare hundreds of thousands of people from experiencing pain just like his.

He turned back to look at the compound, his home for almost two years. About fifty yards southwest of the hangar stood the compound's other building. The square, cinder-block building only looked simple. Its two entry points were facility airlocks that maintained a slight negative pressure. It was a sobering thought — Colding's home was a place designed to keep death in.

The building contained state-of-the-art labs for genetics, computers and veterinary medicine as well as a small cafeteria, rec room and nine 600-square-foot apartments. It was a good-sized facility, but after twenty isolated months even the Trump Tower would seem claustrophobic.

Between the hangar and the main facility stood a metal platform that supported a ten-foot satellite dish. The platform, the hangar and the facility were the sum total of civilization at Genada's Baffin Island base.

A distant, rapid growl of rotor blades echoed off the landscape. Colding turned to see a dark speck on the horizon. The speck quickly grew into the familiar image of a Sikorski S-76C helicopter. Colding loved the sight of that machine. If you took a typical TV news chopper, removed all the logos and painted it flat black, you'd have a twin to Bobby's Sikorski. With twelve seats and a range of over four hundred nautical miles, the Sikorski could get the entire staff to safety in case of an emergency.

The heli closed in, then swooped down to the mile-long landing strip like a noisy shadow, kicking up clouds of powdery snow. The landing gear extended. Bobby Valentine set her down gently.

After a short pause, a metallic rattling sound echoed across the snowy landscape. The hangar's massive doors — 240 feet wide and 70 feet high — split in the middle and slowly opened just enough for the fuel truck. Brady drove it out and stopped close to the Sikorski. Colding walked toward the helicopter, watching the hangar doors to see if they would close.

They stayed open. Which meant, obviously, that Andy Crosthwaite was not in the hangar to shut them.

The main building's front airlock opened. Colding expected to see Andy, but instead Gunther Jones trotted out into the cold. At six-foot-two, Gunther stood eye to eye with Colding but was much skinnier, his black Genada jacket always drooping from his rail-thin frame like a loose shirt on a wire hanger.

"Gun, where the hell is The Asshole?"

"Asleep. I didn't want to leave you guys shorthanded." He handed Colding a walkie-talkie. "That's punched in to Andy's room vid-phone."

Colding sighed and pressed the *transmit* button. "Andy, pick up."

No answer.

"Andy, come in. I'll keep squawking until you answer."

The handset crackled back. "Do you mind? I'm trying to sleep."

"Get your ass out here, Andy. Gunther's supposed to be off-duty."

"Is Gun there?"

"Yes, he came out to cover for your lazy ass."

"Then it's a reach-around happy ending for all. Leave me alone, Colding."

"Dammit, Andy, come out here and do your job."

"I'll pass. My GAF level is pretty low right now."

GAF? Colding looked at Gunther.

"His give a fuck level," Gunther said.

Colding considered Andy only slightly more useful than a day-old dog turd. He'd served with Magnus, which was the only reason the dangerous little bastard had a job at all.

"Andy, I'm—"

"Uh-oh," Andy said. "I think this thing is broken."

A click, and with it, the conversation was over. Colding didn't bother hitting the *transmit* button.

"Don't sweat it," Gunther said. "I don't mind. Let me say hi to Bobby and I'll close up the hangar, crank the heat. Cool?"

Colding nodded. The two men reached the Sikorski as the rotor blades started their slow spin-down and Bobby Valentine hopped out.

Bobby was the Pagliones' private pilot and all-around errand boy. He pushed his heavy brownish-blond hair away from his eyes and flashed the smile that seemed to get him laid everywhere he went. He carried a lunchbox-sized metal case in his left hand. His right he offered to Colding, who shook it firmly.

"P. J., how are you?"

"I'm just fine, Bobby-V," Colding said. "Okay flight?"

Bobby nodded. "It was fine, as the return trip will be if I get out of here before that low-pressure system comes in." Bobby reached out to shake Gunther's hand. "Gun, my man, how's the writing coming?"

"Good, real good! I'm almost finished with the third book. Stephenie Meyer won't know what hit her."

"Go get 'em, tiger," Bobby said.

Gunther nodded, then jogged to the hangar. He ran by Brady, who was dragging a fuel hose to the Sikorski.

Bobby gently lifted the metal case like it was a fragile heirloom and handed it to Colding. "Right there is a regular who's who of extinction," Bobby said. "Caribbean monk seal, Stellar's sea cow, pig-footed bandicoot and a Tasmanian wolf."

"A Tasmanian wolf? Those have been gone since the thirties."

Bobby nodded. "We found a stuffed one in Auckland. Got some DNA out of the fur or something. Okay, package delivered, so let's get me turned around and outta here."

"That soon? Doc Rhumkorrf is dying to go flying with you."

Bobby checked his watch. "Can *Herr Dok-tor* do it right now?"

"He's in the middle of an embryonic immune reaction experiment."

"Sorry, I can't wait," Bobby said. "Besides, Doc Rhumkorrf doesn't really need any more lessons. I'll take him out next time."

Colding checked his watch: 10:50 A.M. Rhumkorrf & Co. had been at it for three hours now and would soon finish. Colding hurried inside, leaving Brady and Gunther to get Bobby turned around quickly.

Hopefully this time, unlike the last fifteen embryonic runs, Colding would be able to report to Danté with some good news.

NOVEMBER 7: SHE'S GOT BALLS

THE TINY, FLOATING ball of cells could not think, could not react. It could not feel. If it could, it would have felt only one thing . . .

Fear.

Fear at the monster floating close by. Amorphous, insidious, unrelenting, the monster reached out with flowing tendrils that touched the ball of cells, tasting the surface.

The floating ball vibrated a little each time one of its cells completed mitosis, splitting from one cell into two daughter cells. And that happened rapidly . . . more rapidly than in any other animal, any other life-form. *Nothing* divided this fast, this efficiently. So fast the living balls vibrated every three or four minutes, cells splitting, doubling their number over and over again.

The floating balls had begun as a cow's single-celled egg. Now? Only the outer membrane could truly be called *bovine.* The interior contained a unique genome that was mostly something else.

The amorphous monster? A macrophage, a white blood cell, a hunter/ killer taken from that same cow's blood and dropped into a petri dish with the hybrid egg.

The monster's tendrils reached out, boneless, shapeless, flowing like intelligent water. They caressed the rapidly dividing egg, sensing chemicals, *tasting* the egg for one purpose only:

To see if the egg was *self.*

It was not. The egg was *other.*

And anything *other* had to be destroyed.

JIAN KNEW, EVEN at this early stage, that failure had come calling once again.

She, Claus Rhumkorrf, Erika Hoel and Tim Feely watched the giant monitor that took up an entire wall of the equipment-packed genetics lab. The monitor's upper-right-hand corner showed green numbers: 72/150.

The rest of the huge screen showed a grid of squares, ten high, fifteen across. Over half of those squares were black. The remaining squares each showed a grainy-gray picture of a highly magnified embryo.

The "150" denoted the number of embryos alive when the experiment began. Fifty cows, three genetically modified eggs from each cow, each egg tricked into replicating without fertilization. As soon as a fertilized egg, called a *zygote*, split into two daughter cells it became an embryo, a growing organism. Each embryo sat in a petri dish filled with a nutrient-rich solution and immune system elements from the same cow: macrophages, natural killer cells and T-lymphocytes, elements that combined to work as the body's own special-ops assassins targeted at viruses, bacteria and other harmful pathogens.

The "72" represented the number of embryos still alive, not yet destroyed by the voracious white blood cells.

Jian watched the counter change to 68/150.

Rhumkorrf seemed to vibrate with anger, the frequency of that vibration increasing ever so slightly each time the number dropped. He was only a hair taller than Jian, but she outweighed him by at least a hundred pounds. His eyes looked wide and buglike behind thick, black-framed glasses. The madder he became, the more he shook. The more he shook, the more his comb-over came apart, exposing his shiny balding pate.

65/150

"This is ridiculous," Erika said, her cultured Dutch accent dripping with disgust. Jian glared at the demure woman. She hated Hoel, not only because she was a complete bitch, but also because she was so pretty and feminine, all the things that Jian was not. Hoel wore her silvery-gray hair in a tight bun that revealed a haughty face. She had the inevitable wrinkles due any forty-five-year-old woman, but nothing that even resembled a laugh line. Hoel looked so pale Jian often wondered if the woman had seen anything but the inside of a sunless lab for the last thirty years.

61/150

"Time?" Rhumkorrf asked.

Jian, Tim and Erika automatically looked at their watches, but the question was meant for Erika.

"Twenty-one minutes, ten seconds," she said.

"Remove the *failures* from the screen," Rhumkorrf said through clenched teeth. Tim Feely quietly typed in a few keystrokes. The black squares disappeared. Sixty-one squares, now much larger, remained.

Tim was Jian's assistant, a biologist with impressive bioinformatics skills. He wasn't on Jian's level, of course, but his multidisciplinary approach bridged the gap between Jian's computer skills and Erika's biological expertise. He was bigger than Rhumkorrf, but not by much. Jian hated the fact that even though the project had two men and two women, she was always the largest person in the room.

Jian focused on one of the squares. The tiny embryo sat helpless, a gray, translucent cluster of cells defined by a whitish circle. At sixteen cells, the terminology changed from *embryo* to *morula*, Latin for *mulberry*, so named for its resemblance to the fruit. It normally took a mammalian embryo a few days to reach the morula stage — Jian's creatures reached this stage in just twenty minutes.

Left alone, the morula would continue to divide until it became a hollow ball of cells known as a *blastocyst*. But to keep growing, a blastocyst had to embed itself into the lining of a mother's uterus. And that could never happen as long as the cow's immune system treated the embryo like a harmful foreign body.

54/150

Jian focused on a single square. From the morula's left, a macrophage began oozing into view, moving like an amoeba, extending pseudopodia as it slid and reached.

All along the wall-sized monitor, the white squares steadily blinked their way to blackness.

48/150

"Dammit," Rhumkorrf hissed, and Jian wondered how he could speak so clearly with his teeth pressed together like that.

The macrophage operated on chemicals, grabbing molecules from the environment and reacting to them. The morula's outer membrane, the zona pellucida, was the same egg membrane taken from the cow. That meant it was 100 percent natural, *native* to the cow, something macrophages would almost never attack. But what lay *inside* that outer shell was something created by Jian . . . Jian and her God Machine.

34/150

"Clear them out *again*," Rhumkorrf said.

Tim tapped the keys. The black squares again disappeared: the remaining grayish squares grew even larger.

Instantly, the larger squares started blinking to black.

24/150

"Fuck," Erika said in a decidedly uncultured tone.

Inside the morula, a cell quivered. Its sides pinched in, the shape changing from a circle to an hourglass. Mitosis. A macrophage tendril reached the morula, touched it, almost caressing it.

14/150

The macrophage's entire amorphous body slid into view, a grayish, shapeless mass.

9/150

The squares steadily blinked out, their blackness mocking Jian, reminding her of her lack of skill, her stupidity, her failure.

4/150

The macrophage moved closer to the morula. The dividing cell quivered once more, and the single cell became two. Growth, success, but it was too late.

1/150

The macrophage's tendrils encircled the ball, then touched on the other side, surrounding it. The tendrils joined, engulfing the prey.

The square turned black, leaving only a white-lined grid and a green number.

0/150

"Well, that was just spectacular," Rhumkorrf said. "Absolutely spectacular."

"Oh, please," Erika said. "I really don't want to hear it."

Rhumkorrf turned to face her. "You're *going* to hear it. We have to produce results. For heaven's sake, Erika, you've built your whole career on this process."

"That was different. The quagga and the zebra are almost genetically identical. This thing we're creating is *artificial*, Claus. If Jian can't produce a proper genome, the experiment is flawed to begin with."

Jian wanted to find a place to hide. Rhumkorrf and Erika had been lovers once, but no more. Now they fought like a divorced couple.

Erika jerked her thumb at Jian. "It's *her* fault. All she can do is give me an embryo with a sixty-five percent success probability. I need at least ninety percent to have any chance."

"You're *both* responsible," Rhumkorrf said. "We're missing something here. Specific proteins are producing the signals that trigger the immune response. You have to figure out which genes are producing the offending proteins."

"We've looked," Erika said. "We've gone over it again and again. The computer keeps analyzing, we keep making changes, but the same thing happens every time."

Rhumkorrf slowly ran a hand over his head, putting his comb-over mostly back in place. "We're too close to it. We've got to change our way of thinking. I know the fatal flaw is staring us in the face, we just don't recognize it."

Tim stood up and stretched. He ran both hands through his short-but thick blond locks, looking directly at Rhumkorrf when he did. Jian wondered if Tim did that on purpose, to mock Rhumkorrf's thinning hair.

"We've been over this a hundred times," Tim said. "I'm already reviewing all of Jian and Erika's work on top of doing my own."

Erika let out a huff. "As if you could even *understand* my work, you idiot."

"You shut up!" Jian said. "You do not talk to Tim like that."

Erika smirked, first at Jian, then at Tim. "Such a big man, Tim. You need a fat old woman to fight your battles for you?"

Tim's body stayed perfectly still except for his right hand, which extended and flipped Erika the middle finger.

"That will be enough, Mister Feely," Rhumkorrf said. "If you're not smart enough to contribute to the work, the least you could do is shut your mouth and focus your *worth*less brain on running your little computer."

Tim's hands clenched into fists. Jian felt so bad for him. All his life, Tim Feely had probably been used to being the smartest person in the room. Here, he was the dumbest — something Claus never let him forget.

"I realize we're all frustrated," Rhumkorrf said, "but we have to find a way to think in new directions. We're so close, can't you all feel it?"

His bug-eyed glare swept around the room, eliciting delayed nods of agreement from all of them. They *were* close, maddeningly so. Jian just couldn't find that missing piece. It almost made her long for the days before the medicine, when the ideas came freer, faster. But no, that wouldn't do — she knew all too well where that led.

Rhumkorrf took off his glasses and rubbed his eyes. "I want you all to think about something." He put the glasses back on. "It took us an hour to conduct this experiment. In that hour, at least four people died from organ failure. Four people who would have lived if they had a replacement. In twenty-four hours, almost a hundred people will die. Perhaps you should consider that before you start bickering again."

Jian, Tim and even Erika stared at the floor.

"Whatever it takes," Rhumkorrf said. "Whatever it takes, we *will* make this happen. We've just failed the immune response test for the sixteenth time. All of you, go work from your rooms. Maybe if we stop sniping at each other, we can find that last obstacle and eliminate it."

Jian nodded, then walked out of the lab and headed back to her small apartment. Sixteen immune response tests, sixteen failures. She had to find a way to make number seventeen work, *had* to, because millions of lives depended on her and her alone.

NOVEMBER 8: GAME . . . OVER?

DANTÉ PAGLIONE SAT behind his massive white marble desk, watching, waiting. His brother, Magnus, sat on the other side of the desk, reclining in one of the two leather chairs, cell phone pressed to his left ear, eyes narrowed. Magnus's nostrils flared open, shut. Open, shut. His thumb constantly spun the Grey Cup championship ring on his right hand. The office lights gleamed off of Magnus's shaved head.

To anyone else in the world, Magnus looked perfectly calm. In truth he *was.* Always. At least on the surface. But Danté had known Magnus all of his life, and he could tell when something chewed at his little brother's guts.

"Continue," Magnus said into the phone.

Danté looked to his office wall, taking in the series of original Leonardo da Vinci sketches. Da Vinci's work was the epitome of control, of calmness, methodical execution of perfection. Things that Danté strived for in all phases of his life.

"Elaborate," Magnus said into the phone. His nose flared again, just a little. He sat up slowly until his back was perfectly straight. Separated by only a year and a half, Danté and Magnus looked extremely similar — both had violet eyes, a big jaw, both were tall and solid, but Magnus had spent far more time in the weight room and it showed.

Although the two were instantly recognizable as brothers, the youngest had another key differentiator — he just *looked* dangerous. The thin scar running from his left eyebrow down to his left cheek was a big part of that look. And when Magnus focused like he was focusing now, staring off into nothing, that cold brain processing all the information, the truth was that Danté's kid brother looked creepy as fuck.

Magnus folded the phone, casually slid it into an inside pocket of his tailored sport coat, then sat back slowly and crossed his left leg over his right knee. "The Novozyme facility in Denmark blew up."

"Blew up? The animal rights activists bombed it?"

"Somewhat bigger than that," Magnus said. "Our little NSA hacker friend isn't sure, but she thinks it was a fuel-air explosive."

Danté let out a slow breath. He didn't have to ask what that meant. There was only one reason to incinerate a billion-dollar facility: a virus had jumped species. "What about Matal and his staff?"

"Dead," Magnus said. "He was in the facility. The entire main staff is gone."

Danté nodded. Novozyme was Genada's primary competitor. Matal had been their answer to Claus Rhumkorrf. You could always build new facilities, but you couldn't replace talent like Rhumkorrf or Matal. In the gold rush for viable xenotransplantation, Novozyme was no longer a factor.

"This works for us," Danté said. "Novozyme is out of the game."

Magnus smiled, just a little. "I'm afraid the *game* is over. For everyone. The G8 are cooperating to shut all of us down. Farm Girl says Fischer is in charge, and he's starting with us."

Farm Girl. The code name for their NSA contact. She would never reveal her real name. Only Magnus spoke with her. Farm Girl's information was always reliable, and she was right — if Fischer was coming their way, it meant major problems.

Anger, annoyance and anxiety all flared up in Danté's chest. Fischer had come after Genada when Galina Poriskova tried to blow the whistle on the surrogate mother fetal experiments. Danté had hired P. J. Colding and Tim Feely to clean up the mess and get rid of any evidence. If those two hadn't succeeded, Fischer would have shut the company down and probably sent Danté and Magnus to jail.

Magnus's smile faded, his blank expression returned. "Kind of ironic, isn't it?"

"What is?"

"That we get shut down over a virus jumping species, and yet our specific line of work ensures that can't happen. If only you hadn't kept that a secret, Danté, the G8 would leave us be."

"We couldn't announce our method. If we had, Novozyme and Monsanto and the others would have tried to copy it."

Magnus shrugged and raised his eyebrows, a gesture that said *oh well*.

It was bad, but perhaps not *that* bad. Danté could find a way to make it work. "What if we tell them now? I can call Fischer. Or better yet, have Colding do it. They have a history."

Magnus laughed. "They're not exactly poker buddies. And anyway, it's too late now. They won't believe our methods are safe, not after Novozyme's accident. It's over."

Danté took a deep breath. He let it out, slow and controlled. There was always a way. He hadn't made Genada one of the world's largest biotechs by sitting around waiting for something to happen. He succeeded because he always thought ahead.

"We knew it might come to this," Danté said. "That's why we have the plane."

Magnus stared for several seconds. His right hand rubbed at his left forearm, the fabric hissing quietly in the silent room. His nostrils were flaring again.

"Danté, you can't be serious about actually using that thing."

"Of course I'm serious. You think we spent fifty million dollars on something so we don't use it when we need it most? Rhumkorrf is close. They could have an embryo within a few weeks."

"Tomorrow, and tomorrow, and tomorrow," Magnus said. "Funny how I've heard the phrase *within a few weeks* for the last six months."

"Rhumkorrf produces results, Magnus. Venter's artificial bacteria, bringing the quagga back from extinction . . . every project he touches ends in success. He's been producing Nobel-quality work since he was ten years old."

"Has he also been racking up billion-dollar debts since he was ten years old?"

"Screw the debt," Danté said. "We've invested far too much money to abandon this."

"*Invested?* Is that what you still call it? We're broke. The well has run dry. Do you have any idea what it costs to actually fly that contraption?"

"I know."

"And what about Sara Purinam and her crew? That makes four new noses deep in our business. The more people, the more chance for infiltration."

"Now you sound like Colding."

The small smile returned. "A rare occurrence, I assure you, but sometimes Colding is right. Every person we add is a risk, or did you already forget about Galina?"

Danté's face felt hot. He didn't like to talk about that girl, not with his brother. "No, I haven't forgotten her. But we have to bring in Purinam and her crew. We just don't have a choice."

"Of course we have a choice. We had a choice with Galina."

It wasn't what Magnus said, but the way he said it. Danté blinked a few times. "That's not funny."

"Odd," Magnus said. "I'm so well known for my sense of humor."

Danté shook his head. Surely Magnus couldn't seriously suggest such a thing. "This is different. These people are loyal to us, so don't mention it again."

"Are you *sure*? Colding and Feely, they're both ex-USAMRIID, same department Fischer works for."

"We wouldn't even have a *company* if it wasn't for Colding."

Magnus shrugged. "And Feely? How do you know Fischer doesn't have him on a string?"

Danté rubbed his temples. "What choice do we have? Colding tells me Feely is the only reason Jian and Erika can work together at all."

"I think we should just end it."

"And then what? Do you want to tell the Chinese that Jian is gone? That their *money* is gone?"

Magnus looked at the da Vinci sketches. "Speaking of money, the Chinese cut us off even before the Novozyme incident. No more spendy-spendy for you, round-eye. The *whole company* is in the red because of Rhumkorrf's project, and now we're *adding* costs with Purinam and the plane? How are we going to pay for this?"

"I have an investor presentation scheduled. Five extremely rich individuals. I just have to ask for more than I originally planned."

Magnus turned back to look at Danté. Magnus rarely showed emotion, but Danté knew how to spot telltale signs of things like anger, frustration. Magnus had another tell, one he only seemed to express for Danté — the half-raised eyebrows of admiration.

"*Five?*" Magnus said. "Think you can get them all?"

"Does a bear shit in the woods?"

Magnus smiled again, a genuine one this time. Magnus possessed many skills Danté did not, but what Magnus *couldn't* do was charm billionaires out of their precious money. Danté could. Every time.

"This project is too important to stop now," Danté said. "We're talking about hundreds of thousands of lives."

"Hundreds of thousands? Being a little grandiose, don't you think? Maybe you're really talking about one life, in particular."

Danté's face flushed red. "That's *not* what this is about," he said, although he knew full well that when you got down to brass tacks, when you got down to the real nitty-gritty, that one life — *his* life — was *exactly* what it was all about. "We're pushing forward, Magnus. This benefits all of humanity. I don't care if we go into the red. This project puts Genada on top, that's what Dad would have wanted."

Magnus stared, but then his eyes softened, just a little, and he nodded.

"Magnus, these are trying times, but the hardest steel is forged in the hottest fires. Do you have my back, or not?"

Magnus drew a deep breath, then sighed and relaxed. "Of course I do. Always. You know you don't have to ask. I'm just not going to rubber stamp everything you say is all."

"We wouldn't be much of a team if you did. Please get Purinam and her crew ready, and you go with them. Load up one of the local backup herds before you take off. The move will be faster if we don't have to load the Baffin Island cattle. When you're thirty minutes out, call Colding and tell him to gather the staff for an emergency evac. Even if Fischer does pick off those signals, I don't think he'll have time to react."

Magnus stood and walked out of the office. Danté would have to watch him. His brother got things done, no question about that, but in stressful times like these he could make bad decisions.

Like the one he'd made about Galina Poriskova.

NOVEMBER 8: RUNNING SUCKS

"I HATE RUNNING," Harold Miller said between big breaths.

"Yeah," said Matt "Cappy" Capistrano, "I fucking hate running."

Sara Purinam shook her head, then wiped sweat out of her eyes. "Three more laps to go, let's dig."

Outside the hangar, winter winds swept across the snowy plains of Manitoba. Inside, however, she kept the temperature nice and warm. The huge plane took up most of the space, but she made sure all equipment was at least six feet away from the hangar walls. That left a nice running track all the way around. Civilians or not, her boys were going to stay in shape.

"Running sucks," Harold said.

"Yeah," Cappy said. "Running sucks."

The Twins, as Harold and Cappy were known, had elevated looking pitiful to an art form. Both jogged along, heads lolling a little bit, hands swinging loosely more than pumping. They ran the same, wore the same facial expressions, and repeated each other like sycophant parrots. They might have actually passed for twins save for the fact that Cappy was as black as an old Al Jolson caricature and if Miller were any whiter, his skin would have been transparent.

Sara looked up at the far wall. Alonzo Barella, the last member of their crew, had a half-lap lead. "Come on, guys, let's catch 'Zo."

"You catch him," Harold said as his already pathetic pace slowed to a walk.

"Yeah," Cappy said. "You catch him and shit."

It was one thing to piss and moan, another thing entirely to quit. Sara felt an automatic diatribe of discipline build up in her head, but she stopped it — they weren't in the military anymore and she wasn't their superior officer. They were all partners. Friends.

Instead of yelling, she doubled her pace, leaving the Twins behind. She reached the corner and turned left, keeping the hangar wall always on her right. Maybe this time, she would catch him.

Unlike the Twins, Alonzo Barella loved to run. The skinny man could go all day. Sara pushed her pace even more, cutting his lead in half, then slowed instantly as her cell phone rang. Not with the normal ring, but with Darth Vader's theme from *Star Wars* — the special ringtone she'd set up for Magnus Paglione.

"'Zo! Hold up!"

Up ahead, Alonzo stopped and turned. Jogging in place. He wasn't even sweating.

Sara answered. Within seconds she had her orders. After a year and a half of getting paid to do nothing but maintenance, it was time to bust out "Fred" and earn their keep.

And, she had to wonder, if she'd finally see that piece of shit P. J. Colding again.

NOVEMBER 8: NOT WIRED THAT WAY

INSIDE THE VETERINARY medicine lab, Erika Hoel cursed under her breath. Sixteen straight failures of the immune response test. Claus had been mad before, but this time his face had turned so red Erika wondered if her former lover might have a stroke.

Claus. That asshole. Erika hated the scientific failure, but couldn't help feeling some satisfaction at seeing Claus so angry. So . . . *frustrated*.

She'd loved him once, back when they worked together on the quagga project. Claus wanted what he couldn't have, and what he'd wanted was for Erika to love only him. But she wasn't wired that way. She had needs, baseline drives and desires that couldn't be ignored and didn't need to be corrected. There was nothing *wrong* with her. She liked men. She also liked women. If Claus had been right for her, he would have understood that, accepted it. But no, for all his brilliance, for all his righteous ego and accomplishments, deep down inside he was a small-souled man who needed to control people. A man who needed to be *the only one*.

She still loved Claus.

She still loved Galina.

And she had neither. Heartbreak is bad enough by itself, but a double dose is exponential agony.

Galina had been a far better assistant than Tim Feely. Not that Tim was stupid, not at all, but some people just operate on a different level. Tim was competent enough, and he also served . . . *other* purposes, true, but Galina he was not.

Erika had already been in love with Claus when Danté hired Galina. A second love had followed. Erika should have told Claus, but she'd known full well what he would say. So she'd kept it secret, and it had ended as badly as it could: when Claus caught them in the act.

Claus forced Danté to kick Galina out of the project. And then Galina had asked Erika to leave as well, so they could be together. And what had Erika chosen? The project. At the time she told herself the project was far more important than romantic dalliances. Oh, that conversation with

Galina, that *last* conversation — how it had shattered the young girl's heart.

Galina hadn't taken it lying down. She'd been willing to fight for Erika. Or so she'd said. Galina threatened to blow the whistle on Genada's human line of experimentation, but after a few weeks, Danté and Magnus had bought the girl off. They gave her millions in hush money and sent her back to Russia. Love, it seems, like everything else, has a price.

I chose the project. That's what Erika had told herself at the time. In the past year, however, she gradually realized the real reason she'd stayed. For Claus. To be near him. But he never forgave her. She had begged him for another chance. He would not cave. He never mentioned the incident, never changed the way he acted around Erika in the lab. In many ways that was even worse — now he treated her like a colleague, and a subordinate one at that, as if their hundreds of nights of passion had never existed at all.

She had chosen the project, and now the project was all she had.

Standard cloning projects had a fairly predictable pattern. First, select a cell from the animal you wanted to clone — usually a stem cell — and *enucleate* it by removing the single cell's nucleus. Second, take an egg from the surrogate mother and enucleate that as well. Third, put the stem cell nucleus into the now-empty egg cell, provide an electrical shock to fuse the two, then wait for the single cell to start dividing in a process called *mitosis*. If that happened, insert the hybrid egg into the surrogate mother and let it develop normally.

The method had originated in the legendary cloning of Dolly, the Scottish sheep. Later came the avalanche of cloned species: fish, birds, goats, cattle, even dogs and cats. The process had become so formulated that elements were taught as early as high school.

The key to all cloning methods revolved around using the same or similar species for both the egg and the creature to be cloned. For the ancestor project, however, the last close relative died out some 260 million years earlier. Jian's computer program, the thing they all called the "God Machine," had provided a genome that actually produced a viable embryo, splitting on its own, undergoing several rounds of mitosis. In a petri dish, that part, the *impossible* part, had already been solved. But you couldn't grow a whole animal in a petri dish — until they could trick the cow's immune system to accept the embryo as *self*, the embryo could not grow into a fetus, and the project was at a standstill.

With the quagga, the answer had been comparatively easy. The animal was closely related to zebras. Once they had cultivated a quagga chromosome out of DNA recovered from hair and other remains, they injected it into the enucleated zebra egg, then put the egg back into a surrogate zebra mother.

It hadn't worked at first. The zebra's immune system rejected the embryo. Erika had found a way around the problem by isolating the gene sequence that produced the antigens — the offending proteins — then replaced the sequence with the corresponding segment from the zebra's DNA. It had been a small section of DNA, and they still weren't sure exactly what it coded for, but the method worked. With the offending antigenic proteins eliminated, the zebra's body handled the pregnancy normally, resulting in the first baby quagga to set foot on the planet in more than a century.

But zebra and quagga DNA were over 99 percent identical. Now, however, they didn't have a mother that was a close genetic match. They had a computer-designed genome and a cow.

Jian's God Machine assigned a "viability rating" to estimate the chances of the hybrid egg passing the immune response test, then developing through surrogate pregnancy all the way to birth. It measured the products of known DNA sequences against those that were lesser known, or even unknown. So far, 65 percent was the highest rate they'd hit. Somewhere in that remaining 35 percent were the proteins that triggered the bovine immune system. That 35 percent amounted to billions of nucleotides, millions of sequences — far too many to eliminate by trial and error. No one knew exactly what genes coded for what traits. She and Jian kept changing these unknown sequences, but couldn't say for sure what the changes would affect — they might be swapping out a protein that affected the color of the animal's eyes, or a protein that was a critical component of brain development. And they *couldn't* know until the animal grew beyond a ball of undifferentiated cells. For the immune system experiment to work, they'd have to reach an 80 percent viability rating, possibly higher.

When they'd started the project with mammal genomes available online, in the public domain, the viability rating had been low. The first thousand genomes generated an 11 percent rating. The thousand after that took them to 20 percent. After they had processed four thousand mammalian genomes, they'd cracked 45 percent viability. From there, Genada's bottomless resources started sequencing uncommon mammals, even extinct species, and with each one the rating ticked a little bit higher.

Would Bobby Valentine's four new specimens be enough to get over

80 percent? And if not, what could she change? Perhaps a new approach and the additional genomes together would get them over the hump. Part of Erika hoped for success, but a stronger part hoped for failure. The last thing she wanted to see was Dr. Claus Rhumkorrf rewarded for being a heartbreaking, small-minded prick.

NOVEMBER 8: EVERY PICTURE
TELLS A STORY

MAGNUS FOLDED HIS cell phone and put it in his left jacket pocket. He took a sip from a glass of Yukon Jack. The ice cubes clinked a little. He set the drink down and put both hands on the desktop. He breathed slowly. In and out. In and out.

In contrast to his brother's da Vinci sketches and priceless works of art, Magnus decorated his office with personal items: dozens of photos, and a single, wall-mounted display case.

Several of the photos showed a smiling, postmission Magnus in various uniforms, some tan and brown, some green, one in a thick wet suit. In all of those, he was posing with other dirty, smiling, dangerous-looking men. Four faces showed up repeatedly: Andy Crosthwaite, Gunther Jones, Brady Giovanni and Bobby Valentine. Those pictures came from Magnus's years in Joint Task Force 2, the counterterrorist division of the Canadian Special Forces. He smiled a lot in those pictures. Things had made *sense* back then.

The largest photo was from Magnus's days as a tight end for the Calgary Stampeders of the Canadian Football League — dressed in the red-and-white uniform, stretching high and long to catch a football just before landing in the end zone. A simpler time, a time between leaving the service and joining Danté at Genada.

The pictures weren't all from the CFL or JTF2. One of them showed Magnus and Andy Crosthwaite holding hunting rifles, kneeling in front of an old well made of black stone, a bloody line of nine severed deer heads spread out before them. Danté kept asking him to take that picture down, said the office wasn't the place for it, but Magnus liked it, so it stayed. There were also postcardish shots, of course: pictures of Magnus and Danté fly-fishing in Montana, at a business meeting in Brussels, together on a yacht in the south of France. Those photos with his brother were true treasures –– nothing mattered more than family. Danté was the only family Magnus had left.

Danté had also asked Magnus to remove the wooden display case, but that simply wasn't going to happen. On the left, the case showed Magnus's unit insignia and rank pins. Stretching out to the right, a dozen Ka-Bar knives mounted point-down, sharp edge facing right. Each of the knives had a story. Five of the knives showed the blackened discolorations of metal heated in a fire. There was enough space for three or four more on the case's right-hand side. Some tales are never finished.

Magnus took one last deep breath, focused, let it out slow, then turned to his computer and called up a spreadsheet.

A lot of red.

His brother was running Genada into the ground because of some altruistic vision. And for what? A replacement organ bought you what, ten years? Maybe twenty? The universe was at least thirteen billion years old — were there even enough decimal places to measure twenty years against that?

Everyone dies.

Some sooner than others.

Danté had smarts, cleverness, business instincts. That was why Dad had left the company to Danté, not to Magnus. A smart decision, the *right* decision. But one thing that Danté didn't have was a real backbone. That was okay, though — that's what brothers are for. When it came time for the hard decisions, Magnus would protect his brother.

Magnus would make sure things got done.

COLDING KNOCKED ON the door to Tim Feely's apartment.

"Enter," Tim called from inside.

Colding tried the handle and found it locked. "It's locked, dumb-ass."

"You know the code."

"I don't know the code to your door, Tim."

"You know my computer password? Same thing, chief."

Colding sighed. He did know that password, as did everyone else. *6969.* The high-security practices of their resident computer expert. Colding punched the numbers into the keypad mounted on the wall next to the door.

Tim sat on the couch of his tiny living room, laptop on the coffee table in front of him. Also on the coffee table, a half-empty bottle of Talisker scotch. Tim loved his scotch.

His apartment looked exactly like Jian's, and every other apartment in the facility: about six hundred square feet of cozy space divided into a living room, a kitchenette, a bathroom and a bedroom.

"Come on, Tim. Why are you working in here instead of with Jian?"

"Because Tiny Overlord Rhumkorrf wants us to *think differently.*"

"Immune response test failed again?"

Tim nodded. Colding walked up to the couch and peeked at Tim's laptop screen.

"Dude," Colding said. "Is scotch and Tetris really part of thinking different?"

Tim shrugged. "Apparently my brain isn't really worth anything. I might as well explore new territories, like a good buzz and a high score."

"Oh come on. Your wallet should be embroidered with the words *smart motherfucker.* How did Rhumkorrf handle it?"

Tim paused the game, took a sip of his drink. "Rhumkorrf is a douchebag, man. A real douchebag."

"I don't see that," Colding said. "He's just an intense guy."

"He'd sell you out in a heartbeat if it got him what he wanted. He'd sell any of us out." Tim and Rhumkorrf had clashed from the beginning.

Tim did a good job of pushing down his dislike and playing his role. Mostly. "Know what really burns my ass?"

"What?"

"That Jian is doing the *real* work. So is Erika. But Rhumkorrf is going to get the lion's share of the credit."

"You gotta let it go," Colding said. "We're here to save lives, change history. Not for glory."

"Hah. I'm in it for the money."

Colding felt a stab of anger, but he shoved it away. Maybe Tim was kidding, maybe not. Didn't matter. As long as Tim helped make the project a success, he could have whatever motivation he liked.

"Should I check in on Rhumkorrf?"

Tim shrugged. "If you like being in the presence of a walking, talking asshole, that's your business. He'll be in the genetics lab, no doubt. But why do that when you can park your ass for a few and have a drink with me, brotha-man?"

"I should check in on everyone first. Maybe I'll have one later tonight."

Tim shook his head. "Naw, can't do later. I'm . . . I'm kind of taking a break now, but in a few hours I'll be locked down in here. Really getting into the research, you know? Tim needs his alone time. And before you ask, I checked on Jian and she's fine. And also, before you ask, I'll make sure she takes her meds in a little bit."

"Gosh, it's like you have ESP or something."

"That or a basic short-term memory," Tim said. "If you're not going to get tanked with me, kindly move along so I can make Tetris my digital bitch."

Colding gave a half-assed salute, then walked out of the apartment.

Just as Tim had predicted, Rhumkorrf stood alone in the genetics lab, staring at a wall-sized screen full of nothing but black squares.

"What's up, Doc?"

Rhumkorrf turned, eyes tight with anger, but seemed to relax a little when he saw Colding. "I fear I am not in the mood for your cartoon references today, my friend."

"Sufferin' succotash," Colding said. "That bad?"

"Yes, that bad. We're at an impasse. I'm convinced we're missing something relatively obvious."

"Did you try turning it off, then turning it back on?"

Rhumkorrf glared, then laughed. "If only it were that simple. Is Bobby still here? I could use some flying time to forget all of this."

"Sorry, he had to take off. If it's any consolation, he left four new samples."

The little man sighed. "Well, who knows. Maybe the answer is in one of those. Please ask Tim to process them right away."

"Tim is very busy," Colding said. "Said he had a puzzling issue."

Rhumkorrf rolled his eyes. "You're a horrible liar. Tetris again?"

Colding nodded.

Rhumkorrf rubbed his eyes. "Have Jian process the samples. The work is beneath her, but maybe she could use the change of pace."

"Speaking of Jian, Doc, her nightmares are getting worse."

"Oh? How often? More intense?"

Rhumkorrf's words came out fast and clipped. He even sounded a little excited. Colding often wondered if the man saw Jian as a person or as a set of symptoms, just another scientific problem to be solved.

"Three nights in a row," Colding said. "I can't really say if they're more intense."

"Any hallucinations?"

"I don't think so. Should you change her dosage again?"

Rhumkorrf shook his head. "No, we need to let the most recent change run its course, see if it corrects the situation before we introduce an additional variable."

"But she's sleeping less and less. I'm worried about her."

"You worry about everyone and everything," Rhumkorrf said. "Trust me, I'll make adjustments before she becomes suicidal again. We can't lose Jian, now can we?"

Colding chewed on his lower lip. Rhumkorrf was the doctor here, and he'd helped Jian before. Maybe the little man was right, maybe these things just took time.

"Okay," Colding said. "I'll give Jian the samples and have her process them. How about you? Can I get you anything?"

"Do you have a Nobel Prize in your pocket?"

"No, that's not a Nobel Prize, I'm just *really* glad to see you."

Rhumkorrf laughed again, then pushed Colding out of the lab.

NOVEMBER 8: OPPORTUNITY
OF A LIFETIME

THE FIVE PEOPLE in Genada's plush meeting room made for quite the Fortune 500 photo op. Two men and a woman from America, one playboy Brit entrepreneur and one Chinese shipping mogul. Both of the American men had made billions in technology — one in software, the other with a search engine — while the woman had turned her family's small line of hotels into the world's second-largest chain.

The shipping mogul was the biggest risk. If word got back to the Chinese State Council, Danté would have much to answer for. They expected to be the sole investor in this project. When it succeeded, the Chinese government would have a way to help its estimated 1.5 million citizens waiting for an organ transplant. With only about a hundred thousand potential donors annually, the People's Republic was desperate to do something to help its populace. The situation was so bad that human rights organizations claimed prisoners were being killed to harvest their organs. China needed a solution. Rhumkorrf's project was it.

Still, the shipping magnate hadn't become one of the richest people on the planet by running his mouth about exclusive investment opportunities. He'd be fine. At least, Danté *hoped* he'd be fine.

Danté greeted the billionaires, gave his most charming smile, then got down to business. "Genada has a cash-flow issue with a critical project. We need capital and we need it now. That gives you a window of opportunity. You've all signed nondisclosure agreements, so I'll just cut to the chase."

He picked up a remote control and hit a button, turning on the large flat-panel monitor mounted on the wall. The screen displayed a chart with a rising, jagged red line.

"The red line represents the growing number of people in the United States with terminal illnesses who are waiting for an organ transplant. Over a hundred thousand right now, up from eighty thousand just five years ago, which was up from fifty-three thousand a decade ago. A new name is added to the list every ten minutes. Only about fifteen thousand organs will become available this year, roughly fifty-five percent from deceased donors, the rest from living donors. In the United States, the average wait for a kidney is over fourteen months. The discrepancy between those needing an organ and available organs increases by about twelve percent each year. Roughly fourteen thousand Americans will die, *this year,* while waiting for an organ that will never arrive.

"Those numbers are just the United States. Worldwide, some estimates range as high as 750,000 people who need a kidney transplant. That doesn't take into account the need for hearts, lungs and livers.

"Genada estimates the average fee for a replacement organ will be around fifty thousand dollars. That means an annual market of over thirty-seven *billion.* And that is the *current* market. With improving living conditions and medical care in India, China, and elsewhere in the developing world, we expect the number of people needing an organ transplant to *double* in the next ten years. Do I have your attention thus far?"

The five investors' heads nodded in unison.

"Several companies are trying to solve this shortfall by a process known as xenotransplantation — transplanting the organs or tissues of one species into another."

"Animal parts," said a small man with thick glasses and a mop haircut. He was one of the American software magnates, and by some standards, the richest man on Earth. "Baboon hearts, pig livers and the like."

Danté nodded and smiled. "With current technology, a xenotransplant can keep someone alive for a few days, weeks at most, and only then if the patient stays in a hospital the whole time. The human immune system, you see, usually attacks the organ. Defeating that immune response is the goal of most companies, but solving that issue leads to a larger, far more significant hazard.

"Xenotransplantation opens up the possibility of a virus jumping species. When you introduce a foreign organ into a human body, you also introduce any viruses that are in that organ. Normally, these viruses die quickly, as they aren't designed to attack a human host. But if those viruses adapt to infect human cells, we can get an infection against which humans have no natural antibodies."

"The H1N1 virus," the shipping magnate said. "Swine flu, SARS, bird flu. Those are species-jumping viruses."

"Or like what just happened in Greenland," said the lone woman. "This doesn't sound like a valid investment to me. It sounds like a way to kill millions."

The comment caught Danté by surprise. The four men looked at the woman — they obviously hadn't heard about Greenland, but their confidence slipped nonetheless. Apparently Genada wasn't the only company with contacts in high places. Danté briefly wondered if Farm Girl might be selling the same information to other parties.

"Genada has the solution," he said. "We are perhaps the *only* valid investment in this area, because our process eliminates any possibility of a virus jumping from the donor species to humans."

He clicked a button on the remote. The picture showed a small creature perched on a rotting log, surrounded by exotic vegetation of some long-gone jungle. The creature had somewhat of a teardrop shape — thick in the middle, narrowing to thin hips and ending in a short, pointed tail. The rear legs stuck out at forty-five-degree angles from those slight hips, resulting in knees and feet farther away from the body than those of a cat or a dog. The front legs also jutted away from the body, but at less of an angle. A sparse layer of silvery fur covered the lithe little body. Although it showed some characteristics of a modern animal, particularly the long whiskers protruding from its pointy nose, it looked unmistakably primitive.

"This is a Thrinaxodon, which lived some two hundred million years ago. It's a member of a group of animals known as Synapsids, also called *proto*-mammals. Something like the Thrinaxodon gave rise to all mammals. That something is the ancestor of you, me, dogs, dolphins, every mammal species. That ancestor, my friends, is what Genada is re-creating, and it's going to make all of you a great deal of money."

The mop-haired man stood up, a big smile on his face, his eyes alight with excitement. "So let me get this straight — you're creating this ancestor creature so you can put its organs into people and save lives, and at the same time, *eliminate* the possibility of these dangerous viruses?"

Danté nodded. "We will create an animal similar to the mammalian ancestor. Since the ancestor would be engineered from the DNA up, we can ensure the resulting animal will not carry any naturally occurring viruses that could adapt to infect people.

"Cataloging and working with this computerized biological data is a science called *bioinformatics*. The Human Genome Project and Celera Genomics sequenced the entire human genetic code, right down to every last nucleotide, but humans were only the start. Scientists have sequenced thousands of mammals, storing the digital analysis in public databases like GenBank. These genomes, combined with animals we sequenced ourselves, give Genada the complete genetic code of almost every mammal on the planet."

"I do not understand," the shipping magnate said. "You have genomes of *modern* animals, but not of this ancestor?"

"Genetic mutation is the basis of evolution," Danté said. "But not all genes mutate at the same rate. As species branch out from a common ancestor, some genes mutate faster, some don't mutate at all. By using a *molecular clock,* so to speak, we can gauge which sequences have changed, and by comparing that gene to the same gene of another mammal, we can tell which sequence is older, closer to the original ancestor's genetic code."

The woman smiled. "I'll be damned. That's such a simple concept, just use the lowest common denominator. You take out everything that's *unique,* and you'll be left with everything that's common."

Danté nodded. They were getting it. The woman was the toughest sell. The software mogul was in, Danté could see that as plain as day, but if the woman invested the last three would follow.

"Our staff created an evolution lab inside the computer," Danté said. "This program statistically analyzes genomes based on the probable function of each gene sequence. The computer works with our digitized ancestor genome, predicting final form and function, then makes changes, predicts again, and measures probability for desired traits. It's just like evolution, only in reverse and a million times faster than nature. We create the creature in the computer, one nucleotide at a time. Since it is created from scratch, we know — *for certain* — that it's free of any viral contamination."

The Chinese man spoke. "But that animal on the screen, it is too small. You could not put its heart in me."

"Correct," Danté said. "But that animal on the screen was created only *in silica,* only on the computer, to give us a baseline. We've already done that. From there, the computer added specific virtual genes coding for size and human organ compatibility. Our first living generation won't be perfect, but we can analyze the *phenotype* — the size of the animal and what it looks like — against the *genotype* — the actual DNA coding. Once we have that, we keep modifying the genome until the animal's organs are ideally suited for human transplantation."

The mop-haired man sat back down. "But if you have all this technology, why not just grow the organs individually?"

"Some companies are working on just that solution, but it's not yet possible. And when it is possible, growing an individual organ will require an expensive lab or manufacturing center. Short answer, the cost per organ would be astronomical. Genada's ancestors, on the other hand, will be herd animals. Most importantly, *they will be able to breed.* All we have to do is put them out to pasture and feed them. Organ demand grows? We simply raise more animals."

"What about PETA," the woman asked. "And what about the Animal Liberation Front? They've been targeting xenotransplantation research."

"We think we have the competitive advantage there as well," Danté said. "The ancestors do not occur in nature. We *made* them, down to the last strands of DNA. We will even use that fact to insist other companies abandon research on pigs and primates. If Genada has already solved the problem, there is no longer a need for that potentially dangerous research."

The software magnate laughed. "You want a monopoly. A monopoly on human life."

Danté nodded. "Lady and gentlemen, nothing sells like life itself. When we succeed, we will be the only vendor. We will be able to charge whatever the market will bear. For the millions of people not quite ready for death, the market would bear quite a lot."

Within an hour, all five had left, and all five had given the same decision: *yes*. That gave Genada enough capital for at least one more year.

Magnus would be so pleased.

THE WRISTWATCH BUZZED. It wasn't an alarm buzz, because for alarms, the watch beeped. The buzz only meant one thing.

Contact.

The buzz was a five-minute warning, a notice to go somewhere, be alone before the full message came in. There was no one else in the room. The five minutes passed very slowly.

A tiny chip in the watch picked up certain heavily encrypted satellite signals. The chip decoded those signals, buzzing out the translated message in the simple dots and dashes of Morse code.

-.. . ..., -.-. --- --.,-- -. . --- --
Destroy comm

-.. . ... - .-. --- -.-- .-.-.. .-.. - .-.-. -. ...
Destroy all trans

-.. . ... - .-. --- -.-- .-.- .-.-.. .-. .. -- -.-.-
Destroy all data

... ..- .-. . .--. --- -.- - / .-.. .- -. -.. ... / .- - / .---- --... --... ----- -----
Support lands at 17:00

After all this time, the command to act. How odd, when the project was so close to completion, close to extending life for millions of people. No, not *when* . . . the correct word was *if*. There was no guarantee they would ever overcome the immune response.

And besides, who gave a fuck? Someone would figure this out eventually. As long as Rhumkorrf didn't get the credit, it would all work itself out.

It would be dangerous, true, but the plan was already made and it wasn't that difficult. Quietly take out the transportation and communication to completely isolate the project. Then, destroy the data, both the live set and the backup. After that? Play dumb and wait for Colonel Fischer and his goons to arrive.

At the computer, a few key taps brought up a private menu. Several prepared programs were ready to go, hidden inside a miles-long stream of archived genetic code. No way it was safe to hide the programs in a ready-to-use format, not with Jian on the island. That woman interacted with computers in a way that defied logic — if hacker programs were just sitting there, Jian would have found them somehow.

These programs would cause *some* damage. How much damage depended on whether Jian was awake or asleep. She was the only real variable, which meant something had to be done about her or the plan might not work.

Regardless, tonight it would all be over . . . one way or another.

A
G
C
T

OVER AND OVER again, the endless chains scrolled across the screen, some segments highlighted in yellow, some in green, some in red, other colors. The *special* language. The *true* language of life. A language that for some reason only she could *really* see, really understand.

Biological poetry.

"Tian?"

She blinked. The poetry changed back to scrolling letters. She was in the bioinformatics lab. She looked up to see Tim standing in front of her desk.

"Mister Feely," she said, and as she did she realized that he'd been standing there for several seconds, quietly saying her name over and over. Part of her brain had heard him but hadn't wanted to come out of that special place.

"You're my boss," he said. "Think maybe you can finally stop calling me *mister*?"

She shook her head. No, she could not do that. Sometimes she tried, tried to say *P. J.* or *Tim* or *Claus*, but it always came out *Mister Colding* or *Mister Feely* or *Doctor Rhumkorrf.*

Her seven-monitor computer array here was identical to the one in her room. Tim held up a bottle and a medicine cup, reached around the outside monitors to offer them to her. "You forget something?"

Her meds.

She looked at the bottle, then at her watch. She was two hours behind on her meds. "Ah. I am sorry." She took the bottle and plastic cup.

He walked around the desk to stand next to her chair. "And what are you doing up? You should be in bed. How about you turn in?"

She shook her head, put the medicine bottle down and started reaching for the fridge under her desk.

"Got you covered," Tim said. He pulled a can of Dr Pepper from his lab coat pocket. She smelled alcohol on his breath.

"Mister Feely, have you been drinking?"

"Just a shot or two," he said. "And speaking of shots, the meds are yours, and this can is your chaser. So drink up!"

Tim made her laugh. He was a good assistant, although not as good as Galina had been. But where Galina had spent most of her time with Erika, Tim made sure Jian took her meds, slept, even ate. Sometimes Jian actually forgot to eat, in the times when the code took over and minutes turned to hours turned to days.

Jian poured the lithium citrate into the medicine cup, filling it to the five-milliliter line. She drank the medicine, then immediately drained the whole can of Dr Pepper. Carbonation bubbled up in her mouth, chasing away the lithium's nasty taste. The bad taste was worth it, though, because it made her normal. Made her able to function without seeing . . . *them*. The medicine let her work.

She reached for the fridge again, but Tim produced a second can from his other pocket.

"Got you covered," he said.

Jian blushed a little. Tim and P. J. took such good care of her. It almost made this place tolerable despite Rhumkorrf's pressure and the constant mean comments from that evil bitch Erika.

"Jian, come on," Tim said. "We've failed the immune test before. Give work a rest for a little bit. We'll get back to it in the morning."

"No, we must work. Did you come up with anything?"

"Yes," Tim said. "A bitchin' new high score in Tetris."

"You must be very proud."

"Not really. I reprogrammed it so I could win. Maybe you should try playing some video chess. Let your mind do something else for a little bit."

She shrugged. She wasn't about to lecture a grown man on the value of hard work.

"Come on, Jian. Go to bed."

"I will," she said. "Let me finish sequencing the four new samples first, then I will sleep."

"Promise?"

She nodded.

"All right," Tim said. "Then you're on your own. I'm pooped. Cheating at Tetris will really take it out of you. Night."

He turned and walked out of the room. She rubbed her eyes. She *was* tired. But it wouldn't take that long to finish this process.

They'd long ago collected samples of every living mammal known to man. After that, Danté had started acquiring samples from extinct species. Each time they digitized one of those additional genomes, the God Machine's viability rate went up. Would the four new samples Bobby had delivered take them over 80 percent?

The myriad forms of animals on Earth take many shapes, but every last one is made from a simple set of four nucleotides: *adenine, guanine, cytosine* and *thymine*. Those four basic nucleotides create the double helix structure that is deoxyribonucleic acid, or DNA. Some people didn't understand *double helix*, but everyone got Jian's favorite description — the twisting ladder.

Variety between the strands, across the *rungs* of the DNA ladder, is limited even further, to just *two* combinations: adenine can only bind with thymine, and guanine can only bond with cytosine. But the combinations along the *sides* of the ladder, the four letters *A, G, T* and *C,* combine in infinite ways.

Those infinite combinations were what Jian wanted to analyze, to digitize, so the God Machine could see the full genome of each animal and compare it with the master ancestor sequence.

First, she extracted the cellular DNA of the four extinct mammals and placed each in a vial. To each vial, she added her sequencing master mix. The mix consisted of a DNA polymerase, random primers and the four basic nucleotides. The mix also included dideoxynucleotides, which were nucleotides with a slightly different chemical structure that contained a fluorescent section critical to the final stage of the process.

She slid the vials into a polymerase chain reactor, a machine designed to produce billions of copies of the target DNA. First the PCR machine "unzipped" the DNA by heating it to ninety-five degrees Celsius, which broke the hydrogen bonds in the rungs. That split the double helix, leaving two single strands of DNA. The machine then cooled the mixture to fifty-five degrees Celsius. This brought the prefabricated random primers into play. A primer is to a strand of DNA what a foundation is to a brick wall: DNA strands can't form at random, they have to begin with a primer. Lowering the temperature allowed the primers to lock in to complementary sections on the single DNA strand, so that a primer with the combination ACTGA would make rungs that created a combination of TGACT on the other side of the ladder. *A* binds with *T*, *C* binds with *G*, and click, a starting point locks down.

Then, more heat.

As the temperature rose to seventy-two Celsius, the DNA polymerase started at the random primers and moved down the open strand, locking free nucleotides onto the open-ended single DNA strands — just like a train engine building the track underneath it as it goes. The end result was two perfect copies of the original DNA strand. From there, the process quickly repeated over and over — two copies became four, then eight, then sixteen, an exponential increase that added up fast.

In years past, there had been more steps she had to follow, but now the entire process was automated. Her machine created *millions* of identical copies, peppered with the little fluorescent dideoxynucleotide chunks that marked segments. The computer used a laser to make those chunks fluoresce, then counted off the segments. End result? A nucleotide-by-nucleotide analysis of the animal's DNA. The millions of copies provided an extremely high degree of accuracy.

The resultant data fed automatically into the supercomputer known as the God Machine. There, Jian's programming would take over. She closed the lid on the PCR machines and set them to run automatically.

In just a few hours, the four new DNA sequences would join the thousands they had already sequenced. She called up the current genome database.

GENOME A17 SEQUENCING: PROCESSING
PROOFREADING ALGORITHM: PROCESSING
PROJECTED VIABILITY PROBABILITY: 65.0567%

Over and over again the powerful God Machine processed trillions of combinations of DNA, looking for the magical set that would produce a viable embryo. They were close now. A few more samples, a few more mammalian species, perhaps, and they would have it.

She still had her secret experiment, the one she hadn't revealed to Rhumkorrf. Colding had insisted on destroying all elements of the human surrogate mother program. Jian had saved just a little bit. A *special* little bit. She had an ancestor genome with 99.65 percent viability probability, one that would beat the immune response for sure.

Not a cow's immune response . . . *her* immune response.

That had been her little secret through the human surrogate phase.

She'd used her own DNA as the primary working template. The irony was that Colding's insistence on eliminating the human surrogates had saved the company, but if they *could* use a human surrogate, they would have successful implantation on the first try. Jian had kept her own modified eggs, hiding them inside the waist-high tank of liquid nitrogen that also held the last sixteen rounds of God Machine genomes. They were *her* eggs, after all, and she couldn't really bear to part with them.

Maybe, if the bovine experiments totally failed, she'd actually use them. Millions of lives hung in the balance. Rhumkorrf would probably even help. He was desperate to make it happen, desperate to make Jian stop being so *stupid*, such a *failure*.

So many people. People dying every day, dying because of her incompetence.

She needed to relax. Maybe Tim was right . . . maybe a little video game. Just for a few minutes. No one would know if she stopped working. Jian quietly turned to her left-lower monitor and called up the Chess Master program. So bad to play now! But she was stumped. Come on, Kasparov level, do your best.

She always beat the Kasparov level. At least the computer program was good enough to make her actually think about her moves, which was more than she could say of playing anyone else in the project. Poor P. J., always trying so hard to win, but he could only see five or six moves into the future. Jian saw entire games played out before the first pawn advanced.

She stared at the black-and-white pieces lined up neatly on the video chessboard. The computer waited for her to make the first move, but for some reason she could only stare at the pieces. The black pieces. The white pieces. Black and white.

Black and white.

Black and white.

They might be another color, and yet the game would still be the same. Blue and red, yellow and purple, and that wouldn't make any difference because the *board's* function didn't change.

The board that lay *underneath* the black-and-white pieces. Black and white . . .

. . . like the fur on the cows.

"That's it," she whispered. "That's it!"

She quit the chess program and called up the bovine genome, her fingers an unrecognizable blur on the keyboard. It was so obvious. Why hadn't she thought of this before? If all that mattered was the internal

organs, the *underneath*, she could eliminate hundreds of potentially prob-
lematic genes by swapping out what was *on top* — the integument.

The God Machine could process that change even while counting off
the genomes of the four extinct mammals. Could all of it be enough to
push the viability rating over 80 percent?

Her main terminal let out an alarm beep, demanding her attention. She
called up the alarm window.

REMOTE BACKUP FAILURE

The off-site backup, the ten-petabyte data drive array that sat in a
temperature-controlled brick building at the end of the runway . . . it had
failed. That system hadn't failed once in the fourteen months since they'd
installed it. The array was designed to survive no matter what, to keep the
experiment alive in the event of worst-case scenarios at the main facility.
Computer crashes, fire, electromagnetic pulses . . . she'd been told it could
even survive a really big explosive called a *fuel-bomb*, although she couldn't
imagine why someone would use such a destructive thing on a harmless
research facility.

The timing couldn't be worse. She had inspiration, the missing link that
might let her solve the immune reaction problem. But she highly doubted
the backup drive failure was an accident — someone was up to something.
She'd just have to do two things at once: deal with the backup failure, and
simultaneously type in the genetic code that had hit her like a blast of moun-
tain wind. She isolated the computer lab from the rest of the network, then
quickly called up a diagnostics program.

NOVEMBER 8: MRS. SANSOME

Margarite's hands moved of their own accord, as if possessed by an unseen demon of passion. She undid the laces on her bodice, slowly exposing her soft, moon-shaped breasts. When the night air caressed her nipples she gasped . . . how could she be so bold?

"Yes, Mrs. Sansome," Craig beckoned heatedly. "Yes, let me see."

"I will, Craig," she cooed sexually.

She stared at him, her eyes passionately out of focus. She wanted him. But he was a vampire! And a stable boy vampire at that!! She had come so far from her servant beginnings, winning the hand of Edward and becoming Mrs. Edward Sansome the Duchess of Tethshire and a very rich woman with money and jewels and many servants of her own. This was wrong, was it not? This was evil! She had to run! Run to Pastor Johnson and do something or she would become an evil denizen of the night and seek the blood of innocents.

However, before she could turn and run, Craig stood up and effortlessly declothed himself of his trousers. His penis sparkled in the moonlight like skin made of crushed rubies.

GUNTHER JONES SAT back and read his words. Not bad, if he did say so himself. Take a bite out of that, Stephenie Meyer. How hard could it be? Some handsome bloodsuckers, some romance, a little forbidden fruit that turns into hot sex, and boom — vampire novel.

The wee hours of the morning were usually his most creative. Tucked away in the security control room, no one bothered him, particularly at 3:00 A.M. Not that he didn't do his job . . . there just wasn't much job to do. Other than making sure Jian didn't try to off herself, he ran through all scheduled procedures and checked that the alarm systems were online. If anything came up that required eyeballs, he woke Brady or Andy or Colding, depending on who was on call.

Closed-circuit cameras blanketed the facility's interior, giving him a view of every possible angle. After almost two years here, he was adept at keeping the monitors in his peripheral vision — if something out there moved, he'd see it. Nothing ever did. That meant Gunther Jones basically got paid damn good money to sit and write for hours on end.

He'd completed two novels in the *Hot Dusk* series already: *Hot Dusk* and *Hot Evening*. As soon as he finished his current book, *Hot Midnight*, he'd have a kick-ass trilogy to push on agents.

The computer beeped, indicating an alert. Gunther reduced his novel (making sure to save it first, he wasn't about to lose those amazing words), revealing a flashing alert message:

SATELLITE UPLINK SIGNAL DOWN

He called up the maintenance screen, hit the *re-link* button, then waited to see the link reconnect like it always did. Colding didn't like losing that signal, although it happened from time to time for some interstellar communications reason they didn't really understand. A new message appeared:

NO SIGNAL DETECTED, RE-LINK FAILURE

Huh. He'd never seen that before. He repeated the step and waited.

NO SIGNAL DETECTED, RE-LINK FAILURE

"Colding's going to be pissed." Gunther called up the diagnostics program and let it run.

HARDWARE FAILURE

He stared at the screen. Hardware failure? That had never happened before. There was only one thing left to do in the repair protocol — send out some eyeballs. He turned to the vid-phone and punched Brady's room.

NOVEMBER 8: A HOT TIME
IN THE OLD TOWN

BRADY GIOVANNI DIDN'T mind the cold, but that didn't mean he was stupid about it. He had been one of those kids who always listened to his mother. Growing up in Saskatoon, listening to your mother meant dressing warm.

When on call, dressing warm meant wearing his thermal long johns and socks to bed, cutting down his response time. After Gunther's call woke him, it took Brady only seconds to pull on the black Genada parka with matching snow pants, military-grade cold-weather gloves, a scarf and the thing that Andy "The Asshole" Crosthwaite teased him about to no end — a wool hat knitted by none other than Brady's mother. The hat fit perfectly over his big head and the headset/mic combo in his ear.

He punched in his access code at the front interior airlock door. It opened and he stepped into the chamber. He closed the door and waited five seconds while the pressure equalized. A beep from the door let him know the cycle had finished.

"Gun, this is Brady, exiting now."

"Roger that," Gunther's voice said in his ear.

Beretta in hand, Brady opened the heavy latch to the outside door and stepped out into the cold night air. The compound's lights lit up the grounds. From the door, he could see the back of the satellite dish. Nothing moving. He double-timed it across the snow, the icy wind pulling at him as he ran. It could blow all it wanted, because Brady was prepared. Maybe a little more than just *prepared*, as proven by the sweat that already trickled down his armpits despite the subzero temperatures.

He kept a sharp watch as he cut a wide circle around the satellite dish. Nothing really happened at the isolated facility. Even something as trivial as this hardware failure brought welcome excitement, gave him a chance to practice good soldiering.

The fifteen-foot-wide satellite array pointed out to the stars, away from Brady. His circle brought him around to the front, where he could see the receiver held up by metal arms that pointed in and up from the concave dish. As he moved, he steadily swept his vision from left to right, then right to left.

Gunther's voice piped into his headset. "You there yet?"

"I'm twenty feet away and you know that," Brady said. "You're watching on infrared, aren't you?"

Gunther's laugh sounded tinny through the small headset. "Yeah, I love this thing. Never get to use it. Nothing moving out there but you, big fella."

Brady came around the front of the satellite dish. Seeing no movement, he closed in until he could examine the receiver. He stared at the gadget for a full three seconds, not really believing what he saw.

Baffin Island wasn't boring anymore.

THE VID-PHONE AGAIN let out its shrill digital blare. Colding groaned and rolled over and looked at the phone — 3:22 A.M. Jian again? Jesus, couldn't a guy just get some fucking sleep around here? Colding clicked the *connect* button.

"What's up, Gun?"

"We have a situation," Gunther said in a rush. "The satellite array has been damaged."

Colding instantly came fully awake. "Define *damaged*."

"Let me patch in Brady," Gunther said. "Brady, Colding's on, tell him what you see."

Gunther's face stayed on the screen, but Brady's girlish voice came from the speakers. "Someone whacked the fuck out of the satellite array. The dish is fine, but the receiver-transmitter unit has been smashed up pretty bad. Looks like marks from an axe."

An axe. There were twelve fire axes spread through the small facility's interior. Whoever sabotaged the satellite dish had come from inside the building.

"Gunther," Colding said, "activate all the apartment cameras and give me a head count, right now."

"No problem, boss." Gunther's eyes looked away from the screen, back to another unseen monitor.

"Let's see . . . Jian is awake and in the bioinformatics lab, typing away. Rhumkorrf is in his bed, looks asleep. Andy disconnected his room camera, but I can hear him snoring over the vid-phone. Hoel is buried in her blankets. Brady is at the dish, I'm here, you're there, and . . . hey . . . Tim's not in his room."

Colding stood up. "Not in his room? Where is he? Do an infrared body count of the whole building."

Gunther's droopy eyes narrowed in concentration. "Um . . . infrared confirms all visuals. Everyone accounted for except for Brady and Tim. And I just checked the access and egress logs. No one has coded in or out for the past two hours."

"But I just went out," Brady said. "Walked right out the front."

"Not showing up," Gunther said. "Someone shut off the tracking. And it looks like the hallway cameras are fixed on a loop. I . . . I can't tell how long it's been since they've shown live video."

Colding started pulling on his clothes. "Call up access to the admin log. Whose code turned off those systems?"

"Uh . . ." Colding heard Gunther's fingers tapping away. "I'm looking."

"Move it, Gun! You're supposed to know how to do this shit!"

"I know, I know! Hold on . . . here it is. Access code was 6969."

Tim's code. But why? Why would Tim do such a thing after all this time? Why . . . unless . . .

"Brady," Colding said, "I want Tim found. He's sabotaging us."

"Yes sir."

"And keep your eyes open. He's got that axe at least, if not other weapons."

"Yes sir," Brady said. "Should I take him out?"

"*No*, for fuck's sake, don't kill anybody," Colding said, shocked at how quickly Brady considered lethal force against a friend. But Brady was thinking like a soldier. Colding needed to think like that as well. If Tim really had taken a payoff from another biotech company, or far worse, he was working with Longworth's special threats biotech task force, there was no telling what the guy might do.

"Protect yourself," Colding said. "But do whatever you can to avoid *shooting* him, okay?"

"Yes sir," Brady said, his voice crawling up another pitch in the excitement.

"Gunther," Colding said, "get Andy up and tell him to guard the rear airlock. If Tim's outside, I don't want him getting back in. And get the internal cameras working."

"Fuck, man, I don't know how to do that."

"You told me you'd studied up on the system, goddamit!"

"I know, I know! My bad, but I can't fix it now. You want me to go outside and search as well?"

Colding punched his leg in frustration. Gunther was too busy writing his fucking vampire romance novels to do the homework that was expected of him. Colding's own fault, really, for taking Gunther's word for it instead of riding shotgun. "Just stay in the control room and get it fixed."

"Yes sir." Gunther's face disappeared from the screen.

Colding jammed his feet into his boots, then reached into his nightstand, pulled out his Beretta and popped out the magazine — full. He made sure the safety was on before he shrugged on his parka. He quietly opened his door and cautiously checked the hallway. Seeing no movement, he headed for the main airlock.

THE ADMIN SCREEN listed five errors.

BACKUP FAILURE
SATELLITE HARDWARE FAILURE
DOOR ACCESS TRACKING SYSTEM FAILURE
CAMERA SYSTEM FAILURE
HANGAR TEMPERATURE LEVEL DANGEROUSLY LOW

Jian's fingers danced across the keyboard, calling up menu after menu, or trying to — most of them were blocked. Her access code had been erased. She had to move fast. Whoever was doing this wanted to wipe out the research. Something had taken out the satellite uplink, so she couldn't even do an emergency data-dump to Genada headquarters in Manitoba. On top of that, the hacker had already erased the off-site backup drive. *Erased it.* The only remaining active data set was in the main drive, located right under her desk in the bioinformatics lab. Jian had caught the attack on that drive, intercepted it in midstream and countered it. If she had been sleeping they would have lost everything the God Machine had produced since Bobby Valentine brought the latest samples.

And that would have been disaster indeed . . . because it was *finally* working.

She split her focus between wiping out the last vestiges of the rampaging computer programs and watching the God Machine's readout. She would handle the other problems as soon as she could. Fixing the cameras would be a snap, but she didn't know what was causing the hangar temperature to drop. Someone had manually shut off the radiant heaters, but why?

The God Machine interrupted her thoughts with a cheerful chime that sounded horribly out of place considering the current situation. Jian looked at the upper-middle-left screen, the one that showed the new announcement.

GENOMES A17 SEQUENCING: COMPLETE
PROOFREADING ALGORITHM: COMPLETE
VIABILITY PROBABILITY: 95.0567%

Ninety-five percent. She had done it. Whatever it took, she had to protect this data set.

HE HUNG IN that space between conscious and unconscious. Bits and pieces came back . . . a sound, his name, the shitty taste in his mouth. Andy Crosthwaite just wanted to stay asleep.

But that rotten cocksucker Gunther would just *not* shut the fuck up.

"Andy, come on, wake up!"

The only light in the room came from the vid-phone, which was damn near blinding to Andy's squinting, sleepy eyes. The phone's screen showed that dickhead Gunther looking like he needed a bathroom pit stop pronto before he dropped the Hershey squirts in his pants.

"Gun, don't you have a fag novel to write, or something?"

"Andy, I'm not kidding, get your ass up now."

"Fuck off."

"*Get up!* Tim's sabotaging the place, you need to guard the back door!"

Andy reached out and put the vid-phone facedown. Then he put his spare pillow on top of it. It didn't drown Gunther out completely, but Andy was a very sound sleeper and it would be enough.

"ANDY, YOU SHITHEAD, wake up!"

The feed from Andy's vid-phone had gone black. Gunther started to scream again, louder this time, when motion on another monitor caught his eye.

The hangar.

"Brady! Brady, come in!"

"Easy, Gun! This headset is *inside* my ear, okay?"

"Right, sorry." Gunther continued in a calm voice. "Infrared shows the cows in their stalls in the hangar, but there is a person moving by the vehicles."

"Just one? You're sure?"

Gunther looked again. The black-and-white monitor showed heat in white, cooler colors in gray shading to black. Aside from the cows and the mystery heat source, he saw only Brady, moving from the satellite dish toward the hangar's front door. "Confirmed, just one target. Gotta be Tim."

"Can you see what he's doing? Where is he?"

"Looks like he's in front of the Humvee. No, he's moving to the back of the hangar. He's going for the cattle! *Move!*"

Colding's voice sounded on the same channel. "Brady, slow down. I'm on my way outside."

Gunther saw Brady's heat signal close on the hangar's front door.

"Gotta take him now," Brady said as he closed the last ten feet. "Can't let Tim kill the cows."

"*No,*" Colding said. "Brady, just wait!"

On the black-and-gray monitor's picture, Gunther saw Tim's white heat signature sprint away from the hangar's back door. The signature stopped for just a second, then Gunther saw a tiny flicker of white moving back toward the hangar. Very small, not human-sized at all, and moving fast.

"Brady, be careful, I've got another heat source . . ."

BRADY BARELY HEARD Gunther's words as he put his big shoulder into the hangar's front door, slamming it open with a clang. He ran through, cut left, then knelt and leveled his Beretta in the direction of the Humvee and the fuel truck, the best spots for cover if there was a second enemy soldier.

But it wasn't his eyes that detected danger.

It was his nose.

What he smelled in that last second of his life told him he had made a really, *really* bad mistake. The thick, rotten-egg scent of natural gas. In a fraction of a second, his eyes flicked to the radiant heater inside the door, to the shattered plastic gas pipe leading into it. Hacked open, he realized, with a fire axe.

Brady didn't have time to see that all sixteen ground-level heaters had suffered identical damage. For thirty minutes, sixteen cracked one-inch PVC pipes had poured gas into the hangar's closed environment, where it floated up to the ceiling, gathering in an invisible cloud.

A gasoline-soaked rope made a simple fuse. The saboteur had left one end inside the back door, then trailed the rope fifty feet outside. One flick of a lighter had done the rest. Just two seconds after Brady Giovanni's muscled mass slammed through the front door, the rope's flame danced into the hangar and kissed the gathered cloud of gas.

The fireball started at the back of the hangar and grew exponentially, lashing out at a pressure of twenty pounds per square inch, the equivalent of a gust of wind traveling at 470 miles per hour. The shock wave smashed into Brady, throwing the big man back. Had he gone through the door he might have lived, but he hit the hangar's inside wall and was knocked cold. He didn't feel the three-thousand-degree Fahrenheit fireball engulf him, didn't see his clothes burst into flame, didn't sense his skin bubble.

The cows fared no better. The shock wave knocked them about like little dogs, not the fifteen-hundred-pound creatures they were. Cows tumbled, burned and smashed into stalls. Some hit the hangar walls with a *gong* audible even over the explosion.

The hangar's huge roof seemed to lift up, balanced on a growing cloud of flame, then crash down, smashing the Humvee and the fuel truck, punching through the truck's tank and exposing aviation fuel to the still-roiling fireball. Dark orange flames shot up from the destroyed hangar, scorching metal and melting plastic.

BEFORE ANDY'S MOTHER had abandoned him to try her hand at whoring for Alberta loggers, she had always said he could sleep through a herd of buffalo stampeding through his room. That was before the military. While there were many things he *could* sleep through, such as Gunther's annoying voice on the vid-phone, a ground-shaking explosion was not one of them. If Andy knew one thing in this world, it was how to wake up fast to avoid getting killed.

He was off the bed, crouched on the ground, Beretta in his hand before he even processed what he'd heard. Gunther had tried to get him up.

"Oops," Andy said.

He started scrambling into his clothes.

IN ERIKA HOEL'S bed, Tim Feely rolled over, the covers falling away from his face. Who was making all that damn noise? And he was hot.

Someone had tucked the covers all up over his head. Damn, the room still spun like crazy. One thing about those Dutch women, they sure could drink. Drink, and fuck like nobody's business. He often wondered what Erika Hoel had been like in her twenties, and he often reminded himself he probably didn't want to know — the woman was forty-five, and he barely lived through their lovemaking sessions.

He reached out for Erika only to find her side of the bed empty. She was probably taking a leak. The room spun again, and Tim Feely dropped back into a deep sleep.

WHAT AN EXPLOSION, what a *rush*. Erika Hoel couldn't believe how well her plan had worked. Simpletons. And the back door wasn't guarded. In her projected timeline, she'd figured Andy would be there by now. She checked her watch, and waited. Another few seconds before the final hacking program kicked in. When it did, she could slip back inside, make sure the bioinformatics lab's petabyte drive was erased, then crawl into bed with Tim and just play stupid. If she ran into Colding along the way, she'd just say she was trying to get away from Tim, who'd suddenly started making threats and acting crazy. The ruse wouldn't last long, of course, but Fischer and his gorillas would be here soon. When Fischer arrived, Erika would be safe — then she could rub it in Claus's face and her former lover would know that *she* had destroyed all of his work.

She stared at her watch and counted down the seconds.

GUNTHER JONES GAVE up trying to reach Brady. The man wasn't going to answer. The hangar fire made the exterior infrared cameras useless. The hallway monitors were still looping, but he had good coverage in all the rooms, and the normal exterior cameras worked fine.

At that moment, *all* of his monitors simultaneously filled with static. His computer terminal beeped a pointless alarm:

CAMERA SYSTEM FAILURE

"No fucking *shit*," Gunther said as he reached under the counter for the system manuals.

———

ERIKA POSITIONED THE axe under one arm and looked at her watch. Her program would have just launched and shut down the cameras. She had to go. Now or never. She peeked in the rear airlock's small window — no one there. She punched *6969* into the keypad, then walked inside and shut the door behind her. The airlock pressure cycle took only five seconds, but it felt like five minutes — Gunther, Andy, Brady or Colding could be anywhere inside, or even following her from the outside. And they had guns.

The five-second cycle finished, the interior airlock door beeped and opened. Erika ran silently into the facility and headed for the bioinformatics lab. If her program had worked, it was over. If Jian had countered it, Erika would have to destroy the petabyte drive by hand.

COLDING OPENED THE front airlock to see flames billowing up from the shattered hangar. Thick smoke twisted in the night wind, blocking out the stars. Even fifty yards away, the heat was damn near blistering. He crouched behind a boulder off to the left, both to take cover in case Tim was out there and to shield himself from the fire's radiating rage.

He still couldn't quite grasp the fact that Tim had waited for *two years*, worked away on the project, really *contributed* to it, pushed for its success, only to suddenly do this. Colding had thought he knew the man.

"Gunther, where the fuck is Tim?" His earpiece let out a burst of static, followed by Gunther's voice.

"All the cameras are out. I can't see a thing. And Brady was in the hangar when that thing went off."

Shit. "Brady, come in," Colding said.

No one responded.

"Brady, if you can hear this, tap your earpiece twice. Anything to let us know you're there."

Colding waited for three slow breaths, but still no response. If Brady had entered the hangar, he was already dead.

And that made Tim Feely a murderer.

Colding had to protect the scientists. That meant neutralizing Tim first, searching for Brady second. A fucked-up prioritization, because if Brady was bleeding out somewhere, unable to respond, delaying a search might cause his death. But Brady Giovanni was paid to put his life at risk if need be — Rhumkorrf, Jian and Erika were not.

Colding scanned the area as calmly and as patiently as he could. He saw nothing.

The front airlock door opened. Colding turned, instantly leveling his Beretta, ready to fire at Tim if the man made one wrong move. Only he wasn't pointing his gun at Tim . . . he was pointing it at Andy Crosthwaite.

Andy Crosthwaite, who was supposed to be guarding the back door.

"Motherfucker," Colding said to himself as he took his aim off Andy and once again knelt behind the boulder.

Andy ran in a half-crouch, reached the boulder and knelt at Colding's left. The smaller man swept his vision from straight out to his left, automatically counting on Colding to sweep from straight out to the right. Andy wasn't panicking; he was calm and patient, doing everything right . . . except, of course, staying by the back door that he'd been ordered to guard.

"Andy, you keep your ass right here," Colding said. "I'm going inside to round up the staff, and I'll bring them back to the front airlock where you watch them. You don't move until I call you. Do you understand?"

"Back off, dick-face," Andy said. "I know what the fuck I'm doing."

A rage grew inside Colding, but there was a time and place for every battle. "Just *stay here*," Colding said, then scooted to the front airlock and slipped inside. Unless Gunther fixed the cameras, he'd have to check each room one by one.

ERIKA SLIPPED SILENTLY into the bioinformatics lab and saw the one thing she did *not* want to see — Liu Jian Dan, sitting at her multiscreened computer station, fat fingers *click-clacking* away.

Jian turned in her chair, heavy black hair falling over her face like a mask. Erika's eyes automatically flicked to the upper-row monitor above Jian's head.

GENOME A17 SEQUENCING: COMPLETE
PROOFREADING ALGORITHM: COMPLETE
VIABILITY PROBABILITY: 95.0567%

"You did it," Erika said. "I don't believe it."

"You . . ." Jian's voice was a chilling whisper. "You put that down."

Erika looked at her hands. She'd forgotten she was holding the fire axe. So close to pulling it off and getting back to her room undetected. But now Jian had seen her. Erika's word against Tim's was one thing, but Colding would automatically believe anything Jian said.

So now they would know it was her. So what? What were they going to do, *fire* her? There was nowhere for anyone to go, and Fischer's men would be here soon.

All that mattered was the data.

Jian stood, reached under her desk, and in one smooth motion pulled out the foot-long petabyte backup cartridge.

The two women stood there, facing off, Jian holding the project's future, Erika holding a fire axe.

"Jian, just give that to me."

Jian stood, shook her head no, then stepped back.

Erika stepped forward.

GUNTHER'S FINGERS TRACED the printed pages of a three-ring binder. He had to figure out how to reboot the system. The support docs said that would clear out Fuck-You Feely's damn loops and hacks.

Colding's voice hissed in his earpiece. "Gun, *come on*, where is that bastard?"

"I'm trying." Wait. There it was. Just call up the prompt window, enter that bit of code . . .

"Gun! *Fix* the *friggin'* camera!"

"Hold on!" Fingers typed the code, then hit *enter*.

The monitors flickered, then all popped back to life. "Got it, hold on!" Once again he had a complete view of the facility's security system. He flipped through the cameras, scanning for motion. Empty hall, Rhumkorrf crouched at the foot of his bed, empty hall, empty genetics lab, Erika's room . . . the blankets thrown back but that wasn't Erika . . . then the bioinformatics lab, *that* was Erika, holding an axe and moving toward Jian.

"Holy *fuck*, Colding! It's not Tim, it's Erika!"

"*What?*"

"Tim's sacked out in Erika's room. Get to bioinformatics, fast, Erika is going to kill Jian."

A new beep joined the cacophony of security room alarms. Gunther knew that sound — the radar system.

"And we've got another problem. One aircraft inbound. ETA . . . five minutes."

"GO AWAY," JIAN said in a childlike voice.

Erika didn't want to hurt anyone, but she was out of time.

Jian backed up until she hit the wall. Nowhere to go. Erika held out her left hand, beckoning for the cartridge. Jian threw herself facedown on the tile floor, her body covering the cartridge as she screamed at the top of her lungs. Erika ran to her, grabbed the bigger woman's shoulder and yanked hard, trying to roll her over.

"Jian, give it to me!" She kept pulling without effect — the woman wouldn't budge. The axe point would punch through the back of her skull like an eggshell, but Erika sure as hell wasn't going to kill the woman.

She straddled Jian's legs, then reached out with her right hand, grabbed a handful of thick black hair and yanked. Jian's head snapped back and she howled in pain. Erika slid the axe head past Jian's throat, then grabbed the handle with both hands and pulled cold wood against warm flesh.

Jian started to choke. She'd have to let go of the backup drive to grab at the axe, then Erika could smash the drive and end all this bullshit. Erika pulled harder, steadily increasing pressure on Jian's fat neck, but the woman just *wouldn't let go*. "Geef me die cartridge, gestoord wijf!"

Jian started thrashing from side to side, sputtering out hoarse choking noises, but held the drive tight.

COLDING SPRINTED INTO the bioinformatics lab to see a bizarre sight: a snarling, skinny, forty-five-year-old woman using a fire axe to choke a 250-pound Chinese lady wearing a Hawaiian shirt. Two middle-aged scientists going at it like a couple of prison inmates during a race riot.

He moved in fast, not slowing down, lowering the gun even as he closed the distance, a flash-thought of wondering where to put it because he didn't have a holster and he wasn't going to fire on an old woman and if he did the bullet might hit Jian. Erika looked up just as Colding grabbed her left shoulder and yanked. The move caught Erika off guard. Her left hand slid off the handle and she fell back, her right still clutching the axe halfway up the shaft. Jian let out a hissing, painful cough.

Colding held the Beretta awkwardly at his right side, more of a hindrance than a weapon. Erika rolled to her ass and saw the gun. Her eyes widened in instant recognition, instant panic, and she even shook her head a little as if to say *no, no that's not supposed to happen*.

"Doctor Hoel! Drop that—"

But that was all he got out before she panicked and swung the axe one-handed with her right arm. The swing was slow, a little clumsy, but he hadn't expected such a snap reaction. The blade's top edge sliced through his down parka. Small white feathers flew into the air. A stinging pain streaked from his left shoulder to his sternum.

The axe's weight and momentum actually turned Erika, still sitting on her ass, pulling her right arm around and stretching her forward like she was reaching out to pick something off the ground. The axe blade dug into the linoleum floor with a *chonk*.

Colding didn't think, he just *moved*, taking one step forward and snap-kicking Erika Hoel in the ribs. He felt and heard something crack. She screamed a strange, sharp scream that cut off almost instantly. The kick's momentum flipped her on her back. The axe remained embedded in the tile floor, handle sticking out at a forty-five-degree angle like some cheap prop from a horror flick.

Pain still stinging his chest, Colding stepped forward and swung the Beretta, aiming for the bridge of Erika's nose. Sanity kicked in at the last second. He pulled back, fighting his own momentum until the top of the Beretta barrel touched Erika's pain-scrunched face with all the force of a mother's goodnight kiss.

Erika Hoel wasn't going anywhere. She tried to move, but the obvious agony of broken ribs kept her fixed to the floor. Colding shook his head, shook away the rage. He already felt horrible about hurting her that bad, but the woman had hit him with an *axe*, for fuck's sake. Damn, did this *hurt*. How bad was he cut?

A hoarse, guttural cough pulled his attention away from Erika.

"Jian, are you okay?"

She paused for a moment, then looked up, her eyes barely visible through the mop of black hair. She scrambled to her feet and threw her arms around his neck, almost knocking him over. She clutched him tight. Silent sobs suddenly racked her body.

"I'm . . . okay, Mister . . . Colding. She . . . she choked me so hard."

Colding kept his left hand down and away from her. The pain seemed to radiate, oddly making his left elbow and right shoulder ache although neither had been touched. He felt his shirt clinging wetly to his skin. He patted Jian gently with his right hand, which was still holding the gun. "Just calm down. You need to let go now, I have to take care of this."

Jian gave him one more squeeze, making his cut scream louder. She let him go and snatched up the thing she'd clutched tight even while Erika had choked her.

"What is that?"

"Petabyte drive," Jian said, her voice a bit more calm. "We have succeeded."

Colding didn't have time to ask what she meant before his earpiece crackled with Gunther's excited voice.

"Boss, great work, but that bogey is almost here."

Who was it? Mercenaries hired by a competitor? No, his gut told him it had to be Longworth's people. "How long till it lands?"

"Less than three minutes."

"Okay, listen closely. That will probably be U.S. Special Forces, maybe Canadian, but either way armed to the teeth. Gather up Rhumkorrf and Tim and get them to the front airlock, leave them with Andy. Then you run the perimeter and see if you can find Brady. I want all of our people calm and visible, with *weapons holstered*, you got that?"

"Weapons holstered, understood."

"Good. If this is an assault team, we *cannot* win, and I don't want anyone else getting hurt."

"Yes sir, I'm on it."

Andy Crosthwaite entered the bioinformatics lab. The thick stench of burning fuel oozed off him, as did a smell Colding had prayed he'd never encounter again — the smell of burning human flesh.

Greasy streaks covered Andy's face, hands and jacket sleeves. He took one look at the scene, then strode forward and leveled his sidearm at the prone Erika Hoel. "You're dead, cunt."

"Goddamit, Andy," Colding said. "You left your post again?"

"Drop the *left your post* bullshit, Colding. This isn't a fucking John Wayne movie. You going to finish this bitch or what?"

"We're not going to *finish* anyone! It's Erika, for God's sake."

"I know who she is. She's a backstabbing twat that worked side by side with us for *two fucking years*, then just went ape-shit and killed Brady."

Colding's heart dropped. "Brady's dead?"

Andy nodded. His upper lip snarled when he spoke. "I pulled his body out of the hangar. He burned alive." Andy glared down at Erika. "So who's paying you, whore? Monsanto? Genetron? How much did you get for killing a man that guarded your ass *every day* for two years?"

Erika's eyes squinted shut, and not just from the pain. Colding could see the guilt wash over her. She'd never intended to kill anyone.

Andy cocked his Beretta, knelt down and put the end of it against Erika's forehead. Her eyes squeezed tighter.

Colding raised his own Beretta.

The movement caught Andy's eye. When he turned to look, he stared straight down a barrel.

"Andy, drop your weapon."

Andy opened his mouth, then closed it. "Fuck a duck, man, what are you doing?"

"I said *drop your weapon*. Nobody else dies today."

For the second time in as many minutes, Colding had moved before thinking, caught up in the situation's express-lane pace. He'd never pointed a gun directly at anyone in his life, and now here he was with a dead man outside, a wounded woman on the floor, a chopper coming in and his pistol in the face of a special forces killer. If Andy got crazy, got mad, if he tried to aim his own weapon, then Colding would have only a split second to pull the trigger or probably be killed himself.

Moving slow, Andy simultaneously stood and pointed his gun to the ceiling. "Okay, okay, chief I'm going."

Colding raised the barrel as Andy stood, keeping it pointed right at the man's face. "I told you to drop your weapon. Take Jian outside."

"But we have incoming. You want me to go out there unarmed?"

Andy meant it as a rhetorical question, but that was *exactly* what Colding wanted.

"Andy, drop your goddamn weapon and get out front . . . *now*."

Andy slowly squatted and lowered his gun to the ground. "You're going to regret this shit. Wait till Magnus hears about this." He grabbed Jian's elbow and guided her to the door. She clutched the petabyte drive to her chest as if it were her only child.

When they left the lab, Colding sighed. No good could come of making Andy Crosthwaite an enemy. But no one else was going to die here, and that was that. He picked up Andy's gun, flipped on the safety, then slipped it into the waist of his pants.

He knelt next to Erika. "Doctor Hoel, I'm sorry I had to do that to you."

SO MUCH PAIN. She suspected it was just some broken ribs, but she'd never had a broken *anything* before. The agony consumed her. It felt like big sticks were jammed into her right side. Or maybe spikes. Jagged ones, made of glass.

"Doctor Hoel," Colding said. "Talk to me. Can you hear me?"

She couldn't even move. The tiniest shift sent waves of near-blackout pain through her chest. As much as her body screamed, it wasn't enough to block out the horrid feeling that she'd *killed* a human being.

It hurt to talk, but she forced out the words. "Is Brady really . . . dead?"

Colding looked away, then looked back. He nodded. "If Andy was that mad, then yeah. Brady's dead."

What the hell had she been thinking? She was a middle-aged woman, not a commando. Was revenge on Claus really worth all this? Certainly not worth Brady's life. Brady had been a nice kid, polite, respectful. Maybe twenty-eight? Twenty-nine? She couldn't remember, and now it didn't matter because the man would never see thirty.

"My God . . . Colding. I . . . I swear . . . I didn't mean it."

Colding nodded. He wasn't gloating, he wasn't angry. He looked sad, like someone who'd just seen a disaster and knew it was real but didn't want to accept it.

"Listen, Doctor Hoel, I need to keep everyone else alive. Tell me what's coming."

She started to shrug, but that hurt even more than talking. "Don't know . . . Fischer . . . will be here soon."

Colding nodded again, as if she had just confirmed his suspicions. "Why is Fischer coming now? We've been here for two years."

She shook her head. "Don't know. Just wanted . . . wanted to ruin Claus. I didn't mean it, I *swear.*"

"Okay," Colding said. He reached out a hand and gently caressed her hair. It felt comforting. "Just stay still. I'll come back as soon as I can with something for the pain."

P. J. Colding stood up and ran out of the room, leaving Erika Hoel crying from shame, shock and sheer agony.

NOVEMBER 8: HITCHIN' A RIDE

COLDING RAN TO a hallway bathroom and tore open a wall-mounted first-aid kit. He grabbed gauze, steripads and a bottle of Advil. Would the Advil help with Erika's pain? He didn't know, but he had to do something. He'd lost it, gone into some kind of rage and kicked that woman's ribs as hard as he could. Like he was some kind of fucking animal. Like he'd been when he attacked Paul Fischer.

Don't forget the axe, big guy. Erika's axe almost killed you.

No, no excuses, he was in charge and that meant everything — Erika's injury, Brady's death, the explosion — was all his fault.

He pulled his parka open and looked in the bathroom mirror. Blood soaked the gray shirt underneath. He gently pulled at the cut fabric to see the gash in his skin. It was still bleeding in spots, but more of a deep scratch than a life-threatening injury. Bad enough to merit kicking a woman's ribs? No, but he tried to check that thought — it was ridiculous to feel guilty for defending himself against that kind of attack.

He started to tear open the gauze pack when the sound of jet engines caught his attention. Erika's pain, his own cut, those would have to wait. He shrugged the bloody jacket back on, puffing up a small cloud of downy white feathers. He ran to the front airlock. Seconds later, Colding stepped into the winter night. The hangar flames had died down considerably. A light wind drove falling snow at an angle, making the exterior lamps look like shimmering cones of light. The approaching jet engines screamed louder than he thought possible.

Fischer was almost here.

Fischer, the man who organized investigations of transgenic companies, who coordinated elements of the CDC, WHO, CIA and USAMRIID. Fischer, who apparently had the ability to reach out and manipulate brokenhearted, bitter women into saboteurs and inadvertent murderers.

Fischer — the man once in charge of the project that had killed Colding's wife.

All of it made Colding long desperately for another round with him, to do far more than just fuck up the man's knee. Colding's rage had no place being directed against a forty-five-year-old woman, but against Colonel Paul Fischer? That was a different matter.

Out by the ruined satellite dish, Gunther and Andy stood with Rhumkorrf, Jian and Tim Feely. Gunther, God bless him, had his gun holstered. Colding walked up and joined them, Beretta in his right hand but down at his side. He kept Andy in sight. Tim looked so drunk he might fall over at any moment. Jian shook with huge sobs.

Twenty feet from the group, a green tarp covered an unrecognizable, smoldering lump. A lump about the size of Brady Giovanni. The night wind made the tarp's edges snap loudly and carried away most of the oppressive stench. Most of it. The odors of burning flesh and burning fuel still hung in the air.

None of them looked at the body. Instead, they looked up into the night sky. The bogey Gunther had warned about was coming in for a landing, but it wasn't a chopper — they saw a massive silhouette, running lightless, flat-black paint soaking up the firelight from the warehouse's flickering flames.

"Mein gott," Rhumkorrf said. "That thing is gigundous."

Colding couldn't believe his eyes. The plane's headlamps flipped on, casting long cones of light onto the snow-covered landing strip. The plane was so big it looked as if it were barely moving. There was only one vehicle that had those massive dimensions . . .

A C-5 Galaxy.

"Sara," Colding said quietly. But it couldn't be. Erika's attack had just happened. How could Danté have responded this quickly?

The C-5 had been Colding's idea. A flying lab to keep the ancestor project mobile in case of something . . . well, in case of something exactly like what had just gone down. One of the world's largest planes, the 247-foot C-5 ran almost from goal line to goal line on a football field. Its wings spread out like the arms of a giant, 222 feet from tip to tip, and the top of the tail towered six stories high. The cockpit looked like a small black Cyclops eye notched into the elongated, rounded triangle of a fuselage. A 450,000-pound monstrosity large enough to move an entire biotech lab — cows and all — to anywhere in the world.

Five sets of massive wheels, each set the size of a Volkswagen Beetle, extended to meet the snowy landing strip. The C-5 seemed to be moving in slow motion, but it was a jet coming in for a landing at around 120 miles per hour.

Gunther moved to stand at Colding's shoulder. "What do you want us to do?"

If not for the burning hangar, the charred body on the ground and the woman in the bioinformatics lab with at least a couple of broken ribs, Colding might have laughed at the question.

"Do? Just get in. Our ride is here."

NOVEMBER 8: WAR ZONE

THE C-5'S TAIL ramp slowly lowered. The wind picked up speed, whipping light snow across the landing strip and sending hands to shield squinting eyes. Lights blared from the plane's twenty-foot opening, a glowing cave that made a hazy, shivering corona against the falling snow. It struck Colding as a giant mechanical monster, jaws agape, waiting to swallow the Rhumkorrf project whole.

As the ramp lowered past the halfway point, a single man walked down its length.

Magnus Paglione.

Andy let out a triumphant "Yeah!" He gave Colding a *now you're in for it* dirty look, then ran to meet his friend. Magnus and Andy reminded Colding of a man and a pet terrier. Andy was hyper, perpetually angry, and worshipped his master. Magnus obviously enjoyed Andy's company, but never hesitated to dish out discipline as needed.

A large black duffel bag hung from Magnus's shoulder. The weight of the contents pulled the canvas straps into taut lines that folded up on themselves, but Magnus carried it with the casual ease of a man carrying a loaf of bread. He walked up to Colding, surveying the people and the damage.

His gaze landed on Brady's corpse. Magnus stared at it for a few seconds.

"Is that Brady?"

Colding nodded.

Magnus looked up, his expression blank. "Who did it?"

Colding swallowed. His heart raced. Magnus's face showed no emotion, but his whole demeanor had changed — he radiated danger.

"It was Doctor Hoel."

"You're kidding," Magnus said. "An old woman did all of this? Why?"

Colding glanced at Rhumkorrf, thought of lying to keep things as calm as possible, but there was no point. "She wanted to get back at Claus for getting Galina kicked off the project."

Claus blinked. Snow stuck to his black-rimmed glasses. He looked down at Brady's corpse, then looked up, taking a subconscious step away from the smoking body as if to separate himself just a bit more.

"That's ridiculous," Claus said. "Erika Hoel is a woman of science. I don't believe it."

"Believe it," Jian said in a hoarse rasp. "She took out the off-site backup and all the data."

Claus's face blanched and his chest puffed up in panic. It wasn't lost on Colding that Claus instantly seemed far more concerned about his project than the dead body on the ground.

"The data? She destroyed our data? How could you let her do that?"

Jian held up the petabyte cartridge. She looked scared, hurt and sad all at the same time, but Colding would have bet a hundo that a part of her bitterly enjoyed the panic she'd just given Rhumkorrf.

"I have it all," Jian said. "And we have done it. Ninety-five percent viability."

Colding felt a surge of excitement, yet another emotion joining the tumult ripping through his head and soul. Had they done it after all?

"Ninety-five . . ." Rhumkorrf said, his face shifting from bluster and anger to shock and excitement. "That is fantastic!"

"Go team," Magnus said. "All's well that ends well, right? As long as we have the precious *data*, I guess it's all good."

Rhumkorrf actually started to agree, then realized that Magnus was being facetious. Rhumkorrf stared at the ground.

Magnus turned his glare back to Colding. "Where is Hoel?"

"In the bioinformatics lab. It's under control."

"If you call my dead friend and millions of dollars in damage *under control*, Bubbah, then you and I use a different dictionary." Magnus loved to call Americans *Bubbah*. Especially Colding. He seemed to find either great humor or great insult in the name.

"I know, right?" Andy said. "Looks like an assault team came in. But no, just some old nympho. Sure glad Colding is in charge."

"Andy, shut up," Magnus said. "We're in a bit of a hurry here. Let's get everyone onboard, we're bugging out."

A fresh gust of wind made everyone duck their head, shield their eyes and take a half step for balance. Everyone but Magnus. He stood still as a stone and stared at Colding. Colding stared right back, his best poker face firmly in place, suspecting Magnus saw right through it.

"Time to move," Magnus said. "Doctor Rhumkorrf, you have enucleated eggs for all the backup herds?"

"Of course. They are in storage in the main lab."

"Get them," Magnus said. "Duplicates of your equipment are on the plane, including the God Machine. You don't have to wait until we land, you can run the immune response during flight."

Jian handed Colding the petabyte drive. "I will get the eggs," she said. She raised an arm over her eyes to block the wind, then ran for the front airlock.

Magnus again stared at the tarp-covered Brady Giovanni. He looked up and nodded, as if he'd accepted the situation. "Colding, get everyone on the plane. We need to move. I'll stay and get a medevac in for Doctor Hoel."

Andy stepped forward. "Are you shitting me, Mags?" The C-5's lights cast strange shadows on Andy's eyes, under his nose, under his chin. It made him look a little demonic. "That bitch *killed* Brady, man. And when I tried to take care of it Colding drew down on *me* and even took *my* gun. He's still *got* my fucking gun, right? You can't possibly tell me you're going to leave him in charge, he has no idea—"

Magnus's left hand shot out and grabbed Andy by the throat, interrupting the smaller guard's rant. The grab was so controlled it looked almost delicate — one second Andy was talking, the next he was choking, his eyes bulging in surprise, a massive hand completely wrapped around his neck.

"Andy," Magnus said. "I thought I told you to shut up."

Andy's hands shot up, tried to isolate a finger and bend it backward. Colding saw Magnus squeeze, just a little bit. Andy's eyes grew even wider, then he held his hands up, palms out. Magnus let go and again looked at Colding, as if nothing had happened. Coughing hard, Andy bent at the waist, hands at his throat. He stayed calm, dealing with it, but it was clear that Magnus could have crushed his windpipe with just a touch more pressure.

"Fischer's on the way," Magnus said. "We have a very limited satellite window and have to go right now. We've been calling you for thirty minutes, but . . ." — he gestured to the broken satellite dish — "looks like your phone is out of service. Our intel says we have about forty minutes to get clear. I want the C-5 airborne in five. Give Andy his weapon."

Colding pulled the Beretta from his belt and handed it back to Andy.

Magnus looked back to the C-5. "Let's move!" He waved his hand. Beckoning someone inside to come down the ramp.

Sara Purinam.

She stood at least five-foot-ten, maybe just a bit taller if you counted her crop of tousled, short blond hair. Light blue eyes were little pinpoints of electric light embedded in her freckled complexion. Just like the last time, Colding didn't see a trace of makeup. Anything covering that skin would only detract from her natural beauty. She looked the very picture of a surfer girl gone air force.

She walked down and stood right in front of Colding. She looked pissed. From the mission? Or from the way he had treated her? Probably both.

He felt an instant and powerful sexual attraction, the same one he'd felt the last time they'd met. He had acted on it and betrayed the memory of his barely cold wife. The thought of Clarissa dredged up a fresh scar of guilt. He had more important things to do than ogle this woman.

"Mister Colding," Sara said in an even tone. "Fancy meeting you here."

"Purinam," Colding said, nodding.

Sara turned to Magnus. "So what the hell is going on? This looks like a war zone."

Rhumkorrf stepped forward. "Yes, what happened? If Erika did want to hurt me, why now? Why is Colonel Fischer after us again?"

Magnus looked at everyone, one by one, seeming to weigh the value of spending more time on the ground. "Novozyme had a virus jump species. Seventy-five percent lethality."

Rhumkorrf's eyes widened. "*Seventy-five* percent? I always knew Matal's method was flawed. That is horrible. Did the virus get out?"

"Contained," Magnus said. "The Americans were on it fast. Fischer fuel-bombed the lab, then moved on to shutting down all transgenic projects. That includes us."

Rhumkorrf shook his head. "No. No, not when we are so close. We have to keep going."

"So get in the fucking plane," Magnus said. "We're taking the project underground. All your competitors will soon be offline. *All* of them. If you don't get out of here before Fischer arrives, your Nobel Prize will be forever lost in the mail."

Sara's eyes narrowed. "Who the hell is Colonel Fischer? Are we talking U.S. military? And there's a fucking dead body right there. We didn't sign up for this shit."

Magnus turned fast and took a step toward her, the motion bringing him toe-to-toe with Sara. She had to look straight up to meet Magnus's eyes.

"You signed up to do whatever we tell you to do," he said. "You've certainly cashed enough of our checks. Now, unless you want to lose your business, get your crew moving and load this plane. You've got four minutes."

Sara held his gaze for just a second, then turned away and shouted in a voice that momentarily drowned out the idling jet engines. "Let's move, boys! Wheels up in four minutes!"

Three men wearing black Genada parkas descended the loading ramp. Colding recognized the short, Hispanic Alonzo Barella. Behind him, Harold and Cappy, the black and white "twins."

"Weapons," Sara said. "The only people armed on my plane are me and my crew, so give your weapons to Harold."

Harold stepped up, hands out. Colding ejected his magazine, checked the chamber, then handed the Beretta and magazine to Harold. Gunther quickly did the same.

Andy laughed at Sara, then grabbed his crotch and shook it. "I'll keep my pistol and give you my *gun*, flygirl. How 'bout that?"

Sara shrugged. "Then you're not getting on the plane. Stay here and fuck a cow or something."

"Enough!" Magnus snapped. "Andy keeps his weapon. Get this damn process moving." He stared at Sara. "That okay with you, *Captain*?"

Sara glared at Andy, who was still laughing, then she turned back to Magnus.

"Fine," she said. "You're the boss."

Magnus checked his watch. "You all have two minutes to grab any personal effects."

Andy and Gunther sprinted for the main building. Colding didn't bother. Neither did Rhumkorrf.

Jian came out the front airlock, night winds rippling her clothes as she struggled to push a dolly loaded with a thick aluminum canister. Alonzo ran to help her. Cappy got under Tim Feely's arm and helped the drunk, sleepy scientist up the ramp. Gunther and Andy soon came back out. Gunther hauled a duffel bag stuffed with books while Andy carried a beat-up brown paper bag. Great. The Asshole thought to save his porno mag collection. The two guards ran up the ramp and into the C-5.

That left Colding alone with Magnus. "So where are we going?"

"An island in Lake Superior called Black Manitou."

"Lake Superior? How in the hell are we going to get *that* thing," Colding jerked his thumb toward the C-5, "through the Canadian air defense grid and then U.S. air defense?"

Magnus looked away, as if the questions annoyed him. "We have a contact at the Iqaluit Airport and a flight plan that shows us as a 747 cargo plane going from Iqaluit to Thunder Bay Airport. We have another contact at Thunder Bay — they don't pay air traffic controllers that much, it seems — and he's going to log us as landing. Flight is about three hours, Bubbah. Once past Thunder Bay, Sara puts the C-5 into night mode: no lights, she flies below the radar deck. There's nothing between Thunder Bay and Black Manitou. It's twenty minutes of low-level flying."

Colding nodded. That sounded like it could work. "Still, isn't Black Manitou a little close to civilization for what we're doing?"

Magnus laughed. "Close to civilization? We'll see what you think when you get there." He unzipped the black canvas duffel bag a quarter of the way, reached in and pulled out a manila folder. He zipped the bag before Colding could get a look inside.

"Here's everything you need to know," Magnus said, holding out the folder. "There's only five people on the island and they all work for Genada. Clayton Detweiler runs the place for us. When you see his son, Gary, tell him to make sure my snowmobile is ready."

Colding took the folder.

Magnus continued. "You're off the grid as of now. No outside communication of any kind, other than a secure comm link to Manitoba. No wireless security gear, no Internet, no nothing. You guys don't exist anymore."

As disturbing as that sounded, Colding also knew it was the only way to keep the project alive. Hell, the C-5 had been *his* idea, a way to keep the project going if anyone tried to shut them down.

He thought about the way Magnus had looked at Brady's corpse, and the deadly vibe he'd given off when he asked *who did it*. If Colding flew off, he'd leave Erika alone with this man.

"What about Doctor Hoel?"

"You mean the old woman who single-handedly fucked up your operation and killed my friend?"

Colding let out a breath that clouded in front of his face, then nodded slowly.

"Don't worry. I'll take care of her."

"Magnus, she didn't mean to hurt Brady. Fischer got to her, she just wanted to destroy Rhumkorrf's work and—"

"You think I'm *stupid*," Magnus said softly. "That's it, isn't it? You think you're smarter than me?"

Colding shook his head, a little too quickly.

Magnus smiled. "Sure you do, Bubbah. You think I'm dumb enough to kill a woman who works for Fischer. This conversation is over. Now get on the plane, or stay here and have a chat with your old buddy Paul Fischer when he lands."

Colding paused one more second, unable to shake a feeling of dread. What choice did he have? If he wanted the project to succeed, he had to trust Magnus. Colding turned and walked up the C-5's loading ramp.

The ramp led into a large cargo bay. At twenty feet across, it was almost wide enough for a two-lane highway. He'd reviewed the engineer's schematics, helped design them, in fact, but he'd never seen the finished product. Once inside, all he could do was stop and stare at the cows. The cows all stared back at him.

He could see all the way down the long fuselage to the front loading ramp, now folded up behind the closed nose cone. Along most of that length ran just over a hundred feet of cattle stalls, seven feet deep, twenty-five to a side with a five-foot aisle down the middle. Clear plastic walls separated each stall. Clear plastic doors completed each cage, with a bin inside the door to hold feed pellets that were dumped in by an automatic system. The outside of each door held a flat-panel control monitor that showed the cow's heart rate, weight and several other factors Colding didn't recognize right off the bat.

Big-eyed black-and-white Holstein cows occupied the stalls, each partially supported by a durable harness that hung from the ceiling. Hooves still touched the deck, but the harnesses carried most of the weight — couldn't have fifteen-hundred-pound animals jostling around during flight. The occasional *moos* helped reinforce the surreal scene. An overwhelming smell of cows and cow shit permeated the place. A labeled plastic tag hung from each cow's right ear — *A-1, A-2, A-3* and so on.

The animals seemed perfectly calm and happy. Calm, but *big*, standing five feet tall at the shoulder. Colding could only imagine trying to control fifty of them inside the plane if something caused a panic.

Just inside the ramp to his right was the aft ladder that led to a second deck containing equipment, computers and lab space for Rhumkorrf and Jian. Up there they had almost all of their equipment from the Baffin facility, just a lot less space in which to work it.

Past the cow stalls and on the right-hand side of the center aisle sat twenty feet of veterinary lab space filled with computers, supply cabinets and a big metal table that ran along the aisle's edge. On the aisle's left side was an open space where a ten-foot-by-seven-foot elevator platform could lower down from the upper deck. Past that were twelve crash chairs arranged in three rows of four. Beyond the crash chairs, the folded-up front ramp and a metal ladder to the upper deck.

Miller and Cappy scurried about, checking readouts and testing the straps securing each cow. The men gave Colding several quick looks, as if they expected him to move forward, but the C-5's interior held him awestruck. The two crewmen quickly walked over to him, both moving nearly in lockstep with the same quick gait.

"You need to get seated, sir," Miller said.

"Yeah," Cappy said. "You need to get seated."

Colding nodded apologetically and walked deeper into the plane. "Sorry, guys, it's just a bit . . . overwhelming. And don't call me sir, call me P. J."

"Okay, P. J.," Miller said.

"Yeah, okay, P. J.," Cappy said.

They led him to the crash chairs where Andy, Gunther, Rhumkorrf, Jian and Tim were already strapped in. Tim was asleep, a little drool trickling down from his lower lip.

The sound of heavy hydraulics whined through the C-5. The rear ramp slowly folded up on itself, tucking away for the upcoming flight. Two outer rear doors closed behind it, returning the plane to a smooth, aerodynamic profile. The C-5's entire nose section could also lift up like a gaping mouth. With both front and rear ramps down, a fifty-seven-ton, twelve-foot-wide M1-Abrams tank could literally drive in one end of the plane and out the other.

Colding sat and reached for the restraints, wincing in pain as his sliced chest and shoulder burned with the new movement.

Sara dropped down the ladder from the upper deck. She turned and saw him fiddling with the restraints. "Let's go, Colding. Buckle up, dammit, we're taking off."

"I, uh . . . I need some help."

Sara walked up to him. In the C-5's bright interior lights, she seemed to notice his torn jacket — and his blood — for the first time.

"That's a mess," she said. "Let's see your wound."

"It's nothing. Can you just help me with the buckles?"

She ignored him, instead reaching out to open his coat and look inside. Sara took in a short hiss of breath when she saw the damage.

"What did that?"

"An axe," Colding said.

Andy laughed his grating laugh. "An *old lady* with an axe, you mean. Better not let you meet my grandma, Colding, she might whip your ass for shits and giggles."

"Andy," Sara said, "*shut* the fuck *up*. Colding, I'll take care of this once we're in the air. For now, try not to bleed all over my plane."

She reached down to both of his sides, grabbed the restraints, buckled him in and tightened him up. Once finished, Sara walked back to the fore ladder and ascended.

Seconds later, the C-5's four giant TF39 turbofan engines hummed with raw power. Colding felt the massive plane start to inch forward. Steady thrust pushed him back into his seat. The plane rattled as it accelerated across the snowy airstrip, then much of the rattling dropped away as the wheels cleared the ground.

NOVEMBER 8: TAKE IT

THREE UH-60 BLACK Hawk helicopters came in low, just thirty feet above the night-darkened snow. The two lead choppers flew in a wide circle around the Baffin Island facility's perimeter. The third Black Hawk hung back, stationary.

Inside that third helicopter, Colonel Paul Fischer looked through binoculars, surveying the damage below. The ruins of a large sheet-metal building lay crumpled like a giant, stomped Pepsi can. Dying flames propelled tendrils of black smoke through the torn metal. The place looked like a war zone. Good thing he was going in with twenty-four soldiers.

Paul wore a bulky, blue bodysuit. He felt ridiculous, but the Chemturion suit would protect him against any infectious agent. At least it would if he'd put on the helmet, which was now sitting at his feet in a tiny gesture of rebellion against strict orders based on ignorance, as issued by one Murray Longworth. Didn't change the fact that Paul looked like a cross between a Smurf and the Stay Puft Marshmallow man.

The eight armed men seated with him in the Black Hawk looked far meaner in their full Mission-Oriented Protective Posture gear. MOPP suits consisted of a mask and a hood that hung down over the neck and shoulders, along with a charcoal-lined bodysuit and gloves. The whole rig provided significant protection against chemical, biological, radiological and even nuclear hazards. Not as much protection as Paul's smurfy Chemturion suit, were it properly worn, but what the MOPP suits gave up in total protection they made up for in mobility. He had no doubt these men could move fast and efficiently use their weapons — mean-looking M249 squad automatic weapons and compact Fabrique National P90s.

Eight more MOPP-suited soldiers rode in each of the other two Black Hawks, sixteen men who would storm the facility and lock everything down. The eight with Paul were part backup, part babysitter. He, apparently, was the baby that needed sitting. He wasn't part of the combat operation. When the men weren't talking directly to him, they referred to him as "the package."

All of this gear was overkill anyway. The odds of another lethal transgenic virus breaking out *right now* were about as high as a cell phone store full of monkeys testing out the complete works of Shakespeare in the next twenty-four hours. But Murray Longworth's orders had been both obnoxious and clear — go in with all due precaution.

Colding had already evaded them once, made an entire research project vanish and eliminated any evidence of Genada wrongdoing. That was why Longworth wanted to go in fast, go in hard, make sure Colding couldn't pull a repeat performance. Looking at the burning hangar, Paul had to wonder if they were already too late.

"Colonel Fischer," the copilot called back. "The outbuilding is destroyed, but the main facility looks intact. The teams are ready to land."

"Tell them to take it," Paul said.

In the distance, the two Black Hawks broke out of their circle and closed in on the facility.

RADAR TRACKED THE distance of the approaching aircraft. One hundred and fifty meters and closing.

Erika Hoel cried. Duct tape held her to the security room chair, the same chair in which Gunther Jones had cranked out two full novels and most of a third. She couldn't slide her hands out of the thick, silver tape, and each time she tried her ribs raged with their stabbing-glass pain.

. . . one hundred twenty-five meters . . .

More of that same roll of duct tape was wrapped around her shins, where it held a fist-sized ball of soft putty against her skin. Magnus had calmly explained the putty was Demex, a kind of plastic explosive. He had walked her through the process, told her exactly what would happen when the incoming aircraft closed to one hundred meters.

. . . one hundred fifteen meters . . .

A coiled wire ran from the Demex to a small router he'd connected to the radar system. That router showed ten red lights, one light for each of ten wires. The other nine wires led out of the security room door, spreading throughout the facility where they connected to much larger balls of Demex.

No one was going to save her. Her petty vindictiveness had killed Brady, and now it would result in her death as well. Cold acceptance finally settled in. She stopped crying. Erika made one final wish that Claus Rhumkorrf and Galina Poriskova would have long, happy lives.

At exactly one hundred meters, the radar system sent a signal to the router.

A COORDINATED EXPLOSION shattered the mostly cinder-block facility. Even though he was five hundred yards away, Fischer flinched back from the blossoming fireball that briefly lit up the night and reflected off the white snow. A solid building one second, a shattered, burning, smoking wreck the next.

"Get clear! Get clear!" he heard the pilot say. Fischer's Black Hawk didn't move, but the other two zipped away from the facility in case there were more explosions or hostiles on the ground that might take potshots.

Colding was a clever fucker, no question, but he wouldn't have done *that*. Magnus Paglione. Had to be. *Dammit*.

"Just stay away from the main facility," Paul shouted to the copilot. "Tell the other Black Hawks to circle wide, look for people on the ground, and use *extreme* caution — some of Genada's staff have special forces training."

Fischer knew the men would find nothing. No research, no evidence. Genada had slipped away again.

TWENTY MINUTES AFTER takeoff, Colding watched Sara descend the fore ladder. She smiled at her passengers and spoke with the mock hospitality of a flight attendant.

"Ladies and gentlemen, we're under way. Please feel free to move about the cabin."

Tim was still out cold, but Jian and Rhumkorrf unbuckled. Rhumkorrf stood and walked slowly past the cattle stalls to the aft ladder, where he climbed up to his second-deck lab. Jian followed him, the petabyte drive still clutched in her arms like a stuffed animal.

Gunther and Andy stood and stretched — for the rest of the flight, they wouldn't have much to do.

"Fucking Brady," Gunther said. "All the garbage we've survived and he dies on *this* job."

"No shit," Andy said, then grabbed Gunther's shoulder in a rare display of camaraderie. "Remember that house outside Kabul?"

Gunther looked away, then down. "Yeah. Yeah, I remember it. I'd be dead if it wasn't for Brady."

"You and me both, brother," Andy said.

Gunther looked up at Sara. Shadows of not-quite-suppressed memories clouded his eyes. "Hey, is there a workstation here or something with a word processor? Where I could plug in this?" He pulled a key ring out of his pocket. A silver flash drive with the red Genada label hung from the end.

Sara looked at the drive. "What's that? Work stuff?"

"It's his faggy novel," Andy said. "That's how Gun escapes memories of all the good times we used to have. Ain't that right, Gun?"

Gunther shrugged and looked down again.

"We have a workstation," Sara said quickly. "All of you, follow me. And Colding, I'm serious about you not getting blood on my plane. I'll get you cleaned up. If any of you want to sleep, I'll show you the bunk room."

Andy leered at Sara. "You want to join me for a nap? Maybe confiscate my weapon the old-fashioned way?"

Sara rolled her eyes. "In your dreams, little man."

Andy laughed, his mouth twisting into a half-smile, half-sneer. He didn't seem that torn up by his best buddy's death, but then again Colding had little combat experience. Maybe the ability to move on quickly was part of what made someone a professional soldier.

Instead of taking them up the fore or aft ladder, Sara pushed and held a button on the inside hull. Machinery whined as the ten-by-ten platform lowered via a telescoping hydraulic pole mounted at each corner.

"We use this for heavy stuff," Sara said. "Or when someone is gimpy and needs to go up to the infirmary."

They walked onto the platform's metal-grate floor. Sara pushed and held a button mounted on one of the hydraulic poles and they rode up.

When the platform reached the top, Colding looked aft at the thousand square feet of second-deck lab space. A large flat-panel monitor, eight feet wide by five feet high, dominated the rear bulkhead. Soft fluorescent lights illuminated gleaming metal equipment, black lab tables, small computer screens and white cabinets, all packed perfectly into the C-5's arcing hull.

Already lost in code, Jian sat in an exact copy of her seven-monitor computer station. Rhumkorrf moved from machine to machine, running his hands over the various surfaces, staring for a second, then nodding with satisfaction and moving on to the next. Colding felt a bloom of pride at seeing his design brought to life, and at seeing Jian and Rhumkorrf's apparent approval.

"You packed this baby tight," Sara said. "I don't know what any of this shit is for, but it sure looks expensive."

Colding nodded. "You have no idea."

"Come on," Sara said. "Bunk room is between the lab and the cockpit." She walked through a narrow hallway and pointed out the C-5's features: a tiny galley, an infirmary with two beds, a bunk room with three bunks, and a small room that had two couches and a flat-panel TV mounted on the wall. A video game console and a rack of games sat in a small entertainment center on the floor below the TV.

"Now we're talking," Andy said. He immediately sat down and fired up a game of Madden.

"Damn," Gunther said. "This plane is huge."

Colding nodded. "That's why we picked it. With our payload it will do over thirty-five hundred miles without refueling. Gives us a massive range. And we're encapsulated — we do all the work right onboard."

Sara pointed to a laptop sitting on a wall-mounted table. "If you want to write, Gunther, there you go."

"Actually, I'm beat," he said. "Think I'll get some sleep."

Maybe Andy could quickly forget Brady's death, but Gunther looked haunted. How long had he known Brady? Five years? Ten? Colding felt the loss like a fist in his chest, but he'd known the man not even two years and they had never been tight friends. Gunther had to be hurting bad.

"Gun," Colding said. "I'm really sorry about Brady."

Gun nodded a silent *thanks*. He shuffled off to the bunk room.

Sara gently grabbed the back of Colding's right arm. "Come on." She walked him the few feet to the small infirmary and pointed at one of the two metal beds. He sat. Without a word, she helped him out of his ruined parka. Bits of white down feathers escaped and floated in the air. She grabbed some surgical scissors and cut away his torn, bloody shirt.

She wore no perfume, but this close the scent of her skin filled his nose. She smelled just like she had two and a half years ago.

He craned his neck to get a good look at the wound. The edge of the axe blade had cut him from his left shoulder to his sternum. He'd been lucky. If the point had gone just a bit deeper, it would have sliced his pectoral in half. Sara cleaned the cut.

"Do I need stitches?"

Sara shook her head. "Basically a glorified scratch."

Her hands moved delicately across his skin, wiping away the still-oozing blood. She picked bits of white down feathers out of the cut before gently smearing antibiotic ointment on the wound. It hurt, but the touch of her fingertips felt relaxing. She quickly finished the job, wrapping gauze across the wound and around his chest, then sealing it in place with surgical tape.

Despite her delicate touch, she radiated hostility. He had to talk to her, smooth things out. "Listen, Sara, I—"

"Don't bother. You got what you wanted — me, and through me, a crew for this plane."

Was that what she thought? That he'd just *used* her? "That's not how it was."

"Oh?" She stood straight and looked him in the eye. With his ass sitting on the table, her head was just a little above his. "That's not how it was? Then how was it, Peej?"

Peej. That strange nickname she started calling him after they'd had sex. He'd thought the name cute then. Now he found it uncomfortable.

"Call me P. J., please."

"Ex*cuse* me?"

"Uh . . . well, you know. The last time you called me Peej, we . . . uh . . ."

She tilted her head and smiled the way you'd smile at some loudmouth in a bar right before you smacked him in the nose.

"Tell you what," she said. "I'll give you a choice. I can call you Peej, or I can call you Mister Rotten Fucking Piece of Shit That Treated Me Like a Used-up Whore. How's that?"

Colding just blinked. "Uh . . . that's not . . . I mean . . . that's not what it was."

She crossed her arms. "Then what was it? Used your magic cock to get me to sign the contract?"

He felt his face get all hot. Clarissa had never talked like that.

"So," Sara said. "Which name would you prefer?"

He just wanted to end this conversation, and right now. "Peej will be fine."

"I thought so. Now go get some sleep. I'll send someone to wake you when we get close to Black Manitou."

Sara strode out of the infirmary and turned left, toward the cockpit. Colding watched her go, watched the only woman — besides his wife — he'd slept with in the last six years.

Maybe she was right. Maybe he deserved it. And then he remembered Brady's dead body, remembered how he'd kicked in Erika Hoel's ribs, remembered that Fischer would keep hunting for all of them. Those things were far more important than worrying about Sara Purinam's feelings.

He hopped off the bed and walked to the bunk room. Gunther was already snoring. The noise didn't keep Colding awake for long.

"STOP IT, HANDS."

Jian's bloody hands ignored her. They kept sewing. The needle pricks were worse this time, each one a piercing sting she felt clear down to the bone. Wet red dampened the panda body's black-and-white fur.

"Stop it, hands."

She finished sewing. Just like the time before, and the times before that, the mishmash creature's big black eyes fluttered to life, blinking like a drunken man awakening to the noonday sun.

Evil.

Jian felt evil pouring off the thing like the acrid stench of a skunk. She wanted to move, to run, but her body obeyed no better than her possessed hands.

Evil enough to kill her. And wasn't that what she truly deserved?

The creature looked at her. It opened its wide mouth.

Jian started to scream.

SARA AND ALONZO sat in the C-5 cockpit. The equipment-packed space smelled of artificial pine thanks to the green, tree-shaped car air freshener Alonzo had hung off the overhead systems panel.

Sara could feel the tension pouring off her copilot, and she'd had just about enough.

"Out with it, 'Zo," she said. "You've been biting your tongue for hours. If you've got something to say, say it."

He examined his instruments, making a show of looking very closely at everything in front of him. Sara let the silence hang. She just stared at him.

The cockpit door opened. Miller and Cappy came in. Normally, they didn't come up to the cockpit during a flight.

"Well, well, well," Sara said. "The gang's all here. I bet you're ready to talk now, hey 'Zo?"

Alonzo nodded. "You actually need us to say it?"

"Say what, exactly?"

Miller laughed a small laugh. "We're *sooooo* reserved and mysterious. See if you can guess what we're thinking."

"Yeah," Cappy said. "See if you can guess and shit."

"Let's see," Sara said, rubbing her chin and looking up. "The spirits tell me . . . you're concerned that we're transporting a genetic experiment that we know nothing about?"

"*Bzzzz,*" Alonzo said. "Wrong, but thanks for playing."

"Come on, guys, enough. Talk to me. Miller, sit your ass down and spill."

Miller took the observer seat, which was right behind the copilot seat. "Sure, the genetics stuff freaks me out," he said. "But I signed up for that. I knew what I was getting into."

Cappy remained standing. He crossed his arms over his chest. "What we *didn't* sign up for, chickee-poo, was flying Fred into a fucking combat zone, complete with burning buildings and dead bodies, then loading up casualties and flying out fast. A *new* Fred isn't built for hot-zone operations like that, let alone a rebuilt one. You know this."

Fred was a nickname for the entire C-5 line — it stood for *Fucking Ridiculous Economic Disaster.* The planes normally required around sixteen hours of maintenance for each hour of flight time. Their modified version was updated with state-of-the-art gear top to bottom, so it was easier to maintain, but Miller was still dead-on: this plane was not designed for combat operations. But what could they do about it now? Sara shrugged, wondering if she looked as nonchalant as she hoped.

Alonzo didn't appreciate the attitude. "Sara, a man *died* back there. This is supposed to be a science experiment, not an action movie."

It was Sara's turn to look away, to overly examine the instruments. She and the boys had been together for seven years. They'd been in her C-5 crew during their days in the air force. When they all got out, they'd pooled their money and bought a 747 that had been converted for pure cargo hauling. There had been plenty of shipping offers from drug smugglers, but Sara and the boys never took those jobs. Most of their income came from FedEx and UPS, when those companies had an overflow of cargo that absolutely, *positively* had to be there overnight.

They owned their own company, controlled their own destiny, and that had been a thrilling feeling. Unfortunately, drops in shipping demands worldwide caught them unprepared. They quickly fell behind on payments and were in danger of losing everything.

Then P. J. Colding had come a'calling. Her knight in shining armor. If Sara and her crew agreed to help rebuild Genada's Frankenstein C-5, the company would pay off the 747 completely *and* give each of them a six-figure salary just to be on retainer. All she and her three closest friends had to do was keep the C-5 in top condition and be ready to fly on a moment's notice.

"We made a deal, guys," Sara said. "We took Genada's money. A *lot* of it. It's not like the Paglione brothers can open the Yellow Pages and just go find another crew for this bird."

"The *Pagliones*?" Alonzo said. "You sure you don't mean *Colding*? We're not blind, Sara. We've seen you hook up with guys before, but you had a *major* shine-on for that big geek."

"Fuck you," Sara said. "I screwed up once. No way I'm hitting that again, and even if I do, you know goddamn well that wouldn't influence my decision. Bottom line is we can't be replaced. If we quit, we're leaving Genada in the lurch."

"I know that, boss," Miller said. "But people are willing to *kill* for this shit."

"Yeah," Cappy said. "Willing to *kill*. And the freakin' U.S. government? Military, maybe? Who is this Colonel Fischer cat, anyway?"

"And how about that burning body?" Alonzo asked. "That kind of thing ain't our business."

She put her fingers on her temples and rubbed. Alonzo was right. They were *all* right, but they were also fresh out of options. "Guys, this situation sucks for us, but if we just stay cool and finish the job, we *own* our 747 free and clear. I'm willing to take risks to make that happen. If we bail, we lose everything we've struggled for. Me? To be blunt, I'd rather die first. But if you guys want out, say the word and we walk as soon as we land."

She stared at each of them in turn. It had to be a group decision. She couldn't coerce them one way or another, nor would she. These men were her family, the brothers she'd never had.

They all looked at the ground, the equipment, anywhere but at Sara. None of them wanted to work for someone else ever again. But how far were they willing to go for that?

She leaned out of her seat and stared hard at Alonzo. "Well? I can't decide this for you. Make a decision."

Alonzo seemed to shrink into his seat. He hated to be put on the spot. "I like being my own boss. But you have to promise us that if it gets crazy, that this whole burning body thing was anything other than a onetime fluke, then we're out. Deal?"

Sara nodded.

"Well then, fuck it," Alonzo said. "We all look out for each other. We finish the job. I'm in."

Sara turned to stare at the Twins, but she already knew their answer.

"I agree with 'Zo," Miller said. "Fuck it, I'm in."

Cappy gave a thumbs-up. "Me too. I'll even throw in a mandatory *fuck it* just so I can swear like all the cool kids."

Sara laughed. "Okay, now that we have that cleared up, let's do our jobs. I'm going to check on Jian and Rhumkorrf. 'Zo, you keep flying. Cappy and Miller, go check on that drunk-ass Tim Feely. If he's still out, just leave him in the crash chair."

Sara followed Cappy and Miller out of the cockpit. They descended the fore ladder to the lower deck while Sara walked to the upper-deck lab.

THE TIGER ARM and the baby arm simultaneously reached up, toward her face. Bent sewing needles sprouted from the finger/paw tips.

"No," Jian whimpered. "No, please no . . ."

Needles sank into her shoulders. The wide mouth opened and leaned in toward her face.

Breath like a puppy's.

Long teeth wet with saliva.

Jian lost her grip on the stuffed monstrosity. The creature fell to the grass. It landed on all fours and started to scramble toward her, hissing in anger, black eyes narrow with hatred and hunger.

Finally, all her pain and suffering would end . . .

SARA ENTERED THE lab to find Jian asleep on her computer desk, head and arms lying heavily to the left of a computer keyboard. Her glossy hair seemed to melt right into the desk's black surface. She was asleep, but not motionless — the woman twitched and whimpered.

Rhumkorrf was sitting at a terminal across the lab, either ignoring Jian's nightmare or oblivious to it.

"Doctor Rhumkorrf?" Sara said. "Is she okay?"

He looked up from his computer, then looked at Jian. He waved a hand dismissively. "She does that all the time." He bent back to his work.

What an asshole. Sara gently shook Jian's shoulders. The woman snapped up and awake, looked at Sara and flinched away as if Sara were some creature straight from the nightmare.

"Take it easy," Sara said in a soothing voice. "It's okay."

Jian blinked, took a deep breath, held it, then let it out in a long, slow exhale. This chick was a total mess. Must have been a humdinger of a dream. Jian's eyes suddenly darted to the right, to her multiple computer screens, then she twisted her body to look under the desk.

"Jian, what is it?"

"Did you see it?"

"See what?"

Jian looked around the lab quickly, eyes hunting. "I thought I saw one of them."

"One of what, honey?"

The woman jammed her fists into her eyes and rubbed. "I thought I saw something. But nothing is there."

Sara reached out and stroked Jian's long black hair. "Just take a breath, kiddo. You had a nightmare, that's all."

Jian stared back with haunted, hollow eyes. "That all," she said with a whisper, then laughed quietly. It was a high-pitched laugh. Had it been louder Sara might have mistaken it for a scream.

Jian turned to her computer, shoulders hunched, hair hanging in front of her face. She had the carriage of a woman who'd been beaten by her husband or boyfriend. And still, Rhumkorrf was oblivious. *Total* asshole.

"Miss Purinam, may I ask a question?"

"Don't call me *Miss*," Sara said, and smiled. "I work for a living. You call me Sara."

Jian shook her head. "I use respectful terms only."

"Okay, then, Sara it is." Sara put a finger under Jian's chin and gently lifted, tilting the woman's head back. Bright red splotches dotted Jian's neck, precursors to the already-forming dark bruises. "We need to get some ice on your neck."

"I am fine, Miss Purinam."

"*Sara*. And when I get the ice, you *will* put it on. Now, what's your question?"

"Where did you get such a plane? This is a flying lab, everything we need. It is amazing."

"It's a C-5B that once upon a time crash-landed at Dover Air Force Base," Sara said. "Most of the plane was sold for scrap, which Colding bought up through one of Genada's dummy corporations. We got parts from two other crashes and new engines from a quiet contract with Boeing. Colding went to Baffin with you; my crew and I oversaw the reassembly project in Brazil. Pour in money, shake well, Genada has its own hot-rodded, big-ass flying lab."

"You put pieces together to make a new whole," Jian said, then nodded. "That is like what I do for Genada, but I do it inside the computer."

"But you guys chop up cells and DNA, stuff like that," Sara said. "You can't do *that* on a computer, can you?"

Jian hopped up and waddled to a white machine. She looked relieved to have something to talk about, or maybe some*one* to talk to. She gestured at the machine like an auto-show model displaying a new concept car.

"This is our oligo synthesizer. When I make genomes in the computer, this machine creates DNA one nucleotide at a time, the same way you would build chain links, only on a much smaller scale."

The device didn't look that dramatic to Sara — waist high, mostly off-white plastic, bristling with orderly tubes and hoses and plastic jars. It didn't look *that* sci-fi, but what Jian was saying . . . well, that was just *beyond* sci-fi.

"I don't think I get it," Sara said. "You're telling me this is like a biological inkjet *printer*? It can make, I don't know . . . *hot-rodded* DNA?"

Jian nodded. "This is the most advanced machine of its kind in the world. It can build full, custom chromosomes that we create and test inside the computer."

"Holy shit. That's amazing. Imagine the brain that came up with that one."

"That brain is mine," Jian said. She smiled proudly, an expression that seemed to crack a hidden reserve of beauty Sara hadn't seen before. "I invented it. I call my computer the God Machine, so this oligo machine is like the hand of God. Isn't that funny?"

No. It wasn't funny. In fact, the name sent a chill down Sara's spine. *The God Machine.* And right smack-dab in the middle of her plane.

Sara didn't like it. Not one damn bit.

"Let me get some ice for your neck," Sara said. "I'll be right back."

SARA GENTLY WRAPPED gauze around Jian's neck. The gauze held a small ice pack in place over darkening bruises. Jian tilted her head to accommodate, but she never stopped typing. Her eyes flicked across her half hemisphere of screens. Sara couldn't understand what the woman was doing — the only thing on the screens was an endless list of four letters: *C, G, T* and *A.*

"I know you're smart and all," Sara said, "but doesn't the computer handle that coding stuff?"

Jian shrugged. "Sometimes I see things that give me idea. I tweak genome here, tweak genome there. I am hoping I can reload our latest research from the drive I brought onboard." As if to punctuate her point, Jian called up a new window, typed in a few lines of code, then returned to the endlessly scrolling list of *A, G, T* and *C.*

The computer gave off a loud, single beep. Jian took in a sharp breath and held it. She stared at the screen with a spooky intensity. Jian reminded Sara of a hard-core gambler waiting for the dice to stop tumbling.

Jian clicked the mouse, and Sara saw actual words appear on the screen.

RESTORE FROM BACKUP: COMPLETE
GENOME A17: LOADED
VIABILITY PROBABILITY: 95.0567%
BEGIN SYNTHESIS? YES/NO

Rhumkorrf's head popped out from behind his terminal.

"Is it loaded?"

"Yes, Doctor Rhumkorrf," Jian said.

He ran over. *Scurried* was a better word, because the fidgety man reminded Sara of a rat with glasses.

"Sara," he said, "please go wake up Mister Feely. Tell him we need to prepare and run the immune response test, immediately."

Sara saw Jian's right hand move the mouse. On the screen, the pointer hovered over YES. Jian's left hand stayed flat on the desktop — she actually crossed her fingers, then clicked the mouse.

A mechanical humming sound came from the oligo machine. The hand of God. Sara quickly left the lab, partly to wake up Feely, and partly because she didn't want to be anywhere near that thing.

THE C-5'S INCESSANT in-flight hum filled the lab's stillness, but Claus barely noticed it. All of his attention rested on the bulkhead monitor, as did that of Jian and Tim.

Once again, the grid of 150 squares. Black filled only nineteen of them.

131/150

They all kept checking watches, looking at the time counter on the monitor, even scanning for other clocks in the room. It had never gone this long — usually this far into the test, there were fewer than ten eggs left.

Another panel went black.

130/150

Three people held their breath, waiting for the inevitable cascade of black squares. A cascade that did not appear.

"Mister Feely," Claus said. "Give me the time." He could have gone by the clock on the screen, but he couldn't let himself believe it. There had to be a mistake. Tim had the *official* time and that was what Claus wanted. Erika had kept the official time before, but she was no longer part of the project. Now her duties — all of them — fell to Tim.

"Twenty-four minutes, thirteen seconds," Tim said.

Claus felt a flicker of hope. Maybe . . . *maybe.* He watched, waited. No more black squares appeared. The embryos vibrated as their cells split and split again, taking them well into the morula stage. In some of the squares, the lethal macrophages actually sat side by side with the morulas.

But no more attacks.

No one spoke. Claus suddenly noticed that the jet-engine hum was the only sound in the lab.

"Time?"

Tim started to talk, then gagged and covered his mouth. Erika had not only been the superior intellect, she also, apparently, could hold her liquor better.

"Twenty-eight minutes and thirty seconds," Tim said, recovering. "Mark."

In square thirty-eight, an egg quivered: another successful mitosis. The macrophages moved around aimlessly.

Claus had done it. He had beaten the immune response.

His strategy had been risky — shorting Jian's meds brought on her manic/depressive symptoms, but it also freed up her mind. Her most creative solutions had always come when she was on the edge of madness. Soon, perhaps, he could get her to her normal medication level, but not now, not when he needed her at her best. The implantation process came next. If that brought more problems, they would need fast solutions. They were on the run from world governments, for God's sake — speed was of the essence.

Besides, Jian's nightmares were getting worse but her hallucinations had only started recently. He probably had a week or so before she got suicidal. Maybe less. But that was the kind of gamble you took when immortality was on the line.

He counted off sixty more seconds, just to be sure.

No more black squares.

"It is a success," he said. "We need to prepare the eggs for implantation."

He wished Erika could have been here for this. Despite her horrible actions, she was a brilliant scientist. Oh well, she'd just have to read about it in the journals. Maybe he'd even leave her name on some of the lesser research papers.

Jian, however, would get full secondary credit. She'd earned it. He saw her fingering the bandage around her neck, the bandage covering the bruises Erika had given her. Women. They were *all* crazy.

"Jian, what changed?" Claus said. "What did you do?"

"The four new samples helped, Doctor Rhumkorrf, but I also had an idea, very simple, that we had not thought. We want internal organs, and we've coded to make those compatible with humans. The rest of the body, we were going piecemeal, replacing small groups of proteins at a time, trying to find the missing piece of the compatibility puzzle. Mister Feely gave me an idea."

"I did?" Feely said.

"Yes. I realized that there was one organ unnecessary to our needs. I told the computer to swap out all DNA for that organ, then perform a hundred thousand generations of test evolution. It seems the DNA associated with that organ was the final immune response trigger."

"But which organ . . ." Claus said, his voice trailing off. No. It couldn't be that simple. Could it? He had asked them to step back, think differently. Jian had done exactly that and found something they all should have seen months ago.

"Well?" Tim said. "What organ was it?"

"The *largest* organ," Claus said, getting the words out before Jian could say them. "The integument. The *skin*."

Tim looked from Claus to Jian. "Really?"

Jian nodded, even smiled a little. "The ancestors will have cow fur."

"And that's it?" Tim said. "Problem solved?"

Of course that didn't solve the problem. The boy wasn't even *close* to Erika's brilliance. "Don't be stupid, Mister Feely. All we did was defeat the immune response. That allows us to implant, monitor, measure and modify as we go. We will probably lose all the embryos within a few days of implantation. When we cloned the quagga, we implanted over twelve hundred blastocysts before one survived to birth. That part of the quagga project was Doctor Hoel's, Mister Feely. Now it's yours."

Tim's eyes widened. "But, but I'm Jian's *assistant*. We have to get someone else in here to replace Erika."

"There is no one else," Claus said. "We are isolated, we have to stay hidden. Congratulations, Mister Feely . . . you've just been promoted."

"But, but . . . I can't . . . she brought back species from *extinction*, I can't—"

"You can and you *will*," Claus said. "Time to grow up, Mister Feely. Millions of avoidable deaths now rest squarely on your shoulders."

Tim blinked again. He opened his mouth to speak, but gagged, ran to a trash can and threw up in it.

BOOK THREE

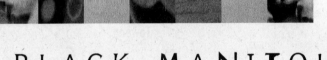

BLACK MANITOU
ISLAND

NOVEMBER 9: FLY BY

THE SUN JUST breaking free somewhere behind its tail, the C-5 approached Black Manitou Island; a tiny sliver of white, brown and green in the midst of Lake Superior's glittering blue splendor. Colding sat in the observer's seat. Sleep fuzzed his eyes. His axe cut hurt.

"Here you go," Cappy said, and put a half-full Styrofoam cup of coffee in his hand.

"Thanks," Colding said. "And thanks for the shirt and jacket."

Cappy ticked off a little two-fingered salute, then walked out of the cockpit. Colding set the coffee down, keeping an eye on it so it wouldn't spill while he opened the manila folder. The liquid vibrated in time with the C-5's engine hum.

He took a sip — *strong brew* — and looked out the front canopy. They were so low the sun sparkled off whitecapped waves, creating a miles-wide cone of flashbulbs reflecting the morning light.

"Middle of freakin' nowhere," Alonzo said. "And they call these things *lakes*? I've seen smaller *oceans*."

"That's why they call them the *Great* Lakes, kid," Sara said. "I can't believe you've never seen them. You gotta get out more."

"Right," Alonzo said. "'Cause Michigan is high up on my list of tourist spots. *Especially* Detroit."

"Most of the state is just fine," Sara said. "I grew up near here, town called Cheboygan."

Alonzo nodded. "You grew up here. Yeah, that explains a lot."

Sara flicked out her right hand and slapped Alonzo's shoulder. He laughed, then turned in his seat and called back to Colding. "How 'bout you, bro? Where you from?"

"Georgia. A little town outside of At—"

"Let's just land the plane, shall we?" Sara said. Colding leaned back. Alonzo let out a long whistle. They were at least five minutes from landing, but no one mentioned that. Seemed Sara wanted to keep the conversation all business, at least where Colding was concerned.

From the observer's seat, Colding had a stunning view out the front canopy. Black Manitou Island looked mostly white, dotted with patches of brown and green. The island ran almost perfectly southwest to northeast. Colding referred to the map in the manila folder. Ten miles from tip to tip, three miles across at the widest point. Deep bays and fjords made it resemble a tropical archipelago. A wide, sandy beach surrounded the coastline.

Alonzo affected a southern drawl. "How close is the nearest *gawddayum* town? Da-na-*neer*-neer-*neer*-neer-*neer*-neer-*neeerrrr*."

"This is Michigan, you idiot," Sara said. "Put away the *Deliverance* banjo."

Colding checked the map again. "You won't be doing much partying with the locals. Closest town is Copper Harbor, about three hours away by boat."

Alonzo groaned. "How far by plane or chopper?"

"Irrelevant," Colding said. "Once we land, no air traffic off the island."

"Fuck," Alonzo said. "Looks like I'll be dating Rosie Palms and her five friends for a while."

"Wrong girl," Sara said. "Around here we call that *Dating Miss Michigan*."

Colding kept flipping through the folder. "It's a bit more accommodating than it looks. Says here the place used to be a four-star resort. Marilyn Monroe supposedly stayed there."

The island grew in size, now filling the forward horizon.

"No radar," Alonzo said. "They have an airstrip but no radar?"

"Uhhh . . ." Colding flipped through more pages. "They only turn it on for landings and takeoffs. Danté doesn't want anyone wondering why an island in the middle of the lake has functioning radar."

As if on cue, a small ping sounded through the cockpit.

"Radar, check," Sara said. "Looks like they're ready for us."

Colding leaned forward again. "Fly the length of the island before you land."

"Please," Sara said.

Colding looked at her. "Please what?"

"Fly the length of the island, *please*." Sara continued to look out the window, never turning to meet Colding's eyes. "Until we land, I'm in charge, remember?"

Alonzo looked at Sara, a funny expression on his face. He craned his head to look back at Colding as if to say, *What's that all about?* Colding just shrugged.

"Eyes on the boat, 'Zo," Sara said. Alonzo turned back to his normal position.

So this was how it was going to be. Well, once on the island, there was plenty of room to steer clear of this woman.

"*Captain* Purinam," Colding said. "If it wouldn't be too much trouble, could you kindly fly the length of the island before landing? *Please?*"

"Why, it's no trouble at all," Sara said. "Standard procedure, really, you didn't even have to ask."

Alonzo gave her that funny look again, then shrugged and turned back to his duties.

Sara took the C-5 north, wide of the island, then banked back and closed in on the northeast tip. Colding traced their path on the map as the C-5 flew over. Rapleje Bay split the northeast end of the island into a pair of mile-long, snow-covered tongues. Rocks peeked through the snow in many places, brown and gray, or black with fresh snowmelt. An inch or two of powder covered the ground, clumped on the bare branches of oaks and poplars and weighed down the boughs of thick evergreens.

Just past the bay, they flew over a neat little farmhouse and a good-sized red barn with a black tar-shingle roof. Gray shingles spelled out the word *Ballantine* in five-foot letters. Colding saw cows milling about a snow-dusted pasture outside the barn, then a running flash of something small and black. Probably a dog.

A road led away from the barn. The C-5 seemed to fly down the road's slightly curving length. To the left of the road, he saw fields long since grown fallow, spotted here and there with young poplars and pines. To the right, the island's center ridge angled up a good five hundred feet. In the dead center of the island, a square wooden tower rose up from that ridge like a small cabin on tall stilts. Next to it stood a thin, metal-frame communications tower painted in red and white, two boxy devices mounted high on its sides. At the top, a compact radar array spun in a steady circle.

Alonzo pointed at the wooden tower. "What's with the Smokey the Bear action?"

Colding flipped through the folder. "It's an old fire watchtower. Has an air-raid siren and everything. The metal tower has the secure satellite up-link to Genada. And a jammer that blocks all communications in or out."

"A jammer?" Sara said. "Then how do you talk to someone on the other end of the island?"

"Regular old telephone poles," Colding said. "Totally self-contained, not connected to any outside system. Look on the right side of the road — landlines running to all the buildings. All the occupied buildings, anyway, which looks like . . . a total of five, including the hangar."

"Five houses," Alonzo said. "Yeah, this place is jumping all right."

They passed the island's center, leaving the two towers behind. To the left, Colding saw an idyllic little harbor on the southeastern coast. Blocks of jagged granite surrounded the island, peeking up just past the water's surface. Only the approach into the harbor looked clear. Massive piles of broken concrete and big rocks made up the harbor wall, turning the endless Lake Superior waves into minor chop. A large white fishing boat, maybe a thirty-footer, sat moored to a long black dock.

Along the road, overgrown trees crowded in among scattered houses. Most of the places looked abandoned. He saw just three buildings that seemed well maintained: a single house, then another barn and house combo. Large swatches of churned-up mud inside fences indicated the barn was a working one.

Not far past that farm, they flew over an open space surrounded by a cluster of small buildings. Colding couldn't make out much, except for a solid-looking gray stone church with a tall bell tower.

Near the island's southwestern tip, the forest gave way to a snow-covered lawn edged with orderly rows of landscaping trees. At the back of the lawn perched a three-story brick mansion that overlooked the estate like some lord's castle from old England. The mansion's high position gave it a commanding view of Black Manitou's southern tip: a sandy beach lined with rocks, then nothing but water as far as the horizon.

A half mile due south of the mansion, a wide, flat clearing snaked through the woods like an oversized golf course fairway. Colding had to look at the paper map to see the logic — if you drew a visual line from end to end, the fairway had a mile-long space down the middle. Just wide enough to land a C-5. Danté Paglione had built a landing strip so that it didn't *look* like a landing strip, at least to any probing satellite.

And that satellite camouflage philosophy bled over to the hangar. Colding actually didn't see it at first, and had to spot-check the map before the visual clicked. The hangar was as big as the one back on Baffin Island, but with wire mesh over the roof that sloped down to the closely surrounding trees. A dense pack of fake pine-tree tips stuck up from the mesh. From the ground it probably looked like the worst camouflage one could imagine, but any satellite or even a plane flying at normal altitude would see nothing other than a wooded hill.

"Sightseeing is over," Sara said. "Let's get her on the ground."

Alonzo nodded. "Roger that."

Sara banked to the left, taking the C-5 back out over the water as she circled around. Surprisingly, the landing was as soft as any commercial flight Colding had ever flown.

The C-5 slowed to a crawl as Sara taxied it into the fake-hilltop hangar.

AS THE C-5'S turbines idled down, the Twins lowered the rear ramp and P. J. Colding walked out of the plane. The place looked and felt oddly familiar: another big-ass hangar, cattle stalls on one end, big-ass open doors looking out into a snowy landscape. And, of course, a fuel truck — he made a mental note to find someplace else to park it.

Just as his feet hit the hangar's concrete floor, a black Humvee and a beat-up old red Ford F150 pulled into the cavernous opening. A painted logo on the Hummer's hood read OTTO LODGE. Two men stepped out, both wearing black parkas with the lodge logo embroidered on the left breast. Colding recognized the men from the personnel pictures in the folder Magnus had given him: Clayton Detweiler and his thirtysomething son, Gary. Clayton maintained the mansion and most of the island. Gary was the driver of the boat the C-5 had flown over on the way in, and was also the island's only regular connection to the mainland.

The Ford truck produced three more people: a taller man almost Clayton's age, and a man and a woman in their early thirties. Colding recognized them from the personnel pages as well: Sven Ballantine, James Harvey and Stephanie Harvey, respectively.

Clayton walked up and extended his hand. He moved with the hitch of an overweight, older man plagued by a bum hip. His every other step brought the clinking of metal from the plus-sized key ring hanging from his belt. The way he carried himself the sound seemed more like the clinking of a gunfighter's spurs than the jangle of a janitor's keys. Colding shook the offered hand, feeling the man's rough skin and thick calluses.

"Welcome to Black Manitou, eh?" Clayton said. "Clayton Detweiler. You must be Colding."

Colding couldn't place the man's accent. He'd never heard anything quite like it. Clayton wore a scowl so deeply entrenched with permanent wrinkles it might have been the only expression the man had ever shown. A three-day growth of bristly gray beard made the wrinkles look deeper, more defined. His thick gray hair was combed straight back, looked oily-wet, and smelled of Brylcreem. Spots of dirt, grease and what appeared to be several mustard stains dotted his black down jacket.

"Nice to meet you," Colding said. He turned to the younger Detweiler. "And you must be Gary, our link to the mainland?"

Gary nodded and shook. The guy looked like a living Abercrombie & Fitch ad. His parka was fresh and clean. Oakley sunglasses hung from a cord around his neck. A deep tan covered skin that was already turning leathery. He wore a hemp necklace and a small gold loop in his right ear. Gary had a little bit of an odd, rich smell about him, something that Colding knew but couldn't place.

Colding shook hands with Sven and James. Each managed a fifty-cow backup herd. Sven was a heavyset older man, perhaps sixty, his old-fashioned mustache and sandy blond hair liberally peppered with gray. The mustache mostly hid a rather disturbing crop of nose hairs. Mostly. Sven looked like he should be riding shotgun with Sam Elliott in some old western.

James had the big-necked look of a former football player — a lineman, not a quarterback — and could have been a poster boy for the phrase "corn-fed." Stephanie had a wide-eyed smile and, of all things, curlers in her red hair.

Colding reached out to shake Stephanie's hand, but couldn't because she thrust a Saran Wrap–covered plate at him.

Brownies.

"Here ya go," she said in an accent just like Clayton's. "My family recipe, eh?"

"Uh, thanks." Colding took the plate.

James poked his wife in the shoulder. "Since when is our family name Duncan Hines?"

Stephanie put her hands on her hips and gave her husband a dirty look. "I'll have ya know *I* put in da walnuts."

"You're a walnut," James said.

"Your *face* is a walnut," Stephanie said.

Clayton rolled his eyes. "Oh, for Christ's sake. You two put a sock in it."

"You're a sock," Gary said. He didn't have the strange accent, just a normal midwestern twang.

Clayton shook his head in annoyance. "Sweet Jesus, all of you shut your pieholes. Well, there ya go, Mister Colding. You just met everyone on Black Manitou Island, population five. Time for all of us to get back to work. Just wanted to have you meet everyone so you wouldn't be asking me stupid fucking questions all goddamn day."

"Actually, Clayton, there's a lot I need to know. Looks like you guys take great care of the mansion and the grounds."

"What, you're *surprised*?" Clayton said. "You thought an old hick like me couldn't take care of business?"

This just wasn't Colding's day for making friends and influencing people. "That's not what I meant at all."

"I been *in charge* here for thirty years, eh?" Clayton's eyes narrowed beneath bushy gray eyebrows. "Just 'cause Danté said to take care of you don't mean I snap to your orders like a trained dog. You got it?"

Gary rolled his eyes, as if he'd heard his father's shitty attitude a million times before. The others looked around uncomfortably.

"Now hold on just a second," Colding said. "We need to set a few things straight, right now."

Before Colding could continue, Clayton looked away, up into the C-5's rear cargo door. Colding heard light footsteps on the ramp.

"Hey, Peej," Sara said. "Who're your friends?"

"We were clearly having a conversation here," Clayton said. "Who da hell are you, eh?"

"I'm da pilot, eh?" Sara said, her voice a perfect imitation of Clayton's accent.

Clayton leaned back a bit, the scowl still on his face. "You makin' fun of da way I talk?"

Sara laughed. "Only a little bit. I grew up in Cheboygan. Used to spend my summers vacationing near Sault Saint Marie."

"Michigan side or Canadian side?" Clayton asked.

"Da Michigan side, of course. I'm a Troll."

Clayton's face lit up in a genuine, friendly smile. It made him look like a completely different person.

Colding stared, dumbfounded, as Clayton extended his callused hand. Sara shook it and introduced herself to the five Black Manitou natives. Where Colding's intro had been awkward at best, Sara's felt like old friends reconnecting. Her natural charm relaxed everyone around her.

Sara saw the plate in Colding's hands. She lifted the Saran Wrap covering and pulled out a brownie as casually as you please. "Oh my, these look delicious. Who made them?"

"I did!" Stephanie said. "You can come over sometime and have some coffee. I made those brownies and they're my favorite 'cause it's an old family recipe."

The woman's speech reminded Colding of an overly happy machine gun kicking out rapid-fire words.

Sara took a bite, chewed, then laughed. "We must be related. Tastes a lot like *my* family recipe."

"Okay," Colding said. "Enough with the brownies. Captain Purinam, if you could attend to your duties, I want to have a talk with Clayton."

"Not now," Clayton said. "Didn't I tell you I got fuckin' work to do?"

Colding had been through *way* too much in the past few hours to put up with this crap. He felt his temper slipping and started to talk, but Gary spoke first.

"Say, Dad," he said. "You have to run me back to the boat anyway. Mister Colding can ride along, get a feel for the island. Fifteen minutes there and back. He is from *Genada*, Dad. You know, the guys who *pay you*?"

Clayton looked away for a second. He seemed annoyed at his son's logic. "Yah, fine," he said. "I'll take you, Colding, but only if Sara comes."

"I'm in," Sara said before Colding could manage a word. He felt like his few hours of sleep had slowed his reaction time or something — everyone was beating him to the punch.

"*Captain* Purinam," Colding said. "Don't you have work to do?"

She shrugged. "Nope. The boys have it covered. Let's road-trip."

Clayton reached out and grabbed a brownie off Colding's plate. He bit in, a few crumbs falling and sticking to his stubble. "Good stuff, Stephanie."

Stephanie beamed. "Thanks!"

"Can you and James hang out here and show people da mansion?"

"Sure!" Stephanie said. "I'd *love* to. We can walk back 'cause it's not really that cold out yet and we don't mind at all, do we, James?"

James didn't bother saying anything, because Clayton had already walked away. The old man got into the Hummer and slammed the door shut behind him.

Colding looked at Gary. "Is your dad always like this?"

Gary smiled an easy smile. Colding still couldn't place that smell.

"Unfortunately, he is," Gary said. "But don't worry about it, man. He's the hardest worker you'll ever meet. And if you need something done, it's done. Okay?" He asked the last word as if it were a signature on a contract, a contract Colding would just have to accept because that's the way it was. Gary obviously didn't want his father catching any shit.

"Okay," Colding said. "I'll give him the benefit of the doubt."

Gary smiled and nodded slowly, not just with his head, but also with his shoulders. "All right, man. For being so cool about it, I'll give you shotgun."

"So kind of you," Colding said, seeing instantly that Gary had eyes for Sara. Gary turned and climbed into the back of the Humvee.

Colding glared at Sara. "You're just coming along to piss me off."

"Yep," Sara said. "But don't worry, plenty more where that came from."

"Fine, whatever. And what was with that whole Troll comment, and that *eh* thing?"

Sara laughed. "Clayton and the others are Yoopers."

"What the hell is a *yooper*?"

"People from the Upper Peninsula of Michigan. You know, Upper Peninsula . . . U. P. . . . Yooper, get it? Yoopers have a real thick accent all their own. *Ya* instead of *yes*, *da* instead of *the*, and they end a lot of sentences with *eh?*, which is basically a rhetorical question. You'll get used to it. And if a Yooper is from *above* the bridge, can you guess what they call people who live *below* it?"

"Ah," Colding said. "*Trolls* live beneath the bridge. Wow. What a clever culture you have in these parts."

A blast of the Hummer's horn jolted them both. Clayton had one hand on the steering wheel, the other twirling in an annoyed circle that said, *Let's go already.*

"I seriously do not like this guy," Colding said.

Sara walked around to the left rear door. "That's okay, he clearly doesn't like you, either. Nobody does, really."

Colding sighed and got in the Hummer's passenger seat.

Clayton jammed the vehicle into reverse and squealed out of the hangar. He turned right and stopped fast, throwing everyone around in their seats, then put it in first and shot down the dirt road that ran through the center of the island like a spine.

DANTÉ'S ELBOWS RESTED on his white marble desk, and his hands held his head. How could this have happened? Every time he turned around, they were stepping deeper and deeper into a head-high pile of dog shit.

He looked up. Magnus sat in front of the desk, relaxing in a chair. He seemed not the least bit bothered by his actions.

"Magnus, how could you have done this?" Danté spoke quietly, firmly. For too long, perhaps, he'd ignored the sad truth: his brother was a bona fide sociopath.

"Relax," Magnus said. "The problem is solved."

"Solved? *Solved?* You killed Erika Hoel!"

"And what would you have done, given her a raise?"

Danté's face scrunched in frustration. He felt a pain in his chest. He pounded the desk with his fist, just once. The fist stayed there like a dropped gavel.

"Danté, seriously, you need to relax." Magnus sounded as calm as if this were a budget meeting with the board of directors. That calmness infuriated Danté even more. His own brother, a *killer*.

"I don't see the problem," Magnus said. "Our facility is destroyed, *including* our equipment, *including* the cows. I had Farm Girl send an email to the media — the Animal Liberation Front claimed responsibility for the blast. Gosh, they didn't mean to hurt anyone, but as they said in the email, if you commit atrocities on God's creatures, don't blame the ALF if there is collateral damage."

"Fischer knows that's all total bullshit."

"Of course he does," Magnus said. "But the ALF has grown more aggressive in the past few months, so the story fits. The media buys into it. If they do, so does the G8. Everyone wants to see xenotransplantation shut down, and guess what? Now we're shut down just like everyone else. So what can Fischer do about it?"

"He'll look for Rhumkorrf's project, that's what."

"And he won't find it. Fischer has no idea where Bubbah and the staff have gone. As long as no one on Black Manitou gets stupid and tries to contact the outside world, we're in the clear. It's what you *wanted*, Danté — time for Rhumkorrf to finish the project."

Danté sat quietly. Magnus hadn't just made a snap reaction, hadn't flipped out over his service buddy's death — he'd thought all of this through. In a way, Danté wished it *had* been a reaction, a crime of passion. That would have been easier to understand than premeditated murder.

"This isn't Afghanistan, Magnus. This isn't combat. You killed a woman, for God's sake."

His brother smiled. "Are you going to pretend you don't know what I am? Pretend you weren't secretly relieved when Galina conveniently disappeared?"

Danté leaned back as if he'd been slapped. He hadn't wanted Galina to *die*, not even for a second. "I had nothing to do with her death. *You* did that, not *me*." He felt his heart hammering in his temples. His skin felt hot.

Magnus rubbed his right forearm. "You told me you wished Galina could just go away. What did you think I was going to do when I heard you say that? Did you think I wouldn't come through for you?"

Danté looked away. Magnus was wrong. It hadn't been like that. It *hadn't*. Danté had just wanted the project to continue, to benefit all of humanity. Of *course* he'd wished for Galina to go away, but he'd said as much in front of Magnus. Said it . . . seen the cold look in his brother's eyes . . . and said no more.

"Danté, you know I love you, but let's be honest, you really don't have a lot going on in the balls department. You have Dad's skill at running a company, the fund-raising, the public panache, all of that good stuff. When I watch you do your thing at board meetings or the media, it blows me away. I *can't* do those things. But when it comes to the other stuff? The *off-camera* stuff? You just don't have Dad's stones. I do. Together, we make a great team, wouldn't you say?"

Danté felt that pain in his chest again. Sharper this time. His brother's eyes, so cold, not a shred of emotion.

"Get out, Magnus. Just get out of my sight."

Magnus stood and walked out, leaving Danté alone with his stress and his shame.

NOVEMBER 9: THE FAIRY

CLAYTON'S HUMVEE FOLLOWED the same road they'd flown over. No surprise, since it was the only road. Arching trees walled up either side. Brown, half-bare branches dripped from their inch-deep coat of melting snow. Many trees had black-flecked white trunks with peeling, paperlike bark. Pine trees stood out the most, thick and full compared with their anemic hardwood cohorts.

Almost no sign of man...it was achingly beautiful. Unkempt dirt roads branched off from time to time, leading to the small, dilapidated houses Colding had seen on the way in.

They passed by what had to be a road to the old town with the big church. Not far after that, the forest thinned a bit. The road quickly crested at a steep dune spotted with tall grasses. The dune's downslope led to the island's small harbor.

Beach smells filtered into the open window, complete with a strong odor of dead fish. Up and down the shore, heavy purplish-gray rock outcroppings led right up to the water, some sliding in at an angle, others standing as small cliffs. Patchy, dry orange lichens covered the top of the rocks, adding texture and depth. In the long spots between the rocks, there was nothing but sand, grass and a few scraggly trees reaching out from twenty-foot-high sloping dunes. Thick logs dotted the beach. Some had gnarled roots still attached, white and stripped free of bark. They looked like the bleached bones of desert animals unable to survive an endless sun.

The road ended at the blackened wooden dock, which ran forty feet into the harbor's calm waters. A small black metal shed sat near the base of the dock. At the end of the dock, Colding saw Gary's boat. A thirty-six-foot Sharkcat cruiser with a flying bridge. The perfect boat for deepwater fishing or a dockside party with fifteen of your closest friends. Black and gold script spelled the words DAS OTTO II on the boat's aft.

Gary hopped out of the Hummer, as did Colding. They both walked down the dock to the boat. This close to him and in the sunlight, Colding saw that Gary's irises looked dilated. Colding finally placed the smell, the sleepy look, the constant half-smile . . . the guy was baked.

"Gary, have you been smoking marijuana?"

The man giggled a little, a soundless thing that made his shoulders shiver. "Yeah. I've been *smoking marijuana*, Mister Narkie Narkerson. Why, you want some?"

"No," Colding said. "Just how stoned are you?"

Gary shrugged. "I don't know, man . . . how high does the scale go?"

Goddamit. *This* was their only support on the mainland?

Gary's smile faded. "Listen, brah, don't sweat it. Just because I boof a bit doesn't mean I can't handle my business."

"I'm not a fan of drugs," Colding said. "Or people who do them."

Gary rolled his eyes. When he did, Colding seemed to hear his own words through Gary's ears. When the hell had he started talking like a high school guidance counselor? Still, he had to probe a little, see just how much of a liability Gary Detweiler might be.

"Magnus tells me you can take care of yourself."

Gary shrugged. "I do what Magnus tells me. That's why I'm always carrying this stupid thing." He unzipped his coat and opened it a bit, allowing Colding to peek inside at a handgun — Genada's preferred weapon, a Beretta 96 — nestled in a shoulder holster.

Colding nodded. "You ever had to use that on the job?"

Gary laughed. "Do I look like Clint Eastwood? My preferred weapon is a bottle of single malt. I get more done drinking in the bars at Houghton-Hancock than I ever would with this stupid gun. I talk to strangers. I ask questions. I find out why people are in town. I see if people have any interest in Black Manitou, which they shouldn't, because only locals even know it's out here. The only shooting this kid does involves tequila and bourbon."

Colding could hear the sincerity in Gary's voice — the man hated carrying the weapon. "So if you don't like the gun, why work for Genada?"

Gary nodded toward the Humvee. "My dad has lived on this island for fifty years, man. He's not leaving. This is where I'll wind up burying him. I need to be here for him, you know? And if I work for Genada, well, then I get *paid* to be here for him. I make crazy money, and all I do is drive this beautiful boat and bang tourists. Once or twice a year, Magnus and Danté come around. I say *yessir* and *nosir* and take them wherever they want to go. Maybe I'm not a gunslinger, but this is more like a permanent vacation than a job."

"But you'll use that gun if you have to," Colding said, his voice low and serious. "If my people are in danger and I call you out here, you're prepared to do what I tell you?"

"My dad is now one of *your people*. I'll do whatever it takes to protect him."

Colding extended his hand. "Gary, I think you and I see eye to eye."

Gary's easy smile came back. They shook. "Anything you need from the mainland, just use the supersecret megaspy radio in the security room. Dad will show you how to get hold of me."

"Thanks. Oh, and Magnus had a message for you. He said to make sure his snowmobile is ready."

"It is. It's in that shed with mine." Gary pointed to the black metal shed at the foot of the dock. "I keep it there so when we've got five feet of snow, I can get to the mansion and back to the docks."

"Five *feet* of snow," Colding said, and laughed. "Whatever, dude, I wasn't born yesterday."

Gary just smiled his stoner smile and nodded.

Colding stopped laughing. "Wait, you're serious? Five *feet*?"

"Sure," Gary said. "If it's a mild winter."

The Humvee's horn blared.

"Can you two stop grab-assin'?" Clayton shouted from the vehicle. "I've got work ta do."

Gary threw his dad a snappy salute, then untied the boat and hopped in. He climbed up a ladder to the flying bridge. Seconds later the Sharkcat's engines gurgled to life — they sounded big and powerful. The boat had plenty of room, easily enough to evacuate the entire staff if it came to that.

Gary waved to Colding and shouted to be heard over the engine. "Good luck, chief. I'm just a call away if you need anything." With that, Gary gunned the engine, trailing a strong wake as he headed out of the harbor.

Colding walked back to the Hummer and hopped in.

Clayton stared after the boat, then shook his head. "Such a show-off, that guy. I love him, but it's hard when your son is a fairy."

"A *fairy*?" Colding said. "You think your son is gay?"

Clayton shrugged. "He's got an earring, eh? Pillow-biter for sure."

"My *word*," Sara said. "An earring on a man? Well, he's *got* to be one of them there homosexuals."

Colding rubbed his eyes. "Clayton, you are truly a man of culture and learning."

"Ain't that da truth," Clayton said. "Okay, let's get this shit finished so I can get on with my day. I get paid for maintenance, not for being a fuckin' taxi driver."

The term *salt of the earth* didn't go far enough to describe Detweiler. More like the rock on which that salt might crystallize. "Clayton, I think you need to relax."

"Ya? Well, think about this, eh?" Clayton leaned onto his left cheek and ripped off a loud, barking fart. The rotten-egg smell immediately filled the Hummer.

"Oh, for crying out loud," Colding said as he leaned his head out the window. Sara let out a gagging noise, but she was laughing as she rolled down both the backseat windows.

"Oh, Clayton!" she said, breathing through her shirtsleeve. "What crawled up your ass and died?"

Clayton's shoulders bounced up and down in a chuckle. He breathed in deeply through his nose. "Oh, that was a good one, eh, Colding? Welcome to Black Manitou, city boy."

"Just take us back to the mansion," Colding said. "I want to see the security room."

Clayton backed the Hummer off the foot of the dock, then drove over the sand-covered pavement and crested the dunes. He was still laughing when he drove onto the road leading to the mansion.

INSANITY. TIM FEELY had worked with Jian for two years, so he felt confident knowing insanity when he saw it. And all of this? Yeah, insanity.

Less than twenty-four hours ago, Erika Hoel had been licking single-malt scotch out of his belly button. Slowly. That was good. That was hot, and fun, and sexy. Sure, being stuck on a frozen island for months on end was crap on a cracker, but being there with a wild-ass Dutch cougar made it a tad more palatable.

Since then? Explosions. Sabotage. Brady Giovanni burned extra crispy. That same wild-ass Dutch cougar nearly choking out Jian with a fire axe. Colding all bloody. A gigantic plane and a secret frickin' base filled with "Yoopers." It was like a James Bond movie featuring inbred hicks.

And, perhaps worst of all, being awarded Erika's duties.

He needed a drink. Maybe somewhere in this mansion he'd find one, and hopefully before he found a gun — because if he had to listen to this way-too-happy woman with the curlers in her hair for one more minute he was going to shoot himself right in the face.

"This is my favorite view on da whole island," Stephanie said. "It's da back porch."

"Really?" Tim said. "I guess that's a good name for a porch on the back of a house."

Stephanie laughed. Her ex-jock husband did not. He shot Tim a glare that clearly said, *Watch it, asshole.* Guy wasn't as big as Brady had been, but he was big enough. Tim decided he'd watch it.

Hangover or no hangover, the view from the sprawling veranda simply took Tim's breath away. The mansion was a jewel atop a crown of snow-spotted golden sand dunes that sloped gently toward the shore.

Flecks of sand and snow blew across cut-stone steps that led almost to the beach. Whitecaps frosted the water all the way to the horizon. Hundreds of frothing spots stood stationary against the roiling waves — ship-killing chunks of granite. Two hundred yards out from shore, a towering rock rose sixty feet out of the water before it seemed to fold over on itself. "What's that big rock that looks like a horse head?"

"That's Horse Head Rock," Stephanie said.

Of course that's what they called it. Black Manitou Island, a place of poetry.

"Come on," Stephanie said. "There's so much more to show you!"

A wide, floor-to-ceiling picture window stood at the back of the veranda. French doors led into an expansive lounge filled with leather furniture and expensive-looking tables. A long mahogany bookshelf packed with old-leather tomes surrounded a large flat-panel TV. A matching mahogany bar with a marble counter and brass trim dominated the room. Behind it *oh thank you, Lord, thank you!* sat a well-lit, glass liquor cabinet filled with hundreds of bottles.

Tim walked straight to the cabinet. Lonely glasses were lined up on a long white cloth, just waiting for a friendly handshake. He grabbed one and started looking through the bottles.

"A little early for a drink, isn't it?" James said.

"There's always room for Jell-O, big fella."

Tim saw that one brand of liquor dominated, taking up an entire shelf. "You've got enough Yukon Jack to last through the second coming. Assuming, of course, that Christ likes to drink till he Yukes."

"I'd leave those alone," Stephanie said quietly. "Those belong to Magnus."

Ah. Magnus. Well, Tim would just go ahead and leave those alone, then.

"Oh my," Tim said as he pulled out a bottle of Caol Ila scotch. "Come to Poppa." He poured a glass and drained it in one go. Burned going down. The first glass was just hangover medicine, really. The second glass was for taste.

"Mister Feely," James said. "Do you mind? We've got work to do."

Tim left the bottle on the counter. He followed James and Stephanie out of the lounge. The rest of the building reeked with turn-of-the-century high class. The twentieth century, mind you, not the twenty-first. Teak paneling, mahogany trim, every room sported a crystal chandelier. Back in the day, this place must have been the hotness.

But all the style and warmth couldn't quite hide the building's age. The floor dipped here and there, some teak wall panels didn't quite line up. Every hall and room held the visible signs of minor repairs — decades of settling had taken their toll.

"Thirty guest rooms," Stephanie said. "Dining room kitchen all that stuff. Da basement has all da old servants' quarters, which are pretty much storage now, eh? Also houses da security room but we can't get in 'cause only Clayton has da door's secret code. We'll show you your room, then take off."

His room. Perfect. Nap time, and not a nap in some godforsaken air force chair designed by the Marquis de Sade. A couple more drinks, then delicious slumber. He drained his glass.

"Mister Feely, I need you!" A gruff German accent — the voice a dagger in Tim's ear. His heart sank as if his parents had just caught him looking at nudie magazines. He turned to see Claus Rhumkorrf, hands on hips, standing in the hallway.

"Mister Feely! Are you *drinking*?"

Tim looked at the empty glass in his hand as if he was surprised to see it there. "What, this? Why, I just found this lying about and I'm being a good citizen. Cleanliness is next to godliness, you know."

"We are ready to start implantation," Rhumkorrf said. "Come with me back to the plane. *Now.*"

Rhumkorrf turned and stormed down the hall. Stephanie shrugged and held out her hand, palm up. Tim gave her the glass, then followed Rhumkorrf.

COLDING FOLLOWED SARA and Clayton through the mansion's halls and down a stairwell.

"Jack Kerouac used to vacation here, ya know," Clayton said. "I used to drink beers with him all da time."

Colding threw Clayton a doubting glance. "You drank with Kerouac?"

"Ya. Hell of a guy. Farted a lot, though. He could clear out da entire bar when he got going."

Colding tried to imagine one of America's greatest literary figures ripping off a loud one in a bar full of Yoopers, but the picture just wouldn't register.

"What about Marilyn Monroe?" Sara asked. "I heard she stayed here. You drink with her, too?"

"She liked to drink alone mostly, eh? I banged her, though. Nice tits."

The utilitarian basement showed far less ornamentation than the two upper floors. There wasn't a speck of dust on anything. Clayton stopped at a door with a small keypad and punched in 0-0-0-0. A heavy deadbolt clicked open inside the door.

"Wow," Sara said. "Pretty crafty password, Clayton."

The old man shrugged and walked into a completely modern room, white walls with fluorescent lighting set into a white suspended acoustic-tile ceiling. A row of security monitors sat on one wall, mounted above a white desk that held a familiar-looking computer. The computer screen showed a slowly spinning Genada logo.

But the desk wasn't what caught Colding's attention. What held his eyes and made him instantly nervous was the three-shelved weapons rack that took up the center of the room.

"This here is Magnus's toy chest," Clayton said.

Colding stared in amazement. He ran his hands along a row of assault rifles: three German Heckler & Koch MP5s, two Beretta AR70s, a British SA80 with a thick nightscope and a triple magazine, four Israeli Uzi nine-millimeters and a pair of Austrian Steyr 69 sniper rifles. Below the rifles hung a rack of Magnus's favorite handgun, the Beretta 96. *Ten* of them. Boxes and boxes of magazines and ammo occupied the lower shelves. Two sets of Kevlar bulletproof body armor hung from the end of the rack.

There were some other supplies: first-aid kits, MREs, four propane canisters with blowtorch nozzles, four lighters and fifteen Ka-Bar knives still in their white cardboard boxes.

"What is all this?" Sara said, concern heavy in her voice. "Is Magnus going to war or something?"

Clayton shrugged. "Something ain't right with that boy."

Colding noticed three small, wooden ammo crates on a middle shelf. He felt his stomach do a flip as he gently pulled out the box, opened it and saw the contents. "Demex? Fucking *plastic explosives*?"

"And detonators," Clayton said. "Doesn't exactly make me happy to have it in my mansion."

Colding saw one more thing. On the bottom shelf, a long, black canvas bag. He unzipped it. Inside was a five-foot-long case, painted a drab military green. Four metal latches held the case shut.

"No way," Sara said quietly. "Please tell me that isn't what I think it is."

Colding flipped the latches and lifted the lid to reveal a five-foot-long metal tube, blocky on one end, all of it painted olive green. A handle stuck out from the blocky part. In front of the handle, Colding saw a metal rectangle that folded out into an *IFF* antenna, an acronym for *Identify Friend or Foe*. A useful feature, considering this weapon could blow just about anything out of the sky.

"It's a Stinger missile," he said.

"I told you not to tell me," Sara said. Her voice sounded alarmed, not a surprising reaction for a pilot looking at a plane-killing weapon. "Anyone want to tell me why Magnus needs a surface-to-air missile?"

Colding didn't know the answer. He zipped the bag, slid it back into place, then stood and walked over to the desk and its bank of security monitors. The setup was identical to the one they'd left behind on Baffin Island.

"Clayton, what's our video coverage like?"

Clayton walked to the counter and started pushing buttons. A series of views flashed across the screens: the outside of the mansion, the harbor, the ballroom, guest rooms, the kitchen. It surprised Colding to see the ease with which Clayton worked the controls — the old man obviously knew his way around the security systems.

"Good coverage," Clayton said. "We even have that crazy infrared crap. We got regular video all over, including everyone's rooms."

"Turn off all room cameras," Colding said. "Everyone but Jian."

He watched as Clayton started flipping switches. "Done," Clayton said. "Why leave Jian's active? You like them big-girl peep shows?"

"I . . . no, Clayton, I do *not* like big-girl peep shows. Jian's tried to kill herself before. She has to be watched at all times. And as soon as we're done here, please go in her room and remove all glass, any mirrors. Take down the chandelier and put up a simple fixture, nothing she could hang herself from."

For once, Clayton didn't have a smart-ass comment. "I'll make sure da room is safe," he said.

"What about the hangar?" Sara said. "That covered, too?"

Clayton pushed more buttons. Multiple views of the hangar, both inside and out. He stopped when the screens showed the mammoth C-5. "There's connections for cameras inside da big plane. Sara, your boys hook those up yet?"

"If it was on the fly-in checklist, probably."

Clayton pushed more buttons. Monitors now showed Alonzo in the C-5 cockpit, Claus and Jian in the second-deck lab and Tim Feely in the veterinary station across the aisle from the crash chairs. Clayton changed the view to show Harold and Cappy walking from cow stall to cow stall, opening the clear plexiglass doors. The press of a button lowered the harnesses, putting the animals' weight back on their hooves. The Twins led the cows out of the C-5 two at a time.

"Yep," Clayton said. "They got it done. That's all da coverage we got. No wireless, no cell phones, no Internet. Landlines connect to James's place, Sven's, my house, da hangar and every room in da mansion has its own extension. Only way to reach da mainland is da secure terminal." He pointed to the small computer at the end of the desk. It was a duplicate of the one Colding had used at Baffin Island.

"That calls my son or Manitoba," Clayton said. "We take care of each other out here, and we're careful, eh? But anything goes wrong, help is three hours away at best."

"I want to see the island tomorrow," Colding said. "All of it. Will your Hummer take us all over?"

Clayton shook his head. "No way. A lot of swamp on Black Manitou. But don't you worry, eh? Me and Da Nuge will show you everything?"

"The Nuge?"

Clayton nodded. "Ted Nugent. Da *Nuge*, eh?"

"Well then," Sara said. "Slap my ass and call me Sally. If Deadly Tedly is involved, I'm in."

Great. The last thing Colding needed was that woman tagging along again. "Uh, Sara, there's no need for you to go this time. Just stay here."

She shrugged. "Gotta go. It's the *Nuge*, man."

"That's right," Clayton said, smiling his bristly smile. "But no sleeping in, eh? You both have your asses on da front steps at 8:00 A.M., got it?"

"Got it," Sara said. "I have to check in with my crew. Drive me back to the hangar, Clayton?"

"I'd be dee-lighted, eh? Colding, your room is number twenty-four. See you tomorrow."

Colding nodded, barely paying attention to Sara and Clayton as they left him alone in the security room. Whatever a "nuge" was, he'd see soon enough.

He moved to the weapons, checking the action on each and every one. His mind swam with possibilities, mapping out contingencies. Three hours to the mainland by boat, only there was no boat here. Other than Gary Detweiler and the Paglione brothers, no one knew they were on Black Manitou. *No one.* But, he reminded himself, that was the way it had to be if they wanted to complete the research, bring the ancestor to life and give hope to millions.

JIAN STUMBLED A little, but Colding's strong arm held her up. "Mister Colding, I don't want to go to sleep. We have more work to do."

"Still not buying it," Colding said. "Keep walking, kid, you're turning in."

He led her down the mansion's hall. She, Rhumkorrf and Tim had finished implantation. Every cow had a blastocyst in its uterus. Those blastocysts would soon implant into the uterine wall, forming an embryo and a placenta. After that, more of her coding would force the embryos to split and form monochorionic-monoamniotic twins. Mister Feely called it *the blue-light special of genetics, two for the price of one.* Some might even split a third time, creating triplets. All of this, of course, assumed the immune response continued to accept the embryos as *self.*

Movement.

Over there, to her left. Jian looked fast. Nothing. Had that been a streak of orange?

"Jian," Colding said. "Are you okay?"

She stared for a second, but there was nothing there. "Yes. I am fine, Mister Colding."

They walked on. Colding was really her only friend, the only true friend she'd had since the government decided she was a seven-year-old genius. That's when they'd removed her from her home in the mountains, taken her away from her family, put her in special schools.

It hadn't taken her long to show even more promise, outstepping her colleagues at the Chinese Academy of Sciences. At age eleven, she published her first genetics paper. By age thirteen, she was speaking at conferences, and her face was all over the news as the poster child for China's scientific ascendance.

Then two things happened. First, she started to see the bad things. Second, she discovered computers.

At first, those *bad* things were really just *strange* things. Shadows at the corners of her vision, things that hid when she looked for them. The visions grew worse. Sometimes they looked like little blue spiders. Sometimes they looked like big orange spiders. Sometimes they crawled on her. And sometimes, they *bit* her.

Even when she showed people the marks on her arms, no one believed her. They gave her the drugs. Sometimes that helped. Sometimes it didn't. What almost always did help, though, was the computer. Jian was among the first people in the world to truly exploit computers for digitizing gene sequences, to understand that the world of silicon and electrons could mimic the submicroscopic world of DNA. And when she was lost in the code, she saw nothing *but* the code. No spiders.

Years had rolled on, some worse than others. Medicines changed. The spiders went away for a while, replaced by green, long-toothed rats, but then the spiders came back and the rats stayed as well. When four-foot purple centipedes joined the spiders and the rats, that was the first time she tried to end it all. People stopped her. Stopped her and put her back to work, but it's hard to work when the spiders and rats and centipedes are biting you. Eventually, her bosses ceased asking her for work she couldn't complete. They left her alone to explore her computerized world of four letters: *A*, *C*, *G* and *T*.

Somewhere along the way, she wasn't sure when, she started producing papers again. Most focused on a theory of digitizing the entire mammalian genome, creating a virtual world that would show how species interconnect. There was no real commercial or medical benefit, so her bosses just let her write more papers. If nothing else, her genius showed the glory of the People's Party.

And then one day her bosses told her she was leaving. They'd sent her to Danté Paglione and Genada, to work with Claus Rhumkorrf. *Keep playing with the computers,* they told her, *if this works, they will build statues of you.*

She started with the human experiments, putting her computer-created genomes inside the wombs of volunteers who really didn't know what was going on. Jian had known it was wrong, but when you can't sleep because there are a dozen hairy spiders crawling on your face, right and wrong don't matter all that much.

Those experiments had ended badly. Some of the results were even *worse* than the spiders and rats and centipedes. Jian tried hard to forget those results.

Then Danté hired Tim Feely and P. J. Colding. Colding made Genada stop the human experiments. He made Rhumkorrf prescribe new medicine for Jian.

And the spiders went away.

"This is your room," Colding said. "Do you like it?"

She touched the maroon wallpaper, feeling the texture of the velvet patterns. A plastic light fixture looked out of place on the high ceiling, as if another fixture had just been removed. A beautiful, wooden, four-post bed awaited her, its thick white comforter calling to her like a lover.

Most important of all, of course, was another seven-monitor computer desk. Just like the one in the C-5, just like the one back on Baffin Island. Danté understood. He always made sure Jian could work no matter where she was.

"This used to be a hangout for the rich and famous," Colding said. "That's what you'll be soon. Rich and famous."

Jian sighed as she crawled onto the mattress, marveling at the softness of the thick down comforter. She laid her head on the pillow. Colding pulled the comforter up around her shoulders.

She looked up at Colding. "You like Sara, don't you?"

He opened his mouth, then closed it.

"Mister Colding, she is very nice. You should date her."

"But I can't date, Jian. I mean, my wife died only . . ." His voice trailed off.

"Over three years ago," Jian said, finishing his sentence for him. "That's a long time, Mister Colding."

"Three years," Colding said quietly, as if trying the words on for size.

"You go see Sara right now. You go to her room, talk."

She waved him away and was already asleep before he made it out the door.

NOVEMBER 9: THIS IS MY WEAPON, THIS IS MY GUN

A KNOCK AT her door. Sara's pulse quickened. Maybe it was P. J. *Peej.* Come to give her a proper apology. She wanted to hate him, but riding with him in the Hummer had been a mistake. It made her remember why she'd wanted him in the first place, two years ago.

A glance at the clock showed 11:15 P.M. She quickly checked herself in the room's full-length mirror. According to Stephanie, Marilyn had been a frequent visitor to Black Manitou, always stayed in Room 17 and had used this very mirror many times. But Marilyn probably hadn't had bags under her eyes, or worn a rumpled flight suit or been all dirty and sweaty from a long flight.

What did it matter? Sara wasn't going to sleep with Colding. She could control her hormones. Colding was a user, and that was that. She wasn't interested in his brown eyes. Or the way he kissed.

Knock it off, idiot. Fool me once, shame on you, fool me twice, go fuck yourself.

She took a deep breath, then walked to the door and opened it . . . to see the leering face of Andy Crosthwaite.

"Hiya, toots. Still wanna confiscate my gun?"

Sara felt a combination of revulsion and disappointment.

"Andy, it's time for bed."

"Ex*actly*," he said, and started to slide through the half-open door.

Sara Purinam hadn't risen to the top of a man's world without learning a thing or three. She blocked the door with her body. The motion brought their two bodies together, so close they could have kissed. Andy's leering smile widened.

"Yeah," he said. "That's what I'm talkin' about."

"Last warning, Andy. You should walk away."

He laughed in her face.

Sara brought her knee up fast, catching Andy square in the nuts. She could have done it much harder, but she only wanted to stun him a little, not put him in the infirmary. He let out a little *whuff* and half doubled over. She put a hand on his head and pushed. He stumbled back two steps, enough for her to shut the door and lock it.

She peeked through the peephole. Andy stared at the door. He wasn't leering anymore. Now he looked like someone who might bomb a government building for shits and giggles. Even through a locked door, Sara felt a small flutter of fear.

Then Andy stood and smiled. He knew she was looking. He turned and walked down the hallway, right hand still on his testicles.

NOVEMBER 9: BLUE-LIGHT SPECIAL

Implantation +0 Days

AS THE GENADA staff slept, the experimental creatures moved to the next stage. Inside each of the fifty cows, the implanted blastocysts had floated through the void of the uterus until they brushed softly against the uterine wall.

At the contact point, cells rapidly changed into trophoblasts. The specialized trophoblast cells divided, penetrating the uterine wall, almost like anchors diving into the soft seafloor. The process was common to all mammals — except no mammal, not even the smallest mouse, went through the process that fast. Trophoblasts linked up with the cow's cells to begin creation of the placenta, and also spread around the rest of the blastocyst to create the amniotic sac, a membrane that would surround the embryos and contain a fluid to protect its contents from shocks and bumps.

Less than three hours after that delicate landing, another set of cells distanced itself from the trophoblast. This set of cells, the *embryoblast,* would become the ancestor itself. When the embryoblast separated, a piece of Jian's coding caused it to cleave in half. Inside the amniotic sacs, halves quickly started developing into individuals.

Blue-light special, two for the price of one.

And the cows' immune systems? No response. Nothing at all.

Once upon a time, a man named Roger Bannister shocked the world by running a mile in less than four minutes — a feat that experts had declared "impossible." Jian's process was a biological equivalent of that feat, or would have been, if Roger had run his mile in thirty seconds flat.

Less than twenty-four hours after the enucleated egg first fused with the artificially created DNA, *gastrulation* occurred. In human pregnancies, gastrulation does not occur for two weeks.

Gastrulation is a fancy word that means that cells stop being copies of each other and start taking on the specialized functions of tissues and organs. From a ball of undifferentiated cells, three distinct cell layers form: the ectoderm, the endoderm, and the mesoderm.

The mesoderm becomes the structure of the animal, including the muscles, bones, circulatory system and the reproductive system. The endoderm eventually grows into the digestive and respiratory systems. The ectoderm generates skin and the neural system — that includes the brain.

While all three layers combined to create an ancestor, the ectoderm would turn out to be the real troublemaker.

NOVEMBER 10: ROTTED SQUIRREL

Implantation +1 Day

COLDING STOOD ON the mansion's front steps, shivering in the early-morning cold despite his thick down parka. He checked his watch. Seventeen minutes after eight. Sara stared at him. He tried to ignore her.

"Hey, Colding," she said. "Unless that watch is some kind of *Star Wars* teleporter, it's not going to make Clayton get here any sooner."

"*Star Trek* had teleporters, not *Star Wars*."

"Oh, *snap*. Thank you for the nerd correction, fan boy."

"Give it a rest. Clayton's late, okay?"

She put both hands on her cheeks and affected an expression of shock. She looked out at the mansion's snow-covered front lawn and the long curving driveway — both of which, of course, were completely empty. "Looks like we're going to get all caught up in the morning-commute traffic jam. We'll be late for the Trekkies convention!"

That biting, sarcastic tone. It was really starting to get on his nerves. "Don't you have other shit to do, Purinam? Or do I get another full day of your attitude."

"I cleared my calendar just for you, Peej."

The nickname again. It made him remember her naked, remember the cool smoothness of her freckled skin.

Over three years ago, Jian had said. *That's a long time, Mister Colding.*

No. This wasn't going to happen. Sara clearly despised him, and with good reason. Sometimes Colding wondered if he'd cornered the market on finding things to feel guilty about, but this was right up there with the best of them.

"Look, Sara. I . . . I'm not normally . . . well, I don't normally act like that. With women. The way I did with you, I mean."

"You don't normally hump-and-dump?"

"Uh . . . no."

"Oh, I see. Just with me, then. How nice it must be for all the other women you treat with respect and dignity."

Colding started to say *there aren't any other women*, but he stopped. He was just sounding more and more like an idiot.

The gurgle of a diesel engine saved him from further embarrassment. Sounded like a big truck. The trees past the curving driveway hid it from view for a few seconds. The sound grew a bit louder as the source cleared the trees and turned down the snow-covered drive.

Sara laughed and clapped.

Colding looked at the strange vehicle, then at Sara. "What the fuck is that?"

"That *has* be the Nuge. How awesome."

Colding stared at the thing rolling toward them. A lumbering, two-part vehicle painted white — white, with black zebra stripes. The front half looked like a four-door metal box set on top of short tank treads, with room inside for front and back bench seats. A stubby down-slanting hood ended flat with heavy headlights and a metal-grate bumper. The roof had a hatch above the front passenger side, and a second above the entire rear seat.

The rear section looked like a modified flatbed riding on its own set of squat tank treads. In that flatbed was a small aerial lift with a man-sized white plastic bucket (also painted with zebra stripes), like the kind on telephone repair or utility trucks. When extended, the arm might lift the bucket as high as twenty feet. An articulated joint connected the front and back halves of the vehicle.

Clayton drove down the curved driveway and stopped in front of the wide stone steps. He leaned out the open driver's-side window and smiled at Sara. "Hiya, doll." He looked at Colding and the smile faded. "Let's go, eh? I ain't got all day."

"Clayton," Colding said, "what the hell *is* this thing?"

"It's a Bv206. Magnus bought it surplus off da Swede military. I use it to mow da landing strip, groom da snowmobile trails and fix da phone lines when storms knock 'em down. Lot of ground to cover, eh? And most of that ground is either swampy, muddy or covered in six feet of snow."

"And you call it Ted Nugent, why?"

Sara raised her hand like a kid in school. She jumped up and down and waved her arm. "Oh! Oh! Teacher, pick on me, pick on me!"

"Miss Purinam," Clayton said. "Please answer for da class."

"It's called Ted Nugent because it can go down *in the swamp.* Just like Fred Bear."

Colding looked back and forth between them. "Who is Fred Bear? What the hell are you people talking about?"

"It's a song," Sara said. "It's a Michigan thing, you wouldn't understand. Just get in."

Sara hopped into the back. Colding walked to the passenger-side seat and opened the door, pausing for a moment to run his hand over the black-striped surface. The armor looked thick enough to stop small-caliber fire. So Magnus had a Stinger, a platoon's worth of weapons *and* a troop transport. Wonderful.

Colding hopped in and shut the door. "You're late, Clayton."

"I slept in. Da benefits of youth." He put the vehicle in gear and pulled away from the mansion.

"You know, Clayton," Colding said. "You can call me *doll,* too. I might blush, though."

"Aw, fuck ya. Listen, I'll take you up da northwest coast, show you da snowmobile trails. They're mostly mud and swamp until everything freezes solid. Then I'll swing you around to North Pointe and, if ya don't mind, Sven would like a word."

Colding shrugged. Why not? He had to see the whole island anyway, even if it was freezing out. Colding started to roll up his window.

"Oh, yah," Clayton said. "Mind leaving that down? I ran over a squirrel a couple of days ago. Didn't quite get all da guts out. It'll stink in here something fierce if you close it."

How about that? Clayton actually asked nicely for something. No pissy tone this time. Maybe the old man was loosening up. Colding shrugged and rolled the window back down.

They headed northwest. Much of the trail looked like an ancient road, now overgrown and pitted, some spots thick with two feet of black, stagnant water. The Bv rolled through all of it. One swamp looked a good twenty feet deep in the middle, but the Nuge proved to be fully amphibious — it rolled into the water and floated, moving across the surface until the tank treads dug into the mud on the far side. One hell of a machine, really.

Through the thick trees, Colding saw the occasional collapsed house. Snow clumped on moss-covered roofs, and a few even had saplings growing up through the angled remnants.

Sara leaned forward, preferring to look out the front window rather than the sides. "Looks like a lot of people used to live here."

"Yah," Clayton said. "Some forty years back we had about three hundred year-round residents. Mostly copper mining, but also summer people, tourists."

"So what happened?"

"We had . . . an incident. At da copper mine. Twenty-two people died. This trail goes right by it, I'll show ya."

He cranked the Nuge forward at a punishing twenty miles an hour. Branches scraped the vehicle's sides and roof, but Clayton effortlessly avoided the tree trunks.

They popped out at a clearing near the island's high rocky spine. Colding saw a small shed made of bone-dry wood, bleached almost white from decades of sun. Like a set from an old silent movie, a barely discernible sign had the word DANGER written on it in faded, paintbrush-scrawled letters.

"That's da old mine," Clayton said. "Used to be tons of copper across da whole U.P. Boomtowns rivaled anything from da gold rush days out West."

"Spooky," Sara said. "Is that where the people died?"

"Most of 'em," Clayton said. "Those men are still in there, at least their bones. At night, when it's quiet, you can hear them calling for help."

Colding would have mocked a woo-woo superstition like that, but Clayton's memories clearly ran deep to a place of pain, maybe also of fear.

"The cave-in kind of broke da town's heart," Clayton said. "People moved away over da years. There was only about fifty of us left when Danté came in and bought everyone out. He kept me and Sven. James and Stephanie are new, brought in to manage a backup herd. Enough of this shit. I don't like this spot much."

Clayton put the Bv206 in gear and they drove back into the woods, the rough road jostling everyone inside. His mood seemed to lighten the farther they got from the mine. "I think I smell squirrel guts," he said. "Your window down all da way, Colding?"

"Yeah, you can see it is."

Clayton looked and nodded. "Okay, eh? Well, keep it down. I'm a little cold so I'm rolling mine up. You know us old guys can get chilly." He cranked the handle to raise his window just as they broke out of the trees at the edge of a small farm. Colding recognized the barn with the roof shingles that spelled out *Ballantine.* This was where the island's only working road started. Or ended, depending on how you looked at it.

Clayton stopped in Sven's driveway. He got out, then, inexplicably, stepped on the metal-grate bumper and hauled himself on top of the vehicle. Colding looked up at the roof for a moment, then leaned out the passenger window to ask Clayton just what the hell he was doing.

As he leaned out, he caught a blur of movement coming from the right. He turned in time to see a wide-eyed black shape flying through the air, teeth flashing inside a gaping mouth. The assaulting animal sailed cleanly through the open passenger window and hit Colding full speed, knocking him flat on the seat.

A dog. A *wet* dog. Colding's adrenaline burst of panic dissipated as a tongue furiously licked at his face. He tried to push the dog away, but it dove at him as if its life depended on it. Despite the animal's loud whines of joy, Colding heard Clayton's loud, sandpaper laugh.

"Oh my *God*," Sara said from the backseat, "he's adorable!"

"*She's* adorable," another man called out. "Mookie! You get off that man and out of that car, eh?"

The wide-eyed, black-furred cattle dog managed one last sloppy lick, then turned and dove back out the window as gracefully as a leaping gazelle.

"What a little *sweetheart*," Sara said.

Colding sat up, using his jacket sleeve to wipe dog spit from his face. "Oh, for crying out loud. I've been slimed."

Sven Ballantine walked up and stopped about five feet from the Bv206. Mookie sat next to him, head forward and big eyes open wide, as motionless as a statue except for the long-haired tail that *swish-swished* quietly in the snow.

Clayton was still standing on the hood, and still laughing.

And then, Colding smelled it.

"Oh God," Sara said from the backseat. Her laugh gave her words a staccato sound. "What . . . *stinks*?"

The horrible odor, it seemed, was coming from Colding's hands and clothes. His nose wrinkled involuntarily.

"You'll want to clean up," Sven said. "Mookie found something dead this morning. She likes to roll in stuff like that. Sorry."

Clayton's laugh came even louder.

"It's okay," Colding said. "Jesus, this stinks, what the hell is this?"

"Dead . . . squir . . . rel!" Clayton called out from the roof. His laugh had turned into a hysterical, wheezing cough. "Gonna . . . piss myself . . . that's why I was late. Found . . . dead . . . *squirrel,* knew that damn dog would roll in it . . . jump on you . . . so *funny!*"

"Sorry," Sven said. "Really sorry you stink so bad and all. Mookie has a knack for getting into trouble. She's a real pain in da ass."

Colding noticed that despite Sven's words, his big hand was absently scratching the black dog's stinky head. Either Sven loved the dog unconditionally, or the old man couldn't smell a thing. Mookie looked up at Sven with blissful reverence.

Colding banged on the inside of the Bv's roof. "Let's go!" He managed a smile at Sven. Sven just nodded. Mookie's mouth opened and her tongue hung out the side, the big smile of a happy dog.

Clayton climbed down. No sooner had his feet hit the ground than Mookie took off like a shot. Damn, that dog could *move.* Clayton slid through the driver's door with surprising agility, shutting the door just before the smelly dog could follow him in. Mookie jumped at the high window, showing amazing air-time. Her slobber streaked the glass. She barked and whined, desperate to say *hello.*

"Not today, you stinky girl," Clayton said, still chuckling lightly. "I'll come see ya after your daddy gives you a bath, eh?"

"Back to the mansion," Colding said.

Clayton laughed some more, a sound that would have been infectious if Colding weren't the butt of the joke.

"What's da matter, *doll?*" Clayton said. "I thought you wanted to see da old town."

"Tomorrow," Colding said. "You got me good, now get me back to the friggin' mansion so I can shower and burn these clothes."

Clayton put the Nuge in gear, then headed back down the road. When Colding stepped out of the vehicle and walked up the mansion's front steps, the old man was *still* laughing.

NOVEMBER 11: TWO FOR
THE PRICE OF ONE

Implantation +2 Days

INSIDE THE C-5'S lower deck, Jian watched Tim move the handheld transducer across Cow 34's belly. An overhead harness looped under the cow's legs, hips and chest, holding her off the ground and supporting all of her weight.

The transducer fed data into the portable ultrasound workstation positioned just outside Cow 34's stall. Doctor Rhumkorrf sat in front of the workstation, his small behind parked on a wooden stool, his hands toying with buttons and absently caressing a black trackball.

Above those controls sat a video monitor that showed nothing but a blue progress bar, just over half full, with words above it that read 52 PERCENT.

In her career, Jian had seen ultrasound evolve from grainy, two-dimensional, black-and-white images to three-dimensional representations showing depth from a top-down perspective, then to what they had now: full, rotatable 3-D models with animated images showing the natural movements of an in utero animal.

75 PERCENT

No mistaking the electricity in the air, the satisfaction at seeing years of work move steadily closer to the final product.

82 PERCENT

"Let's not get excited," Rhumkorrf said, even though he was the only one talking. He absently swayed a bit from side to side as he waited for the image to process. "When Erika . . . I mean, when Doctor Hoel and I brought the quagga back from extinction, it took fifty-two implantation cycles before we corrected the genome enough to produce a live birth."

88 PERCENT

Jian felt relieved, invigorated ... even *light*. She'd lost some weight in the past few weeks, partly from forgetting to eat, partly from the haunting stress that kept her stomach pinched all the time. Just two days after implantation, a normal mammalian embryo would be nothing but a tiny red dot jutting from the uterine wall. Kind of like a big wet pimple. But according to her calculations, and the astronomical growth rate they'd seen in the in vitro embryos, what lay inside Cow 34's womb would be much bigger.

94 PERCENT

Tim's hand continued to move the transducer across the suspended cow's belly. He looked sleepy. Maybe a little drunk. Again. He hadn't smiled since they had landed. Back on Baffin, Tim was *always* smiling.

100 PERCENT ... PROCESSING ...

The progress bar filled up, then a golden-hued image flared to life.

She stared at the screen.

Tim walked out of the stall, saw the screen and stopped cold. "Oh, fuck me running," he said quietly.

Jian slowly shook her head in disbelief. She'd known they would grow fast, she'd *coded* for it, but this?

"Jian," Rhumkorrf said. "You are even more talented than I imagined."

The ultrasound image revealed two fetuses pushed into a tight face-to-face embrace. Rhumkorrf slowly moved his right hand over the trackball, turning the 3-D image to examine the tiny fetal features. Oversized heads had already formed, each bigger than the rest of their respective bodies. Big black spots showed developing eyes. Tiny limb buds sprouted from the bodies. She saw the ghostly shape of forming internal organs.

"Feely," Rhumkorrf said. "How big would you say those embryos are?"

"Umm ... at least eight ounces." Tim's voice dropped to barely a whisper. "Maybe even a little more. Normal embryonic growth for a two-hundred-pound mammal should be less than a tenth of an ounce."

"*Eighty times* the normal growth rate," Rhumkorrf said. "That's even higher than you projected, Jian. Fantastic!"

Fantastic. Was that the right word to describe it? No. It was not. From a single cell to half a pound in less than forty-eight hours. She should have felt elated. But instead, she felt afraid.

And she wasn't quite sure why.

NOVEMBER 11: IT'S ALL ABOUT THE BENJAMINS

Implantation +2 Days

COLONEL PAUL FISCHER stood on the edge of a Brazilian rain forest, staring up into the dark canopy. Never in all his days had he felt this drained, this utterly exhausted. His feet hurt. His eyes burned. This kind of sleep deprivation and world-hopping schedule would grind a twentysomething into the ground, and Paul was pushing fifty.

Amgen had built its xenotransplantation facility in the middle of the deep jungle. A stunning view surrounded the compound, mostly because there were no roads to tarnish the tree line. Amgen had used helicopters to bring everything in and out. Behind Paul, the special threats CBRN team was moving through the compound, completing their mission of seizing the facility and shutting down Amgen's research.

A bird sailed from one tree to another. Paul wondered what kind it was. Maybe after all this crap was over he could retire, come back down here and spend months cataloging all the bird species just for the fun of it. Before he could contemplate retirement, however, he had to finish the job.

Approaching footsteps called his attention away. He turned to face the approaching special threats soldier. This one was bigger than most and put off a more frightening vibe than anyone Paul had ever known. He wore a MOPP suit without the hood, exposing his thin blond buzz cut and a mass of scar tissue where his right ear should have been. The man carried an FN P90 in his right hand and a sat-phone in his left.

"Colonel Fischer, *sir.*"

Fischer tried in vain to remember the man's name, then cheated and looked at the name patch on the man's left breast. "What is it, Sergeant O'Doyle?"

"Mister Longworth would like a status report." O'Doyle handed over the sat-phone. Paul took it. O'Doyle took a step forward and stared out at the tree line, both hands now on the P90 submachine gun.

Paul lifted the sat-phone. It felt like it weighed eight thousand pounds. "This is Fischer."

"Colonel," Murray Longworth said. "How's it look?"

"We've secured the place. No biohazard warnings, everything looks fine." Of course everything looked fine. The Novozyme accident had been a fluke. Paul and the special threats team had flown to four continents and shut down five facilities in the last three days, and he'd known there wouldn't be an issue as long as no one was dumb enough to put up a fight.

"Nice work, Colonel," Longworth said. "The only one left is Genada, wherever the hell they went."

"Any progress on that?"

"Nothing," Longworth said. "Like they vanished. Colding is good."

Paul nodded to no one. Colding was good. Back when they'd worked together in USAMRIID, Paul had never suspected just how good Colding could be. "Nothing on freezing Genada's accounts? Can't we flush them out that way?"

"Switzerland, Cayman Islands and China refuse to cooperate with that. All three countries believe the ecoterrorist attack was real, and that Genada is out of the game. Danté Paglione does a lot of business in those countries, so they won't freeze his assets unless we have something concrete to show that Genada is still doing xenotransplantation research. Keep digging, Colonel. Find me something tangible to take to those governments. Anything from the Russians on Poriskova?"

"Nothing yet, sir," Paul said. "But their effort is encouraging."

For over a year, Paul had been trying to get the Russians' help in tracking down Galina Poriskova, former Genada employee and whistle-blower. Russian authorities had been mostly unresponsive, but all of that had changed in the last three days. Several Russian agencies had called Paul directly, asking what he needed and how they could help. Near as Paul could estimate, the Russians had at least fifty investigators searching for any sign of Poriskova.

"Well, that's something," Longworth said. "How long until they find her?"

"They think maybe four or five days."

"Good. I'll keep bird-dogging on my end. I have Interpol and other agencies cooperating. We'll figure this out, Colonel, just stick with it."

"Yes sir," Paul said, then handed the sat-phone to O'Doyle. Paul wondered just how tired he had to sound if Murray Longworth felt the need to bust out a pep talk. But however tired he sounded, it wasn't half as tired as he felt.

Implantation +2 Days

ANDY CROSTHWAITE SHIFTED his brown grocery bag to his left hand, sighed contentedly, and punched in the code 0-0-0-0 on the security room door. Inside, the familiar rack of weapons was waiting for him.

Real weapons that could do *real* damage.

Not that the Beretta 96 was a toy. The magazine held eleven .40-caliber rounds, plus one in the chamber (Andy *always* had one in the chamber), for twelve shots of solid stopping power. It wasn't his favorite, but the 96 was better than a poke in the eye with a sharp stick.

Still, he far preferred the Heckler & Koch MP5 submachine gun. Magnus provided the .40-caliber variant, providing for consistent ammo with the Beretta sidearms. The MP5s had thirty-round magazines and fired at eight hundred rounds a minute. Accurate at a hundred meters, the thing turned deer into hamburger-on-the-hoof and killed humans dead.

Andy pulled one of the MP5s out of the rack and carried it over to the security monitor table. He tossed down his tattered brown paper bag. It landed on its side and tipped, spilling copies of *Juggs* and *Gallery* across the desktop.

He sat, hands caressing the weapon's well-known curves and angles. He'd break it down, clean it and put it back together. At least it was something to do while taking his completely unnecessary shift. What a fucking joke. No one was going to find them here.

He scanned the monitors anyway. The desk setup looked identical to the one on Baffin Island. More of Magnus's consistency. Why pay money to train people on multiple systems when you can just train them once and install the same system in all locations? Made sense. Everything Magnus did made sense.

Andy checked the infrared feeds of the area surrounding the mansion and the hangar. The infrared worked just fine — and showed nothing. He switched back to the black-and-white pictures of the grounds, the inside of the mansion. Several of the little five-inch monitors were blacked out — typical Colding, no monitoring private rooms except for that suicidal Chinese bitch.

But what about the mythical *Room 17*? Sara's room. Yep, the camera was off.

He set the MP5 on the desktop, then flipped a switch. Sure enough, the screen lit up, showing the inside of Sara Purinam's room. There she was, on her bed. Too dark, though. He scanned the controls . . . ah yes, night vision. He pushed a button and saw Sara Purinam's naked upper body gleam in green-tinged glory. Just a B-cup, but he'd still do her.

She, however, would not do him. The dyke.

"Paybacks are a bitch, you tall twat."

He watched her sleep. He would keep an eye on her, wait for her to slip up. One way or another, figuratively or literally, Sara Purinam was going to get fucked.

NOVEMBER 12: THE THING IN THE CAR

Implantation +3 Days

THE NEXT MORNING, Colding, Clayton and Sara rode along in Clayton's Humvee. No Nuge that morning, but regardless, Colding kept his window rolled up tight.

They reached the fork that led to the harbor. This time Clayton took the road on the left. More trees, more snow, more collapsed houses. Five minutes later the trees ended, giving way to the old town. Clayton pulled into the town center, a stone-paved circle about fifty yards in diameter. Some of the snow-dusted stones were broken or just plain missing. A few small trees grew up through some of the gaps.

An old well made up of the same broken stones sat smack in the circle's center. Some of the stones had crumbled away and lay on the ground like rotted-out teeth. The well looked like some B-movie version of a trapdoor to hell.

Clayton stopped the Hummer. The three of them got out and started walking.

"Welcome to downtown Black Manitou," Clayton said. "I'm sure a city boy like you will feel right at home, eh?"

"Sure," Colding said. "I'll bet the opera house is right over the next hill." The town's structures were in marginally better shape than the dilapidated houses out in the woods. Buildings lined the paved area like numbers on a clock. With due north at noon, ten o'clock was the gothic, black-stone church. The thick building dominated the town circle, squatting down like a granite bulldog. It seemed to have so much weight the rest of the town might rise up at any moment, the light end of a lopsided teeter-totter. The few windows looked original, their glass visibly warped, giving the solid structure an almost fluid appearance. A bell tower (noticeably absent a bell) rose like a pinnacle from the steep slate roof.

Clayton pointed to a green building about twenty feet from the church at the eight o'clock position. The window was still decorated with a faded yellow banner cut in the shape of a star that said GROUND CHUCK ON SALE! Inside, Colding saw empty racks and shelves.

"That used to be Betty's," Clayton said. "Combination grocery and hardware store. She was still here when Danté bought everyone out."

At seven o'clock, the road out of town ran between Betty's and a red building with a moth-eaten moose head hung over the door. One glass eye was long since missing. Shreds of moose fur hung down like demonic streamers.

"That was Sven Ballantine's hunter's shop," Clayton said. "He ran it during deer season. Magnus and that surly little prick Andy Crosthwaite came up about five years ago and went wild, killed every last deer. Cut their heads off, took a picture right by that well."

"Jesus," Colding said. "I didn't know Magnus was such a conservationist."

"Pissed me off to no end, eh? Deer been here since 1948, when an ice bridge connected da island and da mainland. Deer just walked over."

Colding gave Clayton an untrusting look. "An ice bridge?"

"Yep."

"From the mainland," Sara said. "Three *hours* away."

"Yep."

Sara shook her head. "Clayton, you are so full of shit you'd float. It can't get cold enough to make ice cover that much open water."

Clayton hawked a loogie and spat it on one of the mottled paving stones. "You'll see ice everywhere in another week. In a normal winter, Rapleje Bay will have ice two feet thick by da end of November. This winter? Gonna be cold. Maybe coldest ever."

He gestured at a rustic building made of hewn logs and rough wooden beams sitting at about four o'clock, directly across from the church. Other than the church, it was the town's only two-story building. "Da mansion you're staying at was for da rich folk, but plenty of regular people came to Black Manitou Lodge here to hunt and relax."

A few more wooden buildings dotted the town circle. All had peeling paint. Some sagged under rotted, moss-covered roofs. There wasn't a soul in sight.

"Clayton," Sara said. "I think you forgot that thing in the car."

The old man looked at her, then nodded. "By *gosh*, I think you're right, eh? Be back in a jiffy."

Clayton turned and walked quickly to the Hummer.

Colding looked at Sara. "The thing?"

"The thing," she said. "In the car."

Clayton reached the Hummer, got in, started it up, then drove down the road right out of town.

Colding watched the black vehicle vanish into the woods, heading for the mansion. "You told Clayton to strand us?"

Sara nodded. "That's right."

"Huh. Wouldn't the joke be better if you were *in* the vehicle with him?"

"No joke this time. I wanted your undivided attention."

He looked at her, looked close. The pissyness was gone. She seemed all-business.

"Okay," he said. "I'm listening."

"Almost right. *I'm* the one who's going to listen. *You're* going to tell me some things. How you came to work for Genada, how you found me and my crew and why you had that one amazing night with me then vanished."

"Sara, we—"

"*Now*, P. J. You will tell me now. We had a connection. I thought I was being a girly-girl about that, deluding myself, but in the past couple of days I'm pretty sure my initial instinct with you was right. We *did* connect, didn't we?"

He could lie. Just say *no*, walk back to the mansion and be done with it. Instead, he nodded.

She smiled a little. Some of the tension seemed to drain out of her. "Good. That's good. So make like a stoolie and spill."

He looked around the town. They really were in the middle of nowhere. At least a thirty-minute walk back to the mansion.

Fuck it. Why not?

"I was in the army. Used to work for USAMRIID, the army's division to protect servicepeople from biological threats. I met my wife there. Clarissa. She was a virologist. We were married for two years, then there was . . . an accident. Have you heard of H5N1?"

Sara shook her head.

"Bird flu. Terrorist cell was trying to bring it into America the old-fashioned way — by infecting their own people and shipping them over. CIA caught them. USAMRIID was called in to see if we could help the carriers. Long story short, proper restraint precautions were not followed. The guy in charge, Colonel Paul Fischer, he decided to treat the carriers like human beings instead of the terrorist animals they were. One of them . . . one of them got loose, tore off my wife's mask and . . . coughed and spit in her face."

Sara's eyes widened with fear. She was probably imagining herself in Clarissa's shoes. Trying to, anyway — who could really know what it felt like to have someone breathe death in your face?

Colding continued. He couldn't stop himself now. "They brought Clarissa to an ICU. She caught pneumonia, got through that, but the bird flu gave her viral myocarditis."

"Which is?"

"Viral infection of the heart. Came on particularly fast for her. Damaged the muscle tissue, made her heart weak, made it swell. Basically destroyed it."

Sara's hand went to her mouth. She was such a tomboy, but that gesture of empathy for a dead woman she'd never met ached with femininity. "Couldn't they give her a transplant?"

"She still had the virus in her system. There was no way to be sure it wouldn't just infect the new heart. They . . . they can't afford to *waste* replacement organs on someone who's a risk."

"Because of the shortage of organs," Sara said, nodding a little. Sadness filled her eyes.

"They put her on a ventilator. After a couple of days they . . . well, they told me there was no hope for recovery. She was in so much pain, so weak. She slipped under before we could make a decision. So I had to make it for her. I knew she wouldn't have wanted to suffer, and it was only a matter of time."

He had to stop for a second. He hadn't talked about it, to anyone, not since it happened. Doing so dredged up vivid memories, like it was happening all over again. Clarissa's hands, so weak they couldn't hold his, so he held hers. Before they put her on the ventilator, he'd told her it would be okay. She'd answered in her weak voice that he was being stupid — she knew what was happening inside her body. Better than anyone, probably, because she was dying from something she'd studied for a decade.

Sara reached out and touched his upper arm. "You ended it for her? You took away her pain?"

He nodded. The tears were coming now. He couldn't stop them anymore. *Her eyes still closed, eyes that would never open again. The nurse pulling the IVs, removing the breathing tube. Her breaths coming in tiny, shallow gasps. The nurse walking out, shutting the door, leaving the two of them together to ride it out to the end. Till death do them part.*

Sara's hand on his arm, gently sliding up and down. "What did you do then?"

More memories, just as vivid. The rage he'd felt. All his sorrow and hurt channeled into pure aggression.

"I got in my car and went to see Fischer."

"To talk to him?"

"No," Colding said. "To kill him. I tackled him as soon as I saw him, really fucked up his knee. His face was a sheet of blood by the time they pulled me off. Army was going to court-martial me, but Fischer pulled strings. Got me a dishonorable discharge, and I was out."

"What did you do then?"

"Nothing," Colding said. "Sat on my ass for six months. Got fat. Felt sorry for myself. Collected unemployment. Missed my wife. Then Danté Paglione called me. Genada was trying to solve the organ-shortage problem. They had multiple lines of experimentation, but one involved getting women to carry transgenic animal pregnancies."

"Carry . . . are you kidding me? Is that even legal?"

"No. A Genada scientist named Galina Poriskova ratted out the experiment to Fischer. Danté had a second line of research that would solve the organ-shortage problem forever, but if Fischer busted them for the human experiments, that second line would never be completed. I offered to come aboard, but only if Danté scrapped the human experimentation for good. Wasn't what he wanted to hear, but Danté needed me. I knew how Fischer worked, how USAMRIID operated. Danté shut down the experiments. By the time Fischer got to Genada, there was no evidence of wrongdoing."

"Danté is smart," Sara said. "Ruthless, but smart. Hire the guy who would do anything to stop people from dying the way his wife died, right?"

"Transparent as hell, but also dead-on."

"And Tim? How did he come into the picture?"

"He did some contracting for USAMRIID," Colding said. "Research stuff. That's where I met him. He was a double PhD candidate in genetics and bioinformatics. I know some of the science, but needed my own guy to make sure Genada was staying honest. I hired him to come along for the cleanup. Once Galina left, Danté threw money at him to make him stay and replace her."

"But how did Danté *find* you? How did he know about you, and Fischer, about your wife?"

"Same way he found you when I had the idea for the C-5. Magnus and Danté have a high-level contact. From the NSA, I think. The contact can get at all kinds of service records, and more. We found you, found out you were behind on payments for your 747. Then I came to talk to you and what happened . . . happened."

"Yeah," Sara said. "I remember. Which brings us full circle. Why didn't you at least call me, or say good-bye?"

"You gotta understand . . . my wife had been dead all of seven months when I met you. You talked about a connection? Well, I felt it, too, but I *couldn't* feel that way when her grave was barely cold. I couldn't betray her memory like that."

Sara stepped forward until their chests touched. She reached up and caressed his cheek, her fingertips somehow warm despite the frigid temperature. "No wonder you're so gung ho for this project, Peej. I thought you were a rotten douchebag, but now I know I was wrong — you're not all that rotten."

Colding laughed. "Wow, am I glad I bared my soul to you."

Her smile faded, and she touched his cheek again. "Any woman would just melt inside if she knew how you felt, Peej. You did what you thought was right, to honor your wife's memory. But now she's been gone a lot longer than seven months. It's okay to move on with your life."

Colding leaned toward Sara and kissed her. Her lips were soft and warm, and he forgot all about the cold.

NOVEMBER 13: I HATE IT WHEN YOU CALL ME BIG POPPA

Implantation +4 Days

ONE OF HIS cell phones buzzed. Lower-left inside jacket pocket. Only one person had that number. Magnus quickly walked to his office and shut the door behind him. He didn't need to share these calls with Danté. Not just yet, anyway.

Danté's will seemed to be faltering. They'd reached that point before. With Galina. Magnus, of course, had fixed that, just like he would fix things now.

He answered the phone. "Go ahead."

"Well helllooooo, Big Poppa."

The incoming area code said 702 — Las Vegas. All he knew about Farm Girl was that she had once worked for the NSA. Maybe she still did. Judging from the crap sound of the call, she had already bounced the signal through a dozen relay points and was nowhere near Vegas.

"You sure know how to throw a party," she said. "Dad is looking for you and your friends in the dairy industry."

Magnus nodded. *Dad* was Fischer. She wouldn't have called for just that. Didn't take a rocket scientist to know CIA assistant director Murray Longworth would still be driving Fischer to track down Rhumkorrf and Jian. Longworth did not like loose ends. "So why doesn't Dad come ask me himself? He knows where I live."

"He is," she said. "He's coming to see your brother."

Magnus felt his eyes narrow and his lip curl. He forced himself to relax. If Fischer tried to screw with Danté, the man had another thing coming.

"How close is Dad to finding my friends?"

"Doesn't have a clue where to start. Heck, Big Poppa, even *I* don't know where they are."

That was as close as you could get to a compliment from this woman — if Farm Girl couldn't find you, you couldn't be found. Colding and Danté had really pulled it off, hiding the project right under the Americans' noses.

"Dad's frustrated," Farm Girl said. "If your friends stay quiet, I don't think he'll find them at all."

"Glad to hear it. Anything else?"

"I need to expand my wardrobe a bit. Things get more costly every day."

Farm Girl wanted more money. Well, fuck it, she could *have* more money. Thanks to her intel, Genada was the only horse left in the xeno-transplantation race.

"That's fine," Magnus said. "Maybe Santa will be nice to you this year."

"I like Santa. I *love* to sit on his lap."

Magnus sighed and hung up. Once she started with the sexual innuendo, she didn't stop. She sounded sexy as hell, true, but he'd heard enough about her in certain circles to know that getting horizontal with Farm Girl could be a very bad experience. The woman was nine shades of psycho.

Fischer and Longworth were clueless. The rest of the G8 nations had no idea Genada was still in the hunt. The Chinese knew, but they weren't about to talk and give up a chance to save millions of their own people.

Genada now had the most valuable resource it could hope for — *time*. The Rhumkorrf project, it seemed, might just pan out after all.

NOVEMBER 14: HOT MIDNIGHT

Implantation +5 Days

COLDING TYPED IN the supersecret password of 0-0-0-0 and entered the security room. Gunther sat at the terminal, his eyes wide and his fingertips flying across the keyboard.

"One sec," he said without looking away from the screen. His fingers never paused. Colding shut the door behind himself and stood there, waiting. Once Gunther got into a writing groove, you had to just let the man do his thing.

"She screamed . . . and grabbed . . . the broken pool cue," Gunther muttered, leaning so close to the monitor that he had to turn his head a little to read from left to right. "Never again, Sansome said . . . never again . . . will you harm my love. He jabbed the cue down . . . like an axe . . . and the point punched through Count Darkon's . . . unprotected . . . chest. As the body . . . vanished . . . no, wait, as the body . . . *disintegrated* . . . yeah, that's the *shit* right there . . . he knew that it was over. Forever."

Gunther leaned way back in the chair until it almost tipped over, pumping his raised fists in victory. "The *end*, bitches!"

"You're done?"

"Hell fuckin' yeah. I just finished *Hot Midnight*. The trilogy is complete."

"Nice work." Colding checked his watch. "Not to muck up your afterglow or anything, but I need to report to Danté."

"Oh, right." Gunther stood, then leaned forward to tap in a few more keys. "Just saving this slice of brilliance."

"Congrats, man. When do you send it to publishers? How does that even work?"

"Screw the publishers," Gunther said. "I'm going to give this baby away."

"Give it away?"

"Yeah, online," Gunther said. "You'll see. I'll rack up so many fans that the publishers *have* to give me a big fat deal."

Gunther walked past, his eyes once again dopey-looking and half-lidded. He held up his hand for a high five, which Colding met, and then Gunther walked out and closed the door behind him.

Give the book away, for free? That was the dumbest thing Colding had ever heard of.

He moved the mouse and clicked the icon labeled MANITOBA, then waited patiently as the encrypted line connected with the home office. Less than a minute later, Danté's smiling face appeared.

"Good morning, P. J. How is the weather out there?"

"Getting colder, sir. Word is we're due for a big dose of the white stuff."

"When it comes, you have to get on those snowmobiles. Fabulous times. What's up?"

"They did it."

Colding watched Danté's reaction. The man looked half hopeful, half skeptical. "They've done *what*, exactly?"

"Implantation."

"Finally," Danté said, more of a breath than a word. "And it's successful thus far?"

Colding nodded. "Forty-seven cows are pregnant. Two failed to implant, one fetus aborted on day two. What's more, *all* of the pregnancies are either twins or triplets."

Danté smiled a wide smile, a *genuine* smile. Colding realized that he had never actually seen a real, heartfelt smile from Danté. It made the man look a bit maniacal.

"How long?" Danté said. "How long until we have an actual birth?"

"Well, we don't know," Colding said. "Getting to this point was a major accomplishment, but Doc Rhumkorrf said there's bound to be complications. The fetuses are growing very fast, which makes it hard to react to problems. It's been five days and they're already around fifteen pounds each."

"If they survive, *how long* until a live animal, P. J.?"

Colding shrugged. "Too early to tell, really, but it could be anywhere from a month to three months."

Danté grimaced. "Just do what you can to get me at least one live animal."

"Will do. Danté, as long as I've got you here, I was wondering if you had an update on Doctor Hoel? Any word on her?"

Danté sat back. His demeanor seemed to change instantly. "She's fine. Don't worry about her and do your job."

That subject was clearly off-limits. And Colding could do nothing about it from Black Manitou. "How about Colonel Fischer? Does he have any idea where we are?"

Danté shook his head. "No. But he's looking. Hard. We must have live animals if we're going to get the media and the public on our side."

"The fetuses will grow at their own rate, Danté. It's up to nature now."

Danté didn't like that answer, but had to accept it. He knew enough about biology to understand things had to run their course.

"Very well, P. J. Keep me updated."

Danté broke the connection. Colding looked at his watch. He could go check up on Jian, or he could see if Sara was around. Jian was with Rhumkorrf and Tim . . . she'd be fine.

He'd go find Sara. Colding walked out of the security room, amazed at once again feeling excited and nervous about talking to a woman.

NOVEMBER 14: TASTE

Implantation +5 Days

THE TWO FORMING creatures floated inside the amniotic sac, pressed face-to-face like sleepy lovers. The liquid environment supported their growing weight. Millions of chemical compounds drifted freely within that liquid. Some of those compounds were strong enough to register as scents.

And others, strong enough to register as *tastes.*

Inside two tiny mouths, those taste compounds landed on tiny tongues. Newly formed dendrites fired off chemical messages, chemical messages that traversed a tiny gap, known as the synapse, to land on the axons of the next nerve cell. This process repeated up the chain, traveling from the tiny tongues to the tiny brains in a fraction of a second.

Those taste signals activated a very primitive area in the newly formed brains. In effect, taste turned the brains *on* for the first time.

There were no thoughts, no decisions, although those things would come soon enough. There was only a short, intense race against time.

For the taste activated an instinct that would drive the creatures' every waking moment.

Hunger.

Implantation +6 Days

HANDS SHOOK HIS shoulder.

Claus Rhumkorrf tried to open his eyes, but they seemed glued shut. Lights blared right through his eyelids.

"Doc, wake up." Tim's voice? Tim, who had replaced Erika. A stab of emptiness. Claus had told himself he didn't feel a thing for that woman anymore. That had been easy to believe when she was around every day, but now that she was gone he felt her absence.

"Wake *up*, dammit." Tim's voice, ringing with stress. His breath, reeking of scotch. And the man's palpable body odor — how long since Tim had bathed?

"Come on, bro," Tim said. "There's a problem with Cow Sixteen."

Claus moaned. His back was so stiff. Where was he sleeping? On a cot. In a plane. He wasn't even bothering to go back to the mansion anymore. Instead, he just slept in the C-5's bunk room. And the body odor? That wasn't Tim. Maybe a shower was in order. Claus opened his eyes to see Tim's blurry, anxious face.

"Cow Sixteen?" Claus said as he reached for his glasses. "That one has twins or triplets?"

"It *was* twins," Tim said. "But now the ultrasound shows only one fetus."

Claus slid his glasses in place. Tim's words hit home. He stood and walked out of the bunk room, Tim following close behind.

NOVEMBER 15: THAT'S NOT NORMAL

Implantation +6 Days

COLDING COULDN'T HELP but wince a little. Sure, it was science, but that didn't change the fact that he was watching Tim Feely slide a tube into a cow's vagina. A harness suspended the cow, keeping her hooves just a few inches off the ground. Tim wore long gloves that were smeared with a clumpy, whitish substance that Colding could only think of as *cow smegma.*

"A little deeper," Rhumkorrf said. His voice had a flat tone but dripped with anger and tension. He sat at a portable fiber-optic workstation, staring intently at a screen showing a fleshy, pinkish tunnel — the view from deep within the cow's womb.

The 3-D ultrasound workstation sat close by, pressed up against the door of the stall opposite Cow 16's. Jian half hid behind the machine, trying to stay out of the way. Rhumkorrf had shoved the workstation there in disgust when the high-tech, gold-tinted image showed only one ancestor fetus where yesterday there had been two. Then he'd started screaming, apparently, which was when Jian sneaked away and asked Colding to come to the C-5.

"Deeper," Rhumkorrf said. "Get it in there."

"Love it when you talk dirty, Doc," Colding said.

Rhumkorrf sighed and shook his head. "This is not the time for your stupid fucking jokes."

"Yikes," Colding said. "Just trying to lighten the mood."

Trying, and failing. Rhumkorrf was mad because the cow had reabsorbed one of its twin fetuses. *Reabsorption* was when the mother's body made some primitive yet calculated decision to not only abandon the small fetus but also break it down and reuse the raw materials. The problem was, reabsorption only happened when fetuses were a few ounces — it did *not* happen when they were roughly twenty pounds.

"Deeper, goddamit!" Rhumkorrf shouted. "I don't have all day!" His comb-over was starting to fray.

In the cow's stall, Tim started to sweat.

"Doc, come on," Colding said. "Just take it easy."

"I don't need your input, Colding. Shut up or I will kick you out of here. *Mister* Feely, you insufferable *idiot*, can you do your damn job?"

That would be just about enough of that. Colding put a hand on Rhumkorrf's shoulder, letting his thumb slide behind the trapezium muscle just to the left of the neck, pointer finger in front, just above the collarbone. He pinched the fingers together.

Rhumkorrf stiffened in his chair and hissed in a short breath.

"We're all under a lot of stress here, Doc. Wouldn't you say?"

"Yes," Rhumkorrf said. "Of course."

"Good. And you know shouting and stress affect Jian, so let's just calm everything down. Tim is doing fine, don't you think?"

Colding relaxed the pinch a little, but kept the muscle firmly between his thumb and forefinger.

"Of course," Rhumkorrf said. "Uh . . . Timothy. My apologies."

In the stall, Tim nodded absently. His attention remained focused on the fiber-optic tube.

Colding released the pressure and gave Rhumkorrf's shoulders a quick, friendly rub. "There you go, Doc. All better."

Rhumkorrf leaned forward, probably already forgetting Colding's rebuke. On the monitor, a crystal clear image flared to life. Colding sensed Jian walk up on his right, Tim walk up on his left, all three of them looking over Rhumkorrf's scattered comb-over at the image.

Rhumkorrf reached out, fingertips touching the screen. "Beautiful, isn't it?"

"It's bigger," Tim said quietly. "It shouldn't be that big . . . *can't* be."

A placental sac filled the screen, translucent pinkish-white lined with thin red and blue veins. Inside the sac, the fetal ancestor in profile. Its head looked twice as large as the rest of the body. Tiny paws folded up under a long snout, which was dominated by the huge, bluish, closed eye. Colding could even see a tiny, fluttering thing . . . the ancestor's beating heart.

"Fetuses average twenty pounds," Jian said quietly. "They grow twenty pounds in *six days*."

Rhumkorrf's fingertips traced the closed eye. He turned and stared at Colding with wild eyes, his anger gone.

"You see? We've done the impossible!"

Colding couldn't find words. Until now, this had been something on paper, a process he administered just as someone might administer an assembly line or a manufacturing plant. Even the gold-tinted image from the 3-D ultrasound had seemed somehow . . . Hollywood. The live image from the fiber-optic camera finally brought it all home in full, wet color — this was a *living creature*. A man-made organism that had germinated somewhere in Jian and Rhumkorrf's genius, then clawed its way into existence.

Colding tore his eyes away from the image to look at the little man who made it all happen. "Pretty frigging impressive, Doc."

Rhumkorrf turned, smiled and started to reply, but a strangled scream from Jian cut him off. Terror wrinkled her face into a disquieting caricature, locked her attention on the workstation's screen. As one, Colding and Rhumkorrf looked back to the monitor.

The fetal ancestor, eyes open, stared right back at them.

Rhumkorrf jerked his fingers away from the screen and almost fell backward into Colding.

An inexplicable wave of fear tingled up Colding's spine before he remembered it was only a computer monitor and this was a picture of a small fetus, not some six-foot-long creature looking at him with a malevolent gaze.

Jian's hands flew to her head and grabbed huge fistfuls of hair. "*Tian a! It is coming for us!*"

"Jian, calm down!" Colding snapped. "Claus, is that supposed to happen?"

"*No*," Tim said. "*Fuck* no that's not supposed to happen."

Rhumkorrf's skin looked even paler than normal, the hue of the walking dead. "I must say it's a bit unusual, but it's nothing to worry about."

"What?" Tim said. "A bit *unusual*? Dude, you are so full of *shit*! Just *look* at the goddamn thing!"

"Mister Feely! I'm not going to —"

Once again Rhumkorrf found himself interrupted, this time by blurry motion on the monitor that drew everyone's attention. The fetal ancestor turned its wedge-shaped head. Now two black eyes stared out from the screen, right through the translucent placental sack. Colding knew the fetus was actually looking at the fiber-optic camera inside the womb, but the tiny eyes seemed to be looking right at him.

"Odd," Rhumkorrf said. "Most animals don't open their eyes until after birth."

The fetus opened its mouth and lurched forward, hitting the inside of the placental tissue and stretching it outward like a wet pink balloon. They all flinched. Jian screamed louder. The tiny head reared back, the sac's stretched and torn whitish membrane sagged. Another violent thrust. The oversized head ripped through the sac in a cloud of swirling fluid. A gaping maw, pointy teeth. Jaws snapped shut and the image blinked into static.

They heard a splashing from the stall. Colding looked back to see fluid spurting out of the cow's vagina, a three-second downpour cascading off the floor. The cow's water had just broke.

Jian shouted something in Chinese, her voice an uneven tremor that rang with easily understood fear. She tangled both hands in her hair and yanked. Clenched fingers came away thick with long black strands.

Colding grabbed her shoulders, turning her toward him. "Jian, *stop it!*"

She stared at him, eyes wide with primal fear. She seemed terrified of him, as if she thought he was someone else. Or some*thing* else. She pulled another double handful of hair from her head, then shoved Colding hard in the chest. The move caught him by surprise. He tried to regain his balance, but his foot caught on Rhumkorrf's stool, knocking it over and sending both men to the rubberized deck. Jian ran, disappearing down the open rear ramp, heavy feet pounding out a reverberating rhythm.

Rhumkorrf was up first, surprisingly nimble. He helped Colding to his feet. "Are you okay?"

"I'm fine. Doc, do *not* try and tell me what I just saw was *normal*."

"It was probably just a reflexive acti—"

"Oh fuck *you!*" Tim said. "Try studying your biology 101, *Doctor* Rhumkorrf."

Colding left them both behind, sprinting past docile cows sitting quietly in their plexiglass stalls. He ran down the rear exit ramp.

"Jian, wait!"

She kept moving, kept heading for the hangar door, fat shaking in time with her panicked waddle. Colding caught her just before she grabbed the door handle. She turned and tried to push him again, but he caught her wrists. She struggled for a moment, but he held her tightly. Her wide eyes stared at him without recognition.

"Take it easy," Colding said. "Jian, just take it easy."

She blinked rapidly, then clarity seemed to return to her vision. She fell forward into his arms. The sudden move and her weight knocked him back a step, but he held her up. She wrapped her arms around him, head buried in his chest, her body shivering.

NOVEMBER 16: AUTOPSY

Implantation +7 Days

RHUMKORRF SIGHED AS he looked down at the fetal ancestor curled up on the dissection tray. The fetus had torn the amniotic sac in order to get at the tiny camera, spilling the life-supporting fluid contained inside. It had died shortly afterward.

They would avoid fiber-optic work now, stick to the 3-D ultrasound for fear of a repeat performance. Additional ultrasounds on the herd had shown that each cow had only one fetus. All second and third fetuses were gone.

Looking at the cat-sized corpse on the autopsy tray in front of him, he had trouble grasping that it wasn't even a week old. Mammalian development didn't happen like that. The word *impossible* flashed through his mind every few seconds, yet the facts lay on the tray before him.

His gloved hands set the little corpse on a scale. Twenty-one pounds. In just *six days*. But why should he be surprised? From the earliest planning stages they'd sought rapid growth. That was how he'd found Jian in the first place.

He'd read her published research and realized she could theoretically create an artificial genome, then experiment digitally until they could alter normal growth rates. It was on reading Jian's second or third paper, he wasn't sure which, that the whole ancestor project came to him in a flash of brilliance. His work on the quagga cloning project, breakthroughs in computing power, advances in oligo machines — the parts clicked, and he knew his destiny. The pieces existed, the required technology just a bit beyond what was already available off the shelf. All it really took, of course, was enough money.

Venter had funded the quagga cloning, but the man wouldn't touch the ancestor project. He had even called the idea *ludicrous*. So Claus had secured a meeting with Danté Paglione, CEO of Genada, Inc.

Danté jumped on the project. He saw the real possibility of Claus's vision. Danté obtained Jian, and the project was born. Erika Hoel's leading-edge expertise in large-mammal cloning was the perfect parallel to Jian's theoretical work, so Danté hired her as well. And now, after several abandoned lines of experimentation, after five long years, Claus's vision was a reality.

Tim Feely came up the ladder to the second deck. He looked sweaty, harried. His nose looked a little red. "What did you find, bro?"

Such a loser. Oh, how Claus longed to have Erika back. Just to see her face again . . .

"I'm still working on it, Mister Feely. And stop calling me *bro*."

Tim poked the dead fetus, then quickly pulled his finger back. "Dude, this is pretty fucked up right here."

"You have such an eloquent way with words."

"Funny," Tim said, "your mom told me the same thing."

"I'd prefer it if you didn't reference my mother."

"And I prefer box seats at a Pistons game followed by a Texas reach-around, but I'm not going to get either."

Claus paused, thought of asking what a *Texas reach-around* was, then shook his head and let it go.

"Goddamn spooky," Tim said. "The physiology looks so familiar, almost first-trimester human if you factor in the large size."

Tim was right. It *did* look a little like a human fetus. Claus cut out the heart. It was already well developed and looked *very* human. So much, in fact, the two might be indistinguishable. Transplanting it into a human would prove exceedingly easy.

The ancestor's limbs were already forming into their final shape. Somewhat disturbing were the tiny, needlelike claws at the end of each finger. *Claws*, like a cat's, not *hooves*, like a cow's. Had Jian coded for that? Maybe it was part of her broad integument swap. As long as the organs were right, the feet didn't really matter.

The size of the head and braincase also surprised Claus. Obviously, Jian had used a great deal of genetic information from higher mammals. But it was far too early to tell if the current body proportions would remain through birth and into adulthood.

"Hey, bro," Tim said. "You wanna hear something *really* scary?"

Claus sighed. "Just say it, Doctor Feely."

"I did some calculations. I'm estimating the fetuses have a fifty percent food conversion rate."

Claus stopped and looked at the younger man. "*Fifty* percent?"

Tim nodded. "Based on the amount of food the mothers have ingested, minus their baseline metabolic rate and factoring in the fetal weight."

Claus looked at his subject in a new light. *Fifty percent* of everything the ancestor took in was converted to muscle or bone or other tissues. Vastly higher than any other mammal.

"That's significant, but not the scary part," Tim said. "What makes my nut sack shrivel up and head for higher ground is Jian's weight projections. According to her tables, a six-day-old fetus should weigh *five* pounds, not *twenty*."

Claus looked up. He'd known the numbers but hadn't stopped to realize that the fetus on the table was more than *four times* the size Jian had coded for. Shorting her meds had produced the needed breakthrough, but Claus found himself wondering what details she might have missed in her creative state. What things might she have failed to document?

Or, possibly, were there things she didn't even *know* she'd done?

But none of that mattered. The bottom line was they had living animals gestating inside the surrogate hosts. From here on out, all they had to do was study the growth patterns and adjust the genome accordingly. Success was a given; the only variable was time.

Claus continued the autopsy, slicing open the stomach. The contents spilled onto the dissection tray.

Neither man said a word.

The mystery of the missing embryos lay on the wax tray in front of them. Rhumkorrf stared at the tiny, half-digested bones. He could clearly make out bits of a skull.

The ancestors were eating each other inside the womb.

Implantation +7 Days

PAUL FISCHER STARED at the sealed envelope on his desk. He was almost afraid to open it. If it didn't contain information that would help him, he had few options left.

Other than the contents of the envelope, his only real lead had been uncovered by Interpol. The agency had discovered a shoestring connection between Genada and a U.K. company called F. N. Wallace, Inc., that had purchased parts from a scrapped C-5 Galaxy. That discovery made the pieces fall into place for Paul; a plane that large could move the entire Rhumkorrf experiment anywhere in the world. But knowing Genada had a C-5 only helped if the plane was out in the open, or if it flew again. Paul knew Colding would make sure neither of those things happened.

No, Paul's best chance now was to find Galina Poriskova.

And that was why he was scared to open the report that sat in front of him. It could be the key to Poriskova's whereabouts. An actual Russian lieutenant, escorted by two MPs, had hand-delivered it just minutes earlier. The Russian had actually asked for Paul's ID and carefully examined it before asking Paul to sign for the report. Galina's involvement could be enough to convince Switzerland, the Caymans and China to freeze Genada's assets. If Paul couldn't make that happen, there was no way to flush out Colding.

Paul couldn't put it off any longer. He opened the sealed envelope, finding two manila folders inside: one thick, one thin. The thick one was on top, so he started with that. It contained page after page of financial records, records that seemed to confirm Galina had been living a lavish lifestyle all across Russia and Eastern Europe. After the financial records, though, came something far more interesting. It seemed that when Russian investigators followed up on the plane tickets and hotel stays purchased in Galina's name, they discovered that more often than not, no one showed up. At times, a tall blonde did purchase big-ticket items like art and jewelry — but Galina was a five-foot-four brunette. Bottom line? Galina hadn't been seen in Russia or anywhere else since shortly after her meeting with Paul two years ago.

Which meant the second report could contain only one thing.

Paul opened it. If the words on the four pages chilled him, the photos damn near froze him cold.

He picked up his phone and hit the extension for his assistant.

"Yes sir?"

"Get me Longworth, please. Immediately."

"Yes sir."

Paul hung up and waited for the callback. The second report changed everything. As gruesome as it was, it provided the leverage he desperately needed. If the C-5 lead panned out, he could combine it with this and make his case for freezing Genada's accounts worldwide. But that would take time. And with Genada's mole inside the U.S. governmental system, Danté might *still* stay one step ahead.

Unless Paul found a way to make sure the mole couldn't find anything at all.

He looked at the Russian report. Not at the contents, but at the report itself, at the folder. *Paper.* A courier. That's what he needed, not emails, databases and phone calls . . . nothing electronic.

The phone rang.

"This is Colonel Fischer."

"What do you have for me, Paul," Longworth said. "You find them yet?"

"I have an interesting lead. If you approve, I'd like to try something different. We have to catch them off guard if we're going to gain the momentum, go on the attack."

"I like the sound of that," Longworth said. "What do you have in mind?"

"I'd rather not say at the moment, sir. I'll have a courier deliver you a memo."

"A courier? Just email me."

"No," Paul said. "I can't."

Longworth paused for a second. "I see. Good, Colonel. Send your memo. And while you're at it, send memos to anyone else you need help from. I'll make a call and ensure you have as many couriers as you need."

"Thank you, sir."

Paul hung up and did some mental math. To do this right would take three days, maybe four. If it went well, he'd soon be making another visit to a Genada facility.

And this time, he'd find much more than an empty building.

Implantation +8 Days

COLDING AND SARA walked along Rapleje Bay. Snow, stones and sand crunched under their feet. The bay's two tongues of land on either side made for a mile-long, water-filled U that pointed northeast toward the unending expanse of Lake Superior. Stars sparkled like diamond chips on a blanket of black velvet.

He had to get some personal time, even if it was only an hour or so. Jian had recovered from her panic attack. Not all the way, but some — she was still twitchy, eyes always darting to corners. She was hallucinating again, even though she denied it. Colding had told Rhumkorrf to up her meds a little bit more.

Rapleje Bay was ten miles away from the mansion, from the hangar . . . from the lab. Sara had borrowed Clayton's crazy Bv206, the Nuge, so they could get away from everyone for a little bit. It was all getting to be too much: the fetus biting the camera, Jian going off the deep end, Danté's evasiveness, Fischer out there hunting for them. But it was all worth it . . . wasn't it? Saving millions of lives, sparing people the pain his wife had gone through — didn't that end justify the means? A week ago, he would have said yes. He wasn't so sure anymore.

A stiff wind blew from the northeast, rippling the nylon of his black Otto Lodge parka. He was ice-cold. Sara seemed perfectly comfortable in only jeans, a sweatshirt and a windbreaker.

"You must be part penguin," Colding said. "I know you were born around these parts and all, but it's freezing out here."

"Technically, thirty-two degrees is freezing. It's at least forty-five out here. Like spring, really."

Colding smiled and shook his head, wondering how she might handle a sweltering summer day in Atlanta.

"Besides," Sara said, "you better soak up this heat wave while you can.

On an island like this you can bet it's below freezing every day from December to February."

Colding shuddered at the thought. "That's horrifying. I had enough of that at Baffin Island."

"Oh come on, Peej. This place is beautiful. This is where the jet set from the fifties came to relax, and you're being *paid* to be here. Do you know what a resort like this would cost you a night?"

"We're in the middle of nowhere. I wouldn't pay a dime."

Sara rolled her eyes. "That's you, Peej, last of the tightwad romantics."

Colding stopped and looked at Sara. Her short blond hair flopped in the stiff breeze. She had a beauty he'd never seen in another woman, including, he realized, in Clarissa. Even when Sara squinted her eyelids against the stiff wind, he found himself admiring her laugh lines.

She turned and met his eyes, then smiled. "I've decided to forgive you for being a rotten douchebag."

"Good news for me."

"Uh-huh. But you still owe me."

"I do?"

"Yeah. *Big* time."

"I see. And how can I ever make this up to you?"

She grinned. "There's a heater in the Nuge. Wouldn't it be fun to know you put Clayton's pet vehicle to . . . *other* uses?"

He felt a tingly rush in his chest, a vibration that reached into his fingers and toes. In the Nuge?

"Uh . . ." he said.

She took his hand and led him back to the zebra-striped vehicle.

Implantation +9 Days

P. J. COLDING KNEW HE had said something very, very wrong. He just didn't know what it was.

Danté stared out from the secure terminal screen, his eyes narrow slits of barely controlled fury. "I can't believe you could be this stupid."

"But I don't understand." All he'd done was give Rhumkorrf's latest update. "Things are going better than we ever expected. The autopsies show incredible, healthy growth."

Danté shook his head the way you might when you hear someone say something so incredibly stupid it barely merits a response. "You're a smart man. Or at least I thought you were. See if you can guess which word in your sentence pissed me off."

Colding's mind raced for an answer. "I . . . I still don't understand."

"Autopsies!" Danté shouted. He banged his fist on the desk to punctuate each syllable. "Aw . . . fuck . . . king . . . top . . . *sies!*"

"But, sir, after the first fetus attacked the fiber-optic camera, the mother—"

"Spontaneously aborted, I know. Of *course* you do an autopsy on *that* fetus, you idiot, but how many more did you murder?"

Murder. Used in association with a lab animal.

"Two," Colding said. "They're growing so fast, Claus wants to properly document their development."

"I don't need *documentation!*" A thin line of spit dangled from Danté's lower lip. "I need living animals! What is there about the phrase *we're running out of time* that you don't understand?"

"Danté, autopsies are vital to the long-term success of the project. The purpose of these animals is to collect human-compatible organs. If the animals are born and the organs have some congenital defect, Jian will need all the data she can get to figure out where that defect occurred in the growth phase. What if there are problems later on?"

"What if there *is* no later on?" Danté stood up and leaned forward. His face filled the screen. Colding couldn't help but think of the fetal ancestor snapping at the fiber-optic camera.

"We can't risk *any* of them," Danté said. "We need at least one live animal to gain the support of the world *and* to get Fischer to back the fuck off." Danté blinked a few times, then again sat in his chair. The back of his right hand wiped across his mouth, clearing away the string of spittle.

So much for Fischer supposedly not having a clue. Either Danté hadn't been honest before, or something had changed. "Danté, let me talk to Fischer. I know him. I can tell him how close we are, get him to ease up."

"Absolutely not. I'm not taking any chance he can find the project."

"But sir, we—"

"No! He *cannot* find Black Manitou. Fischer knows about Hoel. Just take care of the project and let me handle the rest of it. Let me make this perfectly clear." Danté leaned into the screen, violet eyes crazy-wide. "*No . . . more . . . autopsies.* You do not kill a single fetus, for any reason. Do you understand?"

Colding nodded.

Danté broke the connection without another word. The Genada logo spun slowly on the screen.

Colding thought about Danté's reaction. The man was normally so composed, but he'd lost it. Lost it *bad*, and maybe said some things he hadn't wanted to say. *Fischer knows about Hoel.* Of course Fischer knew about Hoel; she had been his operative. Unless . . .

Unless Fischer knew Hoel . . . was dead. And if she was, there was only one person who had the opportunity to kill her before Fischer could have taken her to safety.

Magnus Paglione.

But that was just a theory, and a far-fetched one at that. Thank God Magnus was far away at the Manitoba headquarters.

As long as Magnus stayed there, everything would work out just fine.

Implantation +10 Days

IN THE C-5'S cockpit, Sara Purinam whistled the tune to "Cat Scratch Fever" as she walked through the maintenance checklist on her clipboard. She and Alonzo were doing the weekly walk-through of all cockpit systems. A couple of things needed work, but Big Fred was in solid shape. Even on a military base with full crews, C-5s were maintenance nightmares. Out here? Making sure she was ready to go on a moment's notice was a full-time job.

" 'Zo, you go through the comms check yet?"

Alonzo nodded. "Yes, genius. It was fine. Just like I told you when you asked me five minutes ago."

Ah. That was right, she had asked him.

Alonzo set his clipboard in his lap and looked at her. "If I didn't know you better, I'd swear someone fucked you stupid."

She whipped out her clipboard and bopped him on top of the head. He flinched and laughed, rubbing the spot she'd hit.

"Ouch! I notice you didn't deny it."

She shrugged. He'd already figured it out, no point in lying to him.

"Sara, what happened to *no way I'm hitting that again?*"

"So I was wrong. So sue me."

He fiddled with his clipboard. "Just . . . well, no one cares if you're getting some nookie, but we all saw how messed up you were last time you and Colding danced."

"Well, it's different now." It *was* different. But Alonzo's concern made her see it through his eyes. She had *hated* Colding. Now? She wondered if the opposite was happening, and after only a few days.

"Just use your head," Alonzo said. "I mean, you know, use it for *thinking.*"

She rolled her eyes. "Ho-kay, I think I'm done with your verbal diarrhea. I'm going to check the systems in the barn. You stay here and think about the things you've said, young man, and you feel shame."

She stood and turned. He held up his hand and smiled. She gave him the high five he wanted. Alonzo supported her, but his concern made sense. Made sense to her brain, sure, but not to her heart.

You are in so much trouble, girl. You're falling hard and you know it.

She couldn't help it. To think the reason he never contacted her was that he still grieved for his dead wife. Heart-wrenching, and just so tragically romantic she could barely stand it.

Sara wandered down to the first deck, where Jian, Rhumkorrf and Tim were working on the cows.

"Good morning," Jian said with a welcome smile. She was standing inside stall twenty-five, working on cow, well, Cow 25. The woman's silky black hair looked patchy, rumpled. Colding had talked about the fetus incident, the hair pulling . . . Jian's breakdown.

"Morning, Jian. How are you?"

Jian waved a hand dismissively. *I'm fine,* the gesture said, then she returned to her work.

Sara moved across the aisle to scratch the nose of a cow with an ear tag that read A-34. It was a big cow. Hell, they *all* were big. Sara stood five-foot-ten, and if the cows had their heads up they could look her right in the eye. Thirty-four had an all-white head save for a black eyepatch on the right side. She reminded Sara of that dog "Petey" from the old Little Rascals movies. She scratched the big, bony part of its nose. The cow's eyes narrowed in pleasure. It pushed into her hand, its neck so strong and head so big it made Sara stumble backward.

"Hey, take it easy, old girl," Sara said with a laugh. "Don't go getting greedy on me now."

Tim looked up from his current patient. "Do you fucking mind? We're trying to work here."

Sara felt like she'd been slapped. She just wanted to say hello. Before she could respond, Jian shuffled out of stall twenty-five and scowled at Tim.

"Sara can go anywhere she wants," Jian said in a cold tone. "You just keep your mouth shut or I will shut it for you."

Tim blinked slowly. If Sara hadn't known better, she would have sworn Feely was drunk.

"Well," Tim said. "Look who had her Cocoa Puffs this morning."

Jian's eyes narrowed. "What does that mean?"

"Means you're *koo-koo*," Tim said. "I'll translate into English for you. You're fucking crazy."

"Feely!" Rhumkorrf snapped. "That will be quite enough of that."

"Back off," Tim said. "I've had about enough of your little Nazi mouth."

Rhumkorrf paused, opened his mouth to speak, closed it, then opened it again. "Are you threatening me with physical violence?"

Tim shook his head. "No, I said I've had about enough of your Nazi mouth. That's a statement of preference. But I also want to put my foot so far up your ass you can smell my toes. That, to be clear, *is* a threat of physical violence."

Rhumkorrf blinked. Tim stared. Jian and Sara looked back and forth between them. Sara had to do something to get rid of this tension.

"Jian, give me some paper," Sara said. Jian paused for a second, then did as she was asked. Sara grabbed a black permanent marker and wrote something down on the paper.

Jian read it, then covered her mouth with her hand to try and hide a giggle. She grabbed a roll of Scotch tape, pulled out a strip, and taped the paper to the stall. Written on it in neat, black block letters were the words MOLLY McBUTTER.

"They need names," Sara said. "What kind of a name is *thirty-four*? From now on this one is Molly McButter."

Rhumkorrf started to protest, but Jian grabbed the marker and another sheet of paper. With almost childlike glee, she wrote down a name and taped it to cage forty-three. That cage held a cow with an all-white head, the only all-white head in the herd, who was now apparently named BETTY.

Rhumkorrf sighed, then shrugged. "All right. I suppose this is harmless."

"It's retarded," Tim said. "That's what it is."

Sara gave him a pleading look. He stared back, then rolled his eyes a little. "Retarded, that is, unless you name one *Sir Moos-a-Lot*. Then we're all good in the hood."

Jian grabbed another piece of paper. "How you spell *moozalot*?"

Sara smiled and winked at Tim. He smiled back, then told Jian how to spell it.

NOVEMBER 20: BLOWTORCH

Implantation +11 Days

"WHAT DO YOU mean, *he's here?*"

His secretary repeated her message. Danté Paglione's stomach dropped again, even further than it had the first time. "Send Magnus to my office, now."

Danté leaned back in his chair. His palms slid in circles on the cool marble desktop. This was bad.

Magnus's office was next door. He arrived first, his solid form sliding through the door without a sound. "You beckoned, O master?"

"It's Fischer," Danté said. "He's here."

Magnus stopped and stared. He seemed to process the information for a second, then shrugged. "He could have called first, but then I'm guessing you wouldn't have been in a hurry to set up a meeting. Relax, brother, we can deal with this."

Magnus sat in one of the two chairs opposite the desk. How could he be so damn calm?

"Did Farm Girl call you?" Danté said. "Why wouldn't she warn us Fischer was coming?"

"She would have, if she'd known," Magnus said. "Fischer must have stopped telling people where he's going. He knows someone is picking off his signals, so he's stopped sending signals."

"What else could he have done we don't know about?"

Magnus shrugged. "I guess we're about to find out."

Seconds later, Colonel Paul Fischer walked through the door. He wasn't alone. Two men in Canadian Army uniforms accompanied him, as did three other men wearing civilian suits. Fischer's hat was under one arm. His other hand carried a leather satchel with an open top.

"Colonel Fischer, this is unacceptable," Danté said. "If you're here to continue your witch hunt against Genada, I assure you our lawyers will have a field day."

"I won't be long," Fischer said. "In fact, let's get right down to business. Where are Claus Rhumkorrf, Liu Jian Dan, Tim Feely and Patrick James Colding?"

"In hiding," Magnus said. "Seems some ecoterrorists want to kill them. We've got to protect our people."

Fischer stared down at Magnus. "Protect them? Like you protected Erika Hoel?"

"Sad, that," Magnus said. "We saved four out of five. Wouldn't you Americans describe that as batting eight hundred?"

"Magnus," Danté said. "Let me handle this."

Magnus nodded, but kept his eyes fixed on Fischer. Fischer turned back to face the older Paglione brother.

"Colonel," Danté said, "please leave."

"Let me spell this out first," Fischer said. "The Canadian government, the United States government and several other governments are cooperating to freeze Genada's assets."

Danté's stomach flip-flopped, and he felt that now all-too-familiar pinching in his chest. He'd known this day might come. "You don't have that kind of international pull, Fischer. You can't freeze our assets."

"Not all of them," Fischer said. "Switzerland and the Cayman Islands are still in process, but that will be taken care of by the end of the day. And you're wrong. After the Novozyme incident, I *do* have that much international pull. Even with the Chinese."

Fischer let that last word hang in the air. Danté's mouth felt dry.

"I'm not much of a talker, Danté, so I'll make it simple. We know you're continuing research that potentially threatens all of humanity. You thought you could keep it going while the G8 demands you shut it down. You're known for your smart business decisions, but that one is just stupid."

Magnus leaned forward. "Are you calling my brother *stupid*?"

"How perceptive of you," Fischer said. "The Canadian government is investigating the murder of Erika Hoel. Officially, Rhumkorrf, Feely, Colding and Liu Jian Dan are the primary suspects. They are all wanted for multiple murders."

Danté looked at Magnus, then back to Fischer. "Multiple? What the hell are you talking about?"

Fischer reached into his leather satchel and pulled out a manila folder, which he placed on Danté's desk. "Russian authorities identified the body of a Jane Doe with DNA matching that of a missing woman. That missing woman was Galina Poriskova, former employee of Genada. Although her remains were heavily decomposed, the Russians said she had been burned badly by an intense flame. A blowtorch, probably. They know this because the *bones* were burned in some places. Also, her right pinkie had been cut off. Galina Poriskova was going to shut Genada down, Danté, but she was tortured to death. Now, you and I both know who did that, but Jian, Rhumkorrf and Colding are the *official* suspects. Genada's assets are frozen because, as your brother just admitted, you are now harboring those suspects."

Magnus smiled. Danté recognized a rare expression on his brother's face — respect.

"Colonel Fischer," Danté said. "I assure you that—"

"Save it," Fischer said. "As of right now, Genada is shut down."

He pulled another folder out of the satchel and tossed it on top of the Galina murder report.

"That's what we know about your C-5. Brilliant work, I admit. We want your flying lab, we want *all* of your research, and we want your staff. While I want to see you and your psycho brother in jail, my mission is to find Rhumkorrf and the others. Should we find them, that means Genada is no longer harboring fugitives. Your accounts would be opened up." He put a business card on the desk. "If you need to reach me, that's my number. Otherwise, good luck dealing with the Royal Canadian Mounted Police."

Fischer turned and walked out of the room, limping just a bit. The other men followed.

Magnus sat quietly. Danté pushed the C-5 folder aside and opened up Galina's murder report. There were pictures. The pain in his chest grew stronger, more piercing.

"Magnus . . . how could you do this?"

"She was a threat."

A threat. She was also a human being. Burns down to the *bone*? What kind of an animal had Magnus become?

"It will be okay," Magnus said. "Danté, I'm here to protect you."

"We don't need that kind of protection. We need to get our lawyers going on this right now."

"Come on, Danté," Magnus said. "Lawyers? What do you think they can do against the bureaucracies of the entire free world?"

"We have to do *something*."

"Do we? Wouldn't it be easier if Fischer just . . . went away?"

Danté stared at his brother's cold eyes. Magnus couldn't consider something that drastic. That wasn't even sane.

Then he looked down at the photos again and wondered whether Magnus had *ever* been sane.

"You don't do a thing," Danté said. "You hear me? Not a damned thing. I can fix this. All we need is a live animal. Once we have that, we go public. Everyone will back off. They can't drop the hammer on a company that will save millions of lives. In fact, Magnus, I need you at Black Manitou. You have to make sure there are no problems."

Magnus stared, said nothing for a few seconds. "You want me out of the way?"

"That's not it," Danté said, but they both knew that *was* it. "The project is our only hope. If this round of fetuses doesn't turn out, we don't have the money to fund another. I told Colding not to kill any additional fetuses, for any reason — you make sure he obeys that order. You also have to *make sure* that island is locked down tight. If someone gets off and Fischer finds them, he'll find Black Manitou, and then it's all over. Can you do that, Magnus? Can you do that for me?"

Magnus blinked, and his eyes softened a little. "Damn, you're good at this stuff, brother. My brain knows exactly what you're doing, but the way you sling words, it makes my heart want to obey."

"Will you go?"

He nodded. "Yes. I'll call Bobby and leave right now. I'll be on Black Manitou by tomorrow morning. Do me a favor, call Colding and let him know he's taking over Andy's security shifts for a few days."

Magnus turned and walked out.

Danté breathed in and out, long and slow, until the pain in his chest started to fade. Colding wouldn't be happy about Magnus coming to Black Manitou, but that was just too bad.

NOVEMBER 22: HOT EVENING

Implantation +13 Days

SARA LOOKED BEHIND her as she quietly walked down the basement stairs. No one there. She walked to the security room door, punched in the supersecret code and slipped inside. Colding sat behind the monitors, feet up on the desk, a thick sheaf of papers in his hand. His eyes lit up when he saw her. Such a smile. That boy was nothing but trouble.

"Hey," he said. "Anyone see you come in?"

She shook her head. "I think I lost the tail, Mister Bond."

"Oh, knock it off. I just don't want Magnus finding out about us. Technically, I am your boss, you know."

"You can boss me around anytime." She walked to the desk, pressed against him and stroked his hair. "I'm down for some covert lovin', but what are you doing here? Isn't this Andy and Gunther's gig?"

Colding shook his head. "Not since Bobby dropped off Magnus yesterday. Seems Mags prefers the company of Andy, so the two of them are either snowmobiling or in the lounge getting ripped."

"Bit of a sudden shift in the totem pole order? Andy must love that."

"Yeah. He's walking around like the cat that tortured and killed the canary. But it's not so bad. I can't keep as close an eye on Jian as I'd like to, but I'm watching her on the lab cameras. Other than that, just catching up on my reading."

His pile of papers looked like a manuscript. The header at the top read HOT EVENING — BY GUNTHER JONES.

"Oh, *snap*! Is that Gunther's trashy vampire romance novel?"

He nodded. "Yeah, only it's not all that trashy. The writing isn't that great, but I have to admit I can't put it down. I already read the first one, *Hot Dusk*."

He set his stack of pages down carefully, then reached back on the counter and found another thick sheaf. "Here," he said, handing it to her. "*Hot Dusk*, the first in the series."

"You're serious. You're actually telling me this is good?"

"Good enough to keep me hooked. I'm a little surprised myself, but I've got to find out how Margarite handles Count Darkon." He stopped talking and just stared at her, as if he were weighing his options about something.

"What," Sara said. "Do I have a booger or something?"

Colding smiled and shook his head. "No, no boogers. I just . . . well, I think you should know what's happening with the fetuses. I don't think it's anything to really worry about, but you should know — as long as you promise not to tell your crew."

"Why wouldn't I tell them?"

"Because *you're* not supposed to know," Colding said. "I like those guys, don't get me wrong, but if Miller and Cappy start blabbing and Magnus finds out they know, it's my ass, and . . ."

"And?"

"Well, nothing. I just don't think you need that kind of pressure."

She never hid anything from her crew, but she trusted Peej. "Okay. I promise."

She waited. Eventually, he talked and told her what was happening inside her plane, what was growing inside the cows.

She *did* freak out, but only a little.

NOVEMBER 24: NICE FUCK-FACE

Implantation +15 Days

COLDING WALKED INTO the lounge knowing he'd see the same thing he'd seen for the past three days — Magnus and Andy getting trashed. Sure enough, there they were.

Magnus was relaxing in one of the brown leather chairs. His left hand held a tumbler with amber liquid and ice. A half-empty bottle of Yukon Jack sat on the mahogany table in front of him. Next to the bottle lay the remote control for the lounge's flat-panel TV.

On the chair to Magnus's right sat one Andy "The Asshole" Crosthwaite: shoes off, white-socked feet resting on a coffee table, Rolling Rock beer in his hand, a shit-eating grin twisting his mouth.

"Colding," Magnus said. "Ready to give your report?"

Colding felt his face get a little hot. Every day, he had to stand in front of Magnus and report. Colding had a feeling the daily charade was Andy's idea, some kind of partial revenge for drawing down on him.

"No issues on my security shift," Colding said. "Anything else?"

Magnus took a slow, deliberate sip. "Yes, two more things. How is the progress in the lab?"

"Couldn't be better. Tim estimates the fetuses are all over a hundred pounds. I checked in with Rhumkorrf a few minutes ago — he said he may attempt a cesarean in about a week."

Magnus raised his eyebrows. He looked at Andy, who shrugged and took a pull on his beer. Magnus looked back at Colding. "Let me make sure I understand this. A cesarean, meaning, you cut them out, and the ancestors walk on their own?"

"Hopefully, yes."

"So this isn't hypothetical anymore. You're telling me that we've actually done it?"

"If the fetuses survive the coming week, then yes, we've done it. If not, then Jian and Rhumkorrf revise the genome. But we've come so far this time we know it's not a question of if, but when."

Magnus took another sip, then smiled. "My brother did it." He drained his drink in one pull, then lifted the bottle and refilled the glass.

"You said you had two more things," Colding said. "What's the other?"

"How's Jian, Colding? How's she doing?"

Colding felt a small wash of fear creep across his back. "She's fine."

Andy's smile widened.

"That's not what Andy tells me," Magnus said. "He said she is . . . what's that delightful colloquialism you used, Andy?"

"Crazier than bugshit on burnt toast."

Magnus pointed at Andy, a little gun-finger trigger pull. "That's it. Crazier than bugshit on burnt toast. Funny how I've been here almost four days, Colding, and you haven't told me about that. I gave you plenty of time. I even scheduled daily reports for you to give you the opportunity to be up front, but it seems you don't want to be forthcoming to your boss. Why is that, Bubbah?"

Colding shrugged and looked out the big window at the sprawling expanse of Lake Superior. How much more did Andy know? Did he know Jian might be hallucinating again? "Jian has some issues, but that's the price you pay for dealing with genius."

Magnus nodded. "Right. *Genius.* And she's reliable? Won't have a sudden bout of homesickness, try and get back to the mainland?"

Now he understood Magnus's concern. A crazy Jian was unpredictable, could do anything, including trying to contact the outside world.

"She's good," Colding said. "Trust me."

Magnus stared at him, said nothing. It took everything Colding had to not turn away, to stay locked on those cold, violet eyes.

"Okay, Bubbah, I'll take your word for it." Magnus turned to look out the picture window once again. Colding gathered that he had been dismissed. He started to walk out of the lounge when Magnus stopped him.

"Oh, Bubbah, just one more thing."

Colding stopped and turned. "Yes?"

"As a supervisor at Genada, do you think it's wise to be fucking the help?"

Magnus knew. Colding looked at Andy, who just kept on smiling.

"I figured Sara for a lezbo," Andy said. "But man, that bitch *loves* the cock, eh, Colding?"

Magnus picked up the remote control. The TV's dark screen flared to life with a green-tinged night-vision image. Colding on his back, in Sara's bed, Sara sitting up, on top of him, riding him.

Colding felt his hands ball up into fists.

Magnus raised his glass, saluting the screen. "Impressive. Why, then, can one desire too much of a good thing?"

Colding ground his teeth. "I ordered cameras *off* in the rooms."

"Oh, that," Andy said. "I guess I didn't get the memo. Man, *love* the titties on that bitch."

Colding's rage welled up, threatening to blow wide open. Only once before in his life had he wanted to kill another man — that was the day he'd attacked Paul Fischer. He had to think clearly, stay calm. The whole Erika/Claus/Galina triangle had almost destroyed the project. Magnus might not take kindly to a love affair between Colding and Sara. If Magnus *had* murdered Erika Hoel, the man would have no compunction about killing Sara Purinam.

Magnus hit the pause button, freezing Sara as she leaned far back, her hands behind her on the bed, her breasts standing out. Past her shoulder, Colding could see his own eyes squeezed shut in ecstasy, his mouth a combination of a smile and a snarl.

"Hey, *Colding*," Andy said. "Man, you've got a great fuck-face. Nice."

Magnus shook his head. "And here I thought you were such a straight shooter, Bubbah. Fraternization with a subordinate is prohibited."

"Uh-oh, am I going to get written up? Will this go on my permanent record?" Colding looked at the wall, trying to appear bored with the whole thing. "What do you *want*, Magnus?"

"I want to know if Sara Purinam is your girlfriend."

"I'm fucking her. So what?" The words sounded sick to his own ears.

"That's all, Bubbah? Just *fucking* her?"

Colding shrugged. "Is that against company rules?"

Magnus laughed. "Not against the letter of the law, but you are her boss."

Colding had to be the stereotypical man-pig, convince Magnus he didn't care about Sara. "Are you *ordering* me to stop fucking her?"

"Take it easy, Bubbah. I just want to make sure you aren't falling for her, something that might compromise your judgment."

"No worries there," Colding said.

"So," Magnus said, "Sara's just a whore to you?"

"She sure fucks like a whore," Andy said. "Where do you think she learned to fuck like that?"

"Where indeed," Magnus said. "She give up that pussy to anyone?"

Andy laughed. "Not everyone. She won't give it up to me."

"No surprise there," Colding said. "Your infinitesimal cock wouldn't be enough for her, little man."

Andy's laugh died in his throat.

Magnus chuckled. "*Infinitesimal cock.* In case that's outside of your vocabulary, Andy, it's an insult. You going to just take that?"

Andy stood and tossed his beer aside. It fell to the ground, spilling on Clayton's immaculate carpets. "Fuck a duck, Colding. I'm going to kick your ass right now."

"Sit down, Andy."

Andy looked at Magnus, then back to Colding. "But you said—"

"Sit!" Magnus shouted the word, so loud even Colding flinched. Andy sat.

Magnus raised his glass to Colding in a mock salute. "Fuck who you want, Bubbah, just keep doing your job. But remember, some Cupid kills with arrows, some with traps."

The way Magnus said that made Colding's blood run cold.

"Cupid? Magnus, with all due respect, what the fuck are you talking about?"

That half-smile again. "Didn't they teach you Shakespeare in America?"

"Not really. I wasn't much for the literature classes."

Magnus nodded a little, as if that statement had answered some longstanding question. "Go ahead and take off. I'm sure you've got something, or someone, to do."

Colding walked out of the lounge. Not only were his personal problems magnified, but he'd been slacking on his main job — Jian. Magnus was watching her. Colding had to make sure the woman got the help she needed.

Rhumkorrf had to fix Jian's meds, and fix them *now*.

NOVEMBER 24: YOU UNDERSTAND

Implantation +15 Days

THE SNOW HAD not come with a big, gale-force storm, but it most certainly had come. An inch here, another two overnight there, usually light but fairly steady over the past weeks. Only now did Colding really notice the accumulation of a half foot of snow that covered everything.

And still the flakes came.

He stood at the water's edge, watching Claus Rhumkorrf try to skip stones. Above and behind them stretched the mansion's sprawling back porch. In front of them: water, whitecaps, and Horse Head Rock.

Rhumkorrf picked up a flat stone from the water's edge. It slipped out of his mitten-covered hand twice before he held it firmly enough to throw. The rock skipped once before plunging into a three-foot wave.

"Need flatter water for that," Colding said.

"Now you're a physicist?"

"Come on, Doc. Talk to me. We need to help Jian."

Rhumkorrf shrugged. "Pressure and stress exacerbate her symptoms, and we're under the gun, as they say. There is only so much we can do for her."

"That's a cop-out answer and you know it."

Rhumkorrf kept staring out at the water, seeming to focus on Horse Head Rock some two hundred yards from shore.

"She was fine for months," Colding said. "Now she's struggling. Hallucinating. We have to stop it before she tries to kill herself again."

"I increased her dosage."

Rhumkorrf tried to pick up another rock, but it kept falling out of his oversized black knit mittens. He gave up after the third try, stood straight, and stared out at the choppy water.

Something was wrong here. Rhumkorrf was the visionary, the planner, but nothing in this project happened without Jian's genius. And yet Doc didn't seem remotely concerned that her biochemistry had changed, that he might have to scramble to find a new medicine that worked.

"I'll bring in someone else if I have to," Colding said. "Another physician who can help her."

Rhumkorrf suddenly shifted into a visible state of anxiety just a few degrees below panic. "If you bring another doctor out here, or take her to the mainland, the Americans might find us and shut us down."

Colding held up both gloved hands, palms up. "If you can't help her, what do you want me to do?"

"Do *your* job," Rhumkorrf shouted. "Keep us safe, keep us secret until I finish my work. *Jian's* job is to help me create the ancestor, something that she's doing exceedingly well right now, so maybe we just need to take the good with the bad."

The prick didn't give a rat's ass about Jian. All he cared about was the experiment.

"You're a medical doctor," Colding said. "You're supposed to help people."

"That is *exactly* what I'm doing. Helping millions of them. Haven't you noticed, P. J., that when she gets like this she is at her most brilliant? It's for the greater good. You of all people should understand that."

Colding stared down at the little man, the cold forgotten for the moment. Realization set in. Rhumkorrf wasn't concerned about finding a new medicine, because he knew the current medicine would work just fine . . . if she got the proper dose.

"You motherfucker," Colding said. "You shorted her meds."

Rhumkorrf shrugged and again looked out at Horse Head Rock.

Suddenly it was hard to think. Colding wanted to kick Rhumkorrf right in the teeth. "How long has this been going on?"

"Five weeks. Had to be done, and it worked. You understand."

Colding snapped out his left hand and grabbed the back of Rhumkorrf's neck, squeezed it tight as he pulled the smaller man close.

"Don't you *touch*—"

Rhumkorrf couldn't finish his sentence, because Colding's right hand locked on Rhumkorrf's throat, pressing down on the Adam's apple. Rhumkorrf's gloved fingers tried to pry the hands away but couldn't find purchase. Another memory flashed in Colding's mind, this time of Magnus back on Baffin Island, squeezing just a little bit harder to get Andy to stop struggling. Colding's hands tightened. He also gave one short shake, bobbling Rhumkorrf's head.

Eyes wide with terror, looking up through glasses knocked askew, Rhumkorrf stopped moving.

"Fix it," Colding said. "Or I'll fix *you*."

He pushed Rhumkorrf away, a little too hard. The man stumbled and fell, skidding across the snow-covered sand. Hand on the ground behind him, he looked up at Colding. Colding suddenly saw the scene through Rhumkorrf's eyes — a bigger man, a *stronger* man, towering over him, ready to hurt.

Sanity snapped back into place, and with it, deep embarrassment.

"Claus . . . I . . ."

"Stay away," Rhumkorrf said. "I'll correct her medication, just stay *away* from me." He scrambled to his feet and ran for the steps to the mansion, giving Colding a wide berth as he passed.

Colding didn't know what bothered him more, that he'd flipped out and put his hands on Rhumkorrf, or that for a brief instant he'd used Magnus Paglione as a template for proper behavior.

"Fuck," he said.

He waited a few seconds to give Rhumkorrf plenty of room, then walked toward the steps that would take him up to the mansion.

He'd check in on Jian, and then go find Sara.

NOVEMBER 25: STUPID COW

Implantation +16 Days

AT THREE IN the morning, Jian found herself alone in the C-5's upper-deck lab. She blinked and looked at the work log she'd called up on her computer. It couldn't be. But there it was, the keystroke log didn't lie.

She'd just done a protein analysis. The results had looked familiar. Now she knew why — she had done the same analysis yesterday, and the day before. But she didn't remember doing either of them.

She called up more logs, looking at her work. Some things she remembered doing, some she did not. Maybe it was the lack of sleep. She couldn't even manage twenty minutes of sleep before the mishmash animal of her dreams came for her.

Doctor Rhumkorrf had brought her meds today, not Mister Feely. Rhumkorrf said he had made an adjustment. It would take a little while for her body to acclimate. Three days, maybe four, to get back to normal, he had said. She'd start feeling a little better as early as tomorrow. And when she *did* feel better, could she please please *please* make sure she told Mister Colding?

She knew she wouldn't feel better. Doctor Rhumkorrf was lying. *Everyone* lied to her.

But the *numbers* didn't lie.

Maybe her failure caused the dreams, the spiders. The rats. The *mishmash*. The *numbers*.

Movement on her left. She turned and took a step back all at the same time, then felt a dribble of pee trickle hot down her leg.

An orange spider.

Big as her whole head, staring at her. Jian's hand shot to the desktop, where she'd left her Dr Pepper. She grabbed and threw all in one motion, the open bottle trailing brown and white froth as it shot toward the corner.

The spider scrambled out of the way as the plastic bottle hit the floor and spun, spraying the area.

"Zou kai!" Jian screamed. "Zou *kai*!"

The spider was gone. Must have slipped into a crack or something, even though she couldn't see a crack. Damn spiders.

The *numbers*. She had to fix the numbers, fix the numbers so the ancestors would come out right.

But . . . *ancestors* . . . for people parts?

That was it! How could they expect to produce an *animal* with transplantable organs? Out of a *cow*? She could fix it, she could fix it all, make the whole project work. They just needed a different kind of host.

She put on gloves, then opened the liquid nitrogen container. She carefully pulled out sample trays and set them aside until she found the one she wanted. The one nobody else knew about. She put the other trays back inside, then carried her special sample to the elevator and descended to the empty lower deck.

Some of the cows were asleep. The ones that were awake watched her. Sir Moos-A-Lot had an orange rat on his head. It didn't seem to notice that the rat was gnawing on a black-and-white ear, red blood spilling down the cow's big flat cheek. The cow just stared at her, oblivious.

Stupid cow.

Jian quietly walked down the center aisle, trying to ignore several sets of cow eyes that followed her motion. She opened the storage cabinets in Mister Feely's area. There, a sterile envelope that had what she needed: a catheter that looked like a thin turkey baster.

Jian grabbed the catheter package. She placed it and the sample tray on the lab table.

Embryo transfer in most in vitro procedures was done by a doctor, and guided by ultrasound. Ultrasound would take an extra set of hands. Jian did not have an extra set of hands. Too bad the orange spiders couldn't help. They had lots of hands.

She'd be on her back, but doing it herself would only take about five minutes.

And besides . . . they were *her* eggs. She could do whatever she wanted with them.

NOVEMBER 25: A VALID CONCERN

Implantation +16 Days

CLAUS RHUMKORRF SAT at the ultrasound station, waiting for Tim to finish running the transducer across Molly McButter's belly. Claus had taken a liking to Molly, but that was simply because the cow showed above-average intelligence. And he liked the way she nuzzled against his chest when he scratched her ear (but only, of course, when no one else in the lab was looking).

Jian, thank God, was looking better already. She'd even combed her hair. Two more days, three at the most, she'd be back to her normal, far-less-creative self. That was okay, though, because they were in the homestretch. No question anymore — the ancestors *would* live to term, and all data indicated they *would* walk on their own.

That asshole Colding, manhandling him like that. How *dare* he. And yet Colding had been right. At least somewhat. If Jian killed herself, that didn't help the project. With the most significant problem behind them, Claus could afford to be gracious and correct her meds. She still threw darting glances into the corners, but he estimated that behavior would vanish by the end of the day.

The progress bar filled up. A gold-hued picture flared to life. "Heilige scheisse," he said, the words out of his mouth before he knew it.

Baby McButter had come a long way from its start as a microscopic ball of undifferentiated cells. If Claus hadn't known better, he would have estimated the creature up on the screen to be four or five *months* along, not two *weeks*.

Jian stared at the picture. She shook her head as if to clear it, then stared at it again. "There has to be a mistake," she said. "That fetus is at least a hundred pounds."

"More," Tim said as he came out of Molly McButter's stall. "Try one-thirty."

"*No*," Jian said. "Program say ancestors should be no more than forty pounds right now."

"Your program versus *a scale*?" Tim said. "I think the scale wins, Froot Loops."

"Stop with the names," Claus said, feeling odd about his instant defense of Jian.

"I don't care about Jian's bullshit program," Tim said. "Look at the damn readouts. Well over a hundred pounds in *two weeks*? Nothing grows that fast. Not an elephant, not nothing."

Claus marveled at the life he'd created. The back legs looked much thicker than he'd theorized. The front legs looked strong as well, but were skinnier and longer than the back. That would suggest a creature that moved at somewhat of an angle, like a gorilla on all fours, as opposed to horizontally, like a running dog or a tiger.

The skeletal structure also showed remarkable growth. The ribs looked very thick and extended from the head all the way down to the hips, growing against one another almost like a kind of internal armor.

"Doc," Tim said. "What are we going to do?"

"We observe and document," Claus said. "We prepare for a C-section in a woolt Maybe less."

"That's not what I mean, dude. Based on the growth patterns thus far, in another week these bitches could hit *three hundred pounds*."

Rhumkorrf nodded. "True, and adult weight could reach four hundred, maybe five hundred pounds. You're right, the organs might be too large. We'll adjust the genome for the second generation, but right away we can use livers, maybe even kidneys."

Tim's face wrinkled up as if he were looking at a very, very stupid person.

"What?" Claus said. "*Now* what is your problem?"

"I'm not talking about transplants and organs, you fucking nerd." Tim looked at Jian. "You know what I'm talking about, Fruity Pebbles?"

"Mister Feely," Claus said, "I'm not going to tell you ag—"

"Predators," Jian said. "Teeth. Claws. Maybe three hundred pounds at birth, possibly *twice* that size within days. Where will we put them? What will we *feed* them?"

Claus looked at her blankly, then turned to stare at the workstation's gold-tinted screen. He used the trackball to turn the fetal image, looking at it from every possible angle. Teeth. Claws. Muscle. Aggression. Attacking the camera, killing while still inside the womb.

"Perhaps," he said quietly, "that is a valid concern."

NOVEMBER 26: CHECKMATE

Implantation +17 Days

COLDING STARED AT the chessboard and contemplated his next move. He couldn't screw it up, because he was winning — he was actually beating Jian. No one in the project had ever beaten her. Okay, maybe her brain was still a bit addled from the med shorting, but Colding would take a victory over her any way he could get it.

He had avoided Sara as much as possible in the last two days. After, of course, he'd gone to her room and broken the cameras there. He didn't quite know how to tell her that Andy "The Asshole" Crosthwaite had a video of her, naked, making love.

He explained his distance by telling Sara that he had to focus on Jian, that he'd been slacking off more than a little on that part of his job. Sara understood. And he wasn't lying, because he *did* focus on Jian, monitoring her progress, making sure Rhumkorrf gave the proper dosage. That and playing a lot of chess.

Colding moved his queen's knight and smiled. "Check."

Jian stared blankly out the lounge's picture window. She seemed to have forgotten Colding was even there at all. She looked much better, though — clearly, the proper dosage was working.

"Jian?"

She just sat there, her hands turning a bottle of Dr Pepper over and over until the color was a light brown — the normal dark caramel shade mixed with the white of bubbles seeking escape against the bottle's pressure. When she finally opened it, Colding thought, the thing would explode.

"Hey, kiddo, pay attention — you're in check."

She glanced at the board, then went back to turning the Dr Pepper bottle.

"Jian, talk to me. What's eating at you?"

She looked at him, her eyes once again focused. "It is too big."

"I know, it's okay. Gary Detweiler is getting material for heavy cages.

We'll have them up in a few days. Doc tells me that will keep the animals under control."

She laughed. "Doctor Rhumkorrf wants to see his name on the cover of *Time* magazine. He would risk all of us."

Colding thought of the shorted meds. Jian was more right than she knew. He also thought of the cages, and of a tiny, camera-biting fetus enlarged to two hundred pounds. Or even bigger. Rhumkorrf had assured him everything would be fine, but the man's statements were questionable at best. If Jian was worried, then Colding was worried. "Why are the fetuses so much bigger than you thought they would be?"

She looked down. The bottle turned faster. "I . . . I made projections, but . . . maybe I was not thinking clearly."

Not thinking clearly. He thought about the timeline. She'd had her breakthrough, created the successful batch right when they left Baffin three weeks ago . . . two weeks after Rhumkorrf started shorting her meds.

"Jian, I need you to think. You said you coded for a herd animal. Docile, about two hundred pounds adult weight. But it's not just the size of the ancestors, it's the aggressive behavior, those . . . *teeth.*"

She raised her head, looked him in the eyes. He couldn't quite read her expression. On her face he saw doubt, confusion. "I thought I program for herbivore. But . . . it is predator."

No shit, Sherlock. Herbivores didn't eat each other in the womb. If Genada had more time, more resources, Colding could just scrap this round of fetuses and have Jian start over. Magnus, however, wasn't going to let that happen.

"I want to leave," she said suddenly. "I want to leave this place. Something bad is going to happen, unless we stop it. We need to call someone."

Colding's breath caught in his throat. He automatically looked at the camera in the upper corner. Gunther was in the security room. Did he see Colding and Jian in here? There was no sound . . . but Colding had also thought there was no video capture in Sara's room. Who knew what else he was wrong about? If Magnus found out Jian was talking about leaving, what would he do?

"Jian, don't say that again. Don't you even *think* about saying anything like that, to *anyone.* Do you understand?"

"But Mister Colding, I am afraid that I . . . I . . ." Her voice trailed off.

"These half-sentences of yours are really annoying, Jian. Just tell me."

She looked at the chess piece in her hand and said nothing.

"Jian, just *tell* me. What are you afraid of?"

Her eyes narrowed. Something was going on in that brilliant head of hers, but what?

"I did things I do not remember doing," she said. "I think that . . . I will look at code again, see what I can find."

She set down her rook in a new space that blocked his check. Colding smiled and started to move his knight into attack position, when he saw that by moving her rook, she had put his king in check with her bishop.

"Checkmate in two moves," Jian said absently.

"Fuck," Colding said.

The bottle spun even faster. Without another word, she stood and walked out of the office.

NOVEMBER 27: KILL 'EM ALL

Implantation +18 Days

JIAN HELD HER breath and waited while Claus Rhumkorrf read her report on his computer. They were alone in the upper-deck lab. She was feeling better, but not when she was around him. Stress was bad for her. Made her twitchy. Made the shadows move.

He turned from the screen to stare at her. "But you don't remember doing this?"

She shook her head. "I do not, but look at it. That is the *real* code I used for the genome. That is why my growth projections are so off."

His eyes widened. She'd never seen that look before. A look of doubt, of fear. He turned back to the screen.

"I see," he said. "And now that you know this, you have new projections?" His tone of voice, almost like he didn't want to hear the answer.

"Yes, Doctor Rhumkorrf." She again looked at the printout in her hands, even though she already knew the answer. "Birth weight, approximately two hundred fifty pounds."

He swallowed. She actually *heard* him swallow. Trembling hands reached up to readjust his black glasses. "And your best guess at . . . at the recalibrated adult weight?"

"Over five hundred pounds."

Of all the odd things, he picked his nose for a second. He wiped his finger on his pants leg. "That would be more in line with the growth we've seen in the fetuses. Still, we need to see the adults. We won't know organ functions or dimensions for sure until we have an adult. Then we can make adjustments and try again."

Jian couldn't believe her ears. *See* an adult? Was he crazy? "Doctor Rhumkorrf, we need to kill them."

His head snapped around, anger smoldering in his eyes. "Kill them? But we're succeeding!"

Jian shook her head. "We are creating something bad. Something *evil*."

"We'll have the cages soon. We're not going to kill anything."

Jian started to speak, but was interrupted when Mister Feely's head popped up the aft ladder.

"Bro-ski! Froot Loops! Get down here, pronto!" He disappeared back down the ladder. Rhumkorrf and Jian followed him to the first deck.

Mister Feely stood next to Molly McButter. Molly's head hung almost to the ground. Thin trails of blood ran from her mouth.

Rhumkorrf knelt to look into the cow's mucus-coated eyes. "What's wrong with her?"

Tim shook his head. "I'm not sure. I just got here ten minutes ago and found her like this."

"Ten minutes? You should have been here *hours* ago, Mister Feely. Were you drinking again, or just sleeping off last night's hangover?"

"Fuck *you*, shit-breath," Tim said as he ran down the aisle to his lab area across from the crash chairs and the elevator. He tore through the cabinets and came back with a fluid-filled IV bag and a needle envelope.

"So?" Rhumkorrf said. "What's wrong with her? Doctor Hoel isn't here to wet-nurse you anymore, you drunken idiot."

"Know what, chief?" Tim hung the bag from a hook above Molly McButter's stall, then knelt to work the needle into her neck. "You're about one ounce of lip shy of me pimp-slapping you like a bitch."

"Just tell me what's wrong with the cow!"

"She's sick, it's like her body is feeding on itself. I'd say it's a sudden onset of malnutrition."

Jian had looked over the cows just last night, and they seemed fine. Malnutrition? How could that be? Too much stress. She felt all itchy. She wanted to get out of there, get away from Rhumkorrf, Feely and the cows.

"Ridiculous," Rhumkorrf said. "It can't be malnutrition. Molly's feed bin is full; she hasn't touched it. We've increased their food intake to compensate for the advanced fetal growth. She didn't look like this yesterday . . . did she?"

"Not even close," Tim said. "Whatever made her sick, it made her *so* sick she stopped eating. She's the only one showing these symptoms, so I'll see if something is wrong with the IV setup. Maybe the pump broke or the needle jammed."

Jian looked at the other cows. They all looked fine. Then she saw something move in stall forty-one. Coldness blossomed in her chest. A tiny plastic baby-doll hand reached over the stall divider. A black-and-orange tiger paw appeared a few inches to its left.

"No," Jian said in an inaudible whisper.

The mismatched arms shivered. A black head slowly appeared from behind the wall. Jian shut her eyes tight and jabbed her thumbs into her stomach, sending a wave of dull pain up her body. She gave her head one shake, then opened her eyes.

The thing was gone.

"Jian," Rhumkorrf said sharply. She jumped at the sound of his voice and turned to face him.

"Jian, did you hear me?" He looked annoyed. Mister Feely looked disgusted.

"No, Doctor Rhumkorrf. What did you say?"

"I asked what you thought of this."

Jian quickly looked at the sick cow, then back at Rhumkorrf. "Mister Feely is right, the rapid fetus growth is making the cow sick."

Tim inserted a new IV needle into Molly's neck. "I'm going to crank up her intravenous feeding," he said. "Hopefully that will normalize her metabolism enough for her to start eating again. I'll increase all the cows' food another twenty-five percent. I think that sometime during the night Molly became sick enough to stop eating, and her body started breaking down muscle in order to sustain the fetus. From there, the situation cascaded."

"We need to set up checks every two hours," Rhumkorrf said. "We'll have to create a rotation with the nonimportant staff."

Tim shook his head. "I can do you one better, bro-hem. I'll program their monitors to watch for altered vitals, tie that into the security room computer. Something goes wrong, the security dude on staff gets beeped, zooms in with a camera, then gives us a holler. Easy."

Jian shook her head. "No. Just let them die."

Rhumkorrf glared at her.

Tim nodded slowly. "Fuckin' A right," he said.

"*Wrong,*" Rhumkorrf hissed, the word long and drawn out. Jian took a half step back.

"These animals will not die," Rhumkorrf said. "And if they do, I swear to God that I will destroy both of your careers. Timothy, the only way you will get near a lab is if you're pushing a mop. And Jian, I promise you that when they take you back to China, you will spend the rest of your life rotting away in an insane asylum."

Rhumkorrf's eyes were wide and angry. A sneer bent his upper lip. *Hateful.* She had to look away. And when she did, Rhumkorrf turned his gaze on Tim. Tim looked down — all of his bluster, all of his threats of violence, gone.

Rhumkorrf walked back to the aft ladder and climbed to the second deck. Jian said nothing. She had to do something to stop all of this, but what? Mister Colding wanted her to shut up. Doctor Rhumkorrf just didn't want to listen. Mister Feely was all talk. Sara? She wasn't one of the decision makers.

Jian couldn't rely on anyone. She knew what she had to do. The only question was, did she have the courage to do it?

NOVEMBER 27: NICE ENDO

Implantation +18 Days

COLDING WAS GETTING the hang of snowmobiling, and, he had to admit, he liked it. A swarm of sleds shot down the snowpacked road toward the docks — Magnus and Andy out in front, Alonzo and the Twins next, then Colding, with Sara bringing up the rear.

She hung back a little in case Colding had problems. Wasn't exactly rocket science to drive one, but like anything else a sled took some getting used to. The brakes on a car or motorcycle usually weren't applied while driving thirty miles an hour across snow or ice, for example.

Up ahead, the road crested the snow-covered dune that marked the harbor. Colding's eyes widened as he saw Magnus and Andy accelerate up the dune and fly off it, trailing comet-tails of powder through open air before they vanished behind the dune's far side. 'Zo and the Twins took the crest more conservatively, keeping their sleds on the ground as they went over. Colding slowed and stopped a good fifty yards shy of the dune.

Sara slid to a stop next to him. "You like what you see there?" Her smile blazed in the afternoon sun. Even with goggles covering her eyes and a helmet hiding her hair and ears, she looked stunning. The helmet didn't hide those freckles.

He looked back to the dune. That much air under Magnus's sled seemed terrifying, but it also seemed like a crapload of fun. "How do you land without killing yourself?"

"You push off when you hit the crest. Keep your feet flat on the runners, but keep your knees bent. Push down with your legs when you land, it absorbs the shock."

"Sounds like jumping a dirt bike."

She nodded. "If you've jumped a bike, you know how it works. I'll go side by side with you, just match my speed."

Colding shook his head. "What if I wreck the sled?"

"I'm pretty sure Genada can afford a new one. Don't be a pussy." Sara gunned her snowmobile and shot away, engine whining. Colding squeezed his throttle tight. The sled rocketed forward so fast he almost fell off. These things were flat-out built for speed. He caught up to Sara at the base of the dune. The upward slope pushed him down into his seat. Still accelerating, he hit the crest and pushed off.

Weightless. Exhilarating. The harbor spread out before him, white and blue, the *Otto II* bobbing slowly in the light chop. The sled dropped down. He bent his knees, then pushed.

Jarring impact, body stunned, limp and flopping. More weightlessness, not the good kind, then a smack that rattled his head inside the helmet. Sliding facedown. Something cold in his neck and left shoulder.

No more motion.

"Fuck," Colding said.

"Hey!" Sara's voice. "Are you okay?"

He pushed himself to a sitting position. As he did, he felt packed snow fall from his snowsuit neck down his shirt and over his stomach. Sara crouched in front of him, helmet now off, eyes filled with concern.

"I think I'm okay," he said. He pulled off his gloves, unzipped the suit and started fishing inside his shirt for the ice-cold snow. "Nothing hurt but my pride."

"You looked sexy," Sara said. "You know, right up until that whole landing thing."

Colding laughed and stood. His snowmobile had wound up on its side, clear plastic windscreen cracked from the crash. He put it back on its treads. Other than the windscreen, it looked no worse for wear. Sara's sled, of course, had no damage. "I see you landed like a pro."

"I've been riding since high school," Sara said. "An old boyfriend from Gaylord taught me."

"You dated a gay lord?"

"It's a town, dumb-ass. Just south of Cheboygan. Big rivals in high school football. I was a sophomore dating a senior from a rival school . . . so scandalous. He used to take me snowmobiling all the time."

"What was his name?"

Sara started to speak, then stopped. "Crap, I had it. Man, that was what, almost twenty years ago? Ah! Don Jewell. See? Sharp as a tack despite my advanced years."

"You still in touch with him?"

She shook her head. "Haven't talked to him since high school. No idea what happened to him."

The sound of the Nuge's diesel engines drew their attention. Clayton's snowproof vehicle crested the dune at a modest speed, then continued toward the dock. Out at the dock, Colding saw the others already at work unloading the *Otto II*. Magnus, Andy, Sara's crew, Sven, James and Stephanie Harvey. They hauled metal poles, rolls of heavy chain-link fence and bags of concrete from the ship to the base of the dock. Mookie the dog ran around, barking, kicking up chest-high waves of snow before stopping every twenty or thirty feet, standing tall, snow-covered black ears up high and black eyes searching the tree line for some imagined threat to her master.

"Let's get to work," Colding said. "Last thing I need is Magnus thinking I'm a slacker. And remember, no public displays of affection out here."

"Spoilsport," Sara said.

They walked quickly to the dock, the Nuge close behind. At the base of the dock, Gary Detweiler and Sven Ballantine stacked their loads of cement bags — Gary carried a single forty-pound bag, Sven carried three.

"What's up, Mister Colding?" Gary said. "Helluva endo you had there."

"Endo?"

"He means your landing, eh?" Sven said. "And I use that word loosely."

Colding laughed and shrugged. No way a wipeout like that wasn't going to bring him some ribbing.

Gary patted the pile of concrete bags, already stacked five high and six across. "This is some pretty serious gear for a cow pen."

Sven rolled out his neck. The cracks sounded like breaking ice. "Babies are on the way, Gary. Expensive babies. Best to keep them protected."

Colding nodded. Sara looked away. She knew the real reason they needed heavy-duty enclosures. Clayton, Gary, Sven and the Harveys did not. That had been Magnus's orders — outside of Colding and the scientific staff, no one needed to know.

Sven turned and walked back down the dock to fetch another load.

"I saw a weather report," Gary said. "You better get these cages built fast. Forecast is for a major storm in three days. No way you can do any construction once it comes in. For sure you'll get that five feet of snow I told you about."

"Wonderful," Colding said. "Like Christmas come early."

Gary leaned in. Colding could smell the pot rolling off him. "All this heavy fence, Mister Colding, for *cows*? Come on, what's *really* going on? I just want to know if my dad is safe."

"Piss off, eh?" Clayton walked up, moving with that old-man hitch-stride of his. "I don't need you babysitting me, boy."

"But Dad, all this stuff."

"Yeah, all this stuff." Clayton bent at the knees, grabbed a forty-pound bag of concrete under each arm, then stood. "We need to load all *this stuff* onto da Nuge. Let's get crackin', eh?" He carried the bags to the Bv's rear section and started stacking them in.

Gary pursed his lips and shook his head. Apparently, concern for his father could cut through a marijuana high.

Colding picked up two bags and immediately dropped one. Holy crap, eighty pounds of concrete wasn't exactly a loaf of bread. Clayton had picked up two like they were nothing, and Sven walked around with three. Good, clean country living had its benefits, apparently.

"Stop dickin' around already, eh?" Clayton shouted. "Can you two pillow-biters have your gay moment off da clock, for fuck's sake?"

Gary laughed, then picked up a bag and carried it to the zebra-striped vehicle. Colding adjusted and picked up his two — almost threw his back out, but he'd be damned if Clayton lifted more than he did.

NOVEMBER 28: DEATH FINDS A WAY

Implantation +19 Days

READY TO INITIATE CONTACT SEQUENCE...

THE SAME SENTENCE on all seven screens, surrounding her, engulfing her. Just one push of the *enter* key and she'd have someone who would listen to her. Someone who could act.

Modifying the network had been a simple affair, one for which she'd never be caught. Black Manitou had no outside phone connection, no radios, no Internet. No way to call anywhere but to Gary Detweiler, or to the company headquarters in Manitoba. But inside the Manitoba facility? A whole computer network connected to the Internet, to the outside world.

She had to do something. This was her fault, her coding. What, exactly, *had* she done? Most of the late nights she'd worked alone in the lab, she remembered nothing but a hazy blur filled with orange spiders and purple centipedes. But she remembered enough to know *why* she created the genome now growing large inside the cows.

Why?

Because she had wanted to kill herself again.

No access to knives, no scalpels, no glass in her room, no chemicals, no pills, nowhere to possibly hang herself, and yet her twisted mind had found a way, *found a way* . . .

. . . the ancestors.

But the ancestors wouldn't just kill *her*. They would kill Doctor Rhumkorrf. Mister Feely. Stephanie and James. Sara.

They would kill Mister Colding.

She couldn't tell anyone what she had done. Not ever. It wasn't just a suicide attempt, her insanity put everyone's lives at risk. They would send her back to China. They would send her back to an asylum, like Doctor Rhumkorrf had said.

She couldn't go back. She remembered the sense of hopelessness, of wishing for death but unable to do anything about it because of the stiff straitjacket. She remembered how those places *smelled*.

She had to stop the ancestor project, but she couldn't tell anyone *why* it was so important, or tell them exactly *what* she had done.

The secure connection to Manitoba was her last-resort solution. She could worm through that side of the network, access the Internet, then make a simple voice-over-IP call. The only problem was she'd have to shut off Black Manitou's jammer to activate the secure connection's satellite uplink. If someone was in the security room, paying attention, they would know she was contacting the outside world.

Jian looked at her finger, still poised above the keyboard. It shook slightly, a tiny tremble.

She pulled her hand away. Not yet. Not yet. She'd try once more, try to get someone to listen.

But if they would not, she knew what she had to do.

NOVEMBER 28: FISCHER WAITS . . .

Implantation +19 Days

PAUL FISCHER READ through the printed reports, all of which boiled down to the same one-word summary.

Nothing.

That's what they had: nothing. Multiple law-enforcement, military and intelligence agencies had gone over every last shred of Genada's financial information, corporate history, employee profiles and anything else that might produce information on the whereabouts of Claus Rhumkorrf, Liu Jian Dan, Tim Feely or Patrick James Colding. The agencies were even looking for more people now — Magnus Paglione, who had slipped his tail shortly after Paul's visit to Manitoba, and the suspected crew of Genada's C-5: Sara Purinam, Alonzo Barella, Harold Miller and Matt "Cappy" Capistrano.

A search for *all* of them, and still . . . nothing.

Fischer pushed the papers away and leaned back in his chair. He had to finally admit defeat. Colding had beaten him.

All Fischer could do now was wait and hope that someone in Genada made a mistake.

NOVEMBER 29: FREAKIN' ORCS AND ELVES

A FANTASY NOVEL. Yeah. That was where the money was. Freakin' orcs and elves and shit? Some wizard kids? How hard could *that* be?

Gunther knew the vampire romance novel was a guaranteed home run. Why not whip out some bullshit fantasy novel under a pen name? Jeez, eighteen-year-olds were doing it, making millions by rehashing Tolkien. Nerds would buy anything with a dragon on the cover, and Gunther could rehash with the best of them.

Had to start with a quest. That's how they all started, really, some dopey farmer kid getting sent on some quest, during which he'd have adventures and trudge through a magic swamp or something, then . . .

A beep from the console broke his concentration. That new alarm Tim had set up for alerts about the cows' vital signs. Elevated heart rate from Miss Milkshake. Gunther tapped the controls, switching the monitors to an interior view of the C-5's lower deck.

He started moving the camera remotely when the alarm changed from a beep to a steady drone. Flatline.

"Uh-oh."

He moved the camera until it pointed at Miss Milkshake's stall. On the black-and-white screen, a dark puddle spread out from under the clear plastic door.

Implantation +20 Days

THE 3-D ULTRASOUND was a marvelous invention, but Claus had always thought it looked a little . . . fake. Maybe it was the gold tint, or the way the little computer model rotated with the trackball movements. He knew the images were real, but on the flat-panel screen they still looked like exactly what they were — computer graphics. And computer graphics, no matter how detailed, couldn't touch the real thing.

The real thing, which now sat on the lab table. It wasn't in a dissection tray, because there weren't any dissection trays that big. It didn't even fit on the damn *table*. He, Tim and Jian stood there, looking at the corpse they'd taken out of Miss Milkshake's belly.

"Oh fuck me running," Tim said. "Look at those *claws*."

Claus *was* looking at the claws. And the teeth. And the front and back legs that hung partially off the edges of the black table. He looked at his computer for the tenth time, still amazed at the weight. An *actual* weight, not one of Tim's calculations.

Two hundred ten pounds, six ounces.

Five feet long from the tip of the nose to the end of its tailless posterior. The beginnings of fur were pushing out from the pink skin. The animal had put on fifty-five pounds in the last three days.

What in God's name had Jian created?

"Look at the teeth," she said.

"I am," Rhumkorrf said. "Can't you see that I am?"

Long and pointy, the ancestor's teeth were definitely designed for killing. For ripping off large chunks of flesh and swallowing them whole. A mouth full of canines, without an incisor or molar to be found.

Tim reached out, gingerly, and traced his fingers along the animal's thick head. "This lower dentiary, it's *massive*."

The heavy jawbone was at least two feet wide at the base, giving the head a wide, triangular shape tapering off at the nose. The jaw bulged with attached muscles.

Claus hadn't been ready for this. They hadn't seen a fetus outside of the womb for thirteen days, ever since Danté forbade further autopsies. Thirteen days ago, 115 *pounds* ago.

"Timothy," Claus said. "Start on the autopsy for Miss Milkshake immediately. We have to know why she died. Go."

Tim ran to the ladder and descended.

Claus carefully examined the skull. Two feet wide, two feet long, the last fourteen inches of length were nothing but jaws and teeth. The creature still possessed a proportionately large braincase. The brain-to-body weight ratio ranked alongside that of wolves.

The skull wasn't the only shocking feature. The front legs had retained their relative length advantage over the hind limbs. The creature would move half upright. All claws ended in thick, muscular digits, each tipped with a six-inch-long claw. Sharp, *pointy* claws, like those of a big cat.

"Now you see," Jian said. "Doctor Rhumkorrf, *please*."

"You shut your mouth," he said quietly. There would be no more insubordination from Jian and Timothy, a fact he would have to remind them of from time to time. "It will probably go through more physiological changes before it's ready for birth. What I can't figure out is this protrusion coming out of the back of its head." A two-foot-long strand of cartilage, thin but sturdy, stretched from the back of the fetus's head. He gently lifted the cartilage; still-forming skin ran from it down to the creature's back.

"It almost looks like a variation on the dimetrodon's spinal sail," Claus said. "I don't know what you were coding for with this, Jian. Come now, you've *got* to remember something this unusual. What is it?"

Jian looked at the growth, then up at Claus. Tears filled her eyes. "I do not remember what that is for," she said. "But it does not matter. Please, Doctor Rhumkorrf, we are on an island where no one can reach us. We have to stop this, you can ask—"

"Do you remember what your insane asylum looked like, Jian?"

She leaned away like he'd actually hit her. That reaction, the way she caught her breath. He knew she'd spent a few years in one, before her countrymen got her back to some semblance of sanity. It was the perfect threat to keep her in line.

"Get back to work," he said. "You made this animal. You go through your code, figure out what we have to prepare for. Do you understand me?"

She shrank back, nodding, then turned and waddled to the ladder. He stared at her all the way, in case she looked back with that pathetic, fat face. She did once, saw him watching her, then scurried the rest of the way to the lower deck.

Left alone, Claus stared at the huge corpse. Claws. Teeth. That wide jaw. That spine.

The cages would be enough.

They *had* to be.

Implantation +21 Days

TIM SHIVERED AS he stared up at the bulkhead monitor. He needed a snort something fierce, but he couldn't risk pulling his flask out of his back pocket. Not with Rhumkorrf watching. And maybe this really wasn't the best time to be schnockered.

Jian stood next to the screen, also looking up at it, mumbling in Mandarin over and over again, switching her weight from the left foot to the right foot and back. She didn't look like a scientist anymore — she looked like a lunatic.

Rhumkorrf sat on a stool, alternately looking at the IV needle in his hand and the pictures up on the bulkhead monitor. "So the IV needle came out of the vein," he said, his voice a monotone of detached scientific analysis. "When would you estimate this happened, Mister Feely?"

"About 11:00 P.M.," Tim said. "I checked the logs of the IV pump. It registered a pressure change, but not enough to trigger an alarm, because it was still pumping. Miss Milkshake had a slight hematoma at the insertion point. I estimate the fetus started eating the amniotic sac at around 12:05 A.M., causing the mother internal bleeding. Dude, the fetus actually *ate* the placenta, by the way, as well as a chunk of the uterine wall. Miss Milkshake flatlined at 12:37 A.M., according to the heart rate recorded by the stall's computer. The fetus drowned in her blood at approximately 12:56 A.M."

Rhumkorrf's head snapped around. He had that furious look in his eyes again. "Mister Feely, are you sure about those numbers? As soon as Miss Milkshake died, the fetus would have asphyxiated within minutes — no oxygen from her blood."

And now for the really, *really* fucked-up part. "The . . . uh . . . during the fetus's struggles, its claws punched a few holes in the cow's abdomen. There was a little . . . uh . . . air coming in, which it tried to breathe, I think, but it was also aspirating the mother's blood."

Rhumkorrf looked shocked. "So the fetus outlived the mother?"

"By around nineteen minutes," Tim said. "When the needle came loose, I think that Baby Milkshake got . . . ah . . . it got hungry and tried to eat the first thing it could find."

"This is not good," Rhumkorrf said. "We're going to have to increase the nutrient intake and set up shifts to check each IV on the hour."

"Doctor Rhumkorrf," Jian said, "this has gone far enough. We have to kill the cows, today. Right now!"

"That's *enough*." Rhumkorrf's voice boomed through the confined upper-deck lab. "Jian, you've never been stable to begin with, and now? Well, your meds are clearly not working. I've had it with your paranoid rants!"

"Oh, blow it out your ass," Tim said. Was this guy for real? The evidence of pending disaster sat on the table right in front of him. "Don't be a fuck-tard, bro. Open your damn eyes! We need to kill these mutant freaks, and right now."

Rhumkorrf's small face wrinkled with fury. "I will not stand by while you two . . . *pussies* ruin this. We've been working for this for years! And we're almost there."

"*Please*," Jian said. "Doctor Rhumkorrf, you must listen. We have to—"

Rhumkorrf stamped his foot on the rubberized floor, cutting off her words. "Jian, get out! I won't hear any more of this! Get out of my lab! Get out of this plane entirely! You're fired! Get out, *get out getout*!"

Tim and Jian looked at each other, then back at Rhumkorrf.

"Get out, I say! *Get out now!*" He pointed his finger to the ladder, anger radiating from his body.

Jian descended.

Well, maybe it *wasn't* a good time to get schnockered, but that's exactly what Tim was going to do. He pulled the flask out of his pocket, un-screwed the top and took a long drink. Ah, the power of scotch.

A hand hit his and the flask flew across the lab, trailing scotch as it went. A blur of motion, then a stinging sensation on his right cheek.

Rhumkorrf had slapped him. He stood nose to nose with Tim, his comb-over sticking up in a hundred different directions, eyes wide and unblinking behind the heavy black glasses.

"Feely, did you forget what I said about your career?"

"Screw my career," Tim said. "I just want to get off this island alive."

"I can't believe you're buying into Jian's paranoid delusions."

At that moment, Tim Feely lost it. He pushed Rhumkorrf hard in his chest. The smaller man stumbled back and fell, turning as he did to land on his hands and knees. He started scrambling to his feet, but Tim jumped on his back. They struggled, then Tim got his hands on Rhumkorrf's head, turned it so it faced the big screen.

"Look at it, bro, look at it! It tried to *eat its way out of the womb.* The only one here with delusions is you! What's going to happen when they're born? What are we going to feed them?"

Tim never saw the elbow. He rolled back, jaw radiating pain, split lower lip spilling blood down his chin.

Panting and shaking, Rhumkorrf stood and looked down. "We can feed them the cattle from the other farms. And we'll have Danté bring out more food. This is science, Feely, and we have to make it work. I wish I had Erika, but I don't. I have *you.* Now, you get your ass downstairs and start doubling the nutrient supplement. I will *not* lose another fetus, not when we're so close."

Tim stared for a second before he realized something disturbing. He was afraid of Claus Rhumkorrf. The wee German was right — Tim was a pussy.

Tim stood, face burning with embarrassment, then cautiously slipped past Rhumkorrf and scurried down the aft ladder.

Rhumkorrf had always been obsessed, but this? This was a different level altogether. Anyone could see the danger. Rhumkorrf had to see it as well, *had to,* but still thought he could put those creatures in the new cages. The goddamn things were going to be bigger than *lions.*

Tim walked down the center aisle toward his lab. As he did, he passed each and every cow, staring at each and every massively swollen belly.

Implantation +21 Days

JIAN SHUFFLED DOWN the hall, small steps making for a slow pace, her hands furiously spinning a Dr Pepper bottle top-over-bottom-over-top. She entered her room, shut the door behind her and locked it. She then moved to the dresser. She didn't slide it, but instead picked the whole thing up. Grunting slightly from the effort, she set the dresser against the door. She looked at the big four-poster bed. She slid behind it and shoved. Wooden feet squealed against the polished stone floor. The bed wedged nicely against the dresser.

Jian sat at her computer desk and called up the program she'd written two days earlier. There was nothing else she could do. Rhumkorrf wouldn't listen. Not to her, not to Tim. Colding wouldn't do anything. There was no longer any choice.

She entered some commands. The program flashed up a window with the words READY TO INITIATE CONTACT SEQUENCE.

She hit *enter*.

IN THE SECURITY control room, Andy Crosthwaite was sitting hunched down behind the security monitor. His big bag o' porn sat close by, the brown paper worn down to an almost tissue-paper thickness from its many travels. But Andy wasn't looking at the latest *Juggs* or *Gallery*. He was halfway through *Hot Midnight*. No one was more shocked than he that old Gun could write a hellacious fucking book, *and* that Andy might actually dig some cheesy vampire romance crap. But it wasn't just mushy romance; Gun had thrown in more fuck scenes than a Skinimax after-hours flick.

Andy didn't want anyone to see him reading the book, *especially* Magnus, who always had his nose in Shakespeare this or Shakespeare that. Andy hadn't read much Shakespeare, but he knew damn well the old English dude didn't write about killer vampire stableboys with glittering ruby schlongs. That bit was just genius, Gunther old boy . . . *gen-ee-us.*

A long beep brought his attention to the main monitor. A command-line window popped up. The window listed two lines.

JAMMER SHUTDOWN ACTIVATED
JAMMER SHUTDOWN COMPLETE

"What the fuck?"

He shuffled together the pages of Gunther's novel, set them on top of the big bag o' porn, then scooted up to the keyboard. He called up the main security menu and clicked the jammer icon, launching the control window. Sure enough, the jammer's status said *disabled.* He hit the *enable* button.

ACCESS DENIED

Andy felt a sinking feeling in his chest.

The log monitor scrolled again, this time with the messages:

TRANSMITTER ACTIVATED
PHONE NETWORK ACTIVATED . . . DIALING . . .

Andy turned to the camera monitor and started flashing through the channels. C-5 cockpit: empty. C-5 lab: Rhumkorrf working at a lab table, but not near a computer. C-5's veterinary bay: Tim in stall four, attending to a cow, also nowhere near a computer. Magnus's room: empty. Colding's room: he was asleep in his bed. Jian's room . . .

What was with all the furniture pushed up against the door? And she . . . she was sitting at her wacky computer desk.

"Oh, fuck a duck."

The log line scrolled again.

VOICE CONNECTION ESTABLISHED. CALLER ID: USAMRIID

"Oh, mother*fucker!*" Andy grabbed the phone and dialed the extension for Magnus's room. As it rang, he punched a button on the console, activating the secure satellite uplink monitor.

VOICE OVER IP SIGNAL DETECTED. WOULD YOU LIKE TO MONITOR THE AUDIO?
YES/NO

He clicked *yes* to listen in. He called up the transmitter control window and clicked *disconnect*, knowing what he'd see.

ACCESS DENIED

Magnus still didn't answer.

"Oh, unholy duck fuckers." Andy turned up the sound on the monitors.

A CHEERFUL VOICE answered on the seventh ring. "USAMRIID, how can I help you?" The voice sounded tinny coming from the computer's small speakers.

"I want Paul Fischer."

"Pardon me, ma'am?"

"I need Paul Fischer. Zhe shi hen jin ji."

"Ma'am, I—"

"Fischer! I must talk to Fischer about problems with our transgenic experiment. If you take the time to screen this call, I will be dead before someone can answer."

There was a brief pause. "Hold on one moment, ma'am."

Jian stared at the computer screen but wasn't really looking at it. All her eyes could see was a ghostly vision of the needle-toothed fetus snapping at the fiber-optic camera.

MAGNUS BUTTONED HIS pants, zipped his fly, then walked out of his bathroom to the desk phone that had rung nonstop for over a minute.

"This is Magnus."

"Where the hell have you been?" Andy screamed so loud Magnus flinched and held the receiver away from his ear.

"Stop yelling," Magnus said. "I was taking a shit."

"So is Jian, all over us. I think she connected to Manitoba, and from there she's calling Fischer!"

Magnus reached into his desk drawer and pulled out a Beretta 96. "Can you shut down our transmitter?"

"I can't! She locked me out somehow, turned off the jammer, too. I can't bring it back online."

Magnus pinched the phone between his shoulder and ear, checked the eleven-round magazine — full. "Is she talking to him now?"

"I think she's on hold."

"Where is everyone? Where is Colding?"

A brief pause: "He's sleeping. Rhumkorrf and Tim are in the C-5. Sara and her crew are doing maintenance there. I think Gunther's out for a snowmobile ride. Don't know where Clayton is, maybe he's with Gunther."

Magnus thought for a second, then reached into his desk drawer and pulled out a second Beretta. "Listen to me, Andy. Take a ninety-six out of the security room rack. Get rid of it, *make sure* it won't be found, and make sure there's a blank space in the rack."

"Got it."

Magnus slid the extra Beretta in the back of his pants, then walked into the hall.

"ARE YOU STILL there, ma'am?"

"Yes."

"I'll connect you now, please hold."

The phone sound changed a little, carried a touch of static, then a man's voice answered.

"This is Colonel Paul Fischer."

"This is Doctor Liu Jian Dan. Listen carefully."

She heard a hiss of excitement just before he spoke. "Jian Dan . . . listen, we've been look—"

"Shut up!" Her patience was gone. Time was almost up. Too much stress. They would be there soon, the rats, the spiders, the mishmash monsters with the teeth and claws. "You shut up and you *listen*! They are too big."

"What's too big?"

"*It* is! The code is wrong, I don't know why I made what I did, but it will kill us all."

"Doctor, please calm down—"

Her door shook in its frame, five big slams. *So loud!* Jian screamed and stepped away from the computer. Her hands grabbed big tufts of her uneven black hair. The door rattled again, vibrating with each repetitive, powerful blow.

"Ma'am? Doctor?" Fischer's voice came from the speakers, small and faraway, drowned out by the pounding and by Jian's screams.

MAGNUS GAVE UP knocking and just punched the door, a straight right with all his weight behind it. The wood cracked with the sound of a gunshot. A white, jagged split appeared in the thick brown door. He reared back and hit it again, even harder, and his fist went through. Blood smears streaked the splintery hole. He took a quick look at his fist — the skin had split over his knuckles. A two-inch splinter jutted from between his index and middle finger. Blood ran down his hand.

Magnus pulled out the splinter, tossed it aside, then reached into the hole and tore free a thick, head-sized piece of door.

He stepped forward and looked into Jian's room.

IT HAD BEEN too much for her strained mind. The violent pounding on the door eroded her sanity to the last pebble of rational thought. When Magnus looked in, Jian didn't see a human face at all — she saw a wide black head with smiling, evil eyes and long teeth dripping with saliva.

The mishmash face of her dreams.

Doctor Liu Jian Dan screamed for the last time.

Magnus calmly aimed his Beretta through the hole and fired. The bullet smashed into Jian's temple, just above the left eye. It punched through bone and tumbled through her brain, ripping out the back of her skull in a cloud of pink and red. Gelatinous globs splattered against the wall.

The shot knocked her back a step, froze that last scream in her throat. Chunks of bone and brain hanging from the back of her ravaged head, Liu Jian Dan managed to take one small step forward, regained her balance for just a second, then fell face-first onto the floor.

NOVEMBER 30: FAILURE

Implantation +21 Days

COLDING SAT UP in his bed, blinking away the sleep. Had he heard a gunshot, or dreamed it? An instinctive alarm rang somewhere in his subconscious.

"Jian."

He threw the covers aside and sprinted into the hall, headed for her room.

COLDING FOUND HER door half open. He tried to push it open farther, but something blocked it. A dresser, he saw as he slid into the room . . . slid in, and saw the body.

He brushed past Magnus and Andy. Jian lay on the floor in a still-widening pool of blood. Her left hand was clenched into a fist, strands of her black hair still sticking out from between her fingers. Her right hand held a Beretta 96. He didn't need to check for a pulse — the fist-sized hole in the back of her head said it all.

"She must have snuck into the security area," Andy said. "Stupid Clayton and that code."

"She was a smart woman," Magnus said. "Even if we had a real code, she probably would have figured it out."

Colding knelt next to the body of his friend. The woman he was supposed to protect. Not just because it was his job, but because Jian had *needed* someone to protect her, to help her cope with life.

And he'd failed her.

Just like he'd failed Clarissa.

He should have gotten Jian off the island days ago. She needed help, *real* help, she needed to be away from the stress that messed her up so bad even if the meds were perfect. But no, he'd ignored her needs, because of the *fucking project*. Because of *hope for millions*.

Colding looked up at Andy. "What happened?"

"I saw her on a routine video sweep," Andy said. "She had the Beretta, she was babbling something in that ching-chang-chong talk."

Magnus made a *tsk-tsk-tsk* sound, almost a bad impression of someone expressing sympathy. It made Colding want to rip out the man's tongue.

"Andy called me and I rushed here, but the door was blocked," Magnus said. "I tried to talk to her, but she wouldn't speak English. I couldn't get inside in time to stop her." He held up a still-bleeding hand, as if his blood was inarguable evidence of his efforts to save Jian.

And yet even with the brains of his company's prized genius dripping down the walls, Magnus Paglione didn't show a shred of emotion. Colding remembered his suspicions about Erika Hoel, how Danté wouldn't say anything about her.

He remembered how he'd left Erika with Magnus.

But Erika had tried to destroy everything, she'd been in collusion with Fischer. Jian hadn't done anything like that. Unless . . . unless she'd made good on her desire to contact the outside world.

Colding looked around the room, searching for a phone, a walkie-talkie, even two tin cans connected with strings. But he saw nothing. There was no way to call out, Danté had made sure of that. No way except for the secure connection to Manitoba, and that was locked up tight.

Then his eyes settled on the computer. Somehow, Jian had figured out how to use the computer to call for help. He looked at the blood splatters on the back wall, some droplets still trickling slowly down. He then looked at the hole in the door. Jian had been facing that hole when she died.

She hadn't killed herself at all.

"Such a tragedy," Magnus said. "She tried suicide so many times, and finally pulled it off."

Andy reached down and pulled the pistol from Jian's hand. "So what do we do now?"

I kill you murdering fuckers, that's what we do now. The thought roared in Colding's head with million-decibel volume. He fought for control. Without a weapon he had no chance against either Magnus or Andy. Despite the rage, the hatred, the undeniable need to do *something,* he had to stay calm. Stay smart. Get Sara, Rhumkorrf and the others off the island. Once Sara was safe, then he could think about justice. He had to play along, buy some time.

"We can't tell the others she's dead," Colding said. "They'll lose confidence, and it could compromise the project."

Magnus looked down at him. A small smile toyed at the edge of his mouth. "So what are you saying, Bubbah, that we tell them she's just taking a nap?"

"Something like that. We tell them she's had a nervous breakdown. Everyone knows how stress messes with her. We'll tell them she needs a few days off. By then, hopefully, the ancestors will be delivered and we'll have our live animals."

Andy shook his head. "What about the gunshot?"

Colding gestured to the empty room. "You see anyone else coming to see what happened?"

"Colding's right," Magnus said. "We'll board up the door, say we had to break in to reach her when she flipped out. We'll lock up her room. No one gets in but Colding, because he's the only one she really trusted. Work for you, Bubbah?"

Colding nodded, feeling the extra burst of guilt brought on by Magnus's words.

"Good," Magnus said. "Colding, hurry up and bury her before anyone gets back."

Colding stood up. "Are you joking?"

"We can't leave the body here stinking up the place," Magnus said. "And I'm not putting her in the kitchen's walk-in freezer where Clayton can stumble into it. If you'd been better at your job, she'd still be alive, so this is *your* mess. Do it. Now."

Colding thought for a moment, still fighting to control the rage. All that mattered now was getting Sara off the island. He had to do whatever it took to make that happen.

"You're right," he said. "I'll take care of it."

Magnus turned and walked out the door. Andy followed him, leaving Colding alone with the corpse of his friend.

NOVEMBER 30: ENDGAME

Implantation +21 Days

MAGNUS SAT IN front of the secure terminal, thick fingers drumming a relentless pattern on the desktop — *babababump, babababump, babababump.* He waited for Danté's face to appear. While he waited, he read the email again.

> FROM: FARM GIRL
> TO: BIG POPPA
> SUBJECT: FUNNY STUFF AT HOME
> I HEARD ABOUT THAT FUNNY PRANK CALL TO DAD. CRAZY PRANK CALLERS!
> ROTFL! IT WAS A SILLY THING FOR THE PRANKSTER TO DO. DAD'S GUYS AT
> THE OFFICE ARE GOING TO TRACK THAT DOWN. WILL TAKE FIVE DAYS AT
> LEAST, SIX AT THE MOST. OH, AND I WOULDN'T TAKE THE CAR. DAD'S
> LOOKING FOR IT. LOOKING HARD.
> TTYL — FARM GIRL

It was over now. Even Danté had to see that. No place left to run. Taking the C-5 out again was a crapshoot at best, and even if they got it off the island undetected, they didn't have any more secret facilities. Fischer would have access to satellite coverage. He'd have people watching. He couldn't see everywhere at once, granted, but the word would be out about the C-5 — no more buying off air traffic controllers. If the C-5 passed near an airport radar system, even a small airport, that might be it.

Five days at best, *maybe* six.

Finally, the Genada logo disappeared, replaced by his brother's panicky face.

"Magnus, what the hell is going on? My computer guys told me our system called USAMRIID?"

"It was Jian," Magnus said. "She hacked into the secure terminal, used your end to call Fischer." He watched Danté's face, the predictable wave of emotions — disbelief, anger, then anxiety.

"What . . . what did she tell him?"

"The usual chitchat. What she had for lunch, ancestor research, that kind of thing. The only piece of luck was she didn't get a chance to give our location."

"You broke the connection in time?"

"You could put it that way, sure."

"You . . . you didn't," Danté said. "Magnus, *please* tell me you didn't."

Magnus said nothing.

"But she's the whole project. You idiot! What the fuck are we going to do without her?"

Magnus was the boots on the ground, making real-time decisions, saving Genada's ass, and Danté was calling *him* an idiot?

"So what now?" Danté screamed, shaking his fist at a camera hundreds of miles away. "That's just a brilliant business decision on your part, you fucking *psycho.* What the hell do we do now?"

"We cut our losses," Magnus said. "We cover our trail, move on to the next opportunity."

"What do you mean, *cut our losses?*"

"Big brother, you'd better pull your head out of your ass and do it quick. Don't you get it? *Jian called Fischer.* He wants Colding and Rhumkorrf. He thinks he'll get them to roll over so he can nail us on other charges. But when we give Colding and Rhumkorrf to Fischer, we make sure they won't talk. Ever. He set up the game this way, not us. He gets what he asked for, and the G8 know without a doubt that Genada is out of the transgenic game. That's all the governments really want. Our lawyers unfreeze the accounts. Presto chango, we move on."

Danté leaned in toward the camera until his face filled up the screen. "We can't do that! Those are our people, and we're *so close*! Once the ancestors are born, the public and press won't let anyone get in our way. We've *won,* we just need a few more days!"

Magnus kept his face expressionless, but inside he felt a rare spurt of sadness. Poor Danté. Never able to make the decisions that had to be made.

Danté's face lit up, like the answer to the world's problems had just flashed in his head. It made him look like a special-ed kid who just caught a bug after hours of failed attempts. "Manitoba! Listen, let's move the C-5 to Manitoba. I'll have crews start building facilities that can hold something the size of a tiger."

Magnus nodded. Sure. Why not? "Okay, brother. How do you want to do this?"

"Let's think it out. There's a major blizzard coming across Lake Superior tonight. The fringes of it are probably already hitting Black Manitou. Our weather report says that's going to last the better part of two days, and there's another storm right behind it. I assume you talked to Farm Girl?"

"Got an email from her," Magnus said. "According to her, we have five days."

"Perfect," Danté said. "I'll have to do some travel jumping to lose Fischer's men first. I'll be at Black Manitou in four days, as soon as the second storm fades a bit, with flight plan and strategy in hand. Okay?"

"How big are these storms?"

Danté reached for his keyboard. The picture changed to a weather map of Michigan. The land was brown, the water was blue, and the two-fisted storm was an angry green mass hung like a massive shroud over the northern shore of Lake Superior.

"Well well well," Magnus said. "That *is* a big storm."

The picture switched back to Danté's face. "Almost hurricane-class winds. Nobody will fly in that, and any boat will be a death trap. Just give me four days, Magnus. I'll be there on December fourth. We'll find a way to get the C-5 out of there, in secret, and to Manitoba. We *have* to find a way."

Magnus nodded. "Four days? I think I can handle that."

"Wonderful," Danté said. "You'll see, little brother, we'll pull through this, *together.*"

Magnus smiled, then disconnected. Family was such a funny thing. You can pick who you fuck, who you kill, but you can't pick your own brother.

Fly to Genada headquarters? In a massive plane that Fischer was looking for? Danté had lost it.

Magnus called up the computer's password program, locking out all access except for his own. When he finished, he left the security office and headed for the hangar.

COLDING WIPED THE back of his hand across his forehead. It just smeared dirt on his skin more than it wiped away the sweat. How had it come to this? How?

He bent to scoop up a last shovelful of dirt, dumped it, and patted it down. For all of her genius, for an intellect that should have been celebrated all across the world and in the history books forever and ever, Liu Jian Dan ended up in a shallow, frozen, unmarked grave.

Now she would be nothing more than carbon.

It had to be a shallow grave. Hard as hell to dig through that dirt. He'd pickaxed and shoveled through about eighteen inches of frozen soil. Below that, the ground temperature must have been above freezing, because he saw no more ice crystals. His arms started to give out at four feet deep, so he'd stopped and placed her inside. She wasn't going to be here for long. He'd make sure of that. Soon, snow would cover the broken dirt, and the grave would vanish. But he could find her again. He'd buried her in a small clearing near a single birch sapling that hadn't quite reached ten feet tall.

He lifted the pickax, looked at it, wondered what it would be like to swing the point into Magnus Paglione's head. *Soon enough.* He set it down and pulled on his parka. From the pocket, he pulled out a can of Dr Pepper.

"I'm sorry, Jian. I failed you."

That was all the eulogy he could muster.

Colding gently set the can of Dr Pepper on the pile of loose dirt, shouldered the pickax and shovel, then started the walk back to the mansion.

NOVEMBER 30: A HOTSHOT LIKE YOU

SARA SAT IN the lounge, curled up on a leather chair with a blanket over her legs. She was halfway through the now beat-up printout of *Hot Dusk*. Without Colding to hang out with for the past few days, she'd spent her free time reading Gunther's novel. Not really her thing, but it was fun to read a book by someone she knew. Clearly, though, written by a guy — ruby penises? Seriously?

She liked the book, but her eyes merely grazed over the words, marking the brief intervals between long looks out the window toward the angry water and the ice-covered rocks. The hazy afternoon sun hid behind clouds that blended from gray to a road-mud black at the horizon.

Colding walked into the lounge. Her face lit up, but she saw no return smile. He looked dirty, rumpled and chilled to the bone. His pants were soaked around the legs and streaked with dark, crumbly dirt. He walked straight toward her and stood, looking down. She'd never seen such an expression on his face: a look of anger and concentration and fear all mashed up into one.

"What are you reading?"

He knew exactly what she was reading. He had given it to her. "Um . . . Gunther's book."

"Yeah? Is it good?" He held out his hand. So odd. She handed him the manuscript. He took the pages, then they slipped out of his hands. He bent to pick them up, pushing the loose pages together again.

"Sorry," he said. He handed her the manuscript. "Actually, I'll have to check it out another time. I have some more work to do. Later."

He turned and walked away without another word. She set the book in her lap, and her finger brushed a small piece of paper barely sticking out of the top of the stack. A piece of paper that hadn't been there a second ago.

Sara casually flipped to that page and read the small note he'd slipped into the manuscript.

*MAGNUS KILLED JIAN. I JUST BURIED HER. I THINK HE ALSO KILLED ERIKA.
WE'RE IN A LOT OF TROUBLE. ACT NORMAL. WE MAY HAVE TO MAKE A MOVE
VERY SOON. BE READY TO DO WHAT I TELL YOU WITHOUT HESITATION. YOUR
LIFE DEPENDS ON IT. EAT THIS NOTE SO MAGNUS DOESN'T FIND IT.*

Her eyes seemed to fall out of focus. She blinked, then read it again.
Jian . . . *dead*?
And Erika Hoel, murdered?
Peej wouldn't joke about something like this. Not about murder. Holy *shit*.
As casually as she could, Sara crumpled the note. It was hard not to look up at the cameras, one mounted in each corner of the room. She brought her hand to her mouth and coughed. Mouth filled with the taste of paper, she coughed a few more times, the hand in front of her mouth hiding her furious chewing. She swallowed.
Sara felt a sudden urge to gather up her crew. Run a full check on the C-5 and make sure everything was shipshape. If she had to move quickly, she didn't want any unexpected trouble from the plane. She put the book down and calmly started toward Alonzo's room.

SARA, ALONZO, CAPPY and Miller trudged through the snow, walking the half mile from the mansion to the hangar. The heavy black clouds had closed the distance, pushing the gray aside like a broom slowly sweeping dust. The first flakes of snow swirled around in crazy spirals. More would be coming, and soon.
"You gonna tell us what's up?" Alonzo said, his shoulders in their usual cold-weather position high up at his ears. "Do you really expect us to believe you want a *surprise inspection*?"
"Quit your bitching, 'Zo," Sara said. "Just get it done."
"You're full of shit, boss," Miller said.
"Yeah," Cappy said. "Full of shit."
She stopped. So did they. The snow swirled around them. She looked each of them in the eye. Her friends. Her family. "Do you guys trust me?"
All three nodded.
"Then do the inspection, and don't ask any more questions." She turned and walked toward the hangar. Her friends followed. The less the boys knew, the less chance of someone slipping up, tipping their hand to Magnus. If he had killed Jian, he wouldn't think twice about whacking the C-5 crew.

They entered the plane, leaving the growing wind to howl outside. Once inside, Sara stopped to give everyone instructions.

"Miller, Cappy, do a status check on the flight harnesses for each cow." The Twins exchanged a glance.

"Just in case, right?" Miller said.

"Yeah," Cappy said. "In case we had to *hypothetically* fly in bad weather?"

Sara nodded. The Twins nodded back, then quickly and quietly went about their duties. Sara walked down the aisle between the cows, Alonzo at her side.

"Know what?" he said. "I have this crazy urge to do the preflight checklist."

"I'd start in the lab," Sara said. "You know, make sure all the equipment is locked down. Just in case."

"Just in case, right. Because far be it from me to tell you that storm coming in is going to be a high-toned son of a bitch."

"No way we'd fly out in that," Sara said. "But after the storm passes . . . anyway, doesn't hurt to be prepared."

"Say no more, *mon capitaine*." Alonzo walked to Tim's lab area and got started.

Sara moved through the barn toward the fore ladder, walking past the cows, suddenly very annoyed with the ever-present smell of cattle and the stink of cow shit. Alonzo was right. That storm *was* a high-toned son of a bitch, and by the time they prepped the C-5 for flight it would be right on top of them. They couldn't safely bust out until tomorrow, when the weather broke. That gave her one night to talk Colding into leaving.

She climbed the front ladder, reached the top and walked into the cockpit —

— to find Magnus Paglione sitting in the comm chair. He smiled at her. The cockpit lights played off his freshly shaved head. Sara's heart beat double time. Adrenaline shivered through her body.

"Sara, are you okay? You look like you've just seen a ghost."

"You scared the piss out of me, Mister Paglione. What the hell are you doing in here?"

Magnus shrugged. "Just checking out the plane, making sure everything was in good shape. You don't mind if your boss checks up on you, do you, Sara?"

She forced a smile. "Of course not."

"Is it still getting nasty outside?"

Sara felt sweat trickling down her armpits. Maybe he'd decided she knew too much. Maybe he was here to kill her, too. "Yes sir, still nasty. Wind is already picking up. That storm will be on top of us real fast."

"I'll bet it would be difficult to fly this big bird in weather like that."

Sara nodded, perhaps a little too enthusiastically, grateful to have an actual subject to discuss. "Oh *hell* yes. Taking the C-5 up now would be downright stupid."

"But you could do it," Magnus said. He stood up and walked closer, breaking the three-foot cushion. The killer stared down at her. This close to him, all alone, she felt like a child, home from school after another disciplinary incident, waiting for her father to make her go fetch the belt.

No, not a child . . . she felt like an insect.

Magnus reached up slowly and brushed a flake of snow off her shoulder. "I bet a hotshot like you *could* fly this beast into that storm."

Her voice came out small and thin. "I . . . yeah . . . we could do it. You know, in an emergency, I suppose."

Magnus smiled. "Well, consider this an emergency. Danté has intel that Colonel Fischer could be here as early as tomorrow morning. You're bugging out tonight."

Sara stared up at him, fear vanishing in the face of swelling anger. "You can't be serious, Magnus. I wasn't yanking your chain about that storm."

"I'm serious, too," Magnus said. He leaned down. Sara couldn't help but flinch a little as his scarred face, with its odd violet eyes, stopped only inches from hers. She smelled Yukon Jack on his breath.

"I want you flying off this island by twenty-thirty hours," he said. "Not a second later, you got that?"

His voice was no longer the smooth, calm monotone she'd heard all this time. Now it crackled with authority, a voice that had undoubtedly ordered men to attack, to shoot, to kill.

"Yes sir." The words came out of her mouth of their own volition.

Magnus stepped back, then nodded once with the flair of a Prussian officer snapping his boot heels together. He slipped past her and out of the cockpit.

Sara shivered. Maybe the storm wouldn't be as bad as she thought. And even if it were, it had to be better than being stuck here with Magnus Paglione.

BOOK FOUR

FLIGHT OF THE
C-5

"YOU TWO FUCKTARDS must be on crack to send us up in this weather."

Sara. Such a way with words. And yet Colding did, indeed, feel like a Grade-A Fucktard, because sending her up in said weather was the only way he could think of to get her to safety. Like that made any sense — get her to safety by putting her in severe danger.

Magnus drove Clayton's Bv206. Colding sat in the passenger seat, Sara in the back. That's how bad and how fast the storm had hit — they needed the Nuge to drive down the half-mile road from the mansion to the hangar. Colding had seen many winter storms, but never one from the vantage point of an island in the middle of Lake Superior. Wind seemed to shake the very ground, the clenched fist of a roaring elemental god. The snow didn't fall, really — it permeated. Thick sheets blew in all directions, including up. And this was just the front end of a killing blizzard that had already cut visibility to a mere twenty yards.

Sara leaned forward over the front bench seat. "Let me make this clear. See this snow blowing fuckall over the place? In the air force we'd ground all flights."

"You're not in the air force," Magnus said. "I got your point the third *and* fourth times you said it. The tenth is just overkill." Magnus wore a big black parka, the hood pulled so far forward it hid his face. Colding couldn't help but think he looked like a modernized version of the Grim Reaper — Death drives a Bv206.

Hazy lights grew visible as the Hummer crept forward. Visibility was so bad they were fifty yards away before Colding could make out the monstrous plane's tail, and even then the front of the plane remained hidden by the storm. In the whipping haze, the black plane's dimensions looked even larger, almost otherworldly.

Magnus stopped the Bv206 a few yards from the C-5. The wind's demonic shriek even drowned out the idling jet engines. Colding, Magnus and Sara hurried out and scrambled up the rear ramp, fighting the wind all the way.

Most of the plexiglass stalls held an *extremely* pregnant cow, each suspended in a flight harness, hooves dangling just a half inch off the ground. IV tubes ran into each of their necks. The animals seemed surprisingly calm. Their vacant expressions showed no awareness of the danger around them, of the gale-force winds that would soon shake the plane like a martini mixer.

Sara pulled back her parka hood. Short blond hair stuck up in all directions, much like it did after several hours of lovemaking. "We have to wait." She looked at them both, but Colding knew the words were meant for him. She was begging him to back her play. "I'm telling you it's *insane* to fly out in weather like this. We could lose the whole project, not to mention the collective asses of me and my crew."

Why didn't she get it? This was her shot to get off the island, away from Magnus. "Fischer could be on the way," Colding said. "We have to get you out of here now."

"Come *on*, guys," Sara said. "It's not like anyone is going to land here in this weather. Just wait for the main part of the storm to blow over. We'll fly out while it's shit weather, but still doable."

"I'm *done* with this," Magnus said, his voice suddenly so loud even the docile cows turned to look. "You fly out of here right now."

Colding mentally begged her to stop complaining, to just play ball.

"I refuse," Sara said. "Flights are my call, we're waiting. I just don't like it."

"Shut *up*," Colding snapped. "Nobody said you had to fucking *like it*. Just do your goddamn job and fly the plane!"

She stared at him, her eyes showing more than a bit of betrayal. Colding instantly hated himself, but he had to get her off the island before her complaints made Magnus change his mind.

Magnus smiled, looking from Sara, to Colding, back to Sara again. "And remember, princess — total radio silence. If Fischer is out there, we can't tip our hand. No radio until you're thirty miles out from Manitoba, got it?"

Sara nodded.

"Good," Magnus said. "You're flying southwest to get out of the storm as quickly as possible. From there you'll circle around the storm, then northeast to avoid the radar at Thunder Bay International. After that you'll head for the home office. Jian, Gunther, Colding, Andy and I are staying here for now. Colding, let's go."

Sara looked uncomfortable at the mention of Jian's name, but she said nothing.

Colding followed Magnus out of the cage and down the ramp. Sara's safety, and the safety of the others, now rested squarely on her piloting skills.

A BRUTAL DOWNDRAFT swatted the half-million-pound C-5 Galaxy, dropping the plane a rattling two hundred feet in the blink of an eye. Sara wondered — for the seventh time in the last fifteen minutes, by her count — if this was it. She pulled back on the yoke, fighting the hurricane-class winds. The gust abated as suddenly as it appeared, and she dragged the C-5 back to five thousand feet.

Alonzo looked white as a sheet, an impressive barometer of his nervous state considering his dark complexion. His head moved with sharp, bird-like movements as his eyes flitted from instrument to instrument.

"This is nuts," he said. "We've got to put her down."

"Where exactly would you like to do that? We're over the middle of Lake Superior."

A crosswind slapped the C-5, shaking it, rattling metal hard enough to make Sara's teeth clack. She'd flown in some bad shit before, but nothing like this. "We're here, 'Zo, and there's nothing we can do about it. Now quit whining and help me get through this."

If she could take a step back in time, maybe she'd have pulled her Beretta and taken her chances in a shoot-out rather than flying into this storm. Was Peej's note for real? Was Jian actually dead, or was that just a trick to motivate her to fly out in this ridiculous weather? Was he just using her again?

No. Couldn't be. He wanted to get her and the boys away from Magnus. Peej had no choice — Magnus had already killed Jian, which meant everyone else's life wasn't worth a plugged nickel. If this was her one chance to get off the island, to get her crew to safety, she had to take it.

The plane lurched right, yanking her body against her seat restraints. Even though the cows were another deck down, she heard them mooing, braying. The sound carried tangible terror. She shared the sentiment, wondering at the power of a storm that could knock the C-5 around with such ease.

Alonzo snapped a peek at the instrument panel, then looked at her, his eyes wide. "That last gust was sixty-two knots." Sweat drenched his face, but he kept his hands firmly on the yoke.

"Just be cool, 'Zo. Nothing to it."

She focused on the instruments. She didn't bother looking out the window; there was nothing to see but snow and ice.

THE C-5 FELL again, but only slightly this time. Compared with the roller-coaster ride of the past thirty minutes, the drop was barely noticeable.

"Wind down to forty knots," Alonzo said. He looked better, relieved. They were now on the blizzard's edge, still in significant danger, but it was nothing the C-5 couldn't handle.

"Cue the Barry Manilow," Sara said, "'cause it looks like we made it. I'd better see how the civvies handled that mess. Keep on this heading for another five minutes to get us some distance from the storm, then circle around it. See, 'Zo? I told you there was nothing to it."

He smiled sheepishly. "Right, boss, nothing to it as long as you don't mind wet-vaccing the poo streaks off my seat."

She grabbed the handset to the in-plane intercom. "Deck two, deck two; everything okay back there?"

Rhumkorrf's voice came back. "Are we quite finished with that tumultuous experience? I wouldn't exactly call that the friendly skies."

"You holding up okay, Doc?"

"I'm fine. I'm afraid I had some difficulty in retaining my preflight meal. I assume I am now free to mop about the cabin?"

Sara laughed. "Sure, Doc. Get yourself cleaned up. Don't worry about it — I almost blew chunks myself. How's Tim?"

"One of the cows fell out of the harness during flight. Tim is working on her."

"Bad?"

"Not good," Rhumkorrf said. "Not good at all."

"I'm coming down," Sara said, then put the handset back in the cradle. "Take over, 'Zo. I need to see what's going on down there."

COAT IN HAND, Sara descended the fore ladder. The second deck was a total mess. Two or three cabinets had popped open during the flight. Debris littered the lab like scientific shrapnel: scattered papers, sterile vacuum packs, broken test tubes and petri dishes. Miller scurried about the area, picking up loose equipment and cleaning up in general.

Pitiful cow sounds filled the air. Sound wasn't the only thing that escaped them — the lab smelled like a shithouse. Froth clung to the big animals' mouths and noses, glistening sweat covered their coats. Wide black eyes looked for a way out.

At the far end of the barn near the folded-up rear ramp, Sara saw an open door at stall three. Tim Feely and Cappy were in the aisle, Cappy kneeling and pushing all his upper-body weight on the cow's head to keep it still. Its eyes blinked spasmodically, its tongue lolled. Tim Feely had one knee pressed heavily on the cow's big neck. He held up a vial and tried to slide a syringe needle into it. Bright blood covered the sleeves of his jacket.

Sara ran to them. Standing up, the cows had a decent amount of room in their stalls — lying flat, hardly any. The cow lay on its right side, legs pointed toward the front of the plane. Blood seeped from the cow's ruptured stomach: a ragged, glistening tear ran from the udder almost to the sternum. A small, bloody, clawed foot hung from the tear, flopping limply in time with the cow's twitches. The fetuses. The *predator* fetuses. Holy shit . . . it hadn't seemed real until this second. If the cows gave birth, were the fetuses dangerous? No, even if they happened to be born at this very moment, they were still just babies.

The cow's chest rose and fell in an arrhythmic pattern. A crack in the stall wall told the story — the crack was where the harness's anchor used to be. The rough flying jostled the cow so much that the anchor ripped free and the cow fell, its overly pregnant belly splitting from the severe impact.

A sign, drawn in Magic Marker in Jian's scrawled handwriting, hung from the stall door. The sign said MISS PATTY MELT. Sara felt a sharp pang of loss for her murdered friend.

Tim kept trying to get the needle into the vial. The C-5 still shook and lurched from the storm, but not bad enough to make him miss like that.

"Tim-dog," Sara said, "you need some help with that?"

"I can handle it." His words sounded slurred.

Sara looked down at Cappy, who mouthed the words *he's drunk.*

Oh joy. Great timing, Tim.

He finally slid the needle into the vial, then drew back the plunger. A yellow fluid filled the hypo. He put the bottle in his pocket and flicked the syringe a few times, then gave the plunger a test push. Liquid shot out the needle.

"Hold her," Tim said, and knelt harder on the cow's neck. Sara leaned in next to Cappy, put her hands on the animal's head. Even a halfhearted twitch betrayed the cow's massive strength.

Tim grabbed at the IV line still stuck in the cow's neck. He slid the needle into a port on the IV line and pushed the plunger all the way down. The cow's twitching slowed, then stopped.

Sara watched Tim. The man didn't move, didn't breathe — he just stared at the cow. Finally, after a few seconds, relief washed over his face.

Tim stood and let out a long, cheek-puffing breath. "Well, time for a drink. I was getting very worried there for a—"

The cow lurched to life with an earsplitting bellow. A front hoof snapped out and hit Tim in his right knee, so fast and powerful it knocked the man's legs out from under him. He dropped, his legs in the aisle, his body falling into the stall and sliding down the cow's bloody, torn belly.

Sara dodged the kicking hoof and stuck her left arm into the stall to grab Tim's hand. She pulled and Tim started to scramble out, but the front leg came back hard, the hoof's sharp edge clipping Tim's forehead. His head snapped back, blood instantly pouring from his scalp and sheeting down his face. Sara kept her right hand on the stall wall for balance, her left locked on Tim's hand.

"Cappy, help me get him out of there!"

Cappy hopped up, his hands grasping either side of the open door. He raised his knees high and came down with his shins pinning the cow's front legs. A part of Sara's brain wanted to stop and applaud the brilliant move. Miss Patty Melt's struggles slowed. Cappy reached deeper into the stall and grabbed the front of Tim's jacket.

She and Cappy leaned back to pull Feely free. In the same instant, a bloody *thing* slid out of the cow's ruptured stomach. Sara saw a flash of wet red, a gaping, triangular mouth and long white teeth that *snapped* down on Cappy's left arm. The sound of cracking bones joined the cow's bellows, followed instantly by Cappy's agonized scream.

Within the tiny cage, the fifteen-hundred-pound cow thrashed about in a braying, blood-splashing panic. Tim flopped limply, unconscious, thrown about by the cow's torn body and its kicking rear legs. Cappy's right hand punched madly at the thing biting his left arm.

Sara drew her Beretta and fired at the cow's head, the gunshots thinly echoing through the confined space. The first bullet removed most of the lower jaw in a spray of blood and splintering bone. The second missed Miss Patty Melt's thrashing head and ripped through the floor. The third turned the cow's eye into a gaping red hole of negative space.

Miss Patty Melt convulsed harder, legs and hooves twitching violently. She let out a strange, sad yell that sounded achingly human, a noise Sara would never forget despite the horrors that were to follow in the coming days.

Sara dropped hard, planting her knees on Miss Patty Melt's muscular neck. She put the barrel in the cow's ear and pulled the trigger once more. Blood splashed up, splattering her coat, her face.

The cow stopped screaming.

Cappy did not.

His face contorted in agony, he punched madly with his right fist, raining blows down on the bloody creature locked on his left arm. "Let go let go!" He lurched back into the aisle, pulling the slimy, jaw-locked monstrosity all the way out of the cow's stomach.

Holy shit it's as big as he is holyshitholyshit. Sara reflexively jumped back a step, instinct screaming at her to stay away from the thing.

Suddenly Miller was there, throwing himself on the bloody creature, wrapping his arms around the thing. "Sara, *shoot* it!"

Sara put the barrel against the abomination's skinless head, angled the Beretta so the bullet wouldn't hit Cappy's arm, then pulled the trigger. A baseball-sized chunk erupted out of the skull, spraying blood and brains and bone.

The thing fell limp, its dead jaws opening just enough for Cappy to slide his ravaged arm off the embedded teeth.

Sara wiped the back of her hand across her face, scraping away wetness. Some of it remained, hot but rapidly cooling in the plane's frigid air.

The remaining cows lurched and bucked against their flight harnesses, probably driven to panic by the screams of Miss Patty Melt. Hooftips scraped the floor, filling the plane with a clicking, scratching chorus.

Sara saw Rhumkorrf in the veterinary area, holding tight to the edge of the lab table.

"Help . . . me," Cappy called out in a weak voice, drawing her attention back where it belonged.

"Got you, pal," Miller said. He leaned in to examine his best friend's wound.

Sara stood and took in the carnage — two wounded people, a huge cow, a dead thing the size of a Great Dane and more blood than a slaughterhouse.

"Miller, how bad is it?"

He moved so Sara could see Cappy's arm. She heard her own automatic gasp — the monster's teeth had broken Cappy's radius and ulna in several places. Blood spurted from the wound, spilling on his lap and on the floor where it mixed with the blood of the dead cow and the blood of the creature. His hand wobbled sickly each time Miller moved it, as if only a few strands of muscle kept it attached.

"We need help, fast," Miller said. He tore off his jacket and wrapped it around his friend's wound, trying to stop the bleeding with pressure. He looked at the bloody fetal corpse. "Sara, what the hell is that thing? 'Cause it sure as *fuck* ain't no cow!"

"It's dead, that's what it is," Sara said. "And as soon as we get out of this weather, we're opening the back doors and dumping every last one of these fucking cows out the rear ramp and into Lake Superior."

She rushed to an intercom panel and punched the *cockpit* button. "Alonzo, call Manitoba right away. We need an alternate landing site."

The speaker crackled with Alonzo's voice. "But Magnus ordered radio silence."

"Cappy's hurt bad. Get Manitoba on the line and tell them we need a landing site with medical facilities. We need it *now*. If they can't find us one, tell them we're heading for Houghton-Hancock."

"Got it."

Sara sprinted back to stall three, passing the still-anxious, still-lurching cows. Straps and buckles rattled, hooves clacked hard against thick plexiglass.

The dog-thing remained in the aisle, its blood spreading in a slowly expanding puddle. Redness clung to fur: white with black spots. The heavy, triangular head looked almost as large as the rest of the body. A strange growth stuck out of the back of the skull, like a single antelope horn but parallel to the stubby body. The growth wasn't bone, though; it looked flexible. Skin ran from the growth down to the bloody creature's back.

She tried to think, tried to process. She wasn't trained for this. *No one* was trained for this. She looked back to the vet lab, where Rhumkorrf was still standing, his hands locked on the black lab table.

"Doc! Get your ass over here, we've got wounded!"

He let go of the table with an obvious act of will, then jogged down the aisle. Sara couldn't bear to look at Cappy, so she focused on the fetus. She could see why Miss Patty Melt had kicked that way despite the poison coursing through her veins. Skinless little arms, still folded against its body, ended in paws with six-inch-long needle-claws.

That . . . thing, it didn't want to die. It felt the poison . . . it tried to get away.

Then Rhumkorrf was next to her, kneeling by Cappy and Miller, his knees dipping into puddles of mixed blood. He took one long look at the wound, then started pulling his belt out of his pants.

"Hold him," he said to Miller.

Rhumkorrf looped the belt around Cappy's arm, just above the horrific wound, then slid the tongue through the buckle. Miller grabbed Cappy's good arm and a shoulder. Sara reached over the top of Rhumkorrf and put her hands on the wounded man's ankles.

Rhumkorrf leaned close to Cappy's ear. "I have to put on the tourniquet to stop the bleeding. This is going to hurt very much, yes?"

Cappy's eyes remained squeezed shut, but he nodded.

"Hold him," Rhumkorrf said again, then firmly pulled the belt tight.

Cappy threw his head back and screamed.

Rhumkorrf tightened it further, then looped the free end of the belt around the arm and tied it fast. "Get him to the infirmary. I'll look at Tim and come up as soon as I can."

"Sara," Miller said. "Get Cappy's legs."

She turned her attention to the task at hand. They carried their wounded friend up the aisle, past the stalls to the lift. The elevator platform lowered. Still holding Cappy, she and Miller rode the lift to the second deck.

THEY LAID CAPPY down on the infirmary table. His blood trailed out the door all the way back to the lift, like some twisted version of Hansel and Gretel.

"This fucking *hurts*," he hissed through clenched teeth.

Miller ripped open a cabinet, pulled out gauze and an air splint. "Just hold tight, buddy. You'll be okay." He looked up at Sara. "We need that landing site, now."

Sara walked to the infirmary's intercom and pushed the *cockpit* button.

"'Zo, what's our status?"

No response.

She pushed the button again.

"'Zo, talk to me."

Still no response.

Then she smelled it . . . *smoke.*

She felt the rush of yet another adrenaline surge and sprinted down the short hall to the cockpit.

Thin tendrils of white curled up from the closed cockpit door. She wrenched the door open. Smoke hung in the air, expanding the hazy glow of the multicolored control lights.

"'Zo! You okay?"

"Where the *hell* have you been?" Alonzo kept his hands on the yoke, not bothering to look back at her. "The radio is out. As soon as I tried to transmit I heard a pop. I tried calling you, but whatever it was also took out the intercom. I put out the fire. We're okay, but we're deaf and mute until I can get in there and fix it."

A *pop* . . . as soon as he tried to use the radio.

"Oh, fuck," she said quietly.

She tried to remember where she'd seen Magnus. She looked at the comm station, under the observer's seat, all over the cockpit. Nothing.

Alonzo turned in his chair to look back. "Sara, what are you doing? What the fuck . . . you're covered in blood!"

"Not worried about that now," she said, then ran out the door. She ran into the bunk room, looked under the metal bunks, ripped mattresses off and threw them. Nothing. She tried the head, in the small supply cabinets, under the tiny washbasin . . . still nothing.

Please, please, please, let me be wrong.

She moved to the game room. Her eyes instantly fell on the flat-panel TV. She felt a tingling on her scalp as she ran to it, angled her body to look behind it.

There, wedged between the TV and the hull wall, was more plastic explosive than she'd ever seen in her life.

SARA STARED AT the bomb. So many wires, connected to the hull, to the back of the TV, to the floor. She knelt, careful not to jostle anything, eyes scanning until she found it — a small, LCD timer that read 9:01 . . . 9:00 . . . 8:59 . . . 8:58.

Calm down calm down keep it cool if you don't think clear you die.

Colding and Magnus weren't sending the C-5 to Manitoba; they were sending it to the bottom of Lake Superior. By the time the storm blew over, there would be no trace of the C-5 or anything in it. A thousand feet of water would cover the wreckage forever.

They couldn't even bail out: in this storm their parachutes would foul and they'd drop. If hitting at terminal velocity didn't kill them instantly, drowning in ice-cold water would follow shortly. Even if they managed to get into a raft, they'd be up against twenty-foot swells and seventy-knot winds. SOS or no SOS, no one would reach them in time.

She took a deep breath. *Think. Stay rational, think.* There had to be a way out. Sara synchronized her watch with the bomb — at 9:12 P.M., the plastique would rip the C-5 to shreds. She didn't know anything about defusing a bomb. Neither did her crew. All those extra wires . . . if they moved the bomb, she had no doubt it would blow instantly. She could start pulling wires, but only as a desperate final option. She sprinted to the cockpit where she grabbed a flight map and threw it down on the small table in the navigator's section. Her hands smoothed the map, accidentally smearing blood across the paper.

"'Zo, where are we?"

"Halfway through our circle around the storm. We're only a hundred miles from Houghton-Hancock."

She traced the path on the map. "We're not going to make it to Houghton-Hancock. There's a bomb onboard, we've got nine minutes to live."

Alonzo quickly set the autopilot and scrambled out of his seat to join Sara. "Nine minutes? Who planted a bomb?"

"Had to be Magnus. I saw him in here a few hours before takeoff." She checked her watch: 9:04 P.M. *Eight* minutes. They couldn't reach Houghton-Hancock. Magnus's crazy circular flight path had them dead smack in the middle of Lake Superior — they couldn't reach anything.

Almost anything . . . there was one place they could reach.

"Take us back into the storm," she said. "Gun it, full throttle. We're going back to the island."

"*Back* to the island? Where *Magnus* is? No fucking way!"

Sara's composure disintegrated. She reached out with her blood-smeared right hand and grabbed the collar of Alonzo's parka. "We don't have a choice! Look at the goddamn map. We can't get anywhere else before the bomb blows up."

"But he's trying to kill us—"

Sara's left hand joined her right. She shook his collar with each word, jerking the slick, down-filled fabric.

"I . . . *know* . . . *that*! They only turn on the radar for scheduled takeoffs or landings, remember? It's off, they won't know we're coming, so take us back into the storm!"

She released his collar. He blinked a few times, then he scrambled back to the copilot's chair. The engines whined. She held the table while the C-5 banked.

"Heading back into the storm," Alonzo said. "But they don't need radar to know we're there. Even with this shit visibility, they'll see us land on the airstrip."

There had to be a way, something. Her eyes scanned the map . . . then she remembered Clayton's words. *There.* That would work, would have to, or they would all die. She carried the map to Alonzo. "We're not landing on the strip." Before he could ask where, her finger jabbed out their destination. He took one look at the map, then looked up, a shocked expression on his face.

"Rapleje Bay? No way."

"It's a mile long and frozen over."

"We're landing on *ice*, ice we won't see until we're less than a hundred feet from it, and we don't know how thick it is. I'm taking us to the landing strip, we'll have to shoot it out with Magnus."

"He's got a fucking *Stinger missile*! The strip is only a half mile from the mansion; if he hears us coming in, all he needs is thirty seconds to blow us out of the sky. 'Zo, if you want to live, you've got five minutes to put us on that bay! Land it, then help Miller get Cappy the fuck out fast."

She ran out of the cockpit, tossing the map back on the table as she left. If they reached the bay in five minutes, that would give them two minutes to get off and get clear. She ran down the hall, back into the bloody infirmary. Miller was still working on the unconscious Cappy.

"I stopped the bleeding," Miller said. "Get Doc Rhumkorrf up here already, like *now*."

"No time," Sara said. "Listen carefully. There's a bomb onboard. Strap Cappy down, we're going back into the blizzard, back to Black Manitou. Emergency landing on a frozen bay. Our chances are shitty, but it's the only option we have. Do you understand?"

"Yes ma'am."

"Good. When we hit the deck, 'Zo will help you get Cappy out. Move fast or all of you die."

She took off through the upper-deck lab and scrambled down the aft ladder. Rhumkorrf and the unconscious Tim were still in stall number three. Rhumkorrf had found some surgical thread and was finishing up stitches on Tim's forehead. Even done in crappy flying conditions, the stitches looked tight and tiny.

Rhumkorrf spoke without looking away from his work. "Tim could have internal injuries. We need a hospital immediately, we can't move him."

"I don't care," Sara said. "We're making an emergency landing, and I need Tim in a crash chair, right now."

Rhumkorrf looked up. "Emergency . . . what's going on?"

"Magnus canceled the project, and us along with it. There's a bomb onboard that goes off in six minutes."

Rhumkorrf's jaw dropped. "A bomb? That doesn't make any sense. The Pagliones have invested millions in this project!"

"And now they're cutting their losses."

"But what about the cows, they—"

"*Fuck* the cows! Don't you get it? There *is* no more project. Magnus wants all of this gone, and us with it. Now, go to the cabinets in Tim's lab. Emergency supplies are there. We have to hide in winter woods for I don't know how long. Find blankets and jackets, *move*!"

Rhumkorrf scrambled to the cabinets, leaving Sara with the unconscious Tim Feely. The man looked seriously fucked up. He was still lying next to Miss Patty Melt, soaked in her blood, his head on the cow's rear legs, his calves on her front legs. The skin beneath his twenty-odd stitches looked red and swollen.

Oh shit, his *knee*. No blood, but it had swollen so much that the pant leg material looked tight and strained. Didn't take a doctor to see that Tim Feely wouldn't be able to walk on his own. She grabbed his hands and pulled the unconscious man into a sitting position. She squatted, slid her arms under his armpits and around his back, then stood. Tim rose up like a limp marionette. Hell, he wasn't that heavy at all, maybe a buck forty-five soaking wet.

She clutched his right shoulder, then slid her left arm between his legs and pulled him onto her shoulders in a fireman's carry. Sara carefully stepped over the cow's legs and into the aisle, then up to the flight chairs. She set him down gently and fastened his restraints.

She checked her watch — 9:08 . . . four minutes.

Sara ran across the aisle to Rhumkorrf, who was making piles of first-aid kits, MREs and blankets. They needed everything they could carry. *If* they came down undetected, and *if* they survived the landing, the island was big enough to stay hidden, but for how long?

She found duffel bags and tossed one to Rhumkorrf. He started cramming his piles inside.

"Why?" he said. "Why in God's name would they wipe out the project?"

"Just pack, Doc."

She'd have to take out Magnus, get him before he knew they were back. He had that arsenal in the mansion's basement — if he and Andy and Gunther went on the offensive, Sara and her boys didn't stand a chance.

"They can't do this," Rhumkorrf said. "They can't cancel my project, I simply won't allow it."

"Doc, shut the fuck up!"

She'd have to start at Sven Ballantine's place. It was the closest house to Rapleje Bay. Get Cappy inside, probably take Sven prisoner. No way of knowing what the old man knew, or whose side he was on.

What about Peej? What side is he on?

She had to face facts: Colding was part of the project, and yet *his* ass wasn't on the bomb-laden C-5.

The plane suddenly tilted up. Sara held on to the cabinet door as supplies skidded across the floor. Rhumkorrf fell back and rolled into the black lab table. The cows' big bodies strained against their harnesses, and once again the lower deck filled with their bellowing.

"Doc, you okay?"

"Fine! I'll get more supplies."

"No, get in your chair, now."

The plane heaved sideways even as Rhumkorrf scrambled to the crash chairs and started buckling in. Supplies flew. Sara checked her watch just as the digital number changed to 9:10 P.M. — two minutes to live. They'd be landing any second. She zipped the duffel bags tight and started carrying them to the crash chairs.

The plane simultaneously bucked to port and dropped hard. Sara felt weightlessness for a second. The floor shrank away, then came up fast and slammed into her face. Dull pain filled her brain like an alcoholic buzz. She couldn't focus. She blinked a few times, tried to stand.

Someone calling her name. Rhumkorrf. Sara shook her head, her thoughts slowly coming back into focus.

"Thirty seconds to landing." That sounded like Alonzo ... but he was ... in the cockpit.

"Sara! Get up!" Rhumkorrf, screaming. "Don't move, I'm coming."

"Stay there!" Her wits returned in a flash. Another drop like that might knock him out as well.

"Twenty seconds." Alonzo's voice, coming over the speakers. He must have fixed the intercom. She'd lost precious time. The plane dropped and lifted underneath her. She ignored the duffel bags and crawled, *had* to crawl, because there was no way she could stay on her feet. She pulled herself into the chair even as it seemed to move like a wild animal.

"Ten seconds," Alonzo called out in a shockingly neutral tone.

She slid the first clip home, head screaming, throbbing, hands slow to comply.

"Five ..."

... you won't make it when the plane hits, you'll be thrown around, you'll die ...

"Four ..."

Keep it calm, just find the straps, buckle in ...

"Three ..."

... we'll crack right through the ice, we'll drown in freezing water ...

"Two ..."

Her hands found the final buckle, the harness clicked shut.

"One ..."

... this is it, oh why didn't you save me, Colding, why why wh—

The free-fall elevator ride ended with a smashing jolt that jarred every atom of her body. They'd come in just a little too steep. Her brain ticked off assumed damage — no way the nose cone would open, which meant the front ramp was useless. Had the fuel tanks ruptured? Would they catch and fill the plane with fire? Would the C-5 turn sideways and roll?

The jolts and bounces threw her against her harness. Five eternal seconds rolled by, filled with the shrieks of creaking metal grinding hard against unforgiving ice.

Momentum pulled her harder against the straps as the C-5 slowed. Ten seconds later the skid ended and her body fell back into the seat. She snapped open her harness and checked her watch: still 9:10 P.M. It had felt like a tortured eternity, but the crash landing had taken less than a minute.

She sprinted aft, down the aisle, the sound of braying cows and their lightly kicking hooves filling her ears. She slapped the button to lower the rear hatch. Hydraulic gears whined as the rear doors opened and the metal loading ramp began to slowly unfold and descend. Wind-driven snow blew inside like a billowing gas. The gale howled, almost with delight, as if it had only been waiting for another chance to get at the people inside the huge plane. Sara turned away from the oncoming blizzard and grabbed the intercom.

"'Zo, are you okay?"

"I'm fine. Holy shit, we're alive!"

"Help Miller get Cappy down here, move move move!"

Sara sprinted back up the aisle to the flight seats. Rhumkorrf was already up, walking on wobbly legs, leaning on the lab table as he stumbled toward the rear ramp. She passed him by and rushed to Tim, unbuckling the unconscious man and again lifting him into a fireman's carry. She stood, shouldering his weight . . .

. . . and felt heavy steps vibrating through the floor. She turned to face the rear ramp — a cow, huge and black and white and insane with wide-eyed panic, barreled down the bay toward her. Sara ran across the aisle to the lab table and lunged on top, the move awkward thanks to Tim's extra weight. She lost her grip on the man and he slid over the other side, crashing to the deck. The cow rushed by, hooves slamming on the rubberized deck, its big body grazing her feet before she pulled them up past the table's edge. The cow ran past the crash chairs and smashed into the folded-up forward ramp so hard the entire plane shook from the impact. It stumbled back, then turned violently, cutting itself on one of the chairs. Blood sheeted the black-and-white fur and splattered on the floor as the cow ran the other way, toward the still-lowering rear ramp.

Screaming, hurricane-force winds poured through the twenty-foot rear opening, filling the cargo bay with billowing snow. Two more cows raged toward the ramp, toward freedom from the terror-filled plane. They pushed against each other in a struggle to get out. One cow's hoof fouled on the corpse of Miss Patty Melt; it fell hard, the foreleg snapping like a gunshot. The creature bellowed in fear and pain, struggling to get up, to get out, but the broken leg wouldn't support its efforts.

Sara saw Rhumkorrf moving from stall to stall, opening the gates and slapping the harness release buttons. The heavy canvas harnesses lowered slowly an inch or two, putting the cows' hooves firmly on the deck, then dropped away, straps falling limply to the floor. The animals bolted out of the narrow stalls and stampeded for the ramp.

"What the hell are you doing?" Sara shouted over the screeching gale and the braying cattle.

But Rhumkorrf didn't answer. Wind blew his comb-over back and forth. Some of the cows ran to the ramp. Others stood in place, confused, frightened.

She heard the whine of the lift machinery from above. The platform started to lower. On the metal grate she saw Alonzo and Miller standing, each grasping an end of the gurney that held Cappy. The lift would bring them down on the other side of the aisle opposite the lab table.

"Sara!" Alonzo screamed. She could barely hear him over the wind and the cows. "What the *fuck*?"

"We gotta move, come on!"

The lift slowly lowered, exposing their feet, their shins, their knees.

A panicked cow ran the wrong way, away from the open rear hatch. It slammed against the black lab table, tilting it, dumping Sara on top of Tim. The cow hit the table again and it fell. Sara got her hands up just in time, catching the heavy table's edge before it smashed into her. Her muscles strained as she tried to push the table clear.

She heard a metallic rattle, the alarmed shouts of men, a bellow of animal pain, heard the lift's whine stop, then restart.

No, Alonzo was taking it back up!

Sara screamed and forced her shaking arms to push harder. The table slid back a little and she was able to swing her legs free before she let go. The heavy black top hit the floor like a guillotine. The now vertical table-top sheltered her from the bleeding, insane, fifteen-hundred-pound cow.

"Alonzo, come back!"

Up above, Sara saw just one foot move off the grate, then nothing. She was too late. The lift was back on the upper deck, a corner dripping blood where the cow had slammed into it. Alonzo was taking Cappy to the aft ladder, looking for a safer way down. Sara threw a glance at her watch: 9:11.

One minute.

How much of that last minute had already gone by? Five seconds? Ten? Time was up. Sara felt tears — hot and sudden and uncontrollable — run down her cheeks.

Her crew wouldn't make it.

No time no time no time . . .

Tim was back on her shoulders before she even gave it a thought. She stepped past the table and ran into a stampede. Bellowing black-and-white bodies heaved around her, hitting her, knocking her from side to side, but she *refused* to fall, *refused* to die.

No time no time no time . . .

She felt the footing change as she moved from the rubberized floor to the rear ramp's echoing steel, then her feet splashing into icy, inch-deep water. The C-5's interior lights lit up a cone of swirling snow and a wide, long, wet gouge torn into the snow-covered ice. Water bubbled up from thousands of cracks, a shimmering, spreading surface that ate the falling flakes. Sheets of white soared up and around her, finding ways into her eyes and mouth.

How much longer how many seconds not gonna make it notgonnamakeit . . .

She turned left, past the gouge, found herself fighting through waist-deep snow. She didn't feel the cold, didn't hear the bellowing cows, she just *moved*, moved away from the plane, away from death, toward life.

We're going to die anyway any second now any—

A bang and a roar and she flew through blast-furnace heat. She hit hard and skidded face-first over the snow-covered ice.

Sara struggled to her feet and looked back. The blast had shredded the C-5 just behind the cockpit, and also behind the wings — Magnus had planted a second bomb. Blinding flames shot up thirty feet, lighting up the stormy, frozen bay with flickering brilliance.

Tim lay to her left, prone and motionless. Her crew was either dead or burning to death. There wasn't a fucking thing she could do about it. There was only one person left to save — Tim Feely. Again he went up on her shoulders in the now-practiced move. When had she thought him light? She carried his deadweight, forcing half steps through the waist-deep snow.

Another explosion erupted behind her as the fuel tanks blew. She was farther away this time, and therefore spared the shock wave's crushing effects. She turned for one last, haunted look. The flaming C-5 seemed to twitch like a dying antelope under a lion's killing bite. It took Sara a moment to realize why — the plane was falling through the cracked surface. The tail went first, its weight finally too much for the thinning ice. There was a deep, reverberating *snap* as the sheet gave way, then the groan of metal grinding against the frozen surface, then the hiss of that same red-hot metal sliding into the water. Within seconds the tail was gone.

Sara stared, her eyes hunting through the blinding snow, hoping to see a miracle, hoping to see one of her friends. They might have gotten out, might be on the other side of the plane.

More vibrating cracks. The middle of the broken plane dropped a bit. It stayed on top for a moment, held up by burning wings pressed flat against the ice, then the wings groaned, bent, and finally snapped free at their bases as the fuselage slid into the water. The massive Boeing engines went next, cracking through, dragging most of the remaining bits of wing with them. Parts remained, scattered about the bay's surface, but the snow was already accumulating, covering them in white.

The C-5 had all but vanished. In four or five hours the crash site would be nothing but misshapen white drifts. Sara heard a final hiss as the last piece of glowing metal slid into the water, then nothing but the sound of the blizzard.

No, there was one more sound — the faint call of a mooing cow.

Sara shivered. They were back on an island where someone really, *really* wanted them dead. No blankets, no food, no protection against the blizzard save for their black parkas. And she couldn't even see the shore.

Animals have instincts that I don't . . . the cows will find the shore.

She was already exhausted. She didn't know how much longer she could carry Tim. They had to get off the bay, find some shelter from the wind or die as assuredly as if she'd never gotten off the plane at all. Sara adjusted the human burden on her shoulder, then leaned into the wind, following the cows' faint calls.

THE COWS HUDDLED in a black-and-gray cluster. Too dark for anything to be white. Thick, heavy-limbed pine trees helped block the wind, but not much. Snow continued to fly in great sheets — even in the woods, it was already so deep it melted against the cows' burgeoning bellies.

Sara leaned against a tree, shaking violently, trying to rub hands that the cold had turned into curled, brittle talons. The tips of her fingers stung badly. Stinging was okay. When they went numb, that meant frostbite. She felt like her entire skeleton was made from icy steel.

She had to find shelter. Tim lay in a heap on the ground, snow already drifting on and around his body. Sara had her doubts he would live through the hour, let alone the night. She guessed the temperature at twenty below zero, far beyond that with the windchill.

Rapleje Bay was close to Sven Ballantine's place. If she could find Sven's house, she could save Tim. But which way? Visibility was less than twenty feet. No moon. No stars. The only chance was to strike out on her own, find Sven's place, then come back for Tim.

Sara found a huge pine tree with boughs so laden down by snow they created a small cave underneath. Ice-cold hands reached in and broke off dry, dead branches, clearing out a space. It wasn't much, but it blocked the wind. She dragged Tim inside.

She felt an overwhelming urge to lie down next to him and just sleep. Exhaustion filled her body, as did pulsing pain from running amid the stampede and suffering the explosion's concussion wave. On top of the physical fatigue, her mind nearly choked at the anguish of losing her friends. Had they died quickly in the blast? Had they burned to death?

She'd avoided any serious burns herself, which was the only good news. She ached, she throbbed, she wanted to collapse.

She looked at Tim Feely lying prone amid the pine needles, broken branches and dead twigs. If she didn't find him real shelter, he would die. She started to cry . . . she didn't want to go back out there. No more. She couldn't take any more.

But she had to.

Her frigid hands wiped away the tears. Sara breathed deeply through her nose, mustering her resolve. She pulled her parka sleeves over her brittle hands, then gently pushed back through the limbs so as not to disturb the snow walls.

EVERY FIVE MINUTES or so the hurricane winds died down briefly, only to pick right back up again. In those seconds-long breaks, the blowing snow seemed to relax, improving visibility from about twenty feet to around a hundred — and in those gaps, the small light stood out like a beacon of hope.

Sara leaned on a tree at the edge of the woods, eyes peering across an open field at the flickering glow. She didn't have much strength left. If this light turned out to be nothing, she'd have no choice but to walk back to Tim's tree, crawl under, and let nature decide their fate.

She walked out into the field. Unencumbered by trees, the wind blew far stronger, driving stinging sheets into her face and eyes. She leaned into the wind and fought through the waist-deep snow. With each clumsy step, the light became a little brighter, a little steadier.

A few steps more, another lull in the wind, and she took in a sight more beautiful than anything she'd ever seen.

The light was mounted on a barn.

Sven's barn.

She turned and trudged back through her own waist-deep trail.

FIVE FEET FROM the barn door, Sara's legs finally gave out. After a half mile of carrying a deadweight, 145-pound man through the waist-deep snow, her body couldn't do it anymore. She fell face-first into a fluffy eight-foot bank that had been sculpted by wind whipping off the red barn. Tim all but disappeared, powder puffing up and around and on him until only his feet stuck out.

She couldn't get up. She didn't *want* to get up. Fuck it. So she'd freeze to death, so what? It was only a matter of time before Magnus came for her. Why not get it over with now, just be dead like the friends she'd failed to help?

Alonzo.

Cappy.

Miller.

Why not just give up?

Because she wanted to see Magnus Paglione dead. And that was more than enough reason to fight on.

Sara picked herself up. Not even bothering to brush the snow off her face, she stumbled to the barn's big sliding door. Her numb hands gripped the black handle. Failing muscles pushed, and with a rattle of metal wheels the door opened a couple of feet.

She stepped inside, leaving the storm behind as she entered an oasis of calm.

How did THEY *get in here?*

Through watering eyes, she saw perhaps two dozen cows lying peacefully in hay-filled stalls. She shook her head, trying to clear her thoughts. *Sven's* cows . . . not the cows from the plane.

Sara willed herself back into the storm and grabbed Tim's feet. She pulled the man free of the bank. His face slid across the snow-covered ground, but it was the best Sara could manage. Finally, after all that cold and pain and fatigue, she dragged Tim Feely into shelter.

Sara stumbled to the sliding barn door and put her weight against its black handle. The wind blew snow inside, almost as if it were some supernatural hand making one last grab for the meal that got away. Wheels creaked as the door shut, reducing the wind to nothing more than an exterior howl.

The barn wasn't warm, but it was well above freezing. Sara heard the hum of a gas-powered generator. She looked around the huge barn and saw the orange glow of several portable heaters.

Safety.

She'd done it. With her last ounce of strength, Sara dragged Tim in front of one of the big electric heaters, then collapsed.

Sleep came almost instantly.

BOOK FIVE

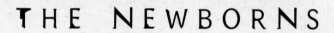

THE NEWBORNS

THE STORM'S FURY had passed, but winds continued to whip powdery snow across the island and drive five-foot waves onto the ice-covered rocks. Colding stood on the sprawling rear porch, staring out across the water. Clayton was hard at work shoveling snow off the porch and salting the half inch of ice that had accumulated during the night.

Colding hadn't slept much. He'd stayed in his room, still dirty from burying Jian in a shallow grave. He had sat on the floor's thick carpet, staring at a window that showed the night's blackness, that rattled with the storm's wind. Sat and thought of his failures. Of Clarissa, Erika, Jian. And if the C-5 hadn't made it, Sara. Next thing he knew, he woke up on the floor, still dressed. He hadn't bothered showering or changing, just put on his coat, boots and hat and walked to the porch.

Each thrust of Clayton's shovel sounded like a gong dragged across broken glass. The old man worked away, his eyes bright and clear, cones of vapor billowing out of his stubbled mouth. He stopped and leaned on the shovel, his chest heaving a little. "Rough night, eh?"

"Yeah," Colding said. "Life really took a dump on us."

"Hell, should have been here in '68, eh? So damn cold da mouth of da harbor froze over. We had to plant dynamite to break up da ice to get boats in. That was da year Paul Newman fell in while we were ice fishing. Me and Charlie Heston had to drag him back to shore."

Clayton paused for a moment. "You're really worried about Sara, eh?"

"Yeah," Colding said. "I am."

"Pretty fuckin' stupid to send them out in that storm." Typical words from the old man, but not a typical tone. He didn't sound insulting, he sounded . . . regretful.

Clayton picked up the shovel again and got back to work, the gong-on-glass sound ripping the air. "When do you expect to hear back from them?"

Colding shrugged. "They should be back in Manitoba already." *Should* be back, but no word yet, at least not that Magnus had shared.

Clayton scraped snow two more times, then he rested the shovel against the mansion wall. He picked up the salt jug and tossed granules down on the freshly cleared ice. He opened the French doors to the lounge, then stopped, turned, and gave Colding a hard, cautious look.

"I wanna know something," Clayton said. "Tell me da truth. You just fuckin' that girl, or you love her?"

The question magnified Colding's misery, his powerlessness. That familiar feeling of tears again, but this time, tears of frustration, maybe even tears of rage.

"I love her."

Clayton nodded, took off a glove and rubbed his mouth. "Thought so. You need anything, you let me know. I've seen a lot of shit come and go on this island. Something's off here, I can feel it." He kicked snow off his boots. "Something's *real* off, eh? And one way or another, we're gonna have to deal with it before too long."

Clayton walked inside and shut the door behind him, leaving Colding alone in the frigid morning to wonder what the words really meant.

HAD SHE SLEPT on a bed of dull nails? Every atom hurt, pulsed, screamed or ached. She smelled of sweat and dirty hay, the odors combining with the unmistakable scent of cows and cow shit so that even her nose found something to bitch about.

Sara pushed herself up on one elbow. She wanted to sleep. Sleep for days, for *weeks*, even, but she had to move. She looked at Tim Feely — and suddenly all the pain was worth it.

He sat on his butt, hugging his knees to his chest, head down and eyes closed. He swayed slightly.

"Tim?" Her voice cracked from a dry throat. "Are you okay?"

He looked up. A huge red and purple bruise covered the right side of his face from hairline to chin. Dried blood clotted the black line of stitches on his forehead. Dark circles ringed both eyes.

"I'm pretty fucking far from okay," Tim said. "How long have I been out?"

Sara took a deep breath, then gave Tim the condensed version of everything she knew — Jian's death, Colding sending the plane out in the storm, Magnus's bomb, the crash landing, and the struggle to reach Sven's barn.

Tim sat quietly for a moment, taking it all in. He gently rubbed his swollen knee. Even the smallest touch there made him wince. "So everyone but you and I are dead. *I'd* be dead if you hadn't dragged my ass a mile through a blizzard?"

Sara nodded.

"Thanks," Tim said. The word couldn't have been simpler, and the look of gratitude and sheer amazement in his eyes couldn't have been deeper. "Sounds like Rhumkorrf really fucked up the works. I hope he's dead."

Sara hoped for the same. Rhumkorrf's actions had caused her friends' deaths. "I got out just before it blew," she said. "I didn't see anyone else."

She looked around the barn, taking in its details for the first time. Fairly standard: fifteen-foot-wide aisle, big enough for a large farm tractor to drive through. Twenty-five stalls on each side. Full haylofts above each row, all under a high arcing roof supported by thick wooden rafters. A few small birds fluttered up there, tiny chirps adding an oddly optimistic feel to their dark situation. Big cow heads peeked out from most of the stalls, vacant black eyes staring curiously at the strangers lying on the ground. Instead of a cow, the first stall to the left of the big sliding door housed a brand-new Arctic Cat snowmobile. Its presence was only a partial comfort — they could use it to get away from Sven's barn, but where would they go?

"We can't stay here, Tim. How's the knee?"

"Fucked up nine ways to Sunday. I think the patella might be broken. Sure as hell can't put weight on it."

She shook her head. "I almost died carrying your ass here. You're coming with me, and you're walking. I'll help you, but you *are* coming with me."

"But what about the storm? It's warm in here."

"I don't hear much wind, so I think the storm is over. That means Sven will be here soon to check on these cows."

"But isn't that what we want? We need help. I'm *hurt,* I need a doctor."

Sara rubbed her eyes. Just one other survivor, and it couldn't be Alonzo or one of the Twins, someone with mettle — it had to be this pussy. "Tim, *listen* to me. If Magnus finds out we're alive, he'll come for us. We're still too close to the plane. We've got to get out of here, try and find Colding. Maybe we can use that snowmobile over there."

Tim looked at the Arctic Cat, but his thoughts were obviously on the bigger picture. "Didn't Colding send us up? How can you trust him now?"

Sara took in a slow breath. She *couldn't* trust Colding. But those nights they'd spent together, the things he'd told her . . . at the very least, he was a far better risk than Gunther or Andy or even Clayton. "I don't know that we can trust him."

A dog bark from outside made them freeze.

The barn door slid open, just a crack. Sara grabbed Tim's hand and yanked him into a stall just as the door opened a little bit more, letting a golden rectangle of brilliant winter morning sunlight spill onto the barn floor.

SVEN BALLANTINE LEANED against the door for a third time. The snow had drifted high against it, half blocking it, half freezing it shut. It opened just enough for him to slide inside. Mookie pushed through his legs and ran into the barn, tail wagging furiously. She darted from cow to cow as if to say *hello!* to the friends she'd missed during the storm, staring at each one briefly to let them know she was there and that she was in charge.

"Take it easy, girl," Sven said. "I'm sure they miss you, too, eh?"

And then Sven Ballantine heard a moo.

At least, he *thought* he'd heard it. But it hadn't come from the barn.

He looked back through the open door, out across the blazing expanse of his snowed-over hayfield. Sunlight roared off the undulating surface, an electric field of frozen white waves running up to the thick pine trees at the field's edge.

Moooooo.

There it was again. And it hadn't been his imagination.

Mookie started barking, a long *ro-ro-ro-ro*, the kind of urgency usually reserved for trespassing squirrels or insolent rabbits. But Sven didn't look, didn't turn around to see Mookie's hackles raised at two battered people hiding in a stall, crouched down by the black-and-white legs of the stall's normal occupant.

Ro-ro-ro-rororo.

"Shut up, girl," Sven said.

Mooooo.

No mistake that time. And it wasn't just one cow, it was several.

Roro-ro-roro-ro.

"God*damit*, Mookie, shut da hell up!"

The scream seemed to hit Mookie like a rolled-up newspaper. Her head dropped to the ground, her tail curled slightly between her legs.

Sven walked out of the barn. He peered across the blinding field, looking for movement. He had to squint to block the worst of the reflected light. There . . . cows. At the edge of his field.

Sven pushed the barn door open a little wider, then walked inside and hopped on the Arctic Cat. It started on the first try. The sound of the engine drew Mookie away from the two people her master didn't seem to notice. The dog barked at the snowmobile and turned three fast circles.

Sven eased the sled out of the barn, then gunned the engine. Mookie followed, barking all the way.

CLAYTON SAT IN the Nuge's toasty warmth. Frank Sinatra blared from the stereo. Sinatra — now, there was a man who could knock back shots of bourbon. Clayton fondly remembered his earliest days on the island, when he and Frank and Dean had drunk Sammy under the table. After Sammy passed out, Clayton had replaced the singer's glass eye with a ball bearing. Sammy had been pissed as hell the next day, but Frank thought it was fucking hysterical.

Always so beautiful after a big storm. The most beautiful place on Earth, really. Not a day went by when Clayton didn't thank the Lord above he'd not only lived here for over fifty years, but been *paid* to do so.

The storms had covered everything in a thick marshmallow coating. Pine trees looked like lumpy white giants out of some paint-by-numbers canvas. The snow changed leafless hardwood branches into soft skeletons. A trillion snowflakes reflected the morning sun, making the landscape shimmer and sparkle.

The Bv dragged its weighted sled along the snowmobile trail. Fourteen inches of snow had dropped in little more than twenty-four hours. A fresh snow meant Magnus would want to take the sleds out, so Clayton had to make sure the trails were properly groomed and ready to go.

Something just *off* with that Magnus boy. His brother Danté wasn't much better. At first, Clayton had thought Colding was yet another Genada doofus, like that ass-wipe Andy Crosthwaite. But maybe Colding was all right. Poor kid was a mess worrying about Sara. And he wasn't the only one. Clayton liked that girl.

Something was wrong on Black Manitou. Way wrong. Fifty *years* on the island. Long enough to know the spirit of a place, to know when something stank worse than a shit sandwich with a side of skunk spunk.

Well, no point worrying until something happened. *Que sera sera*, as Doris Day had said. Now, *she* had been a looker. Too bad she wouldn't put out. The little tease.

Clayton hummed "My Way" as he moved up the trail, wondering if Sara and the others had landed in Manitoba.

SARA RISKED A peek past the stall wall. Through the open barn door, she saw Sven, his dog, and some cows far across the snowy field.

"Get up, Tim. We're moving."

"Moving to *where*?"

The million-dollar question. They could go into Sven's house, wait for him to come back, and then . . . what? Use her Beretta to shoot the old man? Take him hostage? There wasn't any other shelter. Except . . .

"That abandoned town," she said. "Right in the middle of the island. We can lie low there for a little bit, figure out what to do next."

"How far away is that?"

"Maybe five miles."

Tim stared at her like she had a dick growing out of her forehead. "Five *miles*? On foot?"

Sara nodded. "It's our only option."

"We have another option." He pointed to the pistol on Sara's hip.

"No," Sara said. "We don't know that Sven has anything to do with this. I'm not going to hurt him."

"You don't have to shoot the guy, just point it at him and—"

"*No*, Tim. I know guns. You draw this thing on a human being, you better be prepared to use it, and I'm *not* going to blow away some old man. Besides, as far as we know, he has to check in with Magnus every couple of hours or something."

"Or Colding," Tim said.

Sara said nothing.

"I say we take the house," Tim said.

"Doesn't matter what you say."

Sara crept to the barn door and looked out. Sven was still out there with the cows from the C-5. Mookie bounded through the snow, running a long circle around the herd. Sven would come back the same way he'd gone out, which meant Sara and Tim couldn't go out the front — too much fresh snow; Sven would be bound to see the tracks.

She walked deeper into the barn, looking for an exit. Directly opposite the big sliding door she saw a normal, hinged door with a four-paned window on the top half. She used her sleeve to scrape frost away from a small spot, then looked out. Nothing much out there other than snowdrifts, a tiny snow-covered shed and a few snowcapped fence posts.

She pulled the door open, slowly, so that the drift built up on the other side wouldn't fall into the barn. The snow there looked like a waist-high white wall. She stepped over it into the deep snow, then reached back to help the limping Tim Feely. She carefully shut the door. Some snow fell in, but she hoped the still-running heaters might melt it before Sven returned.

She and Tim stood side by side, backs flat against the barn. Before them was a long stretch of undisturbed white marked with high drifts. A single line of footprints led into the shed. Those tracks were covered with less than an inch of snow, making each print look fuzzy and blurred.

"Look," Tim said. "There's no frost on the shed windows. It's heated."

He was right. Probably an electric heater like the ones in the barn. Inviting, but too risky.

"We can't hide there," Sara said. "Looks like Sven went to the shed sometime last night. Means he might be in there again today. It's only six by six, nowhere to hide if he comes out."

"Shit. What now, gunslinger?"

"We just go and hope he doesn't come back to the shed and see our footprints leading out of the barn. Come on."

She put her shoulder under Tim's arm to carry some of his weight. Together, they trudged through the deep snow.

SVEN LOOKED ALL around, searching for any sign of a person. There had to be someone around. Had to. It wasn't like forty-three cows could just appear out of thin air. They weren't James Harvey's herd. As far as Sven knew, James's cows weren't knocked up, and these girls were pregnant with a capital *P*.

Mookie was doing her thing, circling the herd, stopping and staring with her head low to the ground. If her eyes had been lasers, she could have burned a hole clear through the moon. She packed the cows together, waiting for Sven's commands.

He walked up to one of the cows. It had an all-white head with a black eyepatch. The plastic tag clipped through its ear read *A-34*. In permanent marker, someone had scrawled *Molly McButter* underneath the numbers. The tag meant the cows were from the main facility on the south end of the island. How in the hell had the cows traveled some ten miles, during the night, in the midst of a mangler of a blizzard?

"Well, hello there, Molly. I'll bet you've had an interesting night, eh?"

The cow said nothing.

Sven didn't see any tracks. Just a few snow-covered low lines in the snow. That meant the cows had stood here for several hours, tucked into the edge of the woods, waiting out the storm that had covered their path.

Sven kept patting Molly and talking in a low, calm voice. "Well, ladies, I'd better get you all under cover, eh? We've got another storm due soon."

He held up a hand. Mookie's head swiveled, her body motionless, her eyes now only on Sven. The dog radiated intensity. This was her favorite thing in all the world. Except, perhaps, for nap time.

"Mookie, *find*." The lithe dog shot through the snow and into the woods. She'd search for any strays and bring them back.

Sven started the snowmobile and began guiding the cows back to the barn.

CLAYTON STOPPED THE Nuge in front of Sven's barn. He let the vehicle idle and hopped out. A beat later, forty-five pounds of happy-ass black border collie shot out of the barn. Mookie jumped at Clayton, her front paws on his chest, her hind paws hopping up and down as she tried to stretch up enough to lick his face. She whined with excitement.

"Easy there, eh?" Clayton laughed and he twisted his face away from Mookie's insistent tongue. "Take it easy, girl."

"Mookie, *sit*," Sven said firmly. Mookie's rump hit the snow. Her tongue dangled out of her smiling mouth. Her tail kept sliding back and forth across the ground, kicking up wisps of powder.

"Morning, Sven. Thought I'd stop by and see if an old fart like yourself managed to survive da storm."

"I'm fine," Sven said. "You're out here to fix da phone lines?"

Clayton shook his head. "Not yet. Grooming da trails first. Phone lines down, I take it?"

"Yah," Sven said. "I tried calling da mansion to tell them I have their cows."

The words didn't register for a moment. Clayton stared at Sven, then walked up to the barn's open door. Sven walked with him. Mookie heeled to Sven, locked in just a few inches from his feet.

Inside the barn, Clayton saw forty-some cows standing in the open area between the stalls lining either side. He walked up to one and checked the ear tag. *A-13*, it said, with the words *Clara Belle* written in permanent marker.

"An A-tag," Clayton said. "She's from da main herd."

"Yah," Sven said.

"Well, I'll be dipped in meteor shit. I saw these same damn cows loaded onto that big fuckin' plane last night."

"Plane must have come back."

Clayton shook his head. "Can't see how, it didn't land at da mansion."

"Well, unless they make cow-sized parachutes these days, da plane had to land somewhere."

Clayton nodded. Aside from the mansion and the hangar, the C-5 was the biggest damn thing on the island. Couldn't land it on a dime like some helicopter. "You see any people, Sven? Someone had to be with da cows."

Sven shook his head. "Nope."

"Well, this is nuttier than a no-dick stag in mating season. Don't make any sense. You hear anything last night?"

"Slept like a baby, eh? Don't mean there wasn't any noise, though, da wind was screaming."

The presence of the cows meant a landing, or at least a controlled crash. If cows survived, people survived. Which meant the people had either let the cows go, then gone off in another direction . . . or the people were hiding. But hiding from what? From who?

"Sven, I really don't know what to make of this."

"Me neither."

"You mind keeping this to yourself for a little bit? Maybe until I figure out what's going on?"

Sven shrugged. "Don't really matter to me. They're safe here. Besides, I can't call anyone until your lazy ass fixes da phones, now can I?"

Clayton nodded slowly, his eyes still scanning the extra cows that had magically appeared in Sven Ballantine's barn. "I'll fix da lines today. I better finish my swing up to North Pointe and see if I can find anything."

"Just let me know."

Clayton gave Clara Belle one last look. She seemed sick, her eyes glazed over with a thin layer of mucus.

"They don't look good, do they?"

"Nope," Sven said. "They don't look good at all."

Clayton turned and walked back to the Nuge.

SARA AND TIM stood shivering in the woods, a thick, snow-covered pine between them and the road. The storm had passed, but the cold had not. It hung in the air like an ethereal hammer, pounding at them with a constant, numbing pressure.

When the throaty gurgle of a diesel engine had broken the all-powerful winter silence, they'd moved into the woods to hide. On the plowed road the going had been easy, thanks to Ted Nugent and Clayton's early-morning work ethic. Waist-high drifts in the woods, on the other hand, made each step a struggle.

The diesel engine sound grew louder, closer, then the sound changed to an idle.

It had stopped.

Sara peeked around the tree. Clayton and the zebra-striped Ted Nugent. No surprise there . . . but *why* had he stopped?

The vehicle's door opened. A thickly bundled Clayton climbed out. Sara ducked back behind the tree, then slid her hand out of the parka sleeve that doubled as a mostly ineffective glove. Heart pounding in her chest, she unbuttoned her holster strap and pulled out the Beretta. The pistol felt like a block of ice against her bare skin.

"F-f-fuck yes," Tim whispered, his teeth chattering audibly. "Let's whack that old man and t-t-take that tank-thing."

"We're not whacking anyone." She hoped. She didn't want to hurt Clayton any more than she wanted to hurt Sven, but Clayton hadn't stopped in this spot by coincidence. If he found them and told Magnus . . .

She peeked around the tree trunk again. Clayton stopped at the road's edge. He reached into his snow pants, fished out his penis and started urinating on the snowbank. His hips twisted, directing the stream of urine.

"What's he doing?" Tim whispered.

Sara shook her head in amazement. "I think he's writing his name in the snow."

The urine stream slowed to a trickle. Clayton shook once, zipped up his fly, then lifted a leg and cut loose with a fart that echoed off the trees.

"You can come out now," he yelled. "If you don't mind, I really don't feel like marching into da woods after you, eh?"

Sara's hands were cold and brittle. She wasn't even sure if she could actually feel the trigger.

"My truck is nice and warm inside, eh?"

"Sara," Tim said. "Come on . . . I'm . . . so cold."

Other than the black stitches and the purple bruise, Tim's face had little more color than the snow around them. The man shivered uncontrollably. Maybe they *should* have taken Sven's house, but that chance was gone.

And now? She knew they didn't have any choice at all.

Sara stepped out from behind the tree and leveled the Beretta at Clayton.

The man's hands shot up. "Christ on a pogo stick, Sara. Don't point that thing at me, eh?"

"Just don't you move, Clayton, you got me?"

Clayton nodded. Sara reached back and pulled Tim to his feet. They stepped around the tree and trudged toward the road.

"Move to your right," Sara said to Clayton. "Step into that snowbank."

"Where I peed? That's gross."

"Fine, then not there, but get your ass in the snowbank. Any sudden moves and I'll put a round in your kneecap."

"But I already have arthritis in my knees."

"Clayton, shut the *fuck* up! Tim, get in the vehicle and shut the door behind you."

Clayton stepped into the bank, sinking into snow up to his crotch. He wouldn't be able to make any fast moves in that.

Shivering madly, Tim limped through the snow and onto the road. Sara kept the Beretta leveled at Clayton. Tim climbed into the vehicle and shut the door behind him. Once inside, he wrapped his arms around his shoulders and trembled like a puppy in a thunderstorm.

"Sara," Clayton said, "put that damn thing *down*. You're shivering so bad you might shoot me by accident."

Sara looked at her own hand — the pistol seemed to shake like a living thing, as if it, too, were a victim of the island's oppressive cold. She lowered the gun. "How did you know we were out there?"

"Saw footprints in da bank. And seeing as I just saw all da cows that were supposed to be on that plane, I figured some of da crew was around."

"You're a regular fucking Columbo, Clayton."

"Oh, yah, Peter Falk could knock back da soda pops, but now's really not da time for stories, girlie. Where's your crew?"

Sara felt a new stab of loss as the memories of her friends welled up fresh and hot. She shook her head.

"Aw, no," Clayton said. "Only you and Tim made it?"

Was that real sympathy, or just acting? "Clayton, how many people know we crashed?"

"Don't know, eh? We didn't hear anything about it back at da mansion. Can't believe you could bring down something that big without da whole island knowing."

"Yeah. *Real* hard to believe." She raised the gun and aimed it at him again. "When did Magnus send you out to look for us? Did you radio him and tell him you found the cows?"

Clayton shook his head. "You are *really* starting to piss me off with that damn thing. Magnus didn't send me out here, Sara. I plow da road and groom da trails after every storm."

Her whole body shook. Clayton was right, she might just shoot him by accident. He was an old man, for God's sake. He'd been on the island long before Magnus and Danté and Genada . . . or so he said. She had no way of knowing who the hell he was.

"I'm da only one knows you're here," Clayton said. "Now get in da damn tractor before frostbite sets in, eh?"

It was only when Clayton said the word *frostbite* that Sara realized her fingers had stopped stinging.

They were numb.

She took three steps toward the Bv206 before her vision blurred and she fell, unconscious, face-first into the snow.

SVEN STOOD ON his porch, Mookie in her constant position at his side. The salt he'd put down to melt the ice crunched underfoot every time he moved. Winter sucked up all other sounds, hoarded them and refused to share. There was never a time like the dead of winter after a storm, when you couldn't hear anything at all.

Anything, except for the cows.

The new cows were making noises. *Horrible* noises, like they were sick or in pain . . . or probably both. Sven wondered if it had been a mistake to mix the strays with his cows, considering that his herd was a backup in case of main herd contamination. Still, the pregnant cows were worth a fortune — it seemed logical Danté would want them sheltered and cared for.

Sven trudged out to the barn, Mookie automatically at his heels. The dog seemed far more subdued than normal. Sven slid the barn door open and walked in.

Mookie started to growl.

That was a disturbing sound, because while the agile black dog barked at anything that moved, and also most things that didn't, she rarely growled.

"What's got into you, eh?"

Mookie shot into the barn, barking a nonstop *rororororo* at the pregnant cows. She ran behind them, between them, snapped at their feet.

"Mookie! Bad girl!"

What the hell was she doing? The cow with the white head and the black eyepatch stumbled out of the barn, driven by the teeth-baring dog. Mookie was trying to cull the new cows out of the barn.

"*Mookie*, goddamit, stop it!"

Mookie did not stop. She ran back into the barn and nipped at another pregnant, sick cow. This time Sven caught her coming out, his big hand locking down on a neckful of black fur. He lifted her high. She yelped like he'd hit her with a tire iron. The ear-piercing sound was her automatic defense mechanism, her way of getting out of trouble — the yelp always broke his heart.

But that didn't change the fact that she'd lost it with these new cows. He tucked her under one strong arm and held her tight. Dog wasn't going anywhere, and she knew it. Sven scooted in front of Molly McButter. The cow saw Mookie, turned and walked quickly back into the barn.

Once Molly stopped, Sven stayed back and took a good look at her. The cow drooped her head low until her nose was only a few inches off the ground. Thick white mucus covered her eyes and dripped down her cheeks in long, wet, smelly trails. Strands of snot and drool hung from the animal's nose and chin, swaying with motion when the poor creature let out a long and mournful *mooooo*.

Sven looked over his own cows, content in their stalls. They seemed fine and healthy, heads up, eyes normal. But the strays . . . they were all in similar shape to Molly. They hadn't looked this bad just a few hours earlier. Whatever the disease was, it came on fast.

Not much he could do but wait. Clayton would fix the phones soon, then Tim Feely could come out and examine the cows.

Sven used his one free arm to shut the barn door tight. Mookie's tail started thumping against his hip.

"Oh no you don't, you're in *trouble*," he said, but he knew that was a lie and the damn dog probably knew it, too. He set her down. She spun three circles and barked. His dog at his side, Sven walked back to the house, wondering what to do next.

A HAND GENTLY shook her shoulder.

Sara didn't want to wake up. A *bed*, so thick with blankets she was on the verge of sweating. Such heat would have normally felt uncomfortable, but at the moment she'd never experienced anything so luxurious and wonderful.

"Sara, wake up, eh?"

Her eyes fluttered open to see Clayton's salt-and-pepper stubbly face hovering over her own. He was sitting on the bed. Tim looked down at her as well, a crutch under his left arm, his right hand holding a half-eaten chicken leg. Color had returned to his face. While his stitches still looked like shit, some of the swelling underneath had receded.

Sara sat up, reveling in the simple blessing of Not Being Cold. "What happened? Am I naked?"

"You passed out," Tim said. "Clayton put you into the truck, then he drove us to his house. We both undressed you, your clothes were damp. Clayton was a complete gentleman, but I tweaked your nips."

"Like hell you did," Clayton said.

Sara rubbed her eyes. She looked over at Clayton. Her Beretta was stuffed into the waist of his thick snow pants.

"You staring at da gun? I *hope* so, because if you're staring at my thing, Colding might get mad at me, eh?" He pulled out the Beretta and offered it to her butt-first. "You promise not to point it at me anymore?"

Sara nodded and took the gun. At least there was one person she knew she could trust.

Clayton seemed more than happy to be rid of the pistol. "Tim told me about da bomb. I knew that Magnus was a greasy pig fucker rolled in crap-corn, but I didn't think he'd go that far. Where da hell did you land?"

"Rapleje Bay," Sara said. "On the ice."

"No shit?"

"No shit."

"And it's just sitting there?"

"I think most of it melted through when the bomb went off."

"I doubt that," Clayton said. "Too fuckin' big. I'll swing up there and check it out as soon as I can. Magnus could be snowmobiling around any-time now. None of da trails go by Rapleje Bay. If he sticks to da trails, we should be okay, even if da plane is showing a little."

Sara nodded. "Then what? What the hell do we do, Clayton?"

"We have to get you off da island. The cows are at Sven's. If Magnus finds out, he'll come looking for survivors. Phones are down, but you can't keep a thing like that a secret for long."

Sara remembered the monster that had slid out of the cow's ruptured belly. "We have to tell Sven to stay away from the cows."

"Stay away from *cows*?" Clayton said. "How can a cow be dangerous?"

"Not the cows," Tim said. "What's growing inside them."

"And what's inside of them?"

"Monsters," Sara said.

"Oh," Clayton said. "Well, that just fucking clears up everything, then."

"It should be okay," Tim said. "The cows have no IV feeding, so the fetuses are starving. From what we've seen, the cows are just going to die and the fetuses will die along with them."

Sara shook her head. "No, that thing came out and *attacked* Cappy."

"The cow's belly was already torn open," Tim said. "The baby wouldn't have lived long, anyway."

Clayton looked from Tim to Sara. "A monster came out of a cow, bit Cappy, and *then* what happened?"

"It almost bit Cappy's arm off, so I shot it."

"Well, fuck me," Clayton said. "I think I'll tell Sven to stay away from da cows."

Tim tore off another bite of chicken, then talked with a full mouth. "At this point, best to err on the side of caution. Without the nutrition supple-ment the fetuses can't live long. As long as no one goes near the cows, the cows die, fetuses die, done deal. It'll be fine."

Clayton scratched his stubble. It made a sandpapery sound. "I'll tell Sven, but it doesn't change da fact we have to get you off da island. I think I can keep da cows and da crash a secret for a day or two, maybe long enough to get my son out here with da boat and get you two back to da mainland. I'll tell Colding; hopefully he can keep Magnus busy."

At the sound of Colding's name, Sara felt a pang of loneliness, but also one of suspicion. "No. We can't tell Colding."

Clayton's eyes squinted a little and he put a hand on Sara's shoulder. "Are you *sure* you don't want to tell him? He's awfully worried about you."

Sara *wanted* to tell Colding, wanted him here this very second, but that just wasn't the smart thing to do. "P. J. sent us up in a plane loaded with a bomb, yet he stayed on the ground."

Tim opened his mouth to say something, paused, then took another bite of chicken leg. Deep down inside, Sara *knew* Colding would do anything for her, but the facts and her emotions didn't mix . . . and three dead friends made for one hell of a fact.

A fresh gust of wind made the bedroom window rattle slightly. Outside, a few fluffy snowflakes moved from left to right.

Clayton stood up. "If that's da way you want it, fine with me. Another storm is coming in tonight, supposed to hit us pretty hard. Don't know if Gary can get out here in that weather. You two better stay here tonight, get some real rest. Tomorrow I'll hide you in da old town, eh? Right now, I've got to fix da phone lines so Sven can call out if he needs me. Grab some dry clothes out of my closet, eat whatever you want out of da fridge. But keep *quiet*. Anyone knocks, just don't answer."

He patted Sara on the shoulder and walked out of the bedroom. She pushed back the covers and sat up. Tim pretended not to look as he rummaged through Clayton's dresser. He tossed her a flannel shirt and jeans, which she quickly put on.

"Sara," Tim said. "Is this who I think it is?" He was staring at a framed picture on top of Clayton's dresser.

She stood up and looked. "I'll be damned."

In the picture, Marilyn Monroe and a much younger Clayton Detweiler were sharing a passionate kiss.

CLAYTON WALKED INTO the security room to find Colding sitting at the desk, steadily flipping through the monitor channels the way someone would work a TV remote if there was nothing to watch.

"Hey there, Clayton," Colding said. "Come to share a fart or two with me?"

"No gas today. And I ain't here to see you. Da phone lines are down. Computer will tell me where da breaks are."

Colding stood and moved away from the desk. "Be my guest." He walked to the weapons rack and grabbed one of the Berettas, then sat at the edge of the desk and started breaking down the pistol.

Clayton sat and used the mouse to initiate the phone line integrity program. A progress bar started to fill. He was alone with Colding. There were no cameras in the security room, at least none that Clayton knew of. And if there were, where would they be watched? All the Big Brother monitoring was done from this room. Ironically, the security room was probably the only safe place to talk in the entire mansion.

Maybe he could feel it out, see if Colding was to be trusted. "No word from Sara yet?"

Colding's lip curled up in a brief snarl, but the expression disappeared immediately. "Nothing yet." His hands kept removing parts from the pistol, cleaning them with a rag, oiling, polishing, turning. "Magnus has put in new codes and locked me out of the transmitter. I can't call Danté to find out what's going on."

Bad going to worse. "Why would Magnus change da codes?"

Colding shrugged. "He says security is compromised. He wants to be the only one receiving or sending messages." Colding's fingers worked the weapon. This was Clayton's chance to tell him . . . but Sara's and Tim's lives hung in the balance.

"Colding, I . . ." His voice trailed off.

Colding's hands stopped. He looked up. "You what?"

Before Clayton could speak, the computer beeped loudly — the integrity check had finished. In that instant, Clayton's resolve broke. He'd stick to the plan.

"Nothing," he said, and turned back to the computer.

The screen showed four breaks in the landlines — one near his house, one close to the Harveys' place, and two on the line leading from Sven's. Clayton printed the repair map, then left the security room.

SARA GNAWED ON a block of cheese in between gulps from a glass of milk. How could she be hungry at a time like this? She didn't care. Eating gave her hands something to do, even if she couldn't turn off her brain, couldn't turn off the thoughts of her dead friends.

She and Tim walked around Clayton's house, looking at framed black-and-white pictures and faded Polaroids that would have made any paparazzi green with envy.

"Amazing," Tim said. "Here he is drinking with Frank Sinatra."

Sure enough, a black-and-white of Old Blue Eyes holding a half-filled tumbler up to the camera, an incredibly young Clayton Detweiler doing the same with a bottle of Budweiser. To the right of that picture, another black-and-white with an even more famous face.

"Holy shit," Tim said. "Here he is fishing with friggin' President Reagan. And fuck me running, this is Brigitte Bardot back in the *day*. Hot as hell and playing piggyback with Clayton? What is he in this picture, twenty-five?"

Tim kept babbling, but Sara wasn't paying attention anymore. Her thoughts had already drifted away to a darker place, a place where she would know what it felt like to put a bullet in Magnus Paglione's brain.

CLAYTON PATIENTLY RODE the Nuge's zebra-striped lift bucket up to the top of the wooden telephone pole. He was about a quarter mile northeast of the watchtower and the jammer tower. As he rose, he watched the new storm already taking shape. Dull gray-black clouds the color of sour chocolate milk filled the sky, steadily increasing in size and number, choking out the light. The wind had grown steadily all morning, and now was pushing around ten miles an hour.

A fallen tree had snapped the line. He had to repair it to connect Sven to the mansion. But as soon as he repaired that break, Sven might call the mansion, try to get Tim Feely out to check on the cows. And that was just because the cows were *sick* — if Sven found out there were baby monsters brewing in those big bellies, he'd go straight to Magnus. Keeping that info from Sven was a shitty thing to do, but the fact of the matter was that two lives hung on Clayton's every decision.

The lift bucket reached the top. He had no choice — he *had* to keep Sven in the dark until Tim and Sara were off the island. Clayton connected his orange handset and punched in Sven's number.

THE PHONE RANG. Mookie barked at it. Mookie barked at everything.

"Shut up, girl," Sven said as he walked to the phone. "Yah, Sven here."

"Sven, it's Clayton." Clayton's voice sounded scratchy and far-off.

"Clayton, those cows are awfully sick, eh? And they're getting worse fast. Who's coming out to help me?"

"Listen, Sven, there's a problem. Genada is up to no good. Can you just stay out of da barn for a day or so, until this storm passes us over?"

What the hell was that old coot rambling on about? Was this another one of Clayton's tall tales?

"No, Clayton, I can't *stay out of da barn.* I have to take care of my herd, eh?"

There was a pause, no noise but the scratchy connection and maybe some wind on Clayton's end.

"Sven, listen to me, eh? Just trust me on this one."

Clayton clearly didn't understand the state of the strays, or what it meant to be responsible for the safety and welfare of those animals. "Know what, Clayton? How about you just fix da phones."

"Genada is up to no good, I tell ya."

"Well, Genada signs my paycheck every other week. *You* don't. Now fix da phones or I'm driving up to da mansion myself."

Sven heard muttered cursing, and what sounded like someone kicking the inside of a big plastic bucket.

"Sven, you remember when your wife died?"

The question stunned him. What the hell did that have to do with anything? "Of course I remember, Clayton. What's your goddamn point?"

"Remember how I took care of things for you? When you were . . . grieving?"

Sven's big, calloused hand tightened on the plastic handset. *Grieving.* That was one way to describe it. Lying in bed and crying, not eating for a week, unable to lift a finger to help himself . . . that was more accurate. Clayton had taken care of everything.

"Clayton Detweiler, are you trying to tell me that I *owe you*?"

"Yah, and I'm cashing in. Just sit tight. Stay away from da barn, Sven."

What a tit-for-tat son of a bitch. Whatever this was, it was a very big deal to Clayton. "You want to tell me what's going on?"

"I want to, Sven, but I can't."

Wasn't that just perfect? Clayton didn't pull shit like this, ever. Had to be something major. "I'll wait until da storm blows over, but that's it. Tomorrow morning, one way or another, someone is coming out here."

A pause. "Well, that'll have to do. I'll talk to you before then."

Sven hung up and looked out the window, troubled thoughts whirling through his mind like the nasty winds taking shape outside. He'd known Clayton for, oh, thirty years now. Sven nodded — he could wait, wait until the storm had passed. After that, however, he had to fulfill his obligations.

Sven rolled his neck. He heard and felt his old bones crack. The job was tiring enough even without any of this added stress. He felt exhausted. He looked down at Mookie, who looked back, fluffy tail suddenly swishing across the floor.

"You ready for a nap with da old man, girl?"

Mookie barked, then ran for the bedroom. Sven followed. Mookie spun in circles at the foot of the bed. Sven didn't bother undressing, just climbed on top of the blankets and lay down on his side. Mookie jumped onto the bed and curled into her favorite spot, nestled in the crook of Sven's legs.

Both of them fell asleep in seconds.

CLAYTON REALIZED HE hadn't actually done a head count on the cows from the plane. Maybe all of them didn't make it to Sven's. The Harveys' place was fairly close to the crash site; perhaps some cows had wandered there. If James found a stray and simply snowmobiled to the mansion to find out what was going on . . .

Clayton punched in the Harveys' number. Stephanie answered on the second ring.

"Hello?"

"Stephanie, Clayton here."

"Oh, *Clayton*! Are you going to stop by today? I could whip up those brownies you like so much I'll put on some coffee and we can all sit down and—"

"Just let me talk to James. It's important."

"Okay, hold on."

Clayton waited, wondering about the choices he was making. His actions would put Sven, Stephanie and James in *potential* danger in order to save Tim and Sara from *certain* danger. A shit call, either way.

"Hello, Clayton," James said. "Glad to see you got da phone lines fixed this early."

"Not fixed yet," Clayton said. "I'm on a handset at one of da breaks. Say, James, you seen anything weird?"

"Weird like what?"

"Like anything . . . unusual? With your cows?"

"Just came from da barn," James said. "Everything is fine, why do you ask?"

Clayton breathed a sigh of relief. "No reason. Sven said his cows were feeling a little sick."

"Mine are in da pink of health. But don't take forever to fix those phones. If there's some bug going around, I want to make sure I can reach Mister Feely, eh?"

"More storms coming tonight, so no point in fixing da same shit twice. All will be shipshape by tomorrow afternoon. Good day, James."

"Good day."

Clayton broke the connection, happy there was one less thing to worry about.

OUTSIDE SVEN'S BEDROOM window, the storm picked up intensity, swelling, swirling, growing. Loud enough to rattle the windows in their wooden frames, but that wasn't what woke him. No, it was a pair of sounds — Mookie's low, gurgling growl of warning, and the cows.

The screaming cows.

Stay away from da barn, Sven.

He sat straight up in bed. He'd heard sounds like that once when he was a boy in Ontonagon. He'd left the barn door open just enough for a pack of starving coyotes to slink inside in the middle of the night and attack a helpless milk cow. Even as Sven hopped out of bed and quickly pulled on his snow pants and boots, he wondered at the high-pitched sounds of bovine terror, sounds so loud he could hear them over a twenty-mile-per-hour wind from inside a barn some fifty yards away.

Why had Clayton told him to stay out of the barn?

Sickness didn't make cows sound like that. *Predators* did.

He strode to his gun rack and grabbed his Mossberg 500 shotgun. He threw on his coat as he walked to the front door, switching the gun from hand to hand as he shrugged on one sleeve and then the next. The Mossberg was loaded, of course. He always kept it loaded.

Mookie couldn't take it anymore. Her little body shook with violent barks. *Rorororoooooro-ro-ro*

Sven opened the door just a bit and leaned through.

Ro-roro-RORoro-ro

Mookie's slim body tried to squeeze between the door frame and his right leg. Sven turned his knee to block her. Each bark was an ear-piercing blast of animal rage.

"Mookie, calm down!"

Mookie did not calm down.

The cows screamed louder. Sven heard noises like thunder, but it took him a second to realize what those noises actually were . . . fifteen-hundred-pound bodies slamming against stall walls, against the inside of the barn.

He felt Mookie's head suddenly slide between his calves. Sven slammed his legs together, but Mookie's head and shoulders were already through. He squeezed his legs tighter and reached down with his right hand, fingertips sliding inside the dog's collar.

"Mookie, god*damn*it, stay!"

Mookie lurched, yanking Sven forward. The shotgun stock caught on the door frame and the gun fell forward. Sven instinctively reached his right hand to catch it, and just like that, Mookie shot off the porch and tore ass for the barn.

"Mookie! Stay!"

Mookie did not stay.

Sven ran after her. As soon as he came off the porch, away from the house's shelter, the wind cut at him, pulled him. Snow flew so hard it stung his face and hands.

As he ran, Sven pumped a shell into the chamber.

Mookie stood in front of the barn's big sliding door, barking with such violence that spit flew from her shaking head in gloopy strings that arced across her face and nose.

Sven held the shotgun with his right hand as he planted both feet at an angle and slid across the snow. Mookie was preoccupied with the door and saw her master a second too late. She turned to run, but Sven's left hand caught a handful of neck fur and lifted the dog high.

"Bad dog! *Bad!*"

Mookie's long, fluffy tail tucked between her legs and she started yelping.

"Oh, *stop it*, you damn baby. When I say you stay, you *stay!*"

Something smashed into the barn door. Sven's hands flew to the shotgun. Mookie fell to the ground. Sven leveled the Mossberg at the door. Mookie scooted behind him.

Even over the wind, Sven smelled . . . burning fur?

Cow screams, heavy slams, breaking wood, and . . . another noise . . . a kind of growl? Something was in there with his cows. This wasn't sickness at all, and there was no way in hell Sven could walk away from some predator feeding on his animals.

Already breathing hard from an adrenaline surge and a strange feeling of desperation, Sven kept his right hand on the shotgun, finger on the trigger, as his left hand grabbed the sliding door's black handle. He pulled open the heavy door an inch, just enough to peek inside with one eye.

Smells billowed out: shit, animal fear, burnt fur . . . and the heavy scent of blood. Ninety panicked cows in a space built for fifty calm ones. They ran back and forth, as if they might find some way out, slamming into stalls, walls and one another. Blood streaked the walls, bales of hay, the cows themselves. Redness coated the floor in long slimy streaks and spotted hoofprints. Just in front of Sven's boot, a long intestine snaked from one side of the barn to the other. Dirt and hay clung to its wet surface.

Sven moved his head side to side so he could look into the barn at different angles, try to locate the danger. He wasn't going to fully open the door until he knew what he was dealing with. He craned his neck, trying to see past the shuffling mass of cattle. He caught glimpses of mangled cow corpses, so torn up their coats looked bright red with dark-red markings rather than black and white.

BAM

A cow slammed into the door and Sven jumped back. Fear tingling through his chest, he leaned and looked in. The cow crashed forward again: the wood shook as if it had been hit by a lightning bolt.

No ear tag . . . it was one of his.

Two other cows picked up on the first's efforts, perhaps sensing a possible way out.

BAM-BAM-BAM

All three hit the door, almost five thousand combined pounds of desperate animal pummeling forward. Sven stood amazed as the first cow struck again, this time with such force that the skin between her eyes split from the middle of her nose up past her ears. Blood poured down her face, but instead of stopping kept hurling herself forward.

BAM

None of these three had ear tags. They were *his* cows. He had to get his herd out. They'd already seen a way to freedom — even if he shut the door, they'd kill themselves trying to get away from whatever the hell was in the barn. If he let them out, he could shoot the predator, then he and Mookie could round up the herd.

Sven set the shotgun against the door and put both hands on the cold, red-painted wood. The cows kept slamming against it, briefly jamming the roller wheels with each impact. He leaned back hard, digging in his heels, walking the door open with a herky-jerky motion. Each cow impact generated a thundering reverberation of rattling dry wood. The first cow, head bloody, scraps of skin dangling from her nose and face, pushed halfway through the door, shoulders wedging in the narrow opening. She pushed the bottom of the door outward, jamming tight the roller wheels on top. Sven pulled hard, but couldn't budge it. The cows brayed in pure fight-or-flight panic.

Another cow head appeared above the first, thrusting forward, trying to crawl over, push through the narrow opening, sharp hooves driving down on the head below. Sven desperately leaned back with all his weight, but the door wouldn't budge.

BAM-BAM, BAM

A rifle-shot sound of splintering wood. Sven looked up; the left roller wheel had almost ripped away from the door.

BAM-BAM, BAM

All the wheels tore free, spinning out into the snow like shrapnel. Ten feet high, eight feet wide and three inches thick, the door dropped like a drawbridge.

Sven almost made it clear.

The thick wood kicked up a huge cloud of swirling snow when it drove on the ground — and onto his left foot, just above the ankle. His fibula and tibia snapped like fresh carrots.

Eyes wide and white, froth covering their muzzles, the cows roared out like some powerful orgasm of terror. Each pounding step drove the door down onto Sven's broken leg, pinning it, keeping him from pulling free. His screams joined the panicked cries of the stampeding herd.

Some of the cows stumbled and fell. Those behind them plowed forward, sometimes going around, sometimes stepping on the fallen. They spread out like a black and white and red gas, dissipating away from the barn, moving out across the snowdrifted field and into the swelling storm.

Sven lay in the snow, eyes twisted shut, teeth bared and mouth wide open in a silent scream of agony. He tried to pull his foot free, but each tiny motion ripped him with barbed-wire blasts. Swirling black spots clouded his vision. A fierce shake of his head cleared some of them away. Blood poured out of his boots, staining the snow in an expanding red slush.

Pain or no pain, he had to get free, even if he had to tear off his own leg to do so. The thing that butchered the cows was still inside. Fighting through the agony, he sat up and worked his fingers under the door. He only had to lift it a little . . .

His old, well-worked muscles bunched as he desperately tried to lift the three-hundred-pound door. The wood rose, just a fraction of an inch, but it was enough for him to redouble his efforts. It rose another half inch, then suddenly slammed down as if God himself had willed it.

Sven's head snapped back in an involuntary scream. Tears streamed down his face, quickly freezing into glistening trails on his cheeks. He looked up.

A cow stood on the door.

It wasn't braying or panicking, it had just walked a few feet onto the fallen door and stopped. Sven recognized the white head with the black eyepatch — Molly McButter.

"Move, god*damit*! You fucking cow, *move*!"

She didn't. Mookie rushed in, snapped at her feet, but she didn't budge. Molly stood there, snow accumulating on her back, her head bent almost to the ground, glazed eyes staring at nothing, her heavy belly round and distended and hanging low.

Hanging low, and *moving.*

"Get off da door, you motherfucker! Get da fu—"

Sven's epithet died in midsyllable: a long, thick stream of blood poured out of Molly McButter's mouth to splash against the fallen barn door. The flow stopped briefly, just a few drops dribbling down, then it poured free again like crimson vomit. She turned her head to the side, weakly, as if it took some great effort, and looked right at Sven.

Mooooo

That mournful noise was the last Molly McButter ever made. As it faded out, another sound replaced it. The muffled snap of a single cracking rib.

Sven's pain wasn't forgotten, but now it seemed far away, an echo of its former intensity.

Another *crack*.

Molly's ribs . . . *moved*.

A bloody paw ripped out of Molly, six-inch gore-covered claws tearing a huge hole in her belly. Blood and fluid poured forth in gallons, splashing against the barn door, spraying into Sven's horror-stricken face.

"Oh, sweet Jesus."

Molly's knees wobbled. Her eyes rolled back, leaving only half-lidded whites exposed. She fell hard to her side, driving the door even farther onto Sven's nearly severed leg. Pain rolled through his head. A swarm of black bees filled his vision, threatening to take him into darkness.

A bark at his side brought back his focus. Mookie stood next to him, chest out, hackles raised impossibly high, teeth bared, the sound coming out of her mouth more a roar than a bark.

Molly's belly, once swollen and distended, now sagged against her rib cage. The claw came forth again, tearing her from sternum to vagina. A bloody, slime-covered *thing* slid out.

Sven's vision blurred from tears and from pain. Unconsciousness threatened to pull him under. He snarled and dug his fingers under the door — he had to lift, lift or die. Sven threw all his strength into it, until the wood dug into his flesh, until his finger bones started to crack from the strain. The door didn't budge. His muscles weakened, only slightly, and in that moment he knew there was no escape.

Through a haze of semiconsciousness, in the snow-streaked glare of his barn's light, Sven saw the creature lift its blood-smeared head. A big, triangular head, too big for the body. Beneath the red-blood slime, it had fur like a cow . . . a white head, with a black patch surrounding the left eye.

Eyelids opened, blinked, and the thing looked right at Sven. He fell back into the snow, the black bees in his vision now big as sparrows, flying about his head, blocking out everything. With his last ounce of energy, he lifted himself up on one shoulder. He looked for the shotgun — but it was somewhere under the door. The sparrow spots grew to the size of fat crows.

Movement from the barn. Through a waving haze, he saw three creatures step out, one after another. These were also covered with blood, mostly dry except for their mouths and claws, which were lacquered in wet red. Black and white and red. They moved clumsily, each step a new discovery.

One of them opened its big mouth and bit down on Molly's rear leg. The thing shook its head like Mookie shaking a chew toy. Bones cracked, blood splattered, and with a snap the lower half of the leg came free. A lift of the head, a few more crunches, and the leg was gone. The other two started tearing into Molly, ripping free huge chunks.

Molly's mucus-covered eyes were still blinking.

The one that had come out of her belly, though, didn't tear into the still-living cow. It stood on wobbly legs and staggered toward Sven.

Then Mookie attacked it, snarling with lip-curled fury as her white teeth locked down on the creature's big head. The dog jerked and twisted, ripped her mouth away, taking the creature's right ear along with it.

A flash of claws. Mookie's guttural growl instantly changed to a yelp, a *real* yelp, not the fake show she put on when Sven had tried to discipline her. Mookie was knocked away somewhere to the right. Sven didn't see where she landed, because through his spotty vision he saw the creature coming toward him.

Black eyes, locked on his.

Mouth, opening . . . teeth, blazing.

Hot breath in his face, breath like a puppy's. Sven's brain filled with a wonderful memory, of a tiny ball of warm black fur that fit in one hand, a tiny pink tongue kissing his cheek.

Then something stung his neck, a dozen poking knives.

The crows turned into giant buzzards that blocked out all light.

Then nothing.

TED NUGENT ROLLED to a stop in front of the big stone church. The dying storm drove snow off the black stone walls in every direction — down, sideways, even up. Sara, Tim and Clayton hopped out and walked to the door. Sara watched Clayton pull off his mittens and search his over-sized key ring.

The church's black walls looked fortress-solid. If there was any place on the island she could hold out and wait for help, this was it.

Clayton found the key. The twelve-foot-high door opened with a gothic screech. Sara and Tim followed Clayton inside, then shut the door, blocking out the wind. Snow that had blown into the church gently dropped to the floor.

Sara stared up at the wooden beams of the thirty-foot cathedral ceiling. The wood was a warm brown in some places where bits of varnish remained, but blackish gray most everywhere else. Early-morning light filtered through stained-glass windows depicting scenes of the Twelve Apostles. Most of the pews remained, although all were rotting to some degree. Two or three had broken bases, resting with one end on the ground.

A choir balcony hovered above the tall front door. The loft ran along both the church walls and underneath the stained-glass Apostles. At the back of the church, a granite, three-step altar stuck out from the wall like a stage. At the back of that stage stood a twenty-foot-high cross. At the front, a rotted, ornate wooden podium. The whole building smelled of a cold, musty, wet-stone dampness.

Sara pointed to the choir loft. "How do we get up there?"

"Stairs are behind da altar, off to da right," Clayton said. "Narrow, but solid. And before you ask, you get to da bell tower from da loft."

"Magnus come here?" Tim said. "This his spot to tear the wings off baby birds? Maybe skin squirrels alive?"

"I'm da only one with a key to this place. As long as Sven keeps his mouth shut, no one will come looking. Only action here was about forty years ago, when me and Elvis came in after hours and knocked back a pitcher of screwdrivers with Ann-Margret, but now's not da time for stories."

Sara looked up at the stained-glass St. Andrew. The left side of his face had fallen out at some point. Bits of snow blew in through his open cheek. "So what now?"

Clayton scratched his gray stubble. "Well, I've got to use da secure terminal to call my son, see when he can get da boat out here."

"Clayton," Sara said, "won't Magnus be watching that secure terminal?"

He thought for a moment, staring at a dusty, stained-glass image of St. Paul, then nodded. "Yeah, maybe he will. But we don't have a choice."

Clayton was risking his life for them. If Magnus had murdered irreplaceable scientific talent, it certainly wouldn't bother him to kill a janitor with digestive issues.

Clayton slipped out the front door and quickly returned, arms loaded with blankets, a flashlight, a plastic case and a kerosene heater.

"There's a preparatory room to da altar's left. It's small, so that's where I'd put da heater. Knock a hole in da ceiling so da fumes can vent. No windows there, so no one will see da light. There's some food in this case. Keep *warm* — it's going to get cold tonight."

Sara took the heater and the blankets. "When are you making the call?"

Clayton thought and scratched at his ear. "I have to make sure no one sees me. I also can't just stop doing my work, or Magnus might get suspicious, eh? I'll fix da phone line breaks on da south side of the island, keep checking in and see when I can be alone in da security room."

Tim rolled his eyes. "But *how long*, man?"

"Put a sock in it, boy," Clayton said. "I *will* get you off da island. Once I make da call, it's three hours for Gary to get here. You two just stay out of sight."

Clayton handed Tim the rest of the gear, then walked out and shut the creaking doors behind him. Sara and Tim gathered up the blankets, the case and the heater and walked toward the altar.

Tim stopped at the altar and knelt, head dipped in a silent prayer.

"Never figured you for the praying type," Sara said.

"I'll take whatever I can get right now," Tim said. "That includes voodoo. Got a chicken I can sacrifice?"

Sara shook her head.

"Well, then this will have to do."

Sara didn't mind waiting for him to finish.

JAMES HARVEY SLID on his thick Otto Lodge parka. Happily whistling "Cowboy" by Kid Rock, he laced up his snowshoes and started toward the barn. Storm or no storm, there was work to be done.

The morning sun blazed through the blowing snow and reflected brilliantly off long white fields. He guessed another ten inches had fallen during the night. Knowing Clayton, the trails and roads would already be groomed. As soon as he finished the morning's chores, he and Stephanie could take their sleds for a spin or two around the island.

He started the twenty-five-yard trudge to the barn, but stopped when he heard the whine of a dog. He followed the sound around the corner of his house to find Mookie, Sven's dog, cowering and shivering.

"Good God, Mookie . . . what happened to you?"

The poor girl's left shoulder was torn open, bloody and exposed. She held her left paw in the air, as if it hurt to put any weight on it. A long gash on her forehead oozed blood. Snow clumped in her fur, icy bits hung from her whiskers. Mookie limp-hopped to James and leaned her weight against the man. Her whines increased.

James gently brushed the snow off Mookie's face. "Take it easy, girl. It's okay now."

In answer, a low, evil growl burbled forth from Mookie's closed mouth. James pulled his hand back: the dog might be rabid.

Then he realized that Mookie wasn't growling at him. She was growling at something out in the pasture. He stared out across the blazing snow, saw something black and white and red. No, the *something* was black and white; the *snow* was red.

Red with blood.

A dead cow. Was it one of his? Could a wolf have swum over from the mainland? Attacked and wounded a cow, then left? James raised his hand to block the snow's morning-sun glare. Maybe it wasn't dead — the prone cow moved a little with an unnatural, herky-jerky motion.

A head popped up from behind the big body. James couldn't make out much other than some black-and-white fur, marred by the bright red of the cow's fresh blood. Hard to tell from this distance, but the head looked ... strange.

"What da hell is that thing?" he mumbled, squinting his eyes tighter. Didn't *look* like a wolf. Had that thing also torn up Mookie?

The cow's carcass blocked any view of the second creature's body. All James could see was the wolf's big, oddly shaped head.

Then the wolf raised its fin.

James blinked a few times, his brain trying to register what his eyes saw. A *fin*, rising out of the head. The wolf turned slightly, giving James a flash of bright-yellow skin streaked with reddish orange.

That's no wolf. And that sure as FUCK *ain't no cow.*

James turned and walked slowly toward the house, keeping an eye on the creature the whole way. The thing stayed behind the downed cow. Just as James watched it, it watched James. The fin lowered, raised, then lowered again.

What the hell is that thing?

He looked for Mookie, but the dog was nowhere to be seen. James reached the house and walked inside, shutting the door before kneeling to take off his snowshoes. Through his living room window, he could still see the thing in the field. It remained behind the cow, staring back.

Stephanie stood there looking at James, her hair in curlers, a white terry-cloth robe around her and a steaming mug of coffee held in each hand. Her expression was half confusion, half amusement.

"Hey hon weather looks great outside I bet da wind is dying down I made you some coffee maybe after you finish with da cows we can go for a walk in da woods and—"

"Get my Remington."

Her half-smile faded. For once, she didn't say anything. She set the coffee cups down, turned and ran into the den.

James tossed the snowshoes away, scrambled to his feet and followed his wife. She met him at the den door, handed him his Remington Model 870 shotgun and a box of shells.

"James, what's happening?"

A sentence with just three words. For Steph, that had to be a record. "Something out there brought down a cow." He quickly pumped shells into the weapon.

"What is it then a wolf 'cause there ain't no wolves on da island any-more we haven't seen one ever."

"This ain't no wolf. Call da lodge."

Stephanie moved to the end table and picked up the handset. She looked at James, fear in her eyes. "It's still out."

"Fucking Clayton."

Stephanie's scream nearly made him shit his pants. She stared out the living room window. James turned to look and caught a glimpse of the creature he'd seen in the field — huge, all-white triangular head, bloody mouth full of long, pointed teeth, narrow black eyes and that strange fin sticking straight up in the air. Only a glimpse, because he instantly shoul-dered the shotgun and fired.

The window shattered outward. The creature's head snapped back. It fell like a sack of potatoes, a misty cloud of red settling down on the snow around it. Wind blew the curtains inward, accompanied by bits of snow and a blast of frigid air.

James pumped a shell into the chamber, then strode forward

"James, don't!"

Just two words. Apparently Stephanie found brevity only in danger. He kept the gun shouldered and ducked past the flapping curtains to look out the window, squinting his eyes against the wind. Blood poured from the thing's head, staining the snow, bright crimson on bright white. Despite a hamburger-red hole in its head, the creature struggled to rise. James leaned out the window, aimed carefully, and fired again from only three feet away.

The creature fell, limp and lifeless.

He cocked another shell into the chamber and peered out at the dead animal. He'd never seen anything like it. Long front arms ended in large paws tipped with wicked claws. Black-and-white fur, just like the Hol-steins out in his barn. The thick creature had to weigh at least 350 pounds. Looked kind of like a cowhide-covered cross between an orangutan and an alligator. To have looked in the living room window like that, it would have had to stand on its hind legs and lean those big, clawed paws on the sill.

"James honey I'm scared like crazy and it's freezing in here we gotta close that up right now." Stephanie shivered, her terry-cloth-covered arms wrapped tight around her shoulders.

A subzero gust rolled through the window and caught the table lamp's shade like a sea wind filling a sail. The lamp tumbled to the ground, the bulb breaking on impact. The curtains billowed up around his face. James brushed them aside and rested the Remington against the windowsill.

"Come to da basement with me and help me get a piece of plywood."

Stephanie followed him downstairs. "Honey," she said, "I ain't never seen anything like that just what da *hell* was that thing?"

He heard the fear in her voice and realized just how protected their life on the island had been until five minutes ago. No crime, no threats from animals, no danger at all as long as you respected the power of nature and winter.

"I don't know what it was, Steph."

James pulled the piece of plywood from the stack, carefully handing Stephanie one end so as not to give her a splinter.

They heard another crash from upstairs — the wind had knocked something else over. They needed to get that window boarded up fast before a half inch of snow covered the living room carpet.

They brought the plywood upstairs. James walked backwards, guiding them toward the window, but stopped when he heard the muffled crunch of glass beneath his feet. He looked down to see a few pieces of glass lying on the living room carpet.

But the glass would have been blown *outward* . . .

A sudden blast of cancerous realization hit him hard. He dropped the plywood and turned.

In the broken window, the huge head of a second creature, this one with a white head and a black patch on the left eye. A mass of pink scar tissue sat where its left ear should have been. It was just a few feet away, so close James felt the heat of its breath.

Smelled like puppy breath.

James kicked out hard. The thing started to snap, but moved a split second too late. James's boot smashed against its mouth, knocking the head back, out of the window.

James reached for his shotgun.

But his shotgun wasn't there.

He stopped short, knowing damn well he'd left the gun there, wondering where else it could be, then Stephanie started screaming again. Not a scream of terror this time, but a scream of pain, the pain of long, narrow teeth puncturing through terry cloth and into soft skin.

James had one brief moment to realize that there were more of the creatures, *inside* the house. The spotted one scrambled through the window with a speedy urgency, big mouth opening wide, long claws reaching out. James reached for the fallen lamp.

He grabbed it and managed one swing before he went down under the weight of two creatures.

ANDY MOVED HIS king back to king-2. He was on the ropes, unable to keep up with Magnus's methodical attack. The game was already over, but they played it out anyway. Not like there was anything else to do on this fucking island other than choke the chicken, which Andy had already done twice that day. *Juggs* magazine this time. His *Gallery* collection was getting a little old.

They sat in the lounge, Magnus on his leather chair, Andy on a couch, the chess set laid out on a coffee table. Whisky glasses sat on either side of the board, one for Magnus (with ice) and one for Andy (without ice, the way that shit was meant to be). The bottle of Yukon Jack was just under half empty. Andy's buzz made him wonder if he could fall over while still sitting down.

Magnus reached out, his thick right hand hovering indecisively over the pieces.

Andy let out a disgusted sigh. "Come on, Mags, it's boring enough without you pretending you don't know exactly what piece to move."

"The play's the thing, Andy."

"What is that? Another one of those quote-thingees that's supposed to teach me something about life?"

Magnus smiled. "You already know the important stuff, like how to shoot straight. The rest of it? All philosophical bullshit, really."

Magnus moved his queen to king-3, right on top of Andy's king. Andy couldn't take the queen without putting himself in check thanks to Magnus's rook, which sat on queen's-bishop-3.

"I've never liked you," Andy said. It pissed him off to no end that he couldn't beat Magnus. Ever. "Chess is for faggots, anyway. So what now, Mags?"

"Looks like you lose again."

"I meant with the whole plane and everything."

"Oh, *that* what now."

Andy nodded. Sometimes Magnus told him what was going on, sometimes not. All full up with Puke-Jack, maybe he'd let out some secrets.

"Now it's a waiting game," Magnus said. "We declare the C-5 missing. There will be a search, but nothing will be found."

"Without a flight plan? Crash report, anything like that?"

"They know we have a C-5," Magnus said. "Colding ordered it to take off over the big water, and we haven't heard from it since."

Maybe it was the buzz, but Andy couldn't put all the pieces together. "*Colding* ordered it?"

Magnus nodded.

"But what about Fischer? He's got a real hard-on for you and Danté."

"The research is gone," Magnus said. "That's what the governments really wanted. They don't care about Fischer's hard-on for us. Once we fire up the lawyers, make a stink, the governments tell Fischer to back off, and that's that."

"Huh. Is it really that easy?"

Magnus picked up his glass and took a big swallow. "We'll find out, won't we?"

We'll find out. Magnus knew how to plan ahead, how to put pieces in play when others thought he was just standing still. That brand of thinking had kept Andy alive at least a half-dozen times, and in situations far more severe than this. A lot of people had died under Magnus's command, but a lot more had survived when the situation dictated they had no right to do so.

"What about Jian's body?"

"It will be found."

"By who?"

"By us."

"Wait a minute. Then why did you have Colding bury her?"

"So we could dig her up. Part of her, anyway. We leave enough buried so that Fischer's cronies find Colding's DNA all over her. Hair, skin, fingerprints, shit like that."

Andy shook his head. Magnus was just amazing. "So *Colding* gets fingered for Jian's murder?"

Magnus nodded.

"And we found the body?"

"That's right."

"And we knew Colding killed her . . . how?"

Magnus sighed. "Because of his deathbed confession. Which came right after we shot him in self-defense."

Andy moved his king to queen-1. "And Colding attacked us . . . why?"

"You and I were in Manitoba. We'd lost contact with everyone on the island. Clayton, Sven, the Harveys, the scientists. Bobby flew us out here to see what was going on. We discovered Colding had sabotaged the C-5, then killed everyone else after it flew off. He had to make sure there were no witnesses, you see. When we confronted him, he tried to murder us as well."

"Wow," Andy said. "That Colding is a regular psycho."

"Sad, but true."

"Just so I'm tracking here . . . Colding did all of this . . . how come?"

"Because you were fucking Sara."

"I was?"

"You were."

"*Sweet.* Would love to pound on that vaj."

"Jian found out you were doing Colding's girlfriend," Magnus said. "So, like a good friend, she told Colding. Bubbah snapped, killed Jian on the spot. Turns out the boy has a history of losing his temper. He wanted Sara dead, so he sent the C-5 up, put a bomb in it. Then he tried to cover his tracks. Killed everyone. Bobby brings us out here, routine shit, Colding tries to kill us."

"'Cause he's psycho."

"Exactly. But we defend ourselves. As he's dying, he tells us the whole story, including where he buried Jian."

"What a shame," Andy said. "The whole project, wiped out. The only people left are you, me and Gunther."

"Lucky for Gunther he was pulling extended duty up on the fire watchtower. Phone lines were down as well. Crazy how it happens like that. Gunther manned his post like a good soldier, had no idea any of this was going on."

"Will Gun play along with that?"

"Considering his options if he doesn't, yeah, I think he'll play along."

Andy nodded. Gunther was no dummy. "All of this human tragedy, this loss of life makes me sad. Exactly when did Colding snap and kill everyone left on the island?"

"Tomorrow," Magnus said. "You don't mind doing some wet work for me tomorrow, do you?"

"Does a dog mind licking his own balls? I'll get things done. But what does Danté think of all this?"

"Sometimes my brother needs people like us to help him, even if he never knew he needed that help in the first place."

Magnus moved his rook to queen's-bishop-1. Checkmate.

Andy shook his head. "Did I mention I never liked you?"

"You did. Just be grateful that I like you. At least, more than I like Colding."

Magnus refilled his tumbler with Yukon Jack, and Andy set the pieces up for another game.

CLAYTON COULDN'T PUT it off any longer. He had to take his chances. He'd dragged out fixing the phone line breaks, hoping Magnus and Andy would hit the trails for a snowmobile run. No such luck. They weren't leaving the mansion, so he had to figure out how to work around them.

He rolled his mop bucket into the lounge. Magnus sat in his leather chair that faced the big picture window. Andy the Asshole was relaxing in a neighboring chair. A chessboard sat on the table between them.

"Hey, Clayton," Andy said. "Get in here and clean up this pigsty, will ya?"

Clayton looked around the lounge. Dirty plates were everywhere, as were empty beer cans and two empty bottles of Yukon Jack. The jerks hadn't bothered to pick up one damn thing all day. They'd just tossed their trash around as if this were some flophouse.

"You boys even bother to get up to hit da crapper? Or did you just fling your poo around like da fucking gorillas you are?"

Andy raised his whisky glass. "Maybe that can be arranged."

"Maybe you can kiss my ass, you little freak."

"The place *is* a bit dirty," Magnus said. "You sick or something, old man?"

Clayton snorted, his fear forgotten in a brief burst of anger. "I've been freezing my nuts off all goddam day, and I come back to this. I think I'll clean up da rest of da place first so you two rump rangers can sit in your own stink for a bit more."

Magnus slowly turned in his chair to look back at Clayton. "I think you're getting old," he said. "Might have to get someone out here to replace you."

"You wanna fire me, fire me. Until then, I got work to do. I'll start in da security room." Clayton rolled the mop bucket out of the lounge and headed straight for the stairs. Maybe they'd keep playing that chess game, keep drinking. He had to take a shot now, when he knew exactly where those two were.

He carried the heavy mop bucket down to the bottom of the back stairs. Once there, he rolled it to the security room and opened the door. Gunther was sitting in the swivel chair, feet up on the counter, eyes closed in a catnap. The eyes fluttered open when Clayton walked in.

Gunther sat up quickly, as if he'd been caught doing something wrong. When he saw Clayton, he smiled, a smile that quickly turned into a yawn.

"Shit, Clayton, you scared me. I thought you were Magnus."

"Don't worry about it. He's up in da lounge getting hammered with Andy. Hey, I finished *Hot Midnight*. Best of all da three books."

Gunther smiled. "You finished it already?"

"Yah. I liked it. Your main character chick reminded me of Liz Taylor. Liz was a hot one, let me tell you. Liked da backdoor action."

Gunther laughed and shook his head. "Whatever, Clayton. But thanks for reading my book."

"No problem. You'll have da common decency, of course, to not mention to anyone I'm reading a vampire romance novel?"

"Of course."

"You got talent," Clayton said. "More than those fuck-stains you call your friends." He lifted his head to the ceiling, indicating the lounge.

Gunther rubbed his eyes. "Those aren't my friends, Clayton. I served with them, but this is just a job. Man, I'm beat. Been doing sixteen hours a day."

"What, down here?"

"Magnus has me and Colding taking ten-hour shifts up on the fire watchtower, eyeballing for anyone flying in. Andy only has to do four hours at a time, the damn brownnoser."

"Is that right. So, Colding's up in da tower right now?"

Gunther nodded. "Yeah, probably freezing his ass off. Nothing quite like being thirty feet off the ground in a tin shack in the dead of winter."

"Why is Magnus making you guys do that?"

Gunther shrugged. "He thinks Danté might arrive at any second, wants to make sure we talk him in." Another huge yawn opened Gunther's mouth.

"Jeez, author-man. Go grab some coffee from da kitchen. Magnus will never know you're gone. I'll keep an eye on da screens for you, eh?"

"Yeah, coffee would be great. You sure you know how to work this stuff?"

"Who da hell do you think used it before you all got here?"

Gunther smiled, stretched, then stood and walked out of the room, shutting the door behind him.

Clayton sat at the desk and moved the mouse. On the screen, the spinning Genada logo disappeared, replaced by the desktop's blue background and a log-in window. Clayton typed in his user name and password.

The computer let out a sudden beep. The words INVALID PASSWORD flashed on the screen. He closed the window and accessed the administration program. Clayton loved Black Manitou, but never for a moment forgot that if something went wrong his son was his only reliable connection to the outside world. Because of that, Clayton made sure he fully understood the secure terminal and the jammer controls — everything that had anything to do with communications on the island.

"I'm not as old and dumb as I look, you big bald fuck."

Clayton had long ago used the admin program to make himself a superuser, able to override any password protection. He logged in with the password 0-0-0-1, his *fancy* password, and the system came to life. He kept an eye on the security screens: Gunther was walking to the kitchen, Andy and Magnus were still hard at whisky-fueled chess.

Now or never. He clicked the icon marked *Houghton* and waited.

"Come on," Clayton whispered. "Be home, son, *please* be home."

After an agonizing ten seconds that seemed a silent eternity, the screen flashed once, then showed Gary's face.

"Dad? What's up?"

"I need you here right away."

"The weather's bad, Pops. I don't dare take the boat out now."

"Magnus blew up da plane. He's killing people."

Gary blinked a few times. "This better not be another one of your tall tales, Dad."

Clayton shook his head. "Most of da crew is dead. Sara and Tim made it out. He finds them, they're dead, too."

Gary's eyes narrowed and his jaw muscles twitched.

"Tell me what to do, Dad."

Clayton felt a sudden swell of pride. Gary didn't look like a little boy anymore, or like a stoner — Clayton's son suddenly looked like a man.

"I hid them in da church," Clayton said. "Come in quiet with no lights, get them, take them back to da mainland."

"Will you be with them? I gotta get you out of there."

"Never mind about me, eh? I've got to watch out for some other people. Get Sara and Tim off da island, and I'm not going to listen to another word about it, you understand?"

Gary nodded. "Should I call the cops?"

Clayton scratched his beard. "Not yet. Do it when you get them two back. If da local cops show up, even if da fuckin' *army* shows up, Magnus could do anything."

Gary took a deep breath, then let it out slow. "Okay, here's the deal. I can't come tonight; that's just plain suicide. Storms are tearing the lake up. We're talking 'Wreck of the *Edmund Fitzgerald*' weather out there. It's supposed to die down a little tomorrow, not much, but I'll risk it. I'll time it to arrive just after dark. Can you wait that long?"

Gary knew boating, knew the weather. There was a limit to how much risk Clayton expected out of his son. "Yeah, that'll have to do. Be careful. Magnus has da jammer on full-time, so you won't be able to radio in, and I won't be able to warn you if someone is waiting for you, It could be dangerous."

"Dangerous? You really think so?"

"I think you're a smart-ass."

"Your *face* is a smart-ass."

The kid was making jokes, jokes for Clayton's sake. Gary was the one acting like a parent, trying to ease a child's fear.

"It's okay, Gary. I've been through worse. When you get to da church, give two flashes with a flashlight. I love you, son."

"I love you too, Dad."

Clayton broke the connection and logged out. Seconds later he was mopping away. He had the floor half done by the time Gunther walked back into the room, a steaming mug of coffee in his hand.

A SHADOWY FIGURE slipped out of the shed behind Sven Ballantine's barn. The shed's heat had saved his life, but he couldn't stay there forever. He walked toward the house, limping, every step painful from the burns, the bruises and the frostbite.

He hadn't eaten in days. His wounds needed proper care. They'd be infected soon, if they weren't already.

And those . . . *things*. He'd seen them bring down a cow, tear it to pieces.

Besides, surely Magnus didn't want *him* dead. That made no sense, so it simply could *not* be true. He had to get back to the mansion, where they had all those guns.

He passed the front of the barn. It gaped open. He saw no movement. Carefully, quietly, he looked inside. Filled with snowdrifts, but other than that, nothing.

Well, almost nothing. No cows, no people, nothing but scattered hay, broken stalls . . . and piles of feces everywhere he looked. He picked up one of the frozen piles and examined the stool.

What he saw almost made him cry.

He left the barn and limped toward the house, looking everywhere for any sign of movement.

DECEMBER 3, 6:34 A.M.

"REMEMBER, GARY WILL give two flashes," Clayton told Sara. "You answer with two. Anything else, and you lay low. It will be cold, but you need to stay in da bell tower and watch for him."

She nodded. So much sadness in that girl's eyes. Clayton wondered what it felt like to lose all your friends in one shot. He'd lost most of his, and two wives, and a daughter, but gradually over many years. Sven was his only friend left alive.

Sara put her hand on his shoulder. "We can't thank you enough."

Clayton started to say *don't worry about it*, but she grabbed his face and gave him a fast kiss, then threw her arms around him and squeezed. Clayton stood dumb for a moment, then returned her hug. She let go and wiped away a tear.

He locked the church door behind himself. No one would miss the heater, kerosene or supplies he'd stolen for Sara. Still, this was all crazy risky. He'd left footprints in the snow, but that couldn't be avoided. He could only hope that anyone shooting by on a snowmobile wouldn't stop to look around.

Clayton breathed a sigh of relief when he finally climbed into Ted Nugent's heated cab. He put the motor in gear and moved down the trail. He'd finish grooming the road and trails, just to keep up appearances. He passed James and Stephanie's place. Had they been up and on their porch, Clayton could have waved. But he saw no motion at the Harveys' house. Apparently, early morning on this freezing island was a time only for old fools.

The Bv's heavy sled dragged across the six inches of fresh snow, compacting it into a perfectly groomed surface. Clayton turned on the CD player. Some old Bob Seger would be just the thing.

He turned northeast, which would take him within sight of Rapleje Bay. Just southwest of Rapleje Bay, the Harveys' phone line connected to the main line. Clayton checked the latest repair map and drove to the break.

A fallen tree leaned against one of the phone poles. Both ends of the line were still connected, which meant a crack in the line — an easy, quick fix.

Clayton got out of the Bv and pulled a chain saw out of the back section. Poulan, the only kind he'd buy and use. He expertly cut the tree so it fell off the phone line. He climbed into the aerial lift bucket and raised himself to the break. The vantage gave him a clear view of Rapleje Bay. At first he didn't notice anything. Then his eyes caught a few strange, snow-covered bumps out on the ice, some marked with high, curling drifts. Wreckage. Had he just been sightseeing, however, he might have missed the bumps entirely, or at least dismissed them as chunks of ice. Even if Magnus did drive by he probably wouldn't notice. Just a few more hours, hopefully, and Gary would get Sara and Tim off the island.

Clayton turned his attention to fixing the landline, unaware of the hungry eyes that followed his every move.

THREE ANCESTORS REACHED the edge of the trail. Their bellies were full. They felt sleepy. But the food was almost gone — they had to find more.

A noisy thing had drawn them, pulling them through the woods with the promise of new prey. They stared at it, a new shape that made a steady sound much like a low, angry growl. It smelled like the stick that killed. But it *also* smelled like food.

Two of them started to move forward, but Baby McButter flicked her sail fin up and down fast, telling them to stop. This thing smelled too much like the stick. Her two brothers backed up and lowered themselves into the snow so that only their eyes peeked out above the white surface.

Movement, up high, on top of a skinny tree. *That* was prey, *that* was food. The skinny tree bent in on itself, lowering the prey back down to the noisy thing. Then the prey climbed *inside* the noisy thing. The noisy thing started running away.

Baby McButter flipped her dorsal fin high and held it there, signaling them all to move in.

Thick arms plowed through deep snow as they closed the distance. The noisy thing started out slow, but then picked up speed. Baby McButter roared in anger and ran faster, but the noisy thing had heard them and was escaping.

She slowed to a trot, then stopped. Her belly was too full. She couldn't run fast enough. As she watched the noisy thing fade away, she understood why it could move so quickly. No trees here, just a long, wide-open space that led deeper into the woods. The noisy thing liked the wide-open space.

To Baby McButter's right, one of her brothers let out a low, mournful moan. *No food*. Soon they would be hungry, and hunger was the worst sensation any of them had ever experienced.

They sat down and waited. Prey had come this way. Prey would come again.

SARA CARRIED A blanket. She stayed behind Tim, letting him take his time going up the narrow stairs. The crutch helped him walk, but his knee was still pretty messed up.

"This is stupid," he said. "I should just stay in the preparatory room."

Did this guy *ever* stop bitching? "Just climb. You have to take shifts up on the bell tower, Tim. Sooner or later I have to sleep."

Tim sighed and continued up the stairs that led from the back of the altar up to the choir loft. The walls were barely wider than his narrow shoulders. Sara wondered how small people were back when the church had been built . . . what . . . two centuries ago?

Tim made it to the choir loft. "Now what?"

Sara pointed down the loft to a ladder near the church's front wall. "Right there. Figure out how to climb it, I'm not going to carry you."

"Just because you kept me alive doesn't mean you're not a surly bitch. And I mean that in the nicest possible way."

"Just get up there."

Tim crutch-walked to the ladder. The choir loft was made from the same black stone as the church's walls, but with an ornate wooden railing. She looked over that rail down on the dilapidated church proper below. The place must have been beautiful once.

Tim managed the climb up the twenty-foot wrought-iron ladder. He made way more noise than necessary, taking great pains to show Sara just how difficult it was for him.

She slung the blanket over her shoulder and followed him up, going out the trapdoor. The turret was about ten feet in diameter, ringed by four stone pillars rising up from a waist-high stone wall to support the witch's-hat roof. Sara shivered as wind cut through the open turret — this was probably the coldest place on the island.

Tactically, though, they couldn't possibly do any better. She could see the entire town and even down the trail that led to the harbor. Thick stone walls would stop small-arms fire. Fate had put her in the most defensible spot on Black Manitou.

Except, of course, if Magnus decided to use the Stinger.

"Okay," Tim said. "Mission accomplished. Now can I go back down? I'm freezing."

She tossed him the blanket. "Nope. As of right now, you're on the clock. Gary won't come until tonight, but we have to keep an eye out for anyone approaching our position. Get comfy and keep watch. I'll relieve you in four hours."

"Come on, Sara. I'll freeze up here, and I need a drink."

A vision of Tim trying to get the syringe needle into the vial flashed in her head. Had he given the cow the right dosage? Had a drunken mistake cost the lives of Cappy, Alonzo and Miller?

"You've had enough to drink," Sara said. "You pull your own weight, Feely, or else."

He started to complain, but she ignored him and went back down.

"MOTHER DUCK-FUCKIN' MOTHERFUCKER," Andy said, then gently set the phone back in the cradle. This was turning into a crusty-turded shitstorm, and fast. How the hell was it even *possible*?

He sprinted out of the security room, up the stairs and into the lounge. Magnus sat there, fresh bottle of Yukon Jack in hand, staring blankly out the picture window at the blustery winter night.

"Magnus, we've got a big problem. Rhumkorrf just called in."

Magnus turned sharply in his chair. Andy took an unconscious step back.

"If you're bullshitting me, Crosthwaite, I'll give you a million dollars right now."

Andy shook his head. "No bullshit. He called from Sven's place."

Magnus stared for a second, then turned to once again face the window. He took a long swig of whisky, wiped his mouth with the back of his hand. Andy shuffled from foot to foot, waiting for orders.

Magnus finally stood. He capped the bottle and set it on a table. "Have you seen Clayton?"

Andy shook his head. "Not lately."

"Who's in the watchtower?"

"Gunther," Andy said. "Colding is probably sleeping in his room."

"Go get Colding. Tell him Rhumkorrf called in. You don't know what's going on, because Rhumkorrf is supposed to be on the plane. Both of you go to Sven's house. Before you get there, kill Colding."

Fuck yes. *Fuck yes.* "No problem," Andy said. "And then what?"

"You take Colding's Beretta. You kill Rhumkorrf. You kill Sven. When you come back down the trail, you kill James and Stephanie Harvey."

The woman. Hell yeah. He could save her for last, take his time.

Andy felt an iron hand on his neck before he even saw Magnus move. *Fuck,* but that guy was fast. Andy stayed calm and stood very, *very* still as his boss leaned in so close Andy could smell Yukon Jack breath.

"We're in a bit of a pickle here, Andy. All the evidence has to point toward Colding. So if you go dipping your wick in Stephanie Harvey, that will leave evidence that is *not* from Colding. I'll make this so clear even a twisted pervert like you gets it. You *shoot* her, you don't *touch* her. Do you understand? Blink once for no, twice for yes."

Andy blinked twice.

"If Rhumkorrf lived, we assume the others did, too. They have to be hiding somewhere. So do the only thing you're good at — kill everyone you see. This is a good strategy, Andy. If you agree, blink twice. If you disagree, blink once, but if you blink once, I'm going to crush your windpipe, then sit here and sip whisky while you lie on the floor and slowly suffocate."

Andy blinked twice.

Magnus let him go. Andy felt oxygen flood into his lungs. He blinked twice more, just to be sure he'd got the message across.

"Now move," Magnus said.

Andy ran for the door, headed for Colding's room.

TEN MINUTES AFTER Rhumkorrf's call, P. J. Colding held his snow-mobile throttle wide open. Andy was on a sled right behind him, the two of them shooting down Clayton's groomed trails. Headlights played off trees that whipped by as blurs of green and brown and white.

Colding's mind raced even faster than the snowmobile. How could Rhumkorrf be back? Colding had watched the plane take off. Nothing had landed since then. Had the C-5 crashed?

If Rhumkorrf survived, chances were Sara had as well. But if she had, why hadn't she contacted him?

Because she didn't trust him.

That was the only thing that made sense. Andy or Magnus had sabo-taged the C-5 somehow, and Sara had crashed it on Black Manitou. Not *landed*, but *crashed*, as the landing strip was the only place to safely bring down a plane that big. Colding had sent her up. If Sara had survived, she'd think he had betrayed her right alongside Magnus and Andy.

He had to find her. Explain things. But more important, he had to save her from Magnus, which dictated only one sickening course of action — killing Andy Crosthwaite. First Andy, then Magnus.

Colding wondered if he'd be able to pull the trigger. No, that was the type of comment someone might mumble in a badly written movie. He could do it. He *would* do it.

He wanted to get as far away as possible from the mansion and Mag-nus before making his move. Maybe Rhumkorrf could provide enough of a distraction to let Colding slip behind Andy unseen. Andy was a trained killer — Colding knew he'd only get one shot.

He had to make it count.

MAGNUS GUNNED HIS Arctic Cat down the main road. The snow-packed road's perfect condition was a bit ironic, considering Clayton had groomed it, yet Magnus was heading to Clayton's house because the man had seemingly slacked in his duties.

Clayton Detweiler had always been the poster boy of the blue-collar work ethic. Maybe he looked like he'd slept in mustard and didn't know that razors even existed, but the mansion was always clean and all the phone lines worked — everything seemed to just be taken care of as if by some invisible hand.

But for the last two days, Magnus had barely seen Clayton. Not around the mansion, not around the hangar. The roads and trails were groomed, but how much time could that require? Phone line repairs had also taken far longer than normal. Most significantly, the mansion looked dirty. Nothing big, a few papers here and there, but that wasn't normal.

All of it meant that the old man's attention was focused elsewhere. After Rhumkorrf's call, Magnus had a good idea why.

Magnus drove into Clayton's driveway. He walked up to the front door and tried the handle. Locked. He drew his Beretta, then raised a foot and push-kicked. The door flew open, banging against an inside wall.

No one home. He looked in the kitchen, then moved through the living room. Nothing. He moved to Clayton's bedroom. Bed unmade. Clothes covering the floor. Magnus was about to leave when something white in a pile of clothes caught his eye. He bent down and picked it up.

A bra.

"Andy, you were right about one thing," Magnus said to the room. "Sara Purinam is a fucking cunt."

Somehow, Purinam had brought that goddamn plane back. That meant as many as *four* military-trained people on the island. All armed with Berettas.

He walked to Clayton's wall-mounted phone. Next to the phone hung a picture of a young Clayton and a young Clint Eastwood, each holding up a huge steelhead trout, both grinning like mad.

Magnus dialed the mansion's general number. No answer. Goddamned Clayton was out on the trails again, or — more likely — hanging out wherever he'd stashed Sara and the others.

Was Sara and her crew with Rhumkorrf? Was Andy heading into a trap? Magnus dialed another number.

"Watchtower, Gunther here."

"Gun, Magnus. Any sign of Danté?"

"Nope. And no other aircraft, either."

A slice of good news. Magnus needed to clear up all these loose ends before his brother arrived. Danté might turn a blind eye to murder that had already happened, but he wouldn't stand by while Magnus executed people.

"Turn the radar on and leave it on," Magnus said. "I'm out on the sled. You see anything, you hit the air-raid siren."

"Yes sir."

"Have you seen Colding and Andy?"

"Two sleds just went by," Gunther said. "Could be them."

"What about Clayton's Bv206?"

"Saw the zebra-striped thing about five minutes ago, heading southwest, toward the mansion. It's frickin' freezing up here, Mags. How about I come down and work the security room for a while?"

Magnus hung up without answering. Clayton was heading back to the mansion. Was he going for the armory? Did he have Sara and her crew with him?

The Arctic Cat was much faster than the Bv206. Magnus ran out of Clayton's house — whatever it took, he had to get to the mansion first.

COLDING HELD THE throttle open wide, pushing the Arctic Cat to its limits. The Cat's headlights illuminated a narrow cone of the wooded trail's thick darkness. The trail popped out of the trees at Big Todd Harbor, then continued along the coastline. A cloud-covered moon cast down feeble light.

The name "harbor" was a misnomer for this northwest-side beach strewn with huge, jagged chunks of weathered limestone, but it was an inlet, so long ago someone had named it thus all the same. He cast a quick glance out at the water . . . and did a double take. The small inlet looked completely frozen over. At least a half mile of ice stretched out from the coast, as if Black Manitou was growing. The bitter cold wasn't satisfied with claiming just the land — it wanted everything, including the churning waters of Lake Superior.

He looked back up the trail and his hands reactively locked on the brakes: a fallen tree blocked the path. Colding fought to keep the snowmobile under control. The rear end fishtailed to the left, but he brought it to a stop just parallel to the tree. The sled now pointed straight toward the trail's three-foot-high right snowbank.

Dead and free of bark, the tree blocking the road really wasn't much of a tree at all. Maybe a foot in diameter. If he'd hit it full speed, however, it would have demolished his snowmobile and probably killed him. The tree had fallen from the left side of the trail, and only extended about four feet onto the right bank. They could easily go around it.

But there was something odd about the tree.

Behind him, Andy slowed his Polaris to a stop, his headlights illuminating the dead wood. Colding dismounted his Arctic Cat and knelt next to the log. He flipped up his face shield for a better look. Long, deep, parallel white marks covered the old wood.

Claw marks. From . . . a bear, maybe?

Not a bear. You know what it is.

No. No way.

He sensed Andy walking up behind him. Andy had been on Black Manitou many times over the years. Maybe he'd say it was normal, not what Colding already knew it had to be. Colding patted the claw marks with his left hand.

"Andy, look at this. You ever seen anything like this on the island?"

Andy leaned down for a closer look. "Can't say that I have. What is it?"

"Looks like claw marks. Please tell me there are bears on this island."

Andy stood up, shaking his head. "I've never seen any. And I've been in these woods dozens of times."

Colding ran his gloved fingers over the deep marks. The four parallel grooves were almost two inches apart. The claw would be *huge*. He wondered if the thing that had made these marks was moving southwest, toward the mansion, or north, toward Rhumkorrf.

Then his eyes registered the footprints. Everywhere. *Hundreds* of them, pressed into the packed trail. Big prints, eight inches wide and a foot long, clean indentations of claw tips in front of each of the four toes. The snowmobile's lights cast black shadows within the prints, making them look deeper, larger, even more ominous.

If Rhumkorrf made it back . . . then the cows could have made it back too.

The memory of the camera-biting fetus stabbed at him. A few pounds then. Now? Probably over two hundred.

Colding stood and walked back to his snowmobile. "Andy, we've gotta move, fast. I think I know what made those marks." He swung his leg over the Arctic Cat and sat. He paused before hitting the *start* button and looked back. Andy was just standing there.

Andy took off his gloves. "Well, I guess this is as good a place as any."

"For what?"

With a smooth motion, Andy unzipped his snowsuit, reached inside, and came out with his Beretta pointed right at Colding.

"To pay you back for drawing down on me."

Colding stared at the gun. How could he have been so stupid? He should have tried to take Andy out the second he realized the C-5 was on the island. There was no way he could unzip his snowsuit and draw his own Beretta before Andy gunned him down.

"Andy, the . . . the cows, did Magnus tell you what's *inside* the cows? Just listen to me for a second . . . look at the weird footprints all over the ground. It's those *things*."

Andy nodded. "Yeah, that's a problem for sure. But you know what? It's really not a problem for *you*. Not anymore."

This was it. He was going to die, shot to death on this frozen island.

"Andy, *please*." He heard his own voice crack a little. Was that what begging sounded like? Coming out of his own mouth? "Come on, man, this is bad, you don't have to do this."

"Wrong. Magnus told me to do it. It's either me or you. Good, bad, I'm the guy with the gun, so I choose you."

Colding's mind raced for something to say, but words escaped him. What would it feel like to be shot? Holy shit *holyshit* maybe he could dive for Andy's feet, maybe—

Andy cocked the hammer. "You ready, *Bubbah*?"

Colding didn't say anything, *couldn't* say anything.

A crack echoed across the darkness. Colding's body twitched violently, anticipating the lethal pain, but after a fraction of a second he realized the sound had come from the woods. A broken stick.

Andy turned his head to look. His gun remained leveled at Colding.

Colding moved to launch himself at Andy, but he wasn't even halfway out of his seat before Andy turned back, eyes locked on Colding. "Don't bother, duck-fucker."

Colding froze. He was screwed, so utterly screwed.

Another cracking sound, smaller this time but still definitive. Colding thought he saw movement deep in the wood's blackness.

From the trees behind Andy came a low, slow, deep growl.

Colding's skin tingled all over. He felt a new fear, a *primitive* fear, even beyond that brought on by a gun pointed at his face.

Andy took a few steps back, increasing his distance from Colding, then looked into the dark woods. Colding couldn't breathe. *Overwhelming.* He *had* to get away from there, *hadtohadto*, but Andy wouldn't let him move.

"There's a lot of them," Colding said, his words coming fast. "Dozens, maybe forty, you need me or they'll take you down. Two guns, man, *two*."

"You talk too much," Andy said. He once again focused on Colding. "It's been real, dick-weed."

Something erupted out of the woods.

Andy flinched just as the gun fired, throwing off his aim. The bullet hit the seat behind Colding, ripping up the vinyl and tearing out a huge chunk of foam rubber.

Massive.

That was the only word for the thing. White with the black spots of a cow, a lion-sized cross between a gorilla and a hyena, thick shoulders, black beady eyes, a mouth big enough to bite a man clean in half and teeth that looked like they could pierce steel plate. Way over four hundred pounds, easy.

"Fuck a duck," Andy said.

It bounded forward, roaring, huge muscles rippling under the black-and-white fur, heaving chest pushing up snow like the wake from a speedboat. A long fin rose up from the thing's head, revealing a bright-yellow membrane running from the fin to the creature's back.

A single thought dominated Colding's mind: *I'd rather take a bullet.*

He thumbed the *start* button. The engine fired and Colding hit the throttle.

Andy twisted to fire at Colding, then quickly changed his mind and turned to shoot at the oncoming creature, now only twenty yards away and closing fast.

pop-pop-pop-pop-pop-pop-pop-pop

Colding's sled shot up and over the three-foot bank, plunging into the snow beyond. He turned hard left, parallel to the trail.

pop-pop-pop-pop

Each shot made Colding wince, made him wonder if the bullets were tearing into him and he just couldn't feel it. His sled lurched through the deep snow. He couldn't pick up speed. He glanced over at the bloody creature struggling to crawl toward Andy. It had taken at least ten shots at point-blank range, yet still it came on, big jaws snapping on empty air.

Andy turned, his eyes locking on Colding's. The empty magazine dropped free. Andy already had another in hand, and it slid into the Beretta with sickening, professional speed.

Colding looked forward and leaned low as the sled finally accelerated. All he heard was the engine's powerful scream. The fallen tree passed by on his left.

Then he saw them.

To the front and the right, two more of the creatures were coming out of the nighttime woods, barely illuminated by his headlights, ten yards away and closing fast.

A bullet punched a hole in his plexiglass windshield.

Colding angled left toward the trail. He had to jump the bank like Sara had shown him. He already had the throttle opened up, but he squeezed harder anyway.

A sudden, blazing pain exploded in his right shoulder, but he didn't let go.

Closing in from the front right, the first creature leaped for him. Colding hit the bank and pushed down hard on the runners. The sled shot out over the trail, a jet plume of snow streaking behind it. The thing's impossibly long claws reached out and out and out, swinging down in an arc that hit the seat just behind Colding's ass. In midair, the snowmobile's back end lurched to the left. Colding threw his body to the right to counteract the sudden shift just as the Arctic Cat slammed hard on the trail, jarring Colding's body and snapping his head forward. The sled skidded sideways and started to tip, started to roll, but to stop was to die and he savagely brought the machine under control.

On the groomed trail, the snowmobile hit fifty miles per hour within seconds — it shot down the dark trail like a screaming rocket. The creatures gave chase, but only for a few moments before they realized their prey could not be caught.

They turned their attention back to the other prey, the one standing behind the fallen tree.

ANDY FIRED FIVE rounds at Colding before he felt the claw on his leg. He reflexively jumped straight into the air, jerking and kicking, regaining his balance just before tripping over the fallen tree. He stared down at the monster, brain awash in disbelief.

I shot that fucking thing TWELVE times.

And yet still it dragged itself along the ground toward him, leaving a trail of spreading bright-red lit up by his snowmobile's headlight. Andy pointed the gun at the thing's head. It opened its mouth, nice and wide, still reaching for Andy's life.

He pulled the trigger, *pop-pop-pop-pop-pop*

The bullets ripped into the open mouth, breaking a pointed tooth, punching holes in the black tongue before blasting out the back of the skull in a spray of blood.

The head — mouth still open — finally fell still. A last cloud of breath hissed out, crystallizing in the cold before drifting away.

The roar of Colding's snowmobile faded.

Andy heard sounds from the woods. A coppery, acidic feeling blossomed in his stomach as he realized that the dead thing on the ground wasn't alone. He put his third and final clip into the Beretta.

Two long strides brought him to the Polaris. He hopped on and jammed the gun into his open snowsuit. Only a split second to decide between following Colding or turning the machine around and heading back up the trail.

Back up the trail, toward the mansion, toward the big guns.

He gunned the throttle and pulled hard to the right, body leaning far out to aid the sudden, sharp turn. On his back left, past the fallen log, he saw two of the creatures, their white fur a nightmarish red in his taillight's glow. They pounded toward him — heads down, legs pumping hard, black eyes angry with pure hunger.

Andy finished the turn and shot down the trail, toward the mansion. Speed felt like life, like pure safety.

Two more creatures came out of the woods on his right, but they wouldn't be fast enough to stop him. God, but they were so *big*, like shark-finned bears.

"Fuck you and your duck," Andy muttered as he leaned forward. Iraqis couldn't kill him, nor could the Afghans, Haitians, Colombians, Nepalese or the wherever-the-fuck-they-came-from Taliban, and these test-tube rejects sure as hell weren't going to take him out.

Then he saw the tree, leaning, falling, picking up speed as it descended, plumes of snow pouring off branches marking its downward arc. It slammed into the ground with a billowing cloud of powder, completely blocking the trail fifty meters ahead.

Andy's left hand pumped the brake as his right fished in his jacket for the gun. His sled's headlight lit up the trail, the blocking tree and yet another openmouthed creature.

Just like the pair only a few seconds behind him.

The sled still slowing, momentum pulling his body forward, Andy turned in his seat to fire on his pursuers.

They were faster than he thought.

As he came around, he saw an onrushing mass of black and white surrounding a giant, gaping mouth. The teeth closed on his gun hand, punching through skin and bone as if they were tissue-paper-covered twigs. The clawed feet dug in, skidding as the big head ripped to the right, yanking Andy off the seat. He hit the ground, rolled with the momentum, and came up on his feet.

Only then did he realize his arm was gone from the elbow down.

He had just a moment to look, to be amazed at the surreal sight of his *not-there* arm, the splintered bones and shredded flesh, then the second trailing creature smashed into him at full speed. Teeth sank into his chest and shoulder. Andy screamed just once before the two creatures from his right joined the fray.

Less than thirty seconds after the first bite, only bloodstains and an overturned snowmobile marked Andy Crosthwaite's passing.

COLDING BRAKED TO a stop on a rise that gave him a view of both Sven's house and the trail behind him. Ten minutes had passed since that crazy flight for life. His heart still pounded so hard he wondered if his end might not come from a bullet, or a monster, but from cardiac arrest.

He turned to look back, the barrel of his Beretta leading his vision. Nothing right behind him, but how could he be sure? He peered deeper into the dark, shadow-soaked woods on either side, watching for movement or a strange-looking patch of black and white.

Muscles stayed clenched. The barrel wiggled in time with his shaking hand. His stomach was bound up so tight he couldn't draw a deep breath. He saw *hundreds* of the creatures in the darkness, behind every log, lurking under the snow-laden branches of every tree. Waiting to spring, waiting for him to turn away so they could rush him and tear him apart.

Colding held his breath, then forced a long, slow exhale. He had to get control of himself. There was nothing out there. Emotions raged through him — fear of the creatures, frustration from not knowing Sara's fate, humiliation at having begged for his life. He had to calm down. Calm down and *think.* Sara might still be alive, might be with Rhumkorrf, hiding out in Sven's house. Colding had to start there.

He switched the pistol to his right hand, then reached back with his left and checked the right-shoulder wound for the first time. Felt like a burning poker had been permanently fixed to his screaming skin. His fingers came away wet with blood, but not a lot. He slowly rotated his arm. Pain, sure, but full range of motion. Andy's bullet had missed the bone.

Colding had never been shot before, but he didn't think the wound was all that bad. He wiped the blood on the leg of his snowsuit.

He switched the Beretta back to his left hand and drove with his right, down the ridge toward the lights of Sven's barn. He had to get out of sight, and not just because of the monsters — he had no way of knowing if Andy was still out there, hunting, maybe even looking at Colding this very second, lining up a shot.

The gun snapped up when he saw the small man in the black parka standing in the open barn door. Andy? No, this man was even smaller than Andy.

Rhumkorrf.

Colding kept the gun trained on him anyway, then pointed it off. What the hell was he doing? Think, man, have to *think*. He slid the snowmobile to a halt in front of Rhumkorrf but didn't shut off the engine. It idled as he looked the man over.

Claus Rhumkorrf looked like a torture victim. Oozing burn blisters covered most of his face. He wore no hat. The left side of his scalp flaked black where it wasn't raw and red. Tufts of blackened down hung precariously in spots where his parka was nothing more than torn and melted nylon, providing no warmth, no protection. His lips were swollen, cracked and white. His eyes looked vacant and ghostly — soulless.

"My God, Doc, are you okay? Where's Sara and the crew?"

Rhumkorrf didn't answer. He held out his left hand. No gloves. Fingers swollen to twice their normal size, blue from burst blood vessels brought on by frostbite. Second-degree frostbite, probably only a few hours away from the third degree that would demand amputation of those fingers. Colding had to get the man inside. How gone was Rhumkorrf that he wasn't waiting inside Sven's house?

And for that matter, where was Sven?

In the palm of his ravaged hand, Rhumkorrf held something brown with white flecks that gleamed in the barn's light.

"My fault," Rhumkorrf said in a tiny voice. "All my fault."

"Doc, did Sara hide out with you here?"

Rhumkorrf shook his head.

"Did she make it? Where's the plane?"

Rhumkorrf spoke with a far-off, distant voice. "I made it out just before the explosion. The blast knocked me through the air. I . . . I burned a little. I didn't see anyone else — they're all dead."

Pain. Not the physical kind, far worse . . . the same crippling pain he'd felt watching Clarissa die. No. No *way*. Not Sara. "Did you *see* Sara die? See her body? What about the crew, Alonzo and the Twins?"

"I woke up in the snow," Rhumkorrf said. "I told you I didn't see anyone else. I walked here and hid in the shed. Then the fetuses . . . they, they came out. I saw them chase down cows, tear them to pieces. Such *noises*. The ancestors are out there, P. J., you have to believe me."

"Preachin' to the choir. Check out the back of the fucking sled."

Rhumkorrf looked at the ripped seat. Chunks of white foam stuck out from the shredded vinyl. Colding saw Rhumkorrf's eyes moving from cut to parallel cut, could almost hear the calculations clicking away in the man's brain.

"How big?"

"Big," Colding said. "Way over four hundred pounds, maybe four fifty."

"Impossible. They would need . . . tens of thousands of pounds of food to reach that size."

Colding looked back to the barn. "Would fifty cows at about fifteen hundred pounds each do the trick?"

Rhumkorrf stared at the barn, seemingly dumbfounded by the question. "Yes. Yes, that would do it. And if they get the other cows, at the Harveys', they could get even bigger."

The Harveys. *Shit.*

"Get on," Colding said. Rhumkorrf let out a yelp of pain as he sat on the claw-shredded seat. Who knew which of his many injuries had zinged him? Maybe it was all of them.

Colding drove the sled the fifty yards to the house, then stopped on the far side so it wouldn't be visible from the road. He ran inside, feeling the house's warmth on his face even as he scanned for and found the phone.

Rhumkorrf followed him in. "Who are you calling? I already called the mansion and talked to Andy."

"I'm kind of aware of that," Colding said. "I'm calling the Harveys."

The phone rang. And rang. And rang.

"Call the mansion," Rhumkorrf said. "Have them bring that zebra tank-thing, please, get us out of here."

Colding hung up. "Can't do that. I came out here with Andy, under Magnus's orders. Andy tried to kill me."

"Is Andy dead?"

"I don't know. Maybe the ancestors got him, or maybe he's coming after us right now."

Rhumkorrf sagged. He still held the brown rock in his hand. "So Magnus really does want me dead."

"They don't call you a fucking genius for nothing. Come on, we gotta go."

"Go *where*? Magnus will kill us."

"We have to get to the Harveys'. They didn't answer."

"Then they're dead," Rhumkorrf said, shaking his head. "We can't go out there."

"Doc, we *have* to. And I'm not leaving you here, so let's go."

Rhumkorrf shook his head harder, eyes wide, a little drool dripping out of the right corner of his open mouth. "Nein! *Nein!* I watched through the shed window. They caught the cows and killed them, ate them. They eat everything, Colding, bones and all."

He held out his frostbitten hand, again offering up the white-speckled rock. But . . . it wasn't a rock. It was a chunk of dark brown speckled with tiny white ice crystals.

"Doc, what is that?"

"Stool."

"What?"

"Feces. *Scheisse.* From the ancestors."

Colding finally recognized one of the white things — a human tooth, a molar. "Oh, Jesus *Christ.*"

"They ate Sven," Rhumkorrf said. "They ate Sven and all the cows, Colding. Bones and all. Do you understand? *Bones and all.*"

The ancestors were out there, hunting. Could be anywhere on the island. Anywhere. Colding forced his hands to stop shaking. He didn't know where Sara was, if she was even alive at all. But the Harveys? He knew exactly where they were. And Magnus knew where Rhumkorrf was, whether Andy had lived or not. They had to get away from Sven's house, and fast.

"Doc, we're going to the Harveys' house. You can either get on the snowmobile with me, or I will *make* you get on it. I really don't want to put my hands on you again, okay?"

The little man looked at him, shook his head one more time, then he dropped the frozen ancestor shit on the kitchen floor. "You'll get us killed," he said. "Let's go."

MAGNUS FINISHED WRAPPING the duct tape around Clayton's ankles, firmly securing him to the folding chair. He'd already taped Clayton's hands behind him. The security room's harsh fluorescent lighting played off the old man's swelling left eye. Clayton's head hung down, wobbling each time he was bumped.

The head lifted a bit. Clayton blinked rapidly, seemed to snap out of it. "Someone help me! Get this crazy fucker off me!" No confusion. He knew where he was, he knew what had happened.

Magnus slapped him, rocking the old man's head back and drawing blood from his lower lip.

"No one is here, Clayton. Gunther is in the fire tower. Colding is dead by now. The only person coming back here is Andy, and we know how much he loves you."

Clayton spit blood onto the security room's floor.

Magnus had arrived first, then just sat in the dark security room and waited. Clayton had come alone, turned on the lights, then Magnus hit him and it was lights-out. Couldn't have been easier.

Magnus walked to the weapons rack and grabbed one of the compact MP5 submachine guns. He clipped on a gun strap, loaded the weapon, then set it on the ground.

The time for civility had ended. Now it was time to add a new knife to his collection.

Magnus grabbed one of the white Ka-Bar boxes. He opened it and looked at the round handle made of stacked leather washers, looked at the leather sheath. New knives had that *smell*. He dropped the box, then ran his belt through the sheath's loop. It hung nicely on his left side. Only when it was securely in place did he grip the handle and pull.

The seven-inch, flat-black blade seemed to smile at him. The knife reflected no light save for the thin, razor-sharp edge.

"I know you," Magnus said to the knife.

He held the knife with his right hand. With his left, he picked up the

MP5. The weapons felt solid in his hands. Balanced. *Real.* A lot of variables were flying around, for certain, maybe too many things to process all at once. But he always knew what to do with the knife. The knife made decisions easy. He walked in front of Clayton and set the knife on the floor.

The old man stared at it. He was very afraid, clearly, but that angry, defiant attitude still exuded from his every fiber.

"Clayton, I don't have a lot of time. I've done this before. Many times. I know exactly how to get what I want. It's better for you if you just cooperate. Do you understand?"

Clayton said nothing.

"Where did you hide Sara Purinam?"

"Did you look up your asshole? Oh wait, your head is already there, so you'd have seen her by now."

Insolent old bastard. Magnus had something special for him. He slung the MP5 over his shoulder and walked back to the weapons rack. There he screwed a torch tip onto a can of propane. He opened the valve, took a lighter off the shelf and walked in front of Clayton again.

Clayton saw the propane can, heard the hiss of gas, and shook his head. He understood. "Don't you fucking do it, you sick fuck."

Magnus flicked the lighter. The torch's pointy blue flame snapped into existence. He put the lighter in his pocket. Magnus had a philosophy when it came to torture: *Seeing is believing, but feeling is faith.*

He picked up the knife and held the blade in front of the flame. Usually, he did this part in the dark, letting the blowtorch flame be the only illumination up until the blade glowed red. It was a great psychological motivator before the cutting began, but he simply didn't have time for the extras.

"Last chance," Magnus said as he gently moved the flame up and down the seven-inch Ka-Bar blade. "You're going to tell me what I want to know. The only question is how badly you'll be burned when you finally talk."

"Just do it," Clayton hissed, his eyes squeezed wrinkle-tight in anticipation of agony. "Cowards die many times before their deaths, da valiant never taste of death but once, eh?"

The quote came out of nowhere, so random it made Magnus lower the torch. "I'm shocked. You know *Julius Caesar*?"

"Never met him," Clayton said, his eyes still scrunched tight. "Kerouac said that shit to me once when we were nailing some whores down in Copper Harbor."

Typical American. So crude. But crude or not, this old man was tougher than Magnus had suspected. Talking would just waste time unless parameters were established.

Magnus closed the torch valve and set the propane canister on the ground. He walked behind Clayton. He grabbed the old man's right pinkie and slid the hot blade into the skin. Blood poured out, hissing against the blade. Clayton screamed as the blade dug down to the bone. Blood spurted. The smell of burned flesh filled the air. Clayton thrashed in his chair and kept screaming, but Magnus didn't stop — he bent and twisted the pinkie as he cut, pulling it against the base knuckle. Just like bending a hot wing in half. Blood splattered to the floor as something *snapped* and a piece of gristle popped out.

Two more knife strokes through the last bits of flesh . . . the pinkie came right off.

Magnus walked in front of Clayton, tossing the bloody finger up and down in his palm. Tears covered Clayton's cheeks. Blood streamed from a deep cut in his lower lip where he'd bitten through it. He didn't look hateful or insolent or tough anymore.

He just looked old.

"You've got nine left," Magnus said. "Ready to talk?"

Clayton nodded.

"Good. Who is with Sara?"

"Just . . . Tim Feely. Da rest are dead."

"What about Rhumkorrf? Is he with them?"

Clayton shook his head.

"Are you *sure*, Clayton?"

The old man nodded. "He's dead. Sara said he . . . blew up . . . like da others."

Was the old man lying? It *was* possible that Rhumkorrf and Purinam were separated in the crash. "Tell me how the C-5 got back here."

"They crashed on Rapleje Bay. Thick ice. A . . . bomb. They got out and the whole thing blew up, melted through da ice."

That fit. If Sara had brought it down right before the bomb went off, there would be panic as everyone tried to escape. Rhumkorrf could have gotten separated. Sara had put the C-5 on the ice, then let it sink away. That filthy whore had ruined all of his careful plans, all of his meticulous work.

"Tell me where they are," Magnus said.

Clayton did.

Magnus reached inside Clayton's snowsuit, down to his belt, and pulled out the man's thick ring of keys.

"You don't mind if I borrow your ride, do you, Pops?" The Bv206 was enclosed and fairly well armored. A snowmobile was faster, but unprotected, and Sara had a Beretta.

Magnus grabbed a duffel bag and quickly stuffed it with MP5 magazines, a backup Beretta and a first-aid kit. Plastique and timers went in the bag as well, just in case Sara had created a defensible position. And what if he needed info from her? He threw in the propane torch and slung the duffel over his shoulder.

Then his eyes fell to the black canvas bag on the bottom shelf of the weapons rack. Fischer might come early, never knew . . . it helped to be prepared for any contingency. He took that bag as well.

Magnus walked to the door, then turned, taking one more look at the beaten old man. It was always best to leave subjects alive until you were *sure* you had correct intel, leave them in the darkness and silence so they could focus on nothing but the pain. Someone might be tough enough to resist questioning the first few minutes after losing a finger, but after two or three hours of feeling that agony and fearing what would come next? They always told the truth.

"I'm going to leave you here," Magnus said. "I'll come back if you forgot anything." He reached up and flicked off the lights.

Magnus shut the door on the dark security room. He didn't know what was keeping Andy, or if the man was even alive, but Sara Purinam and Tim Feely were just a short snowmobile ride away.

GARY DETWEILER HAD never seen conditions like this. A hard wind kicked up ten-foot swells. Chunks of ice floated everywhere. Although there probably wasn't a chunk large enough to hurt the *Otto II*, he sure as hell didn't want to find out while doing twenty knots.

Once he had the island in sight he turned off his running lights, navigating with GPS and a pair of night-vision goggles. Thick clouds hid the stars and kept the moon to a faint glow, but it was enough illumination for the goggles to show his way in varying shades of neon green.

The closer he got to the harbor, the thicker the ice became. Baseball-sized chunks collected like tightly packed flotsam, making the water look like an undulating solid, rising with each wave, dipping with each trough. The *Otto II* cut through the surface, leaving behind it a path of clear water that lasted only seconds before the churning ice chunks closed in again.

Chunky waves splashed against the pylons at the harbor's entrance. Actually, they splashed against twenty feet of lumpy, solid ice that spread out from the pylons. Gary shook his head in amazement. If this cold continued, the harbor entrance might very well freeze shut in a day or so. After that, the whole harbor would ice over in a matter of hours. That very thing had happened back in the winter of '68, or so his father told him.

Gary pulled back on the throttle, reducing speed and — more important — reducing noise. The wind was loud enough to hide the engine gurgle, unless someone was waiting for him on the dock. The *Otto II* slid through the icy harbor entrance. Beyond the walls, the waves dropped to three feet. He could barely believe his eyes — like the pylons, the shore and dock had extended with a good thirty feet of rough ice. Waves constantly tossed water and fresh chunks onto this frozen, growing shoreline.

And beyond it? A psycho with a gun. Correction, *guns*, and a lot of them. But that didn't matter. Gary's father needed him. Those people needed him. All he had to do was get on the island, make it to the church, then bring them back. Once in the boat and away from the island, they'd be safe.

He couldn't actually dock. The ice was probably too thick there, but it would be thinner out where it met open water. Somewhere in the middle, it would be solid enough to support his weight. He moved the throttle forward, just a bit, increasing speed. The boat crushed the leading edge of ice with a noticeable crackling sound. That sound quickly turned to a definitive crunch, then to a grind as the boat slowed, pushing up sheets of half-inch-thick ice as it went. Finally, fifteen feet from the dock, the *Otto II* stopped.

Gary killed the motor, leaving him alone with the howl of the wind and the steady, Styrofoam-squeaking sound of wave-driven ice grinding against wave-driven ice. He pulled on an orange life jacket. Without it, if he fell through into the frigid water he'd stand little chance of surviving long enough to get back inside the boat's heated cabin.

He grabbed a gaff pole and walked to the bow, testing the tip against the ice. It seemed thick enough to hold his weight.

Keeping his weight on the bow, Gary swung one leg over the edge, pressed his foot against the ice, and pushed. It held. He put his other foot down, but kept his chest and both arms in the boat. He pushed harder, making the surface carry more of his weight. Still the ice held. Waves splashed water and ice chunks at his feet. He swallowed hard and slowly transferred his weight, keeping his hands on the bow railing in case his feet suddenly plunged through.

The ice held.

He slid one foot at a time over the ice, taking care to spread his weight across both feet. The danger zone was likely only the next few yards — at the dock the ice had to be at least six inches thick, strong enough to support a dozen men.

Ten feet from the boat, the ice cracked under his left foot. Water gurgled up through the thin fissures.

Gary stood motionless, waiting in that infinite forever just before the ice would give way. Still it held. He slid his left foot forward, past the watery cracks. After a few more sliding steps, he knew he was safe and strode cautiously toward the dock.

During the day, the snow-covered island might have been a thing of beauty, but in the dark, through the night-vision glasses, it looked like a green-tinted nuclear wasteland. Wind drove wisps of powder across the beach. Snow-covered pine trees looked like heavy monsters trapped in thick green-white goo.

Gary felt for the lump on his left side, under the snowsuit — the gun's firmness gave him comfort. He walked to the shed at the base of the dock. His Ski-Doo snowmobile would quickly cover the one-mile trip to the ghost town. Walking would be quieter, more discreet, but Magnus Paglione was out there and Gary didn't feel like getting into a footrace for his life. Somehow he suspected a former special forces killer was in better shape than a stoner beach bum.

He kicked through a snowdrift blocking the shed and slid inside. The Ski-Doo motor gurgled and died on the first two tries. On the third, it roared to life.

He tossed the life jacket aside. If he had to run or hide, fluorescent orange wasn't the best color. Gary drove out onto the trail, moving slow, trying to keep the engine as quiet as possible. He kept the lights off, using the night-vision goggles to guide his way. The Ski-Doo glided through the inch or two of snow that had accumulated since the road had last been plowed. Dark woods rose up on both sides like canyon walls.

In just over three minutes, Gary saw the church tower through the trees. He took off the goggles. He unzipped his snowsuit, pulled out a flashlight, pointed it at the tower and flashed twice.

SARA AND TIM sat huddled together under three blankets that did little to ward off the cold wind blowing through the bell-tower turret. When Sara saw the double flash come from the dark path leading to the harbor, it seemed unbelievable at first, somehow fake. The second double flash, however, made it real.

"No fucking way," Tim said.

"Way," Sara said. She lifted her own flashlight, a clumsy maneuver thanks to Clayton's thick mittens, and gave two answering flashes. She set the flashlight down and picked up the binoculars, sweeping the dimly lit town square.

GARY SAW THE two flashes. He had to be careful. Could be Magnus up there, tricking Gary into coming in. He patted the gun again, just to be sure it was there. This was crazy, *really* fucking crazy — he was a barfly boat driver who dealt a little pot on the side, not some action star like Uncle Clint.

Gary put the flashlight away and put the night-vision goggles back on.

No way to really know who was in that turret. Setting up for a fast get-away would be smart. He turned his Ski-Doo around, leaving it just past the edge of town with the nose pointed back down the road. He slid off the sled. Now or never. His dad needed him. One quick walk to the church and back, and it would be all but over.

He reached the edge of town before he saw movement.

SARA LOWERED THE binoculars. "What the hell is that?"

"What the hell is what?" Tim reached for the binoculars, but Sara slapped his hand away. She looked through them again. Down there in the darkness, something was moving. Something *big*. Lurking around in the trees at the outskirts of the small town.

"Oh no," she said quietly. "Oh my God, no."

GARY FROZE. HE half hoped there was something wrong with the night-vision goggles, but he knew they were working just fine. At the edge of town, near the lodge, less than a hundred feet away . . . a . . . bear? No, the head was too big. *Way* too big. Through the goggles, the thing's black-patched white fur glowed an unearthly pale green. Something on its back kept popping up and down.

It opened its eyes wide. Gary knew this because the night vision suddenly showed two glowing white-green spots in the middle of that big head.

It was *looking* at him, mouth half open, long, pointed teeth glowing like wet emeralds.

"RUN, YOU IDIOT," Sara whispered. "Goddamit, don't you see them?" The man stayed perfectly still, staring at the shadowy something near the corner of the lodge. He obviously didn't see the others — Sara off-handedly estimated at least twenty — closing in on him from all sides of town.

"Sara," Tim hissed. "What the hell, come on."

She handed him the binoculars and pointed. "Tell me I'm crazy. Tell me those aren't what I think they are."

Tim stared for only a second. "Oh fuck me running. No way."

That wasn't what Sara wanted to hear. She started scanning the town, the horizon, looking for something she could use to help the man.

WIND WHISTLED THROUGH the snow-covered pines. Gary slowly took off a mitten, keeping his eyes focused on the bear-thing by the lodge. If he didn't get Sara and Tim out now, they'd be trapped for days. He didn't know exactly what the animal was, but it was just an *animal*. He was a human with a gun.

He slowly reached into his snowsuit, trying to control his fear, trying to stay calm. He heard a branch break somewhere off to his left. It registered that it would have to be a big branch to be heard over the wind. A *really* big branch. Gary turned, his chest roiling, already knowing what he'd see. Seventy-five feet away, at the edge of the woods, another of the big-mouthed bear creatures glowed green in the night-vision light. It, too, was looking right at him.

What little bravery Gary possessed instantly evaporated. Were there more? How *many* more? Staying very, very still, he swept the landscape.

A third by the hunter's shop.

A fourth and a fifth near the church.

A sixth at the edge of the woods on his right.

Gary Detweiler turned and ran as fast as the bulky snowsuit would allow, his legs *swish-swishing* against each other in a dark parody of a child's wintertime play.

SARA TOOK CAREFUL aim at the lead creature chasing Gary Detweiler. A sudden blow knocked her into a pillar. Strong, bony fingers covered her mouth. Tim had tackled her. Sara angrily brought up her hands to shove the man, but Tim leaned in so close his lips pressed against her ear.

"Don't move!" he hissed. "Keep still, there are more right below us!"

She pushed him off, but stayed quiet. She slowly looked over the parapet and down the side of the church tower. Sara's eyes widened in surprise and fear. Against the suffused gray-white moonlight glow of the snow-covered ground, she counted seven of the creatures. They were all looking up into the church tower.

They're looking right at us.

It seemed that way at first, but Sara realized the creatures were turning their heads, searching. They weren't looking *at* her, but they sure as hell were looking *for* her.

A roar — deep and jagged and hateful and savage — erupted from the path that led to the dock.

WHEN HE HEARD the first roar, his heart seemed to stop but his feet weren't as dumb — they kept pumping. Gary sprinted for his life. Another roar, closer this time. He poured all his energy into the sprint, heavy boots slamming against the snow-covered ground, arms pumping, legs churning.

Like an Old West gunslinger mounting his horse, Gary leaped and spread his legs, landing butt-first on the soft Ski-Doo seat. The now-warm machine fired up on the first try and he gunned the throttle, shooting down the path.

More of them *oh fuck how many are there* poured out of the tree-canyon walls, coming at him from all sides. Speed carried him past their muscular, heaving bodies. The journey that had taken five minutes while *put-putting* along took just over a minute with the throttle locked wide open. The dune crest rose before him, and beyond it would be his boat.

Another one. It came from the harbor side of the dune, stopped on the crest, crouched like a tennis player waiting to return a serve. Gary slowed, banked hard right and drove at an angle toward the crest. The monster took its own angle down the dune face, trying to cut him off. When it almost reached the sled, Gary opened up the throttle full out. The monster curved its pursuit path to correct, but Gary was already past.

He banked hard left just in time to sail over the dune ridge, catching big air, the boat now before him like a beacon of hope. *So close.* He hit the ground and pumped the brakes. The Ski-Doo skidded and slid — Gary was off it and running before the machine even stopped moving.

Another roar *Jesus oh shit oh God* not more than a few feet behind him. So close that going for his gun would slow him down too much and the thing with the huge mouth would be on him.

Gary sprinted down the dock, his steps vibrating the ice-crusted wood. He counted six steps before he felt the heavy vibrations of the creature's pounding feet.

He reached the dock's end and leaped like a long jumper. Behind him, the dock rattled as something massive pushed off.

In midair, huge jaws closed around his chest. He felt a dozen piercing pokes and a crushing pressure, then he smashed into ice as hard as a concrete floor. The ice seemed to hold for just a second, a *fraction* of a second, then cracked like a trapdoor, dropping them into the frigid water. Cold stunned him. His breath locked in his chest, frozen just like the ice covering the bay.

The biting pressure dropped away.

Swim or die.

He kicked hard. The water soaked into his snowsuit, turning it into a lead coat that pulled him down. He kicked harder. His head popped above the surface. He forced one, short, desperate breath.

Like Jaws coming up from the depths, the creature surfaced next to him, giant mouth gasping for air, huge clawed paws splashing at the water and fighting for purchase on thin ice that shattered from each blow.

Gary tried to swim. His arms and legs seemed slow to react. It was like swimming in quicksand. His head slipped under again. He fought to rise, but the snowsuit seemed to drag him down as surely as an anchor.

Swim or die.

He snarled and kicked harder, forcing his body to the surface. He was so close, only a few feet from the boat.

Behind him, the creature slid beneath the waves for the last time. Gary looked over his shoulder, knowing he only had seconds to live, knowing he had to concentrate, but he couldn't stop himself.

Cow-skinned creatures covered the dock. Diffuse moonlight played off their white fur, soaked into black patches as dark as the night itself. Dozens of monsters, packed at the edge, looking down at Gary with black eyes. They weren't coming in after him. He was almost there . . .

He tried to swim, but his muscles simply stopped obeying his commands. His throat locked up as if plugged by a cork. He couldn't take in air. The waterlogged snowsuit pulled him down again.

He reached out one more time, stretching for the ladder on the back of the *Otto II*. Wet, slick mittens hit the bottom rung and slid off. His hand fell away, and water filled his mouth.

Swim . . . or . . .

SARA AND TIM watched the seven cow-skinned creatures moving around the outside of the church — sniffing, looking, listening. They weren't leaving.

"You're the expert," Sara whispered in an almost inaudible voice. "What do we do?"

Tim slowly shook his head and shrugged.

The ancestors stopped their sniffing. They lifted their heads and looked north. The creatures all seemed to hear something. Sara listened, and a few seconds later she heard it, too . . . a faint, faraway sound.

The sound of an engine.

As a unit, the creatures headed for the noise. Sara watched them go, watched their odd, squat, waddling gait as they disappeared into the woods.

MAGNUS SLOWED THE Bv206. Any closer and Sara might hear the diesel engine, even over the wind. He would approach on foot, slip in and kill her. Magnus preferred to be on foot anyway.

He hopped out and slung the compact MP5 over his shoulder. Extra magazines went into his pocket. Beretta in his right hand, an unlit flashlight in his left, he approached the old mine shaft. He moved carefully, calmly. If Clayton was telling the truth, Magnus was up against a female air force pilot and a small, alcoholic scientist with a bum knee. That seemed like easy pickings, but Magnus was alive because he'd learned long ago that there *was* no such thing as easy pickings — a gun was the world's great equalizer. Sara Purinam had a gun.

Drifting snow almost completely covered the mine's old wooden door. Wind howled through the trees, and the mine itself seemed to moan as well. Clayton had always said that was the ghosts of the men who died there, but in truth it was just wind circulating through some unseen ventilation shaft.

Magnus approached the door, sinking crotch-deep in undisturbed snow. Something was wrong. There were no tracks here. Not even indents in the snowdrift. He tried to think of how much snow they'd received in the past three days. Plenty, but not enough to make the drift completely smooth. Unless Clayton had piled snow in front of the door after letting Sara and Tim in, then the recent storm had smoothed the surface, or unless there was another way into the mine.

Or, more likely, unless Clayton was lying.

"You tough old motherfucker," Magnus said quietly. "I didn't think you had it in you."

A noise in the woods, from the south side of the trail. Magnus dropped flat, his body sinking lower than the waist-high snow. He holstered the Beretta and unslung the MP5. Caught in the open, Magnus lifted his head just enough to look out over the snow's surface. He scanned the woods, but couldn't see anything in the darkness.

Another sound. A strange, throaty noise, coming from the direction of the Bv206. He was cut off. Magnus lowered himself back down, then crawled to his left, closer to the shaft door. There was no one in the mine. That much was obvious. If this was a trap, he didn't want to make himself an easy target by turning on the flashlight.

But he had to know what he was up against.

He gripped the MP5 in his right hand and came up to one knee, still crouched low. His left hand stretched out, held the flashlight against the top of the snowbank. He pointed it at the woods twenty-five meters away, then turned it on.

Along the trees lining the snowmobile trail, down close to the ground, the flashlight's beam reflected off glowing animal eyes. Magnus swept the light in a steady arc from left to right, from the trees all the way back to the Bv206 — everywhere the beam fell, it lit up eyes. At least two dozen pairs, spread out over fifty meters.

Magnus turned off the flashlight. The cows? No . . . the things that had been *inside* the cows. The things for which they'd built the heavy cages. But the plane had crashed only three days ago, how could the babies be that big?

A single roar erupted from the woods, quickly followed by dozens more, a cacophonous animal call-and-answer. In the faint moonlight filtering through the clouds, the creatures burst out of the trees like a line of rushing infantry.

Twenty meters. Closing fast.

Magnus stood and ran to the rickety old mine door. He lowered his shoulder and drove through it, splintering and scattering the old wood. He pointed the flashlight beam down the mine shaft as he sprinted, trying not to slip on the frozen dirt.

He'd covered only ten meters when he heard the monsters ripping through the door's remains. Magnus stopped and spun, pointed both the flashlight and the MP5 back up the tunnel. One-handed shooting would make for shit aim, but in this narrow space it wouldn't matter. He capped off a trio of three-shot bursts, filling the confined stone space with a deafening roar. The first creature to come through the door had a black head with a white nose-tip. Three .40-caliber bullets slammed into its skull, punching through fur and bone. The thing fell, twitching and kicking, its big body partially blocking the door.

The jostling flashlight beam made the nightmare scene shake with jittering intensity. More white-and-black monsters, big heads and black eyes and hissing mouths filled with dagger teeth, pushing through the door, pouring over their still-kicking pack mate.

Magnus turned and ran again, trying to keep his balance on the descending, frozen ground. He followed the shaft as it turned a sharp corner to the right.

And saw the dead end.

His frantic flashlight beam played off the ceiling-high pile of boulders and broken timbers. He scrambled up the side, looking for a way through. On his right, he saw his only chance — a dark crawl space, a coffin-sized dirt pocket.

Without stopping to think, Magnus crammed himself into the tiny space. He kept the MP5 close to his body and dug with the flashlight butt, a rabid badger clawing for cover amid a shaking strobe light. He had to make enough room to turn around.

Roars filled the cave, their echoes bouncing off the fallen rocks with ear-piercing intensity. Magnus grunted as he curled into a near-fetal position, working himself around. His shoulder and face wedged against the wall, like he was being squeezed by a giant earthen fist. Frozen dirt scraped his cheek raw. He ignored the pain, forcing himself around until he sat on his ass, legs straight out in front of him, the shoulder-high dirt-coffin space forcing his head down and to the left.

An over-wide head shoved into the crawl space, filling it. The mouth gaped but couldn't open all the way. The upper jaw knocked dirt from the ceiling, the underside of the bottom jaw pressed down against Magnus's shins and feet, pinning them flat. Hot breath turned to vapor as it billowed out. The shaking flashlight's beam shot all the way to the back of its throat.

Was that a tonsil?

The thing felt Magnus's legs beneath its jaw. Teeth snapped as it tried to twist its head to the left so it could bite down on his knees, his thighs.

Magnus fired three bursts. Nine bullets snapped off teeth, ripped into the tongue, drove into the brain. Blood splattered everywhere, on Magnus's hands, his coat, his legs, even on his face to mix into his own oozing cuts.

The creature made a choking, gurgling noise. Its mouth half closed, revealing wide, black, unfocused eyes. It slid limply from the hole and fell away.

Out in the shaft, Magnus saw another patch of black and white. He fired two more bursts but couldn't tell if he'd hit anything.

He waited.

No more heads appeared to fill his tiny hole.

Magnus contorted his body and dug a fresh magazine out of his pocket. Slapping it home, he waited for the next attack. But none came.

He'd never really been afraid in combat, but this . . . this was something else. Fear was no reason to back down, though. If they came again, he'd fight.

There were far less glorious ways to die.

He heard a sound like a body being dragged across frozen dirt, then noises that reminded him of wolves tearing into a deer on some Discovery Channel special.

His back against the end of the crawl space, he pointed the flashlight out, playing it against the far wall. He saw nothing. Whatever was going on out there, it was a few meters away from his spot.

He could hear them back down the shaft, hear their breathing, occasionally hear small whines and growls that could have easily come from big, playful dogs.

The ancestors were waiting. Waiting him out.

Soaked in the blood of his new enemy, Magnus tried to readjust himself, tried to get comfortable. That was the essence of combat — he'd had his abrupt moment of sheer terror, and now, apparently, it was time for the long period of boredom.

If he made it out of this mess, he knew exactly how he'd celebrate — with a little help from his old friend Clayton Detweiler.

BOOK SIX

DECEMBER 4

GUNTHER PULLED HIS blanket tighter and shivered. This was bullshit. Pure and utter bullshit. He looked out the tower-house windows, unappreciative of the sprawling, predawn view afforded him by the ten-meter-high wooden tower, which itself was perched on a high ridge. He could see almost the whole island — north and south shores each just over a click away, the mansion about eight clicks southeast, North Pointe just under eight clicks northeast.

Floodlights mounted under the tower's small cabin cast a fifty-meter-wide patch of light down on the white snow beneath. Twenty below zero and he was in a wooden shack with only a piece-of-shit kerosene heater to keep him alive. But still, it was better than being around Magnus.

Gunther looked at the spinning green line on the radar system's circular screen. He saw the same thing he'd seen for the last five hours: absolutely nothing. He tried to pull the blanket tighter. He'd had it. When he got off this island, he was quitting Genada. Freezing to death, suicides, crazy transgenic shit, Andy "The Asshole" Crosthwaite, freezing to death, sabotage, waiting for the CIA to storm the place, and freezing to death — just not worth it.

The radar unit beeped.

A green triangle now sat at the screen's outermost circle. Gunther watched as the green line slowly spun around its center point until it hit the triangle and produced another beep. The bogey was approaching from 50 kilometers south.

He picked up the landline phone and dialed the security room extension. It rang. No one answered.

"Come on, come on . . . where the hell are you guys?"

Wherever they were, it wasn't near a phone. Magnus had given specific instructions. Gunther's eyes fell on the button for the old air-raid siren that could be heard anywhere on the island.

He hit the button.

AT JAMES HARVEY'S farm, Colding stood straight up when he heard the siren's far-off echo. He and Rhumkorrf had been going over their crude hand-drawn map of the island, trying to formulate a battle plan for finding Sara while simultaneously avoiding the ancestors.

Rhumkorrf looked out the window. "What is that sound? An alarm?"

Colding had bandaged the man's head and hands with some gauze he'd found in a first-aid kit. The gauze covered up Rhumkorrf's ears, so Colding had taped his glasses onto the gauze with medical tape. Even in these darkest of hours, Colding had to admit that Rhumkorrf looked more comical than ever.

Rhumkorrf had returned the favor, cleaning and dressing Colding's gunshot wound. Not much more than a scratch, apparently. Considering Rhumkorrf was an actual doctor, Colding assumed he got the better of the exchange.

They listened to the siren for a few seconds, staring off like dogs hearing a distant call, then Rhumkorrf spoke.

"Does this mean we're saved?"

"I don't know. I'm guessing someone is coming, either an aircraft or a boat. Gunther must not have been able to reach anyone on the phone, so he set off the fire alarm."

"Wouldn't he have called the mansion?"

Colding nodded.

"So where's Magnus? Where's Clayton?"

"Hopefully Clayton's not in the same place as Sven and the Harveys."

The Harveys' ruined living room and the broken window told the story. There wasn't much blood, mostly because something had eaten the carpet where the big spots might have been. The few remaining splatters told Colding the Harveys were no more. He'd risked a run out to the barn and seen much the same scene. The Harveys and their cows were now just biomass added to the growing ancestors.

A lone sheet of plywood had been sitting in the living room. Colding and

Rhumkorrf had boarded up the broken window, kept all the lights off and stayed as quiet as they could. A brutal night, hiding in the house, wondering if Sara was out there, if she was safe, if she was sheltered from the cold. Searching for her in the dark would have been suicide. The ancestors moved fast, they moved quietly, and their black-and-white fur made for perfect camouflage in the winter night. He'd planned on waiting for full daylight, but the siren changed everything.

"We have to get to the landing strip," Colding said. "If it's Bobby coming in, he'll be in the Sikorski. That's twelve seats. We can use that to get everyone off the island."

"The landing strip is two miles away. The ancestors are out there."

Colding threw on his coat. "So is Sara, Doc. And if we can get that helicopter, we can use it to search for her."

"Is this the part where you tell me I can stay here if I don't like it?"

"No. This is the part where I tell you I will beat your ass until you get on that snowmobile."

Rhumkorrf shook his head and put on his coat.

Colding ran to the door and peeked out — still no sign of the ancestors. Beretta held firm with both hands, he walked off the porch and started the Arctic Cat's engine.

A NEW NOISE.

Magnus had spent the last seven hours listening to breathing, the rustling of movement and the most disturbing noise of all — the growing rumble of the creatures' stomachs. So many, blending together, sounded almost like the purr of a huge cat.

The new noise was faint, a far-off sound, something constant that he couldn't quite make out. The creatures apparently heard it as well, for their hidden rustling sounds increased, faded away, then disappeared.

He waited for five long minutes, but heard nothing other than that far-off drone. He flicked on the flashlight — nothing in the tunnel. Nothing he could see, anyway.

Magnus slowly worked his big body out of the hole, trying to be as quiet as possible. After seven hours mashed into that freezing, confined space, his cramped and sore muscles didn't want to cooperate. He slid out and almost fell, catching himself clumsily. Crouched low, he aimed the MP5 and the flashlight beam up the tunnel, waiting for the rush of creatures to come tearing around the corner.

No attack came.

Magnus walked quietly to the bend and peeked around it.

Empty.

They had finally given up on him. MP5 still at the ready, he trotted up the shaft. When he reached the entrance, he finally recognized the sound — an air-raid siren.

Oh, no. *No-no-no.* Bobby Valentine was coming in, and Danté would be with him.

Magnus looked outside. Still dark, although the light of dawn filtered through the woods from over the horizon. Nothing outside the shaft save for trees, and fifty meters away, the Bv206.

He had to warn his brother. Magnus sprinted to the zebra-striped vehicle. His eyes scanned the woods on all sides, but he saw no movement. He jumped in and slammed the door.

An armored vehicle. A defensible position. That gave him a second to think.

He couldn't call the heli. No radio in the Bv, thanks to his own god-damn security rules. The helicopter would come in, and it would be *loud.* That noise would probably draw the creatures.

He pulled out Clayton's keys to start the Bv, then paused. Clayton had keys for every building on the island, including those in the old town.

Magnus turned on the flashlight and set it on the seat. He held the keys in front of the beam and examined them one at a time. Black Manitou Lodge key — tarnished all over. Sven's hunting shop key, the same. The church key . . .

. . . the flashlight beam played off fresh scratches.

Soon, he would deal with them all, with Clayton, with Sara, with Tim, but first he had to get to the landing strip and protect his brother.

SARA POPPED OPEN the trapdoor and climbed out onto the turret, then helped the limping Tim up top. Stars flickered above, slow in relinquishing their place to the oncoming dawn. The noise that had been faint inside the thick church rang loud and clear in the open air.

"An air-raid siren?" Tim said. "What's up with that?"

"Not sure. But obviously whoever is in that tower wants to let everyone know something's coming."

"Or he's trying to call for help."

Sara shivered from the cold. "Well, if those monsters aren't there already, they'll sure come running. They seem to go after noise. I hope whoever it is moves fast."

"Unless it's Magnus," Tim said quietly.

Sara nodded. If only they could be that lucky.

GUNTHER HELD HIS gloved hands over his ears, but it didn't do much to stop the ear-piercing siren blaring underneath the small shack. Amazingly, he'd found a way to make his shitty situation even worse.

He forced himself to lower his hands so he could scan the horizon through his binoculars. Far off, he saw a tiny black speck. Bobby's Sikorski. Bobby didn't need any help bringing that thing in. Gunther had done his job. Time to head back to the lodge. Time to get *warm*.

He hung the binoculars around his neck, turned off the heater, walked out of the tiny cabin onto the wooden catwalk and started down the tall ladder. He was three meters from the ground when his eye caught movement from his left. Instinctively, he stopped and looked.

A flashing yellow color, but it wasn't a light ... more like a flag or something, like triangular fabric, lifting up and down in an irregular pattern. It was about fifty meters away, just at the edge of the tower's cone of light, centered in an odd-looking patch of snow spotted with black rocks.

Holding the ladder with one hand, he lifted his binoculars, leaned out and looked.

Even in the dim illumination cast off by the tower's floodlights, he saw it. A spear of fear stabbed through his chest. Not a flag in a patch of snow, an animal ... a huge, strange-looking, *dangerous* animal. But what was it? And why was it just sitting there?

He heard movement to his right. Gunther lowered the binoculars and turned.

Another creature running full-tilt in an odd crouch-waddle, like a half-upright Komodo dragon. It gathered and leaped, huge mouth opening wide to reveal rows of long white teeth.

Gunther grabbed a rung with both hands and lifted his legs high.

The creature slammed into the ladder where Gunther's feet had just been. Wide jaws snapped down just before momentum carried the big body *through* the ladder, shattering the cold dry wood into a hundred splintery shards. The remaining upper part of the ladder shook from the impact, so hard that it almost flung Gunther free.

The creature fell clumsily into the snow, its monstrous mouth working the ladder's remnants in short, vicious bites.

Gunther's legs desperately kicked open air as he tried to pull himself up. The ladder wobbled wildly, accompanied by the sound of grinding, splintering wood. He looked above — the right ladder post had snapped. Only the left one remained fixed to the tower.

More motion from below. The creature seemed to realize it had missed its meal. It violently shook away a mouthful of bloody splinters, then turned and gathered for another jump.

Gunther pulled hard, lifting himself enough to plant his foot on the wobbling ladder's bottom rung. He scrambled up just before the leaping creature's jaws snapped on open air.

He climbed, the wood wobbling with each step. His hands grabbed the platform just as the left post snapped loose and the ladder fell away. Feet dangling free again, he kicked them under the cabin, then pulled himself up when his body rocked back. He had to get to the phone.

Down below, the creature roared in frustration, a lonely, deep, guttural sound that echoed off the trees, clearly audible despite the blaring Klaxon. Gunther realized that it wasn't just one roar. He stopped on the catwalk and looked around.

More creatures, *dozens* of them, coming out of the woods from all sides like some childhood nightmare, rushing forward with their strange waddling gait. Big as goddamn tigers. They gathered at the tower's bottom, long claws digging into the wood as they tried to climb up, teeth flashing from mouths as wide and long as a grown man's chest.

His hands squeezed down on the wooden rail. He took in a deep breath, then let it out. Control. Just another kind of combat, that's all it was. Had to stay calm, make logical decisions, just like Magnus had taught him.

Whatever the fuck these things were, they couldn't get to him up here. They couldn't jump ten meters. He ran inside the cabin, grabbed the phone and hit the *page-all* button.

The phone rang.

No one answered.

The tower started vibrating under his feet.

Small tremors at first, but after a few seconds he had to put his hand on the wall to keep his balance.

Someone answer, goddamit, answer!

No one answered.

The shaking grew worse.

He set the receiver down, ran back onto the catwalk and looked.

The creatures were attacking the four thick wooden posts that supported the cabin. Biting and clawing, they tore out big, splintery chunks and tossed them aside before coming back for another try. Rough wooden daggers dug into their noses, their lips, their tongues, coating their black-and-white mouths with fresh spurts of red. Still they bit, they tore, climbing over one another to get at the wood.

Logical decisions didn't cover this. *Nothing* covered this. Fear settled into a waiting pattern in his stomach and balls. He was fucked and he knew it. Gunther drew his Beretta and held it, knowing it would do nothing to help him.

The tower lurched to the left, then stopped. Gunther grabbed at the rail in a desperate grip for survival. His bladder let go, the urine a final, brief sensation of warmth amid the bitter cold.

A second post gave way with a resounding snap. The ten-meter tower tilted to the south, slowly at first, but it quickly picked up speed, dropping like a falling tree. Gunther's scream locked in his throat as the tower slammed into the snowy ground. The cabin shattered, as did Gunther, dozens of bones breaking on impact.

Unfortunately, the fall didn't kill him.

Groggy but still conscious, Gunther rolled to one shoulder and looked back toward the base of the tower. The crash had broken all the tower's lights save for one — that last light projected back toward the tower's base, illuminating oncoming death in a morbid spotlight. They came like a tidal wave, a black-and-white tidal wave with a frothing crest of wide-open mouths and long teeth.

Oh, he wished he could have written that one down . . . that was the shit right there.

Gunther was too weak to scream as they tore him to pieces.

WITH DAWN BREAKING across the angry waters of Lake Superior and wind whipping across their backs, the Arctic Cat screamed like nature herself. Colding couldn't believe how fast the machine moved on the open ice — at eighty miles an hour he felt like a cruise missile streaking across the surface.

This open ice hadn't been there just a few days earlier. Black Manitou continued to grow, reaching out like a spreading stain of white ink.

They had taken advantage of the new ice to circle around North Pointe, searching the snow-covered wreckage dotting the frozen-over Rapleje Bay. No sign of Sara. Now they headed southwest, the coastline passing by quickly on their left. Colding prayed they wouldn't hit a patch of weak ice; any accident at this speed meant certain death. He wondered if the creatures were somewhere up on the coast, just inside the tree line, watching them.

When he reached the snowcapped Horse Head Rock, Colding slowed and stopped, taking stock of their tactical situation. Boyd Bay was frozen over all the way out to Emma Island. What had been treacherous, rocky water two months ago was now solid ice. The mansion perched high up on the bluff, looking like some gothic bulwark straight out of an Edgar Allan Poe story.

He saw the approaching aircraft. A helicopter. He squinted his eyes against the rising sun . . . *yes*, it was Bobby's Sikorski. Danté could be on it. If Magnus was alive he would surely go out to meet his brother, giving Colding a small window of opportunity to enter the mansion and get heavier weapons — for protection both against the ancestors, and against Magnus. If Andy was alive and staying home, then this would end quickly one way or another.

But what about warning Danté and Bobby about the rampaging ancestors? Danté might have known about the bomb plot. Known, and done nothing to stop it. Hell, Danté himself could have authorized it. But Magnus might have acted alone. If Colding didn't do something, would two innocent men die? If he *did* try to warn them, would they kill him? Would Magnus? There were no right answers, and every course of action or inaction led to death.

Rhumkorrf tugged at his shoulder. "Are we going to meet them at the landing strip? They can fly us out of here."

Colding shook his head. "We've got to get some weapons. Those monsters could be anywhere."

"Which means we have to go up the stairs, on foot, and into the mansion, where Magnus could be waiting for us?"

"Exactly," Colding said. "So, you ready?"

"I could not possibly be less ready for this insanity. Let's go."

Colding waited for Rhumkorrf to squeeze tight, then gunned the engine and shot across the ice toward the shore.

COLDING CRAWLED UP the last few steps. He pointed his Beretta just over the stone patio deck, sweeping left to right, looking for any motion. Would he even see Magnus? The man was so well trained, so dangerous. What about Andy? Had he made it back? And where was Gunther? Whose side would Gun be on?

Colding licked dry lips. No choice. He had to get better weapons, and get Claus armed as well. Colding half stood and walked forward. He heard Rhumkorrf following close behind.

They walked across the porch and into the lounge, Colding leading, Beretta up and at the ready. Moving quickly but carefully, quietly, they worked their way downstairs to the closed security room.

He turned to Rhumkorrf and whispered, "You stay behind me. Keep a couple of feet back. If you see me turn, you run like hell. If you see me fall, you run even harder, got it?"

Rhumkorrf nodded quickly. His taped-on glasses bobbled against his bloody head bandage.

Colding punched in 0-0-0-0, then opened the door to a dark room. He heard a grunt.

Fighting back the fear of an ancestor or Magnus waiting inside for him, he reached his hand in and flipped on the light switch . . .

. . . and saw Clayton Detweiler, taped to a metal folding chair that sat in a pool of blood. Colding reached back and grabbed Rhumkorrf, pulled him inside and shut the door. The two men stepped into the puddle of blood to untie Clayton.

"Get him ready to go, fast," Colding said. He ran to the ammo rack, grabbed a first-aid kit and tossed it to Rhumkorrf.

"This is duct tape," Rhumkorrf said. "I need a knife."

Colding tossed him one of the white Ka-Bar boxes. Rhumkorrf started cutting while Colding slid behind the desk and flipped through the security channels. If he could spot Magnus and the others somewhere on the grounds, that would help dictate next steps.

"Wake up," Rhumkorrf said to Clayton. "Come on, wake up."

"Wha . . . ?" The old man's eyes opened, and he blinked a few times.

Colding kept his eyes on the monitors as he spoke. "Clayton, why did Magnus do that to you?"

Clayton coughed, then spit blood on the floor. "Wanted . . . to know where Sara was."

The words hit Colding like a boot in the stomach. "Sara's alive?"

"I stashed her and Tim in da church. I told Magnus she was in da mine, to buy time."

"Time for what?"

"For Gary," Clayton said. "My son, he was coming out on da boat. He probably got them and is already back on da mainland. I can call him on da secure terminal, see if he's back."

Sara might not only be alive, she might already be off the island.

Rhumkorrf rolled some gauze into a small tourniquet. He looped it around the stub of Clayton's pinkie. "This is going to hurt very much, yes?"

In response, Clayton grabbed one end of the tourniquet with his free hand, and put the other end between his teeth. He snarled and jerked tight the tourniquet with a grunt of pain and anger. He wiped blood away from his mouth with the back of his good hand, then stood and walked to the desk. "Let me sit down. I'll call Gary."

Colding stood and made space, but kept his attention on the video monitors. He saw the Bv206 rolling down the road to the hangar, still about two minutes away.

"Clayton, is Magnus driving the Nuge?"

The old man nodded. Colding looked at the next monitor, which showed the view from the front of the hangar. The Sikorski had landed, its slowing rotor blades still kicking up a cloud of powdery snow.

The helicopter doors opened. Bobby Valentine and Danté Paglione got out and walked to the hangar.

And beyond them, in the woods, small blurs of movement.

Colding switched the view to infrared.

The screen lit up with white blobs that glowed brightly against the cold wood's gray and black.

"Dear God," Rhumkorrf said. "We have to help them."

Colding shook his head, wondering if he'd made the right decision. "Nothing we can do, Doc. Nothing we can do."

———

DANTÉ AND BOBBY walked out of the hangar and started up the snowy, one-lane road toward the mansion.

Baby McButter, now 510 pounds and so very, *very* hungry, sat quietly and watched her prey.

She and the others had heard the noisy thing up in the air, stalked it from the cover of the trees. They saw it coming down, saw where it might hit the ground. Baby McButter knew prey liked the open areas, so that is where her pack mates waited.

The other animals, the bigger ones, those had been easy to take down. But the tall, thin ones . . . they could be dangerous. They had a stick. A stick that could kill.

She and her siblings had learned not to rush in when they smelled the stick. They had a new way to hunt, a patient way.

Baby McButter softly flicked her dorsal flap three times, signaling to the others. Saliva welled up in her mouth and dripped onto the snow. Small whines escaped her closed mouth.

Whines of hunger.

MAGNUS KEPT THE gas pedal flat on the floor. The Bv could not go fast enough. Down the hill at the end of the narrow, snowbank- and tree-lined road, he saw the Sikorski's rotor blades spinning down. And walking away from the hangar, Bobby Valentine and Danté.

His brother.

His only family.

"Come on, come on!" All the yelling in the world wouldn't make the Bv206 move any faster.

DANTÉ STRODE UP the trail toward the mansion, Bobby Valentine at his side. Up ahead, Danté saw Clayton's snow-plow machine plodding down the road.

"Not exactly a hero's welcome," Bobby said. "Clayton's shit-mobile. I would have thought Magnus would be here with the Hummer."

Danté said nothing. In all his life, he had never been this angry. The hangar was *empty*. The C-5, gone. Magnus had defied him, moved the lab. The wonderful project was over. Raw fury blurred Danté's concentration.

He felt a hand on his chest. Bobby had reached back in warning, his eyes focused up the trail. Danté followed Bobby's gaze. About ten meters ahead, something was lying half buried in the roadside snowbank. Something black and white. One of the cows? It moved slightly, with the small motions of an injured animal. The snow all around the animal was churned up and lumpy, beaten down to the ground in some places, in others still a meter deep. It looked like the animal had been on the losing end of a fight.

Bobby took one cautious step forward, looked hard, then backed up. "Get to the chopper, and move slow, 'cause that sure as *fuck* ain't no cow." He reached into his leather flight jacket and drew a pistol.

Then Danté made the connection. Cow skin, sure, but the head was too big, too wide. And the body, all muscular, narrow hips . . .

. . . narrow, like a Synapsid.

"It's an ancestor," Danté said. "Rhumkorrf . . . he *did* it."

Years of work, billions of dollars, and they had finally pulled it off. *They had won.*

Spellbound, Danté walked toward his creation.

Bobby's hand on his chest again, stopping him. "Boss, no *way*, back to the Sikorski, right now."

Danté blinked, looked at Bobby, then at the creature. The huge, *powerful* creature. Yes, maybe the helicopter was the best place to be.

"Okay," Danté said. He turned to walk back.

The snowbanks exploded in a cloud of white. Seven huge creatures erupted out of them like demons spawned forth from a frozen hell.

Bobby reacted quickly. He brought his gun up to fire at the closest creature, but it lashed out with long claws that slid through Bobby's neck like knives through a balloon filled with red water. His severed head flipped through the air and landed at Danté's feet. Before the decapitated body could fall, two of the creatures opened their huge mouths and lunged. One creature bit into the midsection. The other clamped its jaws high on the chest. Both yanked savagely, tearing Bobby in half just below the sternum. The first creature violently shook its bloody mouthful, making Bobby's dangling legs flop like those of a cloth puppet. Danté saw internal organs fly through the air. Some landed on the ground, some were caught in mid-arc by the other creatures.

Danté turned and sprinted back down the road.

"NO, FUCK NO, fuck no *fuck no!*"

Just a few hundred yards from the landing strip, Magnus watched the creatures bound after his brother.

COLDING WATCHED THE infrared monitor. The white glow of several huge creatures broke out of the dark-colored woods on either side of the narrow road.

They chased another white blur . . . a human-shaped one. Danté Paglione.

Rhumkorrf's small fist, the one that wasn't frostbitten, lightly punched the desktop over and over. "What have I done? What have I created?"

The first white blur picked Danté off in midstride. For just a moment, the blurs of predator and prey merged, becoming one on the screen. Danté's blur, minus a leg, cartwheeled through the air, a trail of heat-white arcing from the new stump. Like a receiver and a defensive back going for a wounded-duck pass, two of the creatures leaped and caught him before he hit the ground. They jerked their heads, tearing the man apart. Three more animals smashed into the glowing white pile and joined the feeding frenzy.

Just like that, Danté was gone. The pack of monsters sprinted to the Sikorski, surrounding it, noses to the ground.

Rhumkorrf kept pounding the desk. "What have I done?"

Colding switched back to normal vision. The Bv206 had stopped. It stayed still for just a couple of seconds, then turned left, slowly driving down the road that led to the rest of the island, to the old town.

The road that led to the church.

"Clayton, tell me you reached Gary."

"He's not answering, eh? I don't think he made it back to da mainland. I gotta find him."

Colding turned to Rhumkorrf. "Bobby's helicopter, you can fly that thing, right?"

Rhumkorrf nodded.

On the monitors, more ancestors trotted out of the woods to join Danté and Bobby's killers. They surrounded the Sikorski. Colding counted at least thirty of them. The stocky animals sniffed around, dorsal fins twitching up and down. Then, as a group, all their heads turned to look down the length of the landing strip.

Colding switched to a wider view. At the edge of the long, curving strip stood a black dog, left leg held up as if it were hurt, its body shaking with the intensity of its repeated barking.

Like a perfectly trained army, the creatures took off as one unit, sprinting toward Sven Ballantine's dog.

Mookie's body convulsed with one more round of barks, then she turned and ran into the woods at the strip's northeast end. The creatures lumbered down the same curving strip that had once handled the C-5's landing and takeoff. They followed Mookie into the dense trees.

Colding knew they might not get another chance at the helicopter. "Clayton, we've got to move, you good?"

"Good enough. Let's get to da church. Maybe Gary is there with Sara, and if not we go from da church to da harbor."

Colding shook his head. "No, you're going on the helicopter with Rhumkorrf. I can't trust him not to take off on us. Sorry, Doc, but I can't."

Clayton reached up and grabbed Colding's arm. "That motherfucker Magnus *cut off my fuckin' finger* and he could be going after *my son*. I'm taking one of those guns, and I'm going to kill that big bastard. You got that, Colding?"

Colding looked into the older man's eyes, saw fury, hatred, stubborn determination.

"I won't run," Rhumkorrf said. "I . . . I swear it. This is my fault, everyone is dead because of me. I swear, P. J., I won't leave you."

Colding looked at Rhumkorrf. The scientist had a pleading expression on his face. He seemed desperate for at least some shred of redemption. Could he be trusted? Colding looked back at Clayton and knew that he didn't have a choice.

"All right, Clayton. But you fall behind and you're on your own. This isn't some story you made up about bow hunting with Charles Bronson or whatever, and I won't die because you can't keep up."

"Fair enough. But I don't know why you're babbling on about Charles Bronson, never met da guy."

Colding grabbed the British SA80 assault rifle. He stuffed five full magazines in his snowsuit pockets.

Clayton held up one of the Uzis. "This will do just fine. Me and Charlie Heston used to shoot these back in da seventies."

Colding took a Beretta 96 from the rack, loaded a magazine and handed the weapon to Rhumkorrf. "You know how to use that, Doc?"

Rhumkorrf looked at the pistol. "I would imagine I point the small end and pull the trigger."

"Yeah, and if it's one of your monsters coming after you, you keep on pulling it till the slide lock's empty, got it?"

Rhumkorrf's eyes filled with a sick fear, but he nodded.

Colding looked at the rack, then slipped out of his snowsuit. He grabbed a bulletproof vest and threw it to Clayton, then put the second one on himself. He pulled the snowsuit back on, feeling bulky from the thick vest. He had weapons, some protection, a vehicle — what he didn't have was *time.*

"All three of us will ride the snowmobile to the helicopter. Doc, you take the helicopter up. Maybe the noise will draw the ancestors, give Clayton and me a chance to reach the church before Magnus does. Look for me to wave you down after we kill Magnus. You land by the well. Remember, we won't have much time before the monsters come, so be ready to take us up right away. We lift off and head for the mainland."

"That plan is fucked," Clayton said.

"You got a better one?"

Clayton shook his head.

"Then let's move."

All three men ran out of the security room.

MAGNUS PARKED THE Bv206 behind the abandoned log lodge, putting the building between himself and the church. He shut off the engine and hopped out, the MP5 slung over his shoulder.

He was alone.

All alone.

And Sara Purinam was to blame.

If she'd flown the plane like she'd been ordered, blown up over the water, then the ancestors would have died . . . and Danté would still be alive.

He'd never really known loss before. Dad had died, but Dad had been old, with a bad heart. Magnus had years to mentally prepare for that. This . . . his *brother*, his only family. Magnus could have never prepared for this pain, for the anguish that tore through his very being. He *hurt*, and in a way physical pain had never affected him.

Sara. All her fault.

He hadn't seen any ancestors following him, but that didn't mean they weren't coming. He'd driven slowly at first, hoping the engine would be quiet enough to avoid drawing their attention. But after a quarter kilometer, he'd opened it up, pushing the Bv to top speed. Had they heard it? He didn't know. If they had, it would take the creatures at least ten minutes to run from the hangar to here, if they sprinted all the way.

He had enough time to do what needed to be done.

He took a long, 360-degree sweep of the area. No movement. The church was only about 50 meters from the lodge.

Time to get yours, cunt.

"OH NO." SARA crouched lower in the tower, just her eyes peeking over the stone wall. "Tim, keep still, I think that's Magnus."

Tim slowly moved to the edge of the bell tower and looked. "Oh *fuck*. He's coming for us. He's coming this way! *Shoot him!*"

Sara felt Tim's fear, empathized with it because she felt the same thing. The killer strode across the town circle, calm as all get out. His hands held a submachine gun. The morning sun blazed off his bald head. Dirt and bloodstains coated his clothes.

Blood from who?

If Magnus didn't see her up here, she'd get at least one clean shot before he could react. One shot, with a pistol, from almost four stories up, while her hand shook from the subzero cold.

She felt Tim's fear, true, but she also felt a burning rage. That bald bastard had murdered Alonzo, Miller, Cappy. And for that, he had to pay.

Magnus kept coming, moving with his smooth athletic grace. She had to control her fear, be a soldier, take that killer down. She could do it. *Had* to do it. Sara aimed, squeezing her hand against the Beretta's knurled handle, feeling the cold metal press into her flesh. She'd take Magnus halfway between the wooden lodge and the well, where he had no cover at all.

Just a few more steps . . .

MAGNUS STOPPED. SOMETHING was wrong. He could sense it. The hairs on the back of his neck stood on end, and it wasn't from the bitter cold. Grief had blurred his decisions. Grief and a need to lash out, to avenge . . . these things had put him in a terrible tactical position. Open space, no real cover. His instincts told him to turn around, find another approach.

But the ancestors were coming. There wasn't enough time.

And that *bitch* had to pay.

SARA SQUEEZED THE trigger slowly, like her daddy had taught her when they hunted deer in Cheboygan. She squeezed . . . and twitched a little when the gun's roar rang out.

HE HEARD THE pistol's report only a millisecond before the bullet ripped into his meaty left thigh. Pain splashed through his leg, but it wasn't the first time Magnus had been shot. Automatic impulses drove him to his right.

Another shot rang out, a miss.

He landed on his right shoulder, thumbing the MP5 to full auto as he rolled.

A third shot. That cunt was staying calm, aiming, trying to shoot straight, but still she missed. He heard the bullet whiz by his right ear as he came upon his feet.

Magnus fired on full automatic, ripping off ten rounds in less than a second.

SARA BARELY HAD time to duck — bullets sparked off the granite walls, filling the air with flying stone splinters that dropped lightly onto her trembling body. She'd hit him, she *knew* she'd hit him, so why was he still firing back?

"Tim, stay down!" Meaningless advice — if Tim got any lower, he would have been part of the stone floor.

Sara fought to control her breathing. If she could get just one more shot . . .

ONLY FIVE SECONDS since the bullet had ripped into his leg, and the real pain was already starting to set in.

Magnus limped backward, MP5 still pointed at the church tower. He squeezed off another five-round burst. The bullets kicked up little firework flashes when they slammed into the granite tower. He'd been such a dumb-ass. The church was like a fortress against small-arms fire. He needed the plastique. Shit, maybe even the Stinger. That would fix her fucking wagon, and fix it good.

Ignoring his screaming leg, he pulled out the empty magazine and slammed home a fresh one, all while moving backward and never taking his eyes off the black tower.

SARA WANTED ANOTHER shot, wanted to finish him, but she couldn't make her body get up, couldn't bring herself to look over the edge, to expose herself to flying bullets. She told her body to move. It refused.

From somewhere behind the lodge, Magnus's voice echoed out loud and deep.

"You didn't kill me, Sara. You *can't* kill me."

His voice seemed to fill the woods, as if the trees were possessed with a supernatural spirit come to tear her to pieces. She suddenly *wanted* the monsters to come back, come back and bring Magnus down. But they were nowhere to be seen.

"It's going to be bad for you now," his voice rang out. "Real bad."

She shouted back without lifting her head above the rim. "Why don't you come give it to me? Just come and get it on right now?"

"*Reallllll* bad," Magnus yelled. "I'll cut your wrists so you can watch yourself bleed to death. I'll burn you until your bones blacken. I *promise*, you rotten whore, I promise that you'll *beg* . . . and when you do, I won't listen."

Sara squeezed her eyes tight against the tension building in her brain, in her chest. How much more could she take? Now Magnus knew exactly where she was. She couldn't run, not with those creatures out there. Magnus wouldn't be dumb enough to step out in the open again — she had to find another defensible spot.

Magnus would kill her, bleed her out slow, *burn* her . . .

No, she couldn't let the terror take her now. She'd *fight* that fucker, fight him till she had nothing left.

"Tim, get your ass up. We have to get downstairs."

Tim crawled for the trapdoor. He descended gingerly, still troubled by his ruined knee. Sara followed him down, wondering how long it would be before Magnus came after them again.

THE ARCTIC CAT rode heavy under the weight of three men, but it reached the Sikorski. Had the monsters heard the snowmobile's whine? Were they coming?

Colding brought the sled to a stop. Rhumkorrf scrambled off and climbed into the helicopter, mittened hands shutting the door behind him. Clayton stayed on the back of the snowmobile, his good arm wrapped loosely around Colding's waist.

Colding revved the engine, making it as loud as possible. He had to draw them in so he'd know where they were, know they were *behind* him. If he drove right to the old town, the creatures could attack at any point along the way. They might even be in the old town already. And if they were, how could he save Sara?

He scanned the tree line but saw no movement.

Colding revved the sled's engine again. The motor's whine filled the clearing, bounced off the hangar, so loud it hurt his ears. The smell of exhaust filled his nose.

Colding felt Clayton's grip around his waist change from a manly *barely-holding-on-to-you* to a clutching, desperate grip of fear.

"Sweet Jesus," Clayton said.

A quarter mile away, the creatures broke from the trees and poured onto the landing strip. At least thirty of them, huge and strong and savage, a phalanx of muscle and teeth.

"Clayton, hold tight." Colding gunned the throttle.

The Arctic Cat still felt a bit sluggish, but free of Rhumkorrf's extra 150 pounds the machine raced back up the one-lane road toward the mansion. Colding turned right at the main road, following the same path Magnus had taken. He'd outdistance the creatures and have maybe ten minutes to gather up Sara and Tim, if they were still alive. Then, if they could either kill or avoid Magnus, they could wait for Rhumkorrf to come with the helicopter and they'd be off this godforsaken island.

Overall? Shit odds. But it was all they had.

Running wide open, the Arctic Cat pulled away. The monsters gave chase.

MAGNUS SAT IN the Bv's front seat, a first-aid kit open next to him. His right hand held his Ka-Bar knife, his left pressed a bloody ball of gauze against his thigh. Had to stop the bleeding. Blood had already soaked his sock, his shoe, and his pants leg from the knee down. He wondered if the ancestors could track a blood trail.

He'd underestimated her. He'd *deserved* to get shot for being so fucking stupid, walking out in the open like an idiot. First Clayton, now Sara — Magnus had lost his edge.

He'd used the knife to cut open his pant leg. Funny to have his own blood on his knife, but it wasn't the first time. He pulled the gauze back for a look. The torn flesh instantly filled with thick red.

Fuck. She'd hit an artery. He jammed the gauze back in, pushing until the pain radiated through his entire leg. He'd been to this dance before. Pressure alone probably wouldn't do the trick, and he didn't have time to wait.

The wound sat on the outside of his thigh, close to the knee, so he knew it wasn't the femoral artery. Maybe it was the ... what was it called ... the lateral circumflex? Didn't matter, he had to stop the bleeding and go kill that murdering cunt.

He pinched the Ka-Bar between his knees, point up. With his right hand he reached into the back of the Bv, digging around in his canvas bag until he found what he needed — the propane torch.

How ironic.

How many people had he burned with a torch just like this one? How many lives had he taken with it? And now that same device might save his own.

He used his left elbow to keep the gauze jammed into his wound, then opened the valve on the propane tank. He fished the lighter out of his pocket and lit the torch. Magnus pointed the blue flame at the tip of the knife and waited for the blade to heat up.

He'd have to cauterize the wound. Pull off the gauze, stick the knife in and sear the artery. Then a pressure bandage, and he'd be good to go. No telling if the wound would open up on him again, but it would buy him time, let him move.

The blade started to glow red.

"You're going to pay for this, Sara. I'll find a way to make you pay over and over again."

He wondered if this knife would make it back to Manitoba, if it would join the others on his office wall.

He shut off the valve and dropped the propane canister. He held the knife handle with his right hand. The glowing tip hovered just a half inch from the gauze.

"And where the offense is, let the great axe fall."

His left hand pulled the bloody gauze clear, his right stuck the hot knife point into the bullet hole. Blood bubbled and muscle sizzled, filling the Bv's cab with the stench of burning flesh.

CLAUS RHUMKORRF SAT slouched down in the pilot seat. Only his eyes moved as he watched the last of the ancestors filter past the Sikorski and up the road leading to the mansion. They were the last stragglers from the pack that chased after Colding and Clayton.

He was on the helicopter's right side, looking out the plexiglass pilot's door window. And if he could see *out*, they could see *in*, so he had to stay very still . . . hard to do when his body shook from both the cold and piercing terror.

How could he have been so damn blind? From the first moment the embryos started to take shape, he'd known — somewhere deep inside — that they meant *death*, not *life*. It all lined up now, all made a twisted kind of sense. He had shorted Jian's meds to bring out her staggering genius. But doing that also brought back her manic-depressive symptoms, her suicidal urges, and she'd manifested those urges by creating these *things*.

The last of the ancestors turned down the main road toward the old town. He would wait just a few more minutes, make sure he had time to lift off in case the Sikorski's engine noise drew them back.

Only now, with death all around him, did Claus realize what kind of a man he was. The ancestor project wasn't about saving lives. Not really. It was about creating a living creature. *From scratch*. Not some bacterium or a virus, not a simple thing with only a few thousand genes, but a large, advanced mammal.

Creating life was the sole domain of God.

God, and now, Claus Rhumkorrf.

He'd conveniently deluded himself until it was too late. And when there could be no more delusion, when he'd watched his creation almost kill Cappy, he'd had yet another chance to stop everything. When the plane crashed, he should have let the cows die, but his overwhelming hubris controlled his actions.

Claus's breath caught in his throat. Back up the trail, a lone ancestor trotted back out from the main road. It stood at the intersection a hundred yards away from the helicopter.

It seemed to be looking right at him.

"No," Claus whispered. "Please, no."

The ancestor's sail suddenly stood straight up, the translucent yellow membrane catching the morning sun. Its toothy maw opened wide. Claus couldn't hear it inside the cockpit, but he knew the creature was roaring a hideous roar, calling its brethren back.

He sat up straight in the seat, reached over his head and pushed the start button for engine one. His frostbitten finger howled in protest, but he easily ignored the pain. The blades started spinning up.

His body shook uncontrollably. The lone creature sprinted toward the helicopter with the crazy gait of a top-heavy pit bull. A hundred meters away and closing fast.

He turned back to the controls. The N1 gauge read 54 percent and climbing. He hit the button to start the second engine.

He couldn't stop himself from looking up again. The ancestor had closed half the distance, enough that he could see its beady black eyes and massive muscles rippling under black-spotted white fur. But that wasn't what froze Claus's heart in his chest. Behind the monster, the woods seemed to erupt, spewing forth a horrific wave of black and white. They barreled down the narrow road like some barbaric army bearing down on a hated enemy.

He pushed the throttle on engine one to the *fly* position, felt the rotor blades spin up faster. Just a few more seconds and he'd lift off.

Something hit him from the right, driving him into the controls that separated the two front seats. Too much weight to bear, crushing him, then the sensation of something sliding away. He opened his eyes to see a sheet of plexiglass, flopping free and smeared with thick wetness — the window of the pilot door. He started to sit up and push it off when the weight hit him again, driving the back of his head against hard plastic knobs. Plexiglass smashed against his face, flattened his nose until he absently registered his eyelashes brushing against it with each rapid blink. Through the plexiglass, inches from his face, the ancestor's gaping mouth opened wide. It shot forward and snapped shut, but the inwardly curved teeth scraped against the plexiglass. It opened again, snapped again, and again the deadly points couldn't catch. The helicopter lurched with each lunging bite. Claus heard and felt claws scratching at the plexiglass, scrambling like a sliding dog trying to find purchase on a linoleum floor. The abomination slid back out a second time.

The plexiglass slid out with it.

Claus pushed himself up, his glasses gone, his vision a blur. The ancestor had fallen on its ass. Feet kicked against the snow-covered pavement as the big creature awkwardly started to rise.

Oh god oh god oh god . . .

Claus reached into his jacket and pulled out the gun Colding had given him. He held it with both hands, his elbows pressed tight to his ribs.

The ancestor coiled to leap into the Sikorski.

Claus heard the first two gunshots before he realized he was firing. His finger danced on the trigger again and again, faster than he knew a gun could fire. The scientific, observant part of his brain noted with fascination that all eleven shots hit the creature in the face.

The slide locked on empty.

The monster fell, blood gushing nearly neon red against the snow.

And beyond the dying animal he had created, Claus saw the pounding black and white blur of the ancestor horde, now only thirty meters away.

He dropped the gun. Eyes flicked about the cabin even as his hands reached up, moved the engine two throttle to the *fly* position. He saw his glasses on the floor and snatched them up. One arm was broken off. The other arm he jammed into his head bandage. The lenses were a little cock-eyed, but he could see clearly again.

The horde closed to ten meters.

The spinning rotor blades finally lifted the Sikorski. Claus felt his breath rush out as the leading ancestors reached up for the hull . . . reached up, and missed.

He urged the damaged helicopter forward and headed for the ghost town.

The horde of hungry ancestors followed.

COLDING AND CLAYTON stopped in the trees at the edge of town, a good twenty yards from the nearest building. The tattered, one-eyed moose head of Sven's hunter shop stared at them. Colding needed just a minute to think, but didn't know if he had that much time.

He shut off the Arctic Cat's engine and listened. The wind had died away. The woods seemed deathly silent save for the distant sound of the Sikorski's rotors slicing through the air. At least Doc had made it off the helicopter pad.

"Anything behind us?" he asked Clayton.

"Haven't seen them since we got on da road. If they're coming, then we're way ahead of them." Clayton cocked his head to the side and looked up. "You hear that?"

The helicopter sounds grew louder. They were out of time.

"I hear it," Colding said. "If Sara is in the church, where will she be?"

"If I was her, I'd be in that bell tower. Stairs at da back right side of da altar go up to da choir loft, then a ladder up to da tower."

Colding looked up at the tower, hoping to see her face. He saw no movement. Someone could be up there looking right down at him, and if they stayed still he wouldn't see them at all.

He chewed on his lower lip. They didn't even know if Sara and Tim were here. Maybe Gary had made it, taken them off the island. Maybe Magnus had already killed them. No way of knowing. Colding could, however, make sure they weren't still waiting. And all he had to do was risk his life to find out.

"Clayton, we're going as soon as Doc flies over. That might draw Magnus out, give us a chance to kill him."

Clayton leaned out and looked across the open town circle. "We'll be exposed for looks like ten or fifteen seconds. Can Magnus get us that quick?"

Colding nodded. "If he's ready, or if he heard us coming, yeah, he could take us out. Just depends on where he is."

"And if we get to da church and he's already inside?"

Colding paused. Anger started to replace his fear. "Then we kill him."

Clayton nodded fiercely. "That's da first time I've ever heard you say something that made sense. You drive, I'll shoot."

Colding started the Arctic Cat and waited for the Sikorski to fly over.

INSIDE THE CHURCH, Tim looked up at the ceiling.

"Sara, do you hear that?"

Sara listened. "I don't hear anything."

"It's getting louder. I think it sounds like . . ."

She heard it, faintly, but she heard it. "Like a helicopter."

They rushed up the ladder to the turret's trapdoor.

MAGNUS HEARD THE flutter of rotor blades. Helicopter approaching. He'd seen both Danté and Bobby go down — that left only one person who could fly the Sikorski.

Rhumkorrf. The man who had murdered his brother.

"I've got something special for you, Doc. Yes I do."

He reached into the backseat.

THE SIKORSKI'S ENGINE hum doppplered into a roar as it flew directly over Colding's position. The helicopter slowed and started to circle back toward the well.

"Clayton, we're going! If you see Magnus, just start shooting!"

"Ya think? Just drive, asshole."

Colding gunned the engine.

The Arctic Cat shot out into the open.

SARA HAD NEVER seen a sight so beautiful — a Sikorski S-76C. Bobby Valentine's ride, coming in low. And she saw something else, down on the ground, something far better — even bundled up in the snowsuit, she knew it was Colding on that snowmobile. Clayton was on the seat behind him, holding an Uzi with one hand. Hope and love exploded in Sara's chest. They could *make* it. But Magnus was still out there somewhere. He could kill Colding at any second. Sara looked around the town circle, trying to spot the big man.

There, by the old log lodge . . . Magnus.

When she saw what he held, that feeling of hope crumbled and died.

MAGNUS TRACKED THROUGH the Stinger's viewfinder. If Rhumkorrf hadn't made these abominations in the first place, Danté would still be alive.

Claus Rhumkorrf was a murderer.

"Breathe your last, motherfucker."

Magnus pushed the firing button.

SARA, TIM, COLDING, Clayton and Magnus watched the Stinger missile's flashing white trail. Oddly, the intended target was busy trying to readjust his bobbling, broken glasses: Claus Rhumkorrf never saw it coming.

The five-foot missile homed in on the Sikorski's hot exhaust. Rhumkorrf had swung the chopper around to face the town center, just in time for the missile to slice into the cockpit window. The warhead exploded on contact, blossoming into a brilliant orange fireball.

Sikorski pieces and streams of burning fuel rained down on the old town.

THE HELICOPTER EXPLODED above the snowmobile's forward path. Colding yanked the steering handles hard right, away from the church. The sudden movement caught Clayton unaware and threw him from the seat. He slammed into the snowy ground, rolled once, then skidded to a halt.

He didn't move.

Colding managed to stay seated as he fought for control. Burning wreckage rained down around him. He squeezed the brakes and pulled hard left as the tail shaft — rotor still spinning — crashed into the ground in front of him. He'd turned too sharply this time; the snowmobile pitched on its right side. Colding dove free before the machine rolled three full, horizontal, rattling times. It landed on its skids, the fiberglass body shattered beyond repair.

Colding hit hard. He smelled burning feathers before he felt the heat, before he realized his jacket sleeve was on fire. He rolled on the ground, pushing his burning arm into the snow. The flames *hissed* out before he suffered any serious damage.

He stood, smoke and steam rising from his ruined sleeve, a murderous gaze fixed on his face. He unslung the SA80 rifle and looked for his target.

A voice from behind.

"Drop it, Bubbah."

Fury. Fear. Colding shook. He fought the urge to whirl around and open up with the SA80. He wouldn't even make a quarter turn before Magnus gunned him down. There was nothing he could do.

Colding dropped the rifle.

"And the Beretta," Magnus said. "Slow."

Colding slowly pulled the Beretta from inside his snowsuit and tossed it away. It fell into the snow and vanished.

"Now put your hands in the air and turn around. You and I have a date with a hot little lady."

7:08 A.M.

A large gush of burning fuel had set the log lodge ablaze. Sara watched long flames rise up into the morning sky, whipped to and fro by the returning wind. She figured the old wooden structure would be completely engulfed by flames within fifteen minutes. Several of the town's buildings smoldered or burned. The Sikorski/Stinger combo would finish the work begun by a mine accident some fifty years ago.

Far worse, the church itself was about to go up in flames. A chunk of engine had spun wildly into the air, arcing a good thirty yards before slamming into the church roof. Small flames glowed, seeking purchase through the slate shingles to the old wood beneath.

From her spot in the bell tower, Sara couldn't get near the flames. Even if she could, she had nothing with which to put them out. The tower's stone turret wouldn't save them — when the fire caught full force, she and Tim would be cooked from below if the smoke didn't kill them first.

"Tim, we have to move."

"Fuck that," Tim said. "The helicopter, the explosion — the noise will bring the monsters."

"We run or we roast. Let's go."

Tim paused, but only for a second, then crutch-walked for the trapdoor. Sara opened it for him. Tim started his awkward climb down, then they heard death speak out loud.

"Saaaaaaraaaaa." Magnus's voice. From *inside* the church. "Sara, I've got someone here to see you."

Blazing rage pulled Sara's lip back into a snarl, even while an urge to run and hide made her stomach clench. Fear or no fear, there was only one way out, and that was over Magnus Paglione's dead body.

"Stay up here," she said to Tim. "I've got to take care of this."

She descended the ladder.

7:09 A.M.

A gun at his back, Colding stood in the church's center aisle amid the broken and moldy pews. The place already smelled of smoke. Small fires burned the rafters on his left, filling the church with a flickering light. Up above, a few sunbeams filtered through the stained glass of the Twelve Apostles. On his right, up in the choir loft, he caught a glimpse of someone deep in the shadows.

Sara.

Behind him, Magnus saw her, too.

"'Tis the east," Magnus called up to the loft. "And fair Sara is the sun. I brought your boyfriend for a little visit."

Magnus had a tight hold on the hood of Colding's parka, keeping him at arm's length. Magnus was too smart to jam a gun into Colding's back, where a sudden move might point the barrel at empty space. Colding knew the MP5 would be low, on Magnus's hip. If Colding spun and made a move, the MP5 would blow his ribs and stomach to pieces.

More movement from the loft, just a hint, and from a different place. "You think I give a fuck about that piece of shit?" The voice came from the shadows. "That bastard sent me to die."

"Oh, come *on*," Magnus said. "You know that was me."

"Bullshit. I'll shoot both of you right now. And this time, Magnus, I'll finish the job."

Colding looked toward the sound of her voice, but he couldn't see her in the loft's dark depths. Damn, but she was smart. Colding's right hand made a fist, his index finger pointing out, his thumb up — the shape of a gun. He slowly moved his left hand and pointed at his chest. He had no idea if she'd understand, or even do it.

And if her aim was off at all . . .

CLAYTON RAISED HIS head.

"Oh . . . I need a vacation."

The old town burned all around him, he had a broken left leg, the creatures were coming and some Canadian shit-eater had cut off his pinkie. He stayed low and still, trying to take it all in before he did anything.

Movement on his left, about twenty yards away, at the edge of town where the trail led into the woods. A flash of fleshy yellow.

Burning wreckage surrounded him, blurring the air with shimmering waves of heat. If he stayed still, it might hide him from the creatures for a few minutes. But if he didn't move, sooner or later they'd get him.

Clayton slowly turned his head to the right. The lodge was on fire, the dry old wood glowing red from flames that shot thirty feet into the air. No shelter there.

But *behind* the lodge, just past the hazy flames, he glimpsed a small bit of a familiar black-and-white pattern. Clayton grimaced, readied himself for the pain, then started crawling.

7:10 A.M.

The fire in the rafters spread slowly but steadily, filling the church with a spastic, flickering light. Shadows jumped, making the pews and the big crucifix vibrate with evil life.

Do it, Colding thought, as if she might somehow read his mind. *Do it, shoot me.*

Magnus stayed behind Colding, but kept calling up to the loft. "Sara, why don't you send Feely down? I'll trade you for Colding. I don't need you. I just need Feely. You don't know enough to be a danger to me."

"Then why did you try to kill me?" Her voice came from yet another spot.

"I didn't try to kill *you*. I tried to kill Feely and Rhumkorrf. You were in the wrong place at the wrong time."

"So was my crew."

"That's why we gave you hazard pay," Magnus said. "Use your head. Jian is dead. Rhumkorrf is dead. Now all I need is Tim and this is over. You and Colding can go on your way. If you make it off the island, more power to you. At least then you'd have a chance. What do you say to that?"

Silence.

"What good is Colding to me if he's dead?"

"He's not dead," Magnus said. "He's standing right—"

A gunshot roared out. Colding felt a sledgehammer slam into his chest. He instinctively jerked backward. His feet caught on a pew and he toppled into Magnus. Colding landed on his right side, then flopped facedown and didn't move.

MAGNUS SLID HIS body half under a pew, hoping the .40-caliber bullets couldn't punch through it. Another shot rang out — the bullet smacked into the frozen, rotted wood.

"What do you think of that, Magnus?" the loft shadows called out. "Now you ain't got jack *shit* to trade, you sick fuck!"

He popped up from behind the pew and opened fire on the choir loft. The wood railing came apart in a shower of splinters. Sara popped up in yet another new spot — Magnus ducked back down just as she fired again.

SARA STAYED ON her belly, shooting between the spokes of the choir loft's rail. The madly flickering firelight made it hard to target Magnus, who kept crawling around under the pews and popping up to spray the loft with bullets. Sara could barely breathe from the smoke. She had two shots left, maybe three — dammit, she'd lost count.

I shot him. He WANTED me to shoot him.

Colding had to be wearing a bulletproof vest; that was the only reason he would want her to do it. Shooting him had robbed Magnus of the human shield, and in a twisted way taken Colding out of danger. She silently prayed that she hadn't somehow misunderstood his signals — that she hadn't just killed the man she loved.

Sara pushed herself back from the loft's edge so that she was out of Magnus's line of sight. She rolled several times to her left. Had to keep moving. A burning feeling shot up her leg. She kicked, knocking away a smoldering piece of rafter. Flames crawled across the ceiling above her. Sara rolled a few more times, carrying her away from the hot spot. She lay flat and eased herself back to the loft's edge.

7:11 A.M.

Colding coughed. A thin stream of spit and blood landed on his chin. It felt like someone had driven a baseball bat through his chest. He slid a hand under his bulletproof vest. It hurt, hurt like a bitch, but his fingers came away without blood. The blood in his mouth, it seemed, came from the lip he'd bitten through.

He looked under the pews, the only vantage he had from his prone position. He couldn't see Magnus. Pieces of burning rafters dropped every few seconds, little meteors plunging down. Some of the pews danced with fire, some were just smoldering. Flames wiggled across the warped wooden floor. Acrid smoke expanded through the church, choking out oxygen and stinging his eyes.

Colding rose to his knees and peeked over the pew. With this much cover, Magnus could be hiding only a few feet away. Colding knew he had to make a run for the altar and the loft stairs, had to reach Sara, but Magnus could cut him down with ease.

Behind him, the tall, heavy, double doors swung open and smashed against the inside wall, flooding the burning church with morning light. A dozen yellow sail fins rose above the pews, spreading out, moving forward.

The pain in his chest forgotten, Colding stood, rounded the pew's corner, and sprinted for the altar.

WHEN HE HEARD the big doors slam open, Magnus peeked out from behind the altar's thick crucifix. Through the shimmering heat haze and the growing smoke cloud, he saw a dozen nightmares trot into the church — muscles thick like lions on steroids, massive heads with jaws wider and longer than a crocodile's, strange yellow dorsal sail fins flipping up and down in twitching anticipation.

Movement on his left. Human movement. Colding, up and sprinting for the right edge of the altar. Drop him, remove a variable, move on to the rest. Magnus brought up the MP5.

I'VE GOT YOU now, fucker.

Sara had seen Magnus hide behind the thick crucifix, then watched and waited for her shot. In a brief moment of total awareness, the world slowed and she saw everything: the monsters spreading out through the church, Colding sprinting for the stairs, Magnus coming around the cross and raising the MP5.

She squeezed the trigger. Just before it clicked home, a burning chunk of rafter fell onto her leg, pulling her aim slightly to the right . . .

. . . THE .40-CALIBER BULLET tore a huge chunk out of the old crucifix, spraying splinters into Magnus's cheek. He ducked back, his face consumed with pain. He popped around the other side and fired a wild burst, hoping to hit Colding, but the man disappeared up the stairwell. Magnus looked to his right, back out into the church. Maybe twenty of them. Some sprinted up the main aisle, some crawled over the moldy, smoldering pews — all wanted to get him. Magnus moved out from behind the cross and shuffle-stepped toward the stairs, opening up with the MP5. The one closest to him fell hard, blood spurting from a half-dozen fresh bullet holes, but there were so many of them . . .

SARA FINISHED SMACKING the flames on her pant leg, then looked over the edge of the choir loft for another shot. Her eyes stung from the smoke. She fought back a cough. Magnus was shuffling to his left, toward the stairs, his attention occupied by the wave of sail-finned land sharks sprinting for him. No cover for him this time. She raised the gun, a part of her brain telling her it felt funny even as she did.

The slide had locked back.

Empty.

She holstered the weapon and ran for the bell-tower ladder.

BREATH RAGGED FROM stress and exertion, Colding cleared the final stair step. The thicker smoke up on the choir loft made him cough violently. Through the black clouds, he saw Sara at the other end of the loft, her feet on the bottom rung of a metal ladder.

"Peej, come on! Up here!"

Colding ran to the ladder and started up, hoping against all hope that Sara knew what she was doing.

———

MAGNUS FLEW UP the stairs, firing blindly behind himself until the MP5 clicked on empty. As he ascended he tried to pop in a fresh magazine, but the narrow staircase made it hard to bring the gun around while taking the steps two at a time. The wooden stairs shook from something even larger than he was.

He had almost cleared the last step when that something hit him from behind. His face *cracked* into the choir loft's stone floor. The MP5 skidded free. The fresh magazine flew out of his hand, rebounded off the wall and skittered over the loft's edge to fall among the burning pews below.

A slashing pain seared up the back of his left leg.

Magnus rolled to his back, cocked his right leg and kicked with all his power. He felt his foot smash against solid muscle, against skin and bone. The creature roared with anger and pain. In a single motion, Magnus sat up and slid his feet beneath him, leaving him with knees bent, fingers on the floor, weight on his toes. The big animal recovered from the kick, reared back and charged up the final five stairs. Magnus shot forward, ducking under the jaws and driving his shoulder into the monster's throat. The impact shuddered through him, far worse than any hit he'd suffered in the CFL, but enough to keep the creature's body trapped in the narrow stairwell. Sliding off the impact, Magnus moved to the right and locked his thick arms around the ancestor's barrel-like neck, left arm underneath, right arm over the top. Its big body thrashed against the stairwell walls, blocking the way for the others.

Magnus let loose his own savage, primitive roar and squeezed with all his power. The muscular monster thrashed its head back and forth, trying to bring its jaws around for the killing bite, but the stairwell kept it from turning. Magnus timed a thrash left, a pause, a thrash right, a pause, then slid his left hand farther up and jabbed his thumb into the monster's right eye. He pushed the thumb in deep and hooked it, using the inside of the orbital bone like a handle. The giant head pulled away, jaws snapping *clack-clack-clack*, trying to back up, but its pack mates blocked the stairs behind it.

In the split second it took the creature to realize it couldn't retreat, Magnus's right hand drew his knife. Left thumb still deep in the animal's eye socket, Magnus drove the Ka-Bar blade into its throat.

"*You* killed Danté!" Spit flying from his mouth, his face a warped mask of psychotic fury, Magnus twisted the knife, pulled it out, struck again.

Blood gushed across the floor, across his legs, so thick he heard it splatter against stone even over the crackling flames and the roars of this bastard's brethren.

"You *all* killed Danté! You hear that, Colding? I'll kill this thing and then I'm coming for *you*! You murdered my brother!"

The ancestor weakened, and then it shot backward down the stairs. But the things couldn't move that way. Magnus had a moment of confusion before he realized the others had yanked it away. Some of them started biting it, tearing off great chunks as blood and bits of flesh splashed the stairs, the walls and the ceiling. Only *some* of them, though, because another scrambled past both the eaters and the eaten.

Magnus stepped forward to meet it. They could only come up the stairwell one at a time, and he would kill them all.

Hand to hand.

One by one.

7:14 A.M.

Sara climbed through the trapdoor. Just two rungs behind, Colding had stopped, unable to look away from the battle. He couldn't believe his eyes. Magnus turned his body just before a huge head shot out of the stairwell, white teeth clacking on empty air. Magnus kicked out, the sole of his left shoe pinning the monster's head against the corner of the stairwell. Before it could adjust its body to push back, Magnus drove a knife in an overhanded arc, burying it in the creature's left eye. Magnus screamed, pulled the blade out, then rotated in an underhand windup that drove the bloody blade deep into the monster's neck. The creature kept fighting even as its blood shot across the already slick floor.

"No," Colding said quietly. "You don't get to live."

He put his feet on the outside of the metal ladder's poles, then slid down to the bottom. He grabbed a piece of fallen rafter and held it like a torch, the burning end hissing and crackling with flames.

"This is for Jian and Doc."

Colding reared back and hurled the burning wood. It spun three times in the air before the flaming end hit the left side of Magnus's face. The big man screamed, then fell to his back. Colding hurried up the ladder.

A monster walked out of the stairwell and closed in on Magnus.

MAGNUS'S HANDS PRESSED at the seared cheek. Even as his skin bubbled and he howled in pain, he knew he had to move. He sat up fast, trying to bring his feet underneath him, but before he could a wide mouth and long teeth snapped for his face. Magnus brought up his hands and hooked his thumbs inside the skin at the sides of the creature's jaws. Five hundred and ten pounds drove him to his back. He locked his arms straight out, fingers digging in from the outside to grab big handfuls of coarse fur. The jaws *cracked* shut less than an inch from his nose. Sharp claws dug into his massive chest.

He was trying to bring his heels up to hook-kick at the eyes when another creature came from his right, teeth snapping down on his arm, his shoulder, punching into his chest, through his lungs.

His eyes went wide and his body stiffened. The creature *shook* him, snapping bones, rending flesh. Hot blood in his face, again, but this time *his* blood.

Movement from his left. A third creature, mouth open wide, blocking the fire's flickering light. Three-foot-wide jaws smashed shut with crushing power. Teeth punched down through his right temple and up through his left cheekbone, sliding together somewhere in his brain.

COLDING KICKED SHUT the turret's trapdoor. Sara ran into his arms and — finally — he held her close again. Sobs racked her body. He squeezed her tight. Her body molded to his, and he felt his soul breathe a deep, clutching sigh of relief. He kissed her smoke-streaked forehead.

"Take it easy," he said just loud enough to be heard over the roaring fire. Still holding her, he took a quick look around. Fire danced across most of the roof, ten-foot flames pouring up and around the remaining slate shingles. He heard a heavy, wooden crack from inside the church, followed by the sound of something smashing to the ground amid roaring flames. Then came the horrible, deep roar-howls of the ancestors trapped beneath.

The flames had spread almost to the tower. The turret's stone walls wouldn't burn, but they wouldn't have to — heat billowed up like a concussive force, the round tower funneling it like a chimney.

He rubbed Sara's back. "Come on, Sara. We've got to get out of here."

"Oh, let her cry," came a voice from behind him. He turned to see Tim Feely, defeated, resting heavily on his crutch. "Just let her cry, Colding. There's no way out of here. Even if we could get out of this turret, look what's waiting for us."

Colding shuffled Sara a few steps to the left so he could look over the edge. Dozens of ancestors circled the turret's base. Some were trying unsuccessfully to climb the black rock. Others were actually *biting* it, chipping their long teeth as they tried to tear the foundation out from under them. Every few seconds another ancestor ran out of the open double doors. Some were on fire, trailing smoke, their black-and-white hides adding the stench of burnt fur to the ghost town's carnage.

Tim was right. It was over.

"Shhh," Colding said softly as he petted Sara's head. "Everything will be okay."

Tim started to laugh — the sick, demented laugh of someone who's given up all hope. But over his laughter, over the sound of the raging fire, over the sound of the roaring, hungry ancestors, Colding heard something else.

The gurgling growl of Ted Nugent.

7:17 A.M.

Clayton Detweiler grimaced as he worked the clutch with his broken leg. Pain dominated his thoughts, but he pushed it away, focusing on the task at hand. He'd been hurt worse.

"Got somethin' for ya, ya little shits." His left hand held the wheel, his right held the Uzi. "Time to whack 'em and stack 'em."

The Nuge shot around the burning lodge, pivoted on thick tank treads, then rolled toward the church. The ancestors surrounding the turret turned as one and sprinted toward him.

BABY MCBUTTER SAW the strange, noisy animal come roaring toward her brethren. It had been sitting still earlier, still and quiet, and it hadn't smelled like food — but now it did. And it smelled like something else.

It smelled like the stick.

Baby McButter lifted her sail three times, signaling alarm, but some of her brethren didn't notice. Those were the ones too hungry to worry about any danger.

CLAYTON STOPPED THE Nuge near the well. He slid over to the passenger side and stood on his good right leg, pushing his upper body out of the top hatch.

"You hungry?" he shouted to the oncoming horde. "Uncle Clayton's got a snack for ya!"

He opened up with the Uzi, firing short, controlled bursts just like Chuck Heston had taught him. The first burst hit the lead ancestor dead-center, dropping it in midstride. Clayton bagged two more, clearly killing one and blowing the left leg off the second. It fell to the snow-covered ground, writhing in pain.

He slid back inside and pulled the hatch shut, then gunned the engine and drove straight for the wounded ancestor. Clayton Detweiler smiled when the tank tread crushed through the creature's chest, leaving two twitching halves behind.

He drove the Nuge to the bell tower and stopped. Popping in a fresh magazine, he again stuck his head out the roof hatch. A big bastard scrambled around the curved tower, claws digging in for traction. Son of a bitch had to be over 550 pounds if it was an ounce.

"Aw, fuck ya," Clayton said, and held the trigger tight. Twenty-five rounds ripped out in less than three seconds. The creature's skull disintegrated in a cloud of brain and bone and blood. It fell forward, momentum sliding the dead body over the snow until the mangled head mashed up against Ted Nugent's front right tread.

Clayton reloaded with a full magazine and looked for a new target. The monsters now kept their distance, keeping to the shadows or behind smaller fires where the intense heat distorted their visages into shimmering, demonic ghosts. Most of the creatures stayed a good twenty yards back, feasting on the corpses of their fallen pack mates with a savage, shaking desperation.

Clayton looked up the church tower. Peering down over the edge were the joyous, shouting faces of Colding, Sara and Tim.

7:19 A.M.

Colding watched Clayton crawl out of the roof hatch. The old man's face wrinkled with agony, but he moved as quickly as he could and climbed into the rear section. Colding would have never thought Clayton Detweiler beautiful, but seeing him riding up in that lift bucket, an Uzi dangling from a strap around his neck, he could have been Miss America, Miss Universe and the Playmate of the Year all rolled into one fabulous farting package.

The bucket reached the turret. Colding reached out and grabbed Clayton's shoulder. "You're one mean old bastard! You saved us!"

Clayton pushed his hand away, then gave Colding the Uzi. "I'm fuckin' done. Where's Gary?"

"I saw him last night," Sara said. "He took off on his snowmobile. The monsters were chasing him, but . . . I don't know if he got away."

Clayton sagged. Colding stepped into the bucket and slid under the man's arm, keeping him up. Sara got in next, then helped the crutch-wielding Tim do the same. Four people made for a tight fit. Colding worked the simple controls, lowering the bucket to the Bv.

Ancestors darted around but didn't make themselves an easy target. Some lurked just inside the tree line, some hid behind burning wreckage. They were smart enough to block roads, smart enough to use protective cover. He couldn't assume they would behave like animals at all.

Sara scrambled out of the bucket and into the Bv's open rear section, then hopped over the side and ran for the driver's door. Colding helped Tim out of the lift bucket, across to the front section and down into the rear hatch. Clayton crawled out of the bucket on his own, but the old man's left leg looked bad. His snow pants stuck out at a strange angle, anchored by one bloody point. A compound fracture. Colding watched him slide through the rear hatch, trying to imagine just how tough Clayton Detweiler had been to hold that pain in check long enough to rescue them all.

Movement, rustling. The ancestors, getting closer.

Colding dropped to the ground and ran to the passenger-side door. He climbed in and stuck his head out the front hatch, just as he'd seen Clayton do.

An ancestor rushed the Bv from the right. Colding brought up the Uzi and ripped off a hurried burst. Some of the bullets went wide, but at least two hit the thing in the chest. It stopped, skidding slightly, twitching like a kid just stung by a bee. Colding ripped off two more bursts as the thing scrambled off. He wasn't sure if he hit it or not.

Clayton reached up and handed Colding a fresh magazine. "Last one," he said. "Don't waste it."

One full magazine, a second maybe half empty . . . about forty-five rounds total.

"Hold tight," Sara said. She drove the Nuge away from the church inferno. The town square looked like a war zone cluttered with twisted metal wreckage, every building burning bright.

Colding felt a tug on the bottom of his tattered parka. He looked down.

Tim handed up a green canvas bag. Colding looked in the bag with several quick peeks, not taking his eyes off the surroundings for more than a second at a time. Two, no, three pounds of Demex. About two dozen detonators. His heart leaped when he saw four magazines, but it sank again when he realized they were for Magnus's MP5, which was somewhere in the burning church.

Sara pointed the Bv northeast. With his head sticking out of the hatch, buffeted by the wind, the town roaring with flames and the Bv's diesel happily gurgling away, Colding had to scream to be heard.

"Sara, where are you going?"

"The harbor! Gary's boat might still be there. And this thing is low on fuel. We probably can't reach the mansion, so the harbor it is."

She didn't wait for an answer, she just drove. She managed to avoid most of the Sikorski's wreckage. The pieces she couldn't avoid, she simply ran over. The Nuge bounced along as it rolled over twisted metal and through small fires.

Sara drove out of the town and onto the road, thick snow-covered woods on either side, the harbor maybe a mile away.

Three ancestors rushed from the woods on the left. Colding fired off a quick burst at the leader. The monster slowed but kept coming. He let off another three-shot burst. One of the bullets caught the ancestor in the eye. It fell to the ground, thrashing and shaking its head as if it were being electrocuted. Its two companions stopped, looked at the retreating vehicle for a few seconds, then turned and attacked their fallen comrade. Within seconds, three more creatures joined the brutal feeding frenzy. The fallen ancestor fought desperately, lashing out with long claws and drawing blood several times, but finally fell still, its corpse torn asunder and swallowed in giant chunks.

Colding had never dreamed such savagery existed. For the first time he wondered if these things could breed. And if they could, and they got off the island . . . well, quite frankly, that wasn't his fucking problem. Someone with a higher pay grade could sweat it. He just wanted to get these people to safety.

The ancestors kept up the pursuit, running parallel to the Bv but staying in the trees. They were like shadows in the deep woods; a flash of white, the reflection of a beady black eye, but little more. Every hundred yards or so, one of the critters grew bold and attacked. Colding waited until they got so nerve-rackingly close he couldn't miss. He bagged one with a lucky head shot, the bullet likely bouncing around inside the skull and ripping the brain to shreds. The other ones acted little more than annoyed at the bullets — they'd rush, take a few rounds, then turn and dart back into the woods. He didn't need an Uzi . . . he needed a fucking *cannon*.

The wind swept in from the beach at twenty miles per hour. With the Nuge driving straight into it, Colding suffered severe windchill on top of twenty-below weather. His face stung. His ears and nose felt numb.

Sara's steady forward progress started to outlast the ancestors' short sprints. At the half-mile point, the monsters fell behind. That would buy a few precious moments at the dock.

They topped the dune and rolled down the other side, the wide-open expanse of a roiling Lake Superior spreading out to the horizon. Colding saw Gary's snowmobile near the dock. He also saw the *Otto II*. It was at the far edge of the harbor, about twenty feet inside the north breakwall.

The Bv slowed, crunching over jagged shore ice before Sara stopped it near the dock.

Clayton screamed into the heavy wind. "Gary! Son! Are you there?" There was no answer. With the wind so loud, even if Gary was on the boat he probably couldn't hear. Clayton hobbled out of the vehicle, then reached back inside and grabbed Tim's crutch.

"Hey," Tim said.

"Fuck ya," Clayton said, and started limping out onto the ice toward his son's boat.

Colding looked behind the Bv — no sign of the ancestors. They had made it.

Then he looked back to the boat, and he saw it.

They *all* saw it.

Sara stepped out of the driver's door. She stood and stared.

"No," Tim said from inside the cabin, his voice thick with frustration. "No, I can't take any more, I just can't."

Colding looked down at Sara, who shrugged as if the weight of the world hung from her shoulders. He looked back out at the harbor, his mind reeling from this latest blow.

The harbor was frozen solid. Up to and even outside the breakwall entrance, an irregular sheet of snow-covered ice shone like a sprawling, massive field of broken white concrete. The *Otto II* sat in the middle of it, resting at a slight list to port where the ice had frozen unevenly and tilted the boat.

The frigid wind dug deeper into Colding. He really wanted to just lie down. Lie down and sleep.

"Peej," Sara said, "what are we going to do?"

He couldn't quit now. There had to be a way. "The Bv is amphibious, right?"

Sara shook her head. "It is, but there's no way this tin can will make it to the mainland. Look at those waves out there."

Colding looked. Far past the breakwall ice, fifteen-foot waves moved like sea monsters hunting for a victim. "Maybe we can't make it back, but we could drive it out on the ice, into the water, maybe wait for help?"

Sara shrugged. "Maybe. But when we run out of gas, the waves will push us back to the island. You know what will happen then."

Colding's body grew weaker, both from the cold and a growing avalanche of despair. The ancestors would arrive at any second. "We need an icebreaker to get that thing out. Something."

Sara looked at him. "Hopefully that's an icebreaker in your pocket, but maybe you're just glad to see me." No humor in the words, no joy. She had given up.

Colding started to shake his head, then remembered the canvas bag slung around his shoulder. The canvas bag full of plastique and detonators. He looked at Gary's snowmobile. "Clayton! Come here!"

Clayton turned and looked back, sadness visible on his face. He cupped his hands to his face and shouted. "I gotta find my son!"

Colding waved his arm, beckoning Clayton to return. "If we don't break the ice, no one will make it out and the ancestors will climb right into that boat. Get back here and start Gary's snowmobile — do it now!"

Clayton looked at the boat one more time, then started crutch-walking toward his son's snowmobile.

Colding crawled out of the hatch and dumped the bag's contents onto the scattered snow. "Sara, Tim, help me. Either of you know how to make a time bomb?"

They shook their heads, then each of them grabbed a timer and started playing with the controls. Necessity was the mother of invention, and this mother was one mean bitch.

7:28:01 A.M.

Baby McButter cautiously crested the dune and looked down. The prey sat at the water's edge. She sniffed — despite the strong wind, she still caught a faint wisp of the stick. The stick had stung her once already. She did not want to be stung again.

Her stomach churned and growled, but it felt different, not as bad as before. She sensed that change had nothing to do with the chunk of leg she'd eaten back by the fire.

Baby McButter flicked her sail fin into high in a short, definitive pattern. Behind her, the remaining ancestors fanned out along the dune's crest. There was nowhere left for the prey to run.

7:28:12 A.M.

Gary's Ski-Doo idled next to them as Colding, Tim and Sara worked quickly to make more and more fist-sized bombs. The timers proved to be very simple. They'd synced them all to P. J.'s watch, but had yet to set the detonation time. He didn't know how many it would take, and he couldn't risk leaving the job half-finished. Almost done now, just a few more.

Clayton sat in the Ted Nugent's backseat, leaning against the passenger-side window. Maybe he'd passed out, maybe not.

Tim looked up from his pile of plastique balls and detonators. "They're here."

No, it was too soon. Colding and Sara snapped a quick look at the snow-covered dune. They saw small bits of movement from just behind the crest, like sticks blowing in the wind. That, and a few small glimpses of yellow.

The ancestors weren't attacking.

He remembered their intelligence . . . they knew about the guns. He stood and pointed the Uzi at the dune, then snapped a quick glance at his watch.

"Set all the timers for 7:30, do it now! Shove 'em in the bag!"

Sara and Tim didn't argue, they grabbed bombs and started setting timers. Would that be enough time?

Sara thrust the bag at him. "Don't fuck it up," she said. Some women might have said *good luck* or at least *I hope you know what you're doing,* but that just wasn't Sara's way. He handed her the Uzi, threw the bag full of bombs over his shoulder, then hopped on Gary's snowmobile. He gunned the engine, driving the sled out onto the bumpy ice toward the *Otto II*. The rough surface jarred him with punishing ups and downs.

He reached the boat and started a wide circle around it, dropping plastique balls as he went.

7:28:33 A.M.

Sara saw two ancestors bound over the crest and barrel down the snowy dune.

Why only two?

"Tim, get in!"

Sara fired as she backed toward the Bv. She got lucky on the first burst, the bullets smashing into the ancestor's front left leg. It toppled forward, instantly crippled, rolling head over heels in a cloud of snow and sand.

She fired a burst at the second one, now only fifteen feet away, so close she could see its tongue inside the open mouth. The bullets drove into that open mouth.

It kept coming.

Fear pulled her finger tight against the trigger. Bullets sprayed into the ancestor's face. It stopped only five feet from her, shaking its head violently, trying to turn away, but it was too late. It fell heavily to its side, twitching and kicking its powerful limbs.

Sara pointed the Uzi at its head and fired.

Two bullets came out, then the little submachine gun made a *click* sound. Sara blinked a few times, tried pulling the trigger again, her adrenaline-soaked brain not quite comprehending the fact that she was out of ammo.

Again, just a single click.

Dozens of ancestor heads popped up into plain sight. Every yellow sail fin rose high into the air.

"Fuck me running," Tim said. "They know the goddamn gun is empty."

The ancestors rose and charged down the snow-covered dune, their wide-open mouths roaring in long-delayed triumph.

Sara tossed the Uzi aside and jumped into the driver's seat. She gunned the engine, driving straight out onto the ice. It would crack eventually, but the Nuge was supposed to be seaworthy. If she could get them close to the *Otto II*, it might be enough.

It would have to be.

7:28:54 A.M.

Colding pushed the Ski-Doo to its limits, smashing it over the uneven ice. Any second now the jagged crust could crack under him, drop him into a freezing, watery grave.

But the ice held.

He drove to the breakwall entrance, stopping maybe thirty feet from the open water. That was as close as he dared go to the ice's edge. He tossed a Demex bomb. The fist-sized ball bounced once, then came to rest only five feet from the splashing water. Colding looked back toward the *Otto II*. He'd left a line of ten bombs between the boat and the harbor entrance, another six in a circle around the boat itself. He checked his watch: fifty-five seconds and counting.

The sound of a diesel engine and smashing metal drew his attention. The zebra-striped Bv206 pounded across the ice. Tank treads ground over the uneven surface, slowing the vehicle to maybe ten miles an hour. The ancestor pack was only thirty feet behind and closing fast.

A sick, coppery feeling ran through his stomach — he wouldn't be able to make it to the *Otto II* before the ancestors did. He looked in his canvas bag. Still had eight plastique balls.

Plastique balls that were ticking away.

Fifty seconds and counting.

Colding pointed the Ski-Doo at the shore and gunned the engine.

7:29:11 A.M.

They were only twenty-five feet from the *Otto II*. She checked the side mirror: three ancestors at the back bumper.

She heard a deep, splintery cracking, then the Bv dropped through the ice and plunged into the water. The passengers' heads snapped forward as if they'd driven straight into a wall.

Icy water welled up over the windshield, over the roof, and poured through the open upper hatch.

A scream came unbidden, but the cold wetness locked it tight in her throat.

7:29:16 A.M.

Colding saw the Bv drop through the ice into the water. It almost went under, then popped up like a slow-motion cork. The ice broke up under the lead ancestors. Two dropped into the frigid water. The last one leaped into the Bv's rear flatbed and clung to the zebra-striped lift bucket.

Colding couldn't help Sara now. He didn't have a gun, didn't even have a knife, for fuck's sake. She would have to find a way to deal with it.

He banked left, between the shore and the ancestor horde, dropping plastique balls along the way.

Forty seconds and counting.

7:29:21 A.M.

Sara regained her composure. Despite ice-cold water up to her ankles, she punched the gas pedal to the floor. The Nuge moved forward, slowly churning through the harbor.

"Tim, get over here. Keep your foot on the gas!" Tim slid sideways. Sara hopped over him to the passenger side as he took the wheel.

Sara crawled out of the passenger-side hatch, water dripping from her legs. She gathered her feet under herself and crouched, trying to keep her balance on the swaying Bv's slick metal roof. They had to tie off to the *Otto II* to get everyone onboard.

Then she heard the roar.

So close it hurt her ears, so close she felt hot breath on the back of her neck. She knew, finally, that her time had come.

Sara turned to face her fate. An ancestor perched on the Bv roof, long claws scraping into the metal as it struggled to keep from sliding off. Not even two feet away. So big. So *big*.

A snarl twisted Sara's lips. Her hair strung wetly across her face, her eyes hateful slits, she looked as much like an animal as the beast preparing to end her life.

Come on, fucker. Get it over with.

The ancestor opened wide and leaned forward.

Sara closed her eyes.

Five shots rang out.

The ancestor reared backward, blood pouring from an eye, from its mouth, from its nose. Big clawed feet slipped on the wet roof and it tumbled overboard, splashing into the icy water like a boulder dropped from ten stories high.

Sara turned, unable to grasp the fact that she was still alive.

Standing in the bow and wrapped in a thick blanket, Gary Detweiler held a smoking Beretta in his outstretched hand.

"About fuckin' time." Clayton's voice, from inside the Nuge. "Where da hell you been, boy?"

7:29:45 A.M.

Colding tossed the last plastique ball and turned toward the *Otto II*, chancing a quick glance at his watch.

Twelve seconds.

He had only one chance. He opened the throttle and leaned forward, holding on tight as the Ski-Doo slammed toward the boat.

7:29:49 A.M.

They didn't have time to tie off. The Bv's port side ground against the *Otto II*, breaking away ice that clung stubbornly to the starboard hull. Sara and Tim scrambled aboard as Gary pulled his dad out of the hatch. Clayton screamed in pain, but with his son's help made it onto the boat.

Sara looked around for Colding but didn't see him. "Gary! Where's Colding?"

Gary ran to the short ladder leading to the boat's flying bridge. As he climbed, he pointed out the port side.

Sara looked. There was Peej, driving toward them, Ski-Doo bouncing off the broken ice like a Jeep driving through a rutted gully.

She checked her watch. *Two, one . . .*

7:30:00 A.M.

Twenty-four balls of Demex plastic explosive detonated simultaneously. Ice chunks and shards flew like frozen shrapnel, some to land a good mile away.

A six-pointed ring erupted around the *Otto II*. The concussive force ripped inward, powerful enough to hit the ancestors closest to the boat and knock them into the frigid waters. Sara and Tim dove to the deck, ice flying all around them.

Colding was halfway between the ring and boat when the plastique detonated. The shock wave hit him from behind, so powerful it tumbled the Ski-Doo like a toy thrown by a petulant child. He flew through the air, the snowmobile spinning out from under him and smashing into a dozen pieces against the ice.

He landed fifteen feet from the boat's port side, his limp body cartwheeling off the ice. He flew another ten feet to plunge into the newly open water just five feet from the boat.

Sara watched, horrified, as P. J.'s body vanished beneath the surface.

"Rope!" She stripped off her jacket. "Get me some fucking rope!"

The *Otto II*'s engines roared to life. Gary looked down from the flying bridge and pointed to a footlocker.

She opened it and pulled out a long coil of red-and-white nylon rope. Then Gary was at her side, clumsy bandages across his chest showing huge splotches of red, some of them wet and fresh.

She handed him a loose end of the rope. "Tie it around my waist!" She peeled off her sweater and kicked off her boots as Gary tied the rough rope around her hips.

She turned on Gary. "You do *not* pull me up until I tug on the rope, understand?"

Gary shook his head. "You've only got a few seconds in that water, Sara, you can't—"

She reached out and held the sides of his face.

"Pull me up before I tug, and I'll *kill* you. Do you understand?"

Gary nodded.

Sara turned, put her foot on the side rail, then dove into the water.

The cold splash from the Bv's brief submersion had been bad, but nothing like this. She tried to stay under as her body rebelled, instinctively pushed for the surface.

Get out get out get out.

Her head popped out of the water, barely in time for her to let loose a scream of primitive, instinctive fear.

She looked up at the boat. Gary stood there, the white-and-red rope in his hands, a look on his face that said *Should I pull you in?*

Sara didn't answer the unasked question. She drew a huge, rattling breath, then forced herself under once again. The cold scraped her skin like a grater, driving at her with needles of pain. She kicked and kicked. Hard to see anything in the murky water.

So cold . . .

Her lungs screamed from lack of oxygen, but she dove farther. She wouldn't leave him down there. She kept on kicking with all of her quickly fading energy.

Where is he? I can't lose him . . .

She couldn't see. Blood roared inside her head. Her heart banged like a kick drum, faster, faster.

Her hand smashed into a slimy rock at the bottom of the harbor. She couldn't take any more, *had* to go up. She put her hands out to push away from the bottom, and her fingers hit something soft.

Soft like fabric.

She grabbed for it. It was a body — Colding's body.

He's not moving . . .

Sara wrapped her legs around his back and yanked on the rope. She immediately threw her arms under his shoulders, clutching him chest to chest in a desperate, loving embrace. The rope snapped taut around her waist, pulling them toward the surface.

Can't breathe can't breathe . . .

Sara's mouth opened of its own accord. Icy water poured across her tongue, into her throat. She thrashed, panic taking her, yet she refused to let go.

Her head broke the surface. She gasped for air, coughing violently. She barely felt the hands pulling her into the boat. Her body shivered as if from an epileptic fit. Somebody pulled off her pants and wrapped a blanket around her before her thoughts became her own again.

She sat up. Tim was over Colding, performing CPR, blowing air into his mouth, then pumping his chest.

Unable to move, Sara watched while her lungs kicked out deep, chest-rattling coughs. Engines roared. She felt the boat lurch forward.

Colding coughed, sending a splash of water out of his lungs and onto his face. Tim turned him on his side. Colding coughed again, then Sara heard the sweet sound of air rushing into his lungs.

"Help me get his clothes off," Tim said. Sara reached in. She and Tim pulled the waterlogged snowsuit off Colding's body. Colding kept coughing, but he obliged, weakly helping them remove his clothes. Sara moved to him and held him, their two naked, wet, frigid bodies wrapped in the same blanket. Gary threw a second blanket around them. It had blood on it — the same blanket he'd been wearing only moments earlier.

"You two will be fine," Tim said. "I've got to look at Clayton." He limped to the bow, leaving Sara and Colding clinging together, their bodies shivering in unison.

"Guess I owe you one," Colding said through blue lips.

Sara nodded. "Guess so."

They kissed, both sets of lips feeling icy and clammy, but it didn't matter. All the death was forgotten in that moment, because she had life, and she had *him*.

They had won. Not without a heavy price, but it was over.

They had *survived*.

Huddling together, shivering together, they looked back to shore as the *Otto II* pulled away from Black Manitou Island.

COLDING'S LAST EIGHT plastique balls had made an arc behind the ancestor horde. The bombs shattered huge chunks of ice, enough to break off a massive slab that stranded the ancestors in the harbor.

They ran about the slab, looking for a way off, but there was nowhere for them to go. A small piece near the edge broke off under one's weight — it fell into the water, thick limbs splashing uselessly. It lasted only a few seconds before it slid beneath the surface.

The main slab cracked in two. When it did, the seven ancestors at the edge of the left chunk proved to be too much weight — the slab tilted like a large teeter-totter. The seven tried to turn and run back up the ice, but it was too late: they all splashed into the water, doomed by their useless attempts at swimming.

The slab continued to break apart.

Sara and Colding heard the animals' roars even over the wind and the *Otto II*'s full-out engine. One by one, the ancestors fell into the water and disappeared.

One last ancestor remained afloat. It was missing its left ear and had an all-white head save for a black patch on the left eye. It looked at the boat, seemed to look right at Sara and Colding. It opened its mouth and let out a huge, primitive roar of unbridled fury.

Colding saw something moving in the water, something with a wet, black head. Could some of them swim after all? Then the image crystallized in his brain.

"Mookie," Colding said quietly. He shouted up to the flying bridge, "Gary, stop the boat!"

The black Australian shepherd cut through the frigid waters, heading straight for the patch of ice that held the last ancestor.

"Mookie!" Colding shouted. "Get the hell away from there! Come here, girl!"

But the dog ignored him. She reached the ice patch and struggled to climb on top.

BABY MCBUTTER TURNED and saw the small creature. She had seen this prey before. It had been there when she'd torn her way free from the big animal, when she'd taken her first bite of the trapped prey with the wounded leg. This creature had attacked her, *hurt* her.

Baby McButter roared in wide-mouthed fury, challenging this new threat. The prey managed to clumsily scramble aboard the ice patch — it roared back, the *roorooroo* sound pitiful and small in comparison, but no less hateful, no less primitive.

Baby McButter took a step toward the prey, but stopped — the ice shifted with every movement. She'd seen all of her brethren enter the water and not come out. She had to stay still.

The little prey ran toward her, barking, stopping just out of claw-swipe range. Its black lip curled back to show small white teeth. It made threatening lunges.

It wouldn't stop making that annoying noise.

COLDING LOOKED AWAY from the ice-top battle to see Tim helping Clayton move to the back of the boat.

"Dad!" Gary shouted down from the flying bridge. "Are you okay?"

"Good enough," Clayton said. He looked up and smiled. "I'm proud of you, son. Now get me da hell out of here."

Colding pointed out to the ice floe. "Clayton, you know that dumb-ass dog, call her in here! What the hell is she doing?"

Clayton leaned heavily on the rail and looked out. "We haven't seen Sven, eh? I think he's dead, and I think Mookie knows it. She's getting some payback."

Mookie barked so hard her body shook, pure fury encapsulated in wet black fur. The last ancestor took a tentative *snap*. Mookie easily danced away, kept barking, kept snarling.

The one-eared ancestor reared back its head, then lunged at the dog. The ice floe tilted instantly, sending dog and ancestor into the frigid harbor. The ice righted itself, splashing back into the water. A huge white head with a black eye spot surfaced. The ancestor's long claws splashed feebly, hitting the edge of the ice. Chunks broke off with each swipe, giving the creature no purchase. It opened its mouth for one last roar, then slid below the surface.

Colding looked hard, hoping, *wishing*. Finally, he saw a small patch of black cutting through the ice-filled water.

"Come on, girl!"

The dog looked exhausted. She paddled straight for the boat. Waves lifted her, buffeted her. She panted, spitting out water in big, cheek-puffing gasps. Colding reached out as far as he could. Sara weakly held his legs, letting him stretch even farther. Mookie dipped under, then popped back up. She slowed. Colding reached farther . . . and his fingers grabbed the dog's collar. He dragged her to the rail. Sara reached over and helped him pull the exhausted, tuck-tailed dog onboard. Mookie collapsed between Colding and Gary Detweiler, shivering madly, chest heaving: one more exhausted, wounded survivor of the disaster.

Her tail slapped wetly against the deck.

Finally, it was over.

The six survivors of Black Manitou Island headed out into the churning waters of Lake Superior.

EPILOGUE

HE STOOD ON the dune ridge, left paw up and against his chest, watching the prey float away on yet another noisy thing. The wind blew into his face, carrying their scent. He wanted the skinny prey, wanted to tear them to pieces, but now for a new reason.

That reason? Baby Moos-A-Lot wanted to kill them. He wanted revenge. They had killed his brethren and his leader. But he didn't want to eat them because for the first time in his short four-day life he wasn't hungry anymore.

One of the skinny things had stung his mouth with the stick. He pushed his thick tongue against the spot, feeling where a tooth was not. It had also stung him in the paw, so bad it was hard to walk. Baby Moos-A-Lot hadn't been able to keep up with the others. He'd arrived just in time to see the leader fall into the water. Fall in, and not come back up.

Hatred. Hatred for the skinny prey, and it felt much, *much* stronger than even his worst hunger pangs.

A noise behind him. He wheeled, bared his gap-toothed maw, ready for a three-legged charge.

But it wasn't a skinny thing. It was one of his kind. Scorched black skin covered the right side of its head. The right eye was a hollow socket rimmed with wetness. There were more burns on its right shoulder, down the side.

He was upwind and hadn't smelled his own until now. This close, however, the rich stench of scorched fur and burnt flesh filled his wounded nose. He also recognized a signature scent: no other of his kind would smell quite like that. If there were any others of his kind left.

And he smelled one more thing, a smell that affected him in an exciting new way.

It was the smell of . . . a female.

THE RED SQUIRREL stopped and stared at the treasure trove.

A pile of pinecones.

She smelled the seeds inside. So yummy. And she was so hungry.

There were other smells, too. The smell of a dead animal. The smell of another squirrel — faint and strange, but still there.

She looked up, eyes scanning for the silhouettes programmed into her instincts: small head close to wings, long wide tail, the silhouettes of hawks and owls. Nothing. She scurried a few feet closer, then stopped again.

Now she smelled a new smell, a *strange* smell. Some kind of animal, but one she'd never known before. Anything new made her want to run. But such a pile of pinecones! So much food!

She moved closer. The pile of cones sat near a hole in the ground next to a small white tree. A hole like the rabbits made. And next to the hole was a shiny thing just a little bigger than the squirrel herself. Like a piece of tree branch, but thicker, smoother. The round sides were a dark red, with spots of white like the snow. The sun glinted off its top. That sight made her *more* hungry, because usually when she saw that shiny shape, nearby there were crinkly things with salty food inside.

Movement.

She scrambled away, then stopped and looked back. Movement *behind* the pinecones. The fluff of a squirrel tail. One of her own, already eating the pinecones! But those were *her* pinecones!

She sprinted in, came around the pile to drive the competitor away.

A glimpse of horror — nothing *but* a tail! Danger! She turned to flee, but felt a stabbing pain in her back. She squealed and tried to run, but something lifted her into the air. Her feet kicked on emptiness. She twisted her head to attack the pain in her back, bit down on something hard.

Even in her panic, she recognized the taste.

Bone.

A bone, long and thin like a stick. At the other end was the unknown animal that produced the new smell. The squirrel couldn't turn all the way around, but she saw glimpses of white skin and a head covered in long, heavy black fur.

The creature holding the bone was dragging her into the hole. Darkness covered her, just the spot of light shining in from above. Her little feet dug into dirt and scrabbled, pushed, clawed, but it made no difference. The thing in her back pulled her down and down, the stench of death grew thicker.

She saw big, curved white bones scored everywhere with gnaw marks. She was *inside* something dead. The pain!

The spot of light seemed so far away. She felt something grab her, hold her. She squealed and squealed. Her head thrashed, she snapped her jaws, anything to escape, to *survive*.

Crushing pressure on the back of her neck. Her body stiffened, then relaxed. She felt a chunk of herself torn away. Small mouth opening and closing, tiny breaths slowing, she finally stopped moving enough to see her surroundings.

She saw the torn, meatless corpses of her kind, stacked into a neat pile of fur and bones.

ACKNOWLEDGMENTS

From the Author

A VERY EARLY version of this novel was first released as a free, serialized audiobook podcast running from September 2005 to February 2006. *Ancestor* reared its head again as a small-press novel, published on April 1, 2007. With no marketing budget, no advertising and no media coverage, the print version of *Ancestor* hit #7 overall on Amazon.com, and it was the #2 fiction novel behind *Harry Potter and The Deathly Hallows. Ancestor* wasn't there for long, but it was *there,* and that made all the difference.

That success came via word of mouth from my fans, the people who dubbed themselves "Junkies." Those were heady times in the land of Siglerism. That accomplishment directly led to my publishing deal with Crown, a deal that included the major rewrite and re-release of *Ancestor* that you now hold in your hands.

Ancestor represents all phases of my path as an author: from free, online audiobooks to surprise small-press success to bestselling hardcover novelist. This novel is the living metaphor for my dream to become an author, my hard work to reach that goal, my final success in getting an honest shot at the big time — and most important, at entertaining you and proving my worth as a storyteller.

My very career as a writer exists because of the fans who downloaded that free online audiobook, then continued to enjoy my works and support my efforts. I owe all of this to my fans, to my "Junkies." That's why I dedicate this book to you, Junkies — you are all the stuff of dreams, and your FDO™ thanks you.

And to you, the person holding this book? I busted my fanny to make the best story I could. I hope you enjoy *Ancestor,* and I hope I keep you coming back for more.

THE LIST OF awesomeness below pertains specifically to this version of *Ancestor*. Other key contributors were thanked in previous versions.

Team Sigler

- A Kovacs, the Director of Døøm
- Julian "Tha Shiv" Pavia, Editor and Destroyer of Worlds
- Byrd Leavell, Super Agent and Family Man
- Crown Publishing, many thanks to all y'all

Fallen in Battle

- Mookie, in these pages you get to live forever.

The Three Amigos of Biology Research

- Joseph A. Albietz III, M.D., Pediatrics
  and Pediatric Critical Care Medicine
- Jeremy "Xenophanes" Ellis, Ph.D., Developmental and Cell Biology
- Tom Merrit, Ph.D., Virology, Gene Therapy
  and Human Molecular Genetics

Siglerism Military Attachés

- Major Kris Alexander, U.S. Army: WMD counter-proliferation
- Robert W. Gilliland, Major, USAF: C-5 Galaxy
- Chris Grall, Veteran, U.S. Army: Weapons expertise
- JP Harvey: Helicopters
- Renee Jordan: Weapons and CBRN expertise

Foreign Language Phrases

- Sacha Kerckhoffs, Yang Liu, Katharina Maimer, Daniel Morgan, David Perry, Christian Walther, Christian Weihs, Selganor Yoster (and if I missed any here, my apologies)

Design Stars

- Kyle "The Crusher" Kolker, for another kick-ass cover
- Andre Gilbert, sculptor of Baby McButter
- Donna Mugavero, for design reference

CONTACT THE AUTHOR

E-mail: scott@scottsigler.net
Facebook.com/scottsigler
Myspace.com/scottsigler
Twitter.com/scottsigler

Also by SCOTT SIGLER

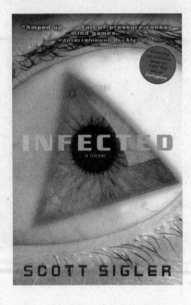

"Part Stephen King, part Chuck Palahniuk, *Infected* blends science fiction and horror into a pulpy masterpiece of action, terror, and suspense. Three recommendations: don't read it at night, or just after you've eaten a full meal, or if you're weak of heart. You've been warned!"
—James Rollins,
 New York Times bestselling author
 of *The Judas Strain* and *Black Order*

INFECTED
A Novel
$14.99 (Canada: $16.99)
978-0-307-40630-9

The stand-alone sequel to *Infected*, *Contagious* is an epic and exhilarating story of humanity's secret battle against a horrific enemy.

CONTAGIOUS
A Novel
$14.99 (Canada: $18.99)
978-0-307-40632-3